also by
SCARLETT ST. CLAIR

When Stars Come Out

HADES X PERSEPHONE
A Touch of Darkness
A Touch of Ruin
A Touch of Malice

HADES SAGA
A Game of Fate

ADRIAN X ISOLDE
King of Battle and Blood

a TOUCH of MALICE

SCARLETT ST. CLAIR

Bloom *books*

Published by Bloom Books, an imprint of Sourcebooks
P.O. Box 4410, Naperville, Illinois 60567-4410
(630) 961-3900
sourcebooks.com

Originally self-published in 2021 by Scarlett St. Clair.

Library of Congress Cataloging-in-Publication Data is on file with the publisher.

Manufactured in the UK by Clays and distributed by
Dorling Kindersley Limited, London
10 9 8 7 6 5 4 3 2
002-331526-NOV/21

To the best Daddy in the whole, wide world.

Before you died, I got to tell you about all sorts of amazing things that were happening for me. We were FaceTiming and you smiled and said, "I am so proud." Not long after, you'd test positive for COVID. I will always be thankful for our final call. I remember that you didn't feel good, and I didn't want to keep you long, but I wanted you to know I loved you—and that was our whole conversation. I miss you, I love you—over and over again.

The next morning, you crashed and went on the vent.

When I saw you in the hospital, I knew it was goodbye. You were struggling and yet, when I took your hand, you opened your beautiful eyes and smiled at me. The next time I saw you, I was picking up your ashes.

I'd give anything to hug you again, to hear your voice and your laugh. To receive a funny text message out of the blue, to rub your bald head and lean on your shoulder, but I know you're still with me and that you are so proud. I owe my perseverance to you—the person who always believed in what everyone else thought was impossible.

REST IN PEACE
Freddie Lee Nixon
December 23, 1948–November 27, 2020

PART I

"Changes of shape, new forms, are the theme which my spirit impels me now to recite. Inspire me, O gods...and spin me a thread from the world's beginning down to my own lifetime."

—OVID, *METAMORPHOSES*

PART I

CHAPTER 1
A Touch of Torment

Rough hands parted her legs and skimmed up her thighs, lips following—a light pressure gliding across her skin. Half-asleep, Persephone arched against the touch, restraints biting into her wrists and ankles. Confused, she tugged on them in an attempt to free her hands and feet but found the bindings would not give. There was something about this, the inability to move, to resist, to fight, that made her heart race and the blood pulse into her throat and head.

"So beautiful." The words were a whisper against her skin, and Persephone froze.

That voice.

She knew that voice.

She'd once considered its owner a friend, and now he was an enemy.

"Pirithous."

His name slipped from between her teeth—laced with rage and fear and disgust. He was the demigod who had stalked and kidnapped her from the Acropolis.

"Shh," he whispered. His tongue, wet and cold, slithered against her skin.

A cry tore from her throat. She pressed her thighs together, twisting against the foreign touch ghosting across her skin.

"Tell me what he does that you like," he whispered, sticky breath bathing her ear, hand skating closer to her center. "I can do better."

Persephone's eyes flew open as she sat up, inhaling sharply. Her chest ached and her breathing was ragged, as if she'd just run across the Underworld with a wraith on her heels. It took a moment for her eyes to adjust, to realize she was in Hades's bed, silk sheets clinging to her dampened skin, fire blazing orange in the hearth opposite them, and beside her was the God of the Dead himself, his energy, dark and electric, charging the air, making it heavy and tangible.

"Are you well?" Hades asked.

His voice was clear, quiet—a soothing tonic she wanted to consume. She looked at him. He rested on his side, his exposed skin burnished by the firelight. His eyes glittered black, dark hair spilling over the sheets like waves in a starless sea. Hours ago, she had clutched it between her fingers as she rode him long and slow and breathless.

She swallowed; her tongue felt swollen.

This was not the first time she'd had this nightmare, nor was it the first time she'd woken to find Hades watching.

"You haven't slept," she said.

"No," he replied and rose beside her, lifting his hand to brush her cheek. His touch sent a shiver down her spine, straight to her soul. "Tell me."

When he spoke, it was as if his voice were magic, a spell that coaxed words from her mouth even when they seized in her throat.

"I dreamed of Pirithous again."

Hades's hand fell from her cheek and Persephone recognized the expression on his face, the violence in his endless eyes. She felt guilty, having unearthed a part of him that he worked so hard to control.

Pirithous haunted Hades just as much as he haunted her.

"He harms you, even in your sleep." Hades frowned. "I failed you that day."

"How could you have known he would take me?"

"I should have known."

It wasn't possible, of course, though Hades had argued that was why he had assigned Zofie as her protector, but the aegis had been patrolling the exterior of the Acropolis during the abduction. She had also not noticed anything out of the ordinary because Pirithous's exit had been through an underground tunnel.

Persephone shivered, thinking of how she'd thoughtlessly accepted the demigod's help to escape the Acropolis, all while he'd been planning her abduction.

She would never trust blindly again.

"You are not all seeing, Hades," Persephone attempted to soothe.

In the days following her rescue from Pirithous's home, Hades had been in a dark mood, which had culminated in his attempt to punish Zofie by relieving her of her aegis duties—a move Persephone had halted.

Still, even after Persephone had rejected Hades's decree, the Amazon had argued with her.

"*This is my shame to carry.*"

The aegis's words had frustrated Persephone.

"*There is no shame. You were doing your job. You seem to think your role as my aegis is up for discussion. It isn't.*"

Zofie's eyes had gone wide as she looked from Persephone to Hades, uncertain, before she relented, bowing deep.

"*As you wish, my lady.*"

After, Persephone had turned to Hades. "*I expect to be informed before you attempt to dismiss anyone under my care.*"

Hades's brows rose, his lips twitched, and he countered. "*I hired her.*"

"*I'm glad you brought that up,*" she'd said. "*The next time you decide I need staff, I also expect to be included in the decision making.*"

"*Of course, darling. How shall I apologize?*"

They'd spent the rest of the evening in bed, but even as he made love to her, she knew he struggled, just like she knew he struggled now.

"You are right," Hades replied. "Perhaps I should punish Helios, then."

She gave him a wry look. Hades had made comments before regarding the God of the Sun. It was clear neither of them cared for one another.

"Would that make you feel better?"

"No, but it would be fun," Hades replied, his voice contradicting his words, sounding more ominous than excited.

Persephone was well aware of Hades's proclivity toward violence, and his earlier comment on punishment reminded her of the promise she had extracted from him after she'd been rescued—*when you torture Pirithous, I get to join*. She knew Hades had gone to Tartarus that night to torment the demigod, knew that he had gone since—but she had never asked to accompany him.

But now she wondered if that was why Pirithous haunted her dreams. Perhaps seeing him in Tartarus—bloodied, broken, tortured—would end these nightmares.

She looked at Hades again and gave her order. "I wish to see him."

Hades's expression did not change, but she thought she could feel his emotions in that moment—anger, guilt, and apprehension—but not apprehension at allowing her to face her attacker. It was apprehension at having her in Tartarus at all. She knew that a part of him feared to show her this side of him, feared what she would think, and yet he would not deny her.

"As you wish, darling."

Persephone and Hades manifested in Tartarus, in a windowless, white room so bright, it hurt. As her eyes adjusted, they widened, welded to the spot where Pirithous was restrained in a chair at the center of the room. It had been weeks since she'd seen the demigod. He appeared to be asleep, chin resting on his chest, eyes closed. She'd once thought he was handsome, but now those sharp cheekbones were hollow, his face wan and ashy.

And the smell.

It wasn't decay, exactly, but it was acidic and sharp, and it burned her nose.

Her stomach roiled, souring at the sight of him.

"Is he dead?" She could not bring her voice above a whisper just in case—she was not ready to see his eyes. She knew she asked a strange question, given that they stood in Tartarus, in the Underworld, but Persephone was aware of Hades's preferred methods of torture, knew that he would give life only to extinguish it through a series of harrowing punishments.

"He breathes if I say so," Hades replied.

Persephone did not respond immediately. Instead, she approached the soul, pausing a few feet from him. Up close, he looked like a wax figure that had grown too soft under the heat, slouched and frowning. Still, he was solid and all too real.

Before she had visited the Underworld, Persephone had thought souls were shades—shadows of themselves—but instead, they were corporeal, as solid as the day they'd died, though that had not always been the case. Once, the souls of Hades's realm had lived a bland and crowded existence under his rule.

Hades had never confirmed what had changed his mind—why he'd decided to give both the Underworld and the souls color and the illusion of life. He'd often said that the Underworld merely evolved as the Upperworld did, but Persephone knew Hades. He had a conscience, and he felt regret for his beginning as King of the Underworld. He'd done those things as a kindness, as a way to atone.

Despite this, he would never forgive himself for his past, and it was that knowledge that hurt her heart.

"Does it help?" she asked Hades, unsure if she wanted an answer. "The torture?"

She looked at the god, who still stood where they had manifested, hair unbound, horns on display, looking dark and beautiful and violent. She could not imagine what being here did to him, but she remembered the look on his face when he had found her in Pirithous's lair. She had never seen his rage manifest in such a way, never seen him look so horrified and broken.

"I cannot say."

"Then why do you do it?" She walked around Pirithous, pausing behind him and meeting Hades's gaze.

"Control," Hades answered.

Persephone had not always understood Hades's need for control, but in the months since they'd met, she was starting to desire that very thing. She knew what it was to be a prisoner, to be powerless, to be caught between two horrible choices—and still choose wrong.

"I want control," she whispered.

Hades stared at her for a beat and then held out his hand.

"I will help you claim it."

His voice rumbled in the space between them, warming her chest. She approached him again and he drew her close, back to his chest.

Suddenly, Pirithous inhaled. Persephone's heart raced as she watched him stir. His head lulled and his eyes blinked open, sleepy and confused.

Again, that fear of seeing his gaze slashed through her, shaking her insides. Hades gave her a reassuring squeeze about the waist, as if to remind her that she was safe, and dipped his head; his breath teased her ear.

"Do you remember when I taught you to harness your magic?"

He was referring to their time in her grove, after Apollo had left with this favor from Hades and a promise from Persephone that she wouldn't write about him. She had sought comfort among the trees and flowers but only found disappointment when she could not bring life to a parched patch of ground. Hades had come then, appearing like the shadows he bent to his will, and helped her harness her magic and heal the ground. He had been seductive in his instruction, lighting a fire wherever he touched.

Her body pricked with chills at the thought and her words hissed from between her teeth.

"Yes."

"Close your eyes," he instructed, lips grazing the column of her neck.

"Persephone?" Pirithous's voice was hoarse.

She squeezed her eyes shut tighter, focusing instead on Hades's touch.

"What do you feel?" His hand drifted down her shoulder, the fingers of his other arm, firm around her waist, splayed possessively.

This question was not so easy—she felt many things. For Hades, passion and arousal. For Pirithous, anger and fear, grief and betrayal. It was a vortex, a dark abyss with no end, and then the demigod said her name again.

"Persephone, please. I—I am sorry."

His words struck her, a lance to her chest, and as she spoke, she opened her eyes.

"Violent."

"Focus on it," Hades instructed, his hand pressed into her belly, the other laced with her fingers.

Pirithous remained slouched in his metal chair, restrained and jaundiced, and the eyes she had feared stared back now, watery and afraid.

They had switched places, she realized, and there was a moment when she hesitated, questioning whether or not she could hurt him. Then Hades spoke.

"Feed it."

With their fingers twined, she felt power gather in her palm, an energy that scorched her skin.

"Where do you wish to cause him pain?" Hades asked.

"This isn't you," Pirithous said. "I know you. I watched you!"

A roar started in her ears, and her eyes burned, the power inside her a heat she could scarce contain.

He had left strange gifts, stalked her, taken pictures of her in a space that was supposed to be safe. He had taken away her sense of security, even in sleep.

"He'd wanted to use his cock as a weapon," she said. "And I want it to burn."

"No! Please, Persephone. Persephone!"

"Then make him burn."

The energy pooling in her hand was electric, and as her fingers slipped from Hades's, she imagined the magic gathered there blasting toward Pirithous in an endless lava-hot stream.

"This isn't—"

Pirithous's words were cut short as the magic took root. There was no outward indication that anything was wrong with him—no flames leapt from his crotch—but it was clear he felt her magic. His feet dug into the ground, he bucked against his restraints, his teeth were clenched, and the veins in his head and neck popped.

Still, he managed to speak through gritted teeth.

"*This isn't you.*"

"I am not sure who you think I am," she said. "But let me be clear—I am Persephone, future Queen of the Underworld, Lady of Your Fate. May you come to dread my presence."

Crimson dripped from Pirithous's nose and mouth, his chest rose and fell rapidly, but he did not speak again.

"How long will he stay like this?" Persephone asked, watching as Pirithous's body continued to arch and strain against the pain. His eyes began to bulge from their sockets and a sheen of sweat broke out across his skin, making him look green in color.

"Until he dies," Hades replied simply, watching with an expression of disinterest.

She didn't flinch, didn't feel, didn't ask to leave until Pirithous was silent and limp once more. She considered her earlier question to Hades—*does it help?* In the aftermath, she had no answer, save for the knowledge that a part of her had wilted and that if she did this enough, the rest of her would wither away.

CHAPTER II
A Touch of Grief

"How is the wedding planning going?" Lexa asked. She sat across from Persephone on a white quilt, embroidered with blue forget-me-nots. It had been a gift from one of the souls, Alma. She'd approached Persephone on one of her daily visits to Asphodel, a bundle in her arms.

"I have something for you, my lady."

"Alma, you shouldn't have—"

"It is a gift for you to give," the soul interrupted quickly, wisps of her silver hair floating around her round, rosy-cheeked face. *"I know you grieve for your friend, so here, give her this."*

Persephone had taken the bundle, and upon realizing what it was—a quilt, lovingly crafted with small, blue flowers—tears sprang to her eyes.

"I don't know that I need to tell you what forget-me-nots mean," Alma continued. *"True love, faithfulness, memories. In time, your friend will come to know you again."*

That evening, after Persephone had returned to the castle, she'd hugged the blanket to her chest and wept. The next day, she gifted it to Lexa.

"*Oh, it is beautiful, my lady,*" she'd said, holding the bundle as if it were a small child.

Persephone stiffened at the use of her title; her brows furrowed, and when she spoke, she sounded more confused than anything. "*My lady?*"

Lexa had never used Persephone's title before. Their eyes met, and Lexa hesitated, blushing.

Lexa never blushed.

"*Thanatos said it is your title,*" she explained.

Persephone recognized that titles had a use, but not among friends.

"*Call me Persephone.*"

Lexa's eyes widened. "*I'm sorry. I didn't mean to upset you.*"

"*You…didn't.*"

As much as Persephone tried to sound convincing, she couldn't imbue her voice with enough reassurance. The truth was, hearing Lexa call her my lady was another reminder that she wasn't the same person as before, and as much as Persephone told herself to be patient with Lexa, it was difficult. Lexa looked the same, sounded the same—she even laughed the same, but her personality was different.

"*Besides, if we are using titles, then you would have to call Thanatos lord.*"

Again, Lexa appeared to be embarrassed. She averted his eyes, and her flush deepened as she answered, "*He said…I didn't have to.*"

Persephone had left that conversation feeling strange and somehow even more distant from Lexa than before.

"Persephone?" Lexa asked.

"Hmm?" Persephone was drawn from her thoughts. Her eyes shifted and met Lexa's eyes—bright blue, beautiful. Her face was paler here beneath the light of Elysium, framed by her thick, dark locks. She was also dressed in a white gown that tied around the middle. It was a color Persephone could not remember her wearing in the time she had known her in the Upperworld.

"Wedding planning—how is it going?" Lexa asked again.

"Oh." Persephone frowned and admitted, "I haven't really begun."

That was half-true. She hadn't begun planning—but Hecate and Yuri had. In all honesty, thinking of planning a wedding without Lexa hurt. If she'd been alive, her best friend would have been online looking for color palettes and dresses and venues. She would have made a plan and lists and explained customs Persephone had never been taught by her mother. Instead, she sat across from Persephone, quiet, subdued, unaware of their history. Even if Persephone had wanted to include her in Yuri and Hecate's plans, she couldn't—souls were not allowed to leave Elysium unless Thanatos deemed them ready to transition to Asphodel.

"Perhaps we can take the planning to her," Persephone had suggested.

Thanatos had shaken his head. *"Your visits leave her fatigued. She could not handle anything more at the moment."*

He had also attempted to ease the rejection with his magic. The God of Death was able to calm those in his presence, bringing comfort to the grieving and easing anxiety. Sometimes, though, it had the opposite effect on Persephone. She found his influence over emotion invasive, even when he meant well. In the days after Lexa's death, Thanatos had used his magic in an attempt to ease her suffering, but she'd told him to stop. While she knew he meant well, she wanted to feel—even if it hurt.

It seemed wrong not to when she had caused Lexa so much pain.

"You don't seem excited," Lexa pointed out.

"I am excited to be Hades's wife," Persephone clarified.

"It's just…I never imagined that I would be getting married. I don't even know where to start."

Demeter had never prepared her for this—for anything. The Goddess of Harvest had hoped to outwit the Fates by keeping her isolated from the world—from Hades. When she'd begged to leave the greenhouse, to enter the world in the guise of a mortal, she'd only had dreams of finishing her degree, beginning a successful career, and reveling in her freedom for as long as possible.

Love had never been part of that dream, least of all marriage.

"Hmm," Lexa hummed, and she leaned back on her hands, head tilted toward the muted sky, as if she wished to sunbathe. "You should start with what makes you the most excited."

It was advice the old Lexa would have offered.

But what made Persephone most excited was being Hades's wife. When she thought of their future, her chest felt full, her body electric, her soul alive.

"I will think on it," Persephone promised as she rose to her feet. Speaking of the wedding, she was due at the palace soon to begin planning. "Although I am sure Hecate and Yuri will have their own ideas."

"They may," Lexa said, and for a moment, Persephone couldn't look away. The old Lexa stared back, thoughtful and sincere as she added, "But it is your wedding."

———

Persephone left Elysium.

She should teleport to Asphodel. She was already running late, but as she left Lexa behind, her vision blurred with tears. She stopped, burying her face in her hands. Her body ached, chest hollow and lungs aflame. She knew this feeling well, as it had crippled her in the days since Lexa's death. It came, unbidden, like the nightmares haunting her sleep. It came when she expected it and even when she didn't, attached to laughter and smells and songs, to words and places and pictures. It chipped away at pieces of her.

And it wasn't just sadness that burdened her—she was also angry. Angry that Lexa had been hurt at all, angry that despite the gods—despite her own divinity—there was no fighting Fate. Because Persephone had tried, and she had failed.

Her stomach knotted, poisoned by guilt. If she had known what lay ahead, she would have never bargained with Apollo. When Lexa lay unconscious in the ICU, Persephone had just begun to understand what it was to fear losing someone. In fact, she had been so afraid, she had done everything in her power to prevent what was ultimately inevitable. Her decisions had hurt Lexa in ways that were only repairable with time—and a drink from the Lethe.

Even with her memories gone, Persephone still had hope that the old Lexa would come back. Now she knew the truth—grief meant never going back, never collecting the pieces. It meant that the person she was now in the aftermath of Lexa's death was who she would be until the next death.

Bile rose in her throat.

Grief was a cruel god.

As she approached the palace, she was greeted by Cerberus, Typhon, and Orthrus, who bounded toward her. The three Dobermans halted before her, energetic but obedient. She knelt, scratching behind their ears and moving to their sides. She'd come to understand their personalities more. Of the three, Cerberus was the most serious and the most dominant. Typhon was mellow but always alert, and Orthrus could be silly when he wasn't patrolling the Underworld—which was almost never.

"How are my handsome boys?" she asked.

They panted and Orthrus's paws tapped the ground, as if he could barely contain his wish to lick her face.

"Have you seen Hecate and Yuri?" she asked.

They whined.

"Take me to them."

The three obeyed, ambling toward the palace. Towering and ominous, it could be seen from just about anywhere in the Underworld. Its shining obsidian pinnacles seemed to go on forever, disappearing into the bright, gray-toned sky, a representation of Hades's reach, his influence, his reign. At the base of the castle were gardens of green ivy, red roses, narcissus, and gardenias. There were willows and blossoming trees and pathways that cut through the flora. They were a symbol of Hades's kindness, his ability to change and adapt—they were atonement.

When she first visited, she'd been angry to find the Underworld so lush, both because of the bargain she'd struck with the God of the Dead and also because creating life was supposed to be her power. Hades had quickly illustrated that the beauty he had crafted was an illusion. Even then, she'd been jealous that he was able to use his magic so effortlessly. Though she was gaining control daily—through practices with Hecate and Hades—she still envied their control.

"We are old gods, my dear," Hecate had said. *"You cannot compare yourself to us."*

They were words she repeated every time she felt the familiar claws of jealousy. Every time she felt the familiar frustration of failure. She was improving, and one day, she would master her magic, and maybe then the illusions Hades had held for years would become real.

The dogs led her to the ballroom where Hecate and Yuri stood before a table of floral stems, color swatches, and sketches of wedding dresses.

"There you are," Hecate said, looking up at the sound of the Dobermans' nails tapping on the marble floor. They ran straight for the Goddess of Witchcraft, who bent to pat their heads before they plopped on the floor beneath the table, panting.

"Sorry I'm late," Persephone said. "I was visiting Lexa."

"That's alright, dear," Hecate said. "Yuri and I were just discussing your engagement party."

"My...engagement party?" It was the first time Persephone had heard anything about it. "I thought we were meeting to plan for the wedding."

"Oh, we are," Yuri said. "But we *must* have an engagement party. Oh, Persephone! I cannot wait to call you queen!"

"You can call her queen now," Hecate said. "Hades does."

"It's just so exciting!" Yuri clasped her hands. "A Divine wedding! We haven't had one of those in *years*."

"Who was the last?" Persephone asked.

"I believe it was Aphrodite and Hephaestus," Hecate said.

Persephone frowned. Rumors had always circulated about Aphrodite and Hephaestus, the most common that the God of Fire did not want the Goddess of Love. During the times Persephone had spoken to Aphrodite, she'd gathered that the goddess was not happy in her marriage, but she did not know why. When she tried to learn more about her relationship, Aphrodite shut down. In part, Persephone did not blame the goddess. Her love life and its struggles were no one's business. Still, she got the sense that Aphrodite believed she was very much alone.

"Were you in attendance at their wedding?" Persephone asked Hecate.

"I was," she said. "It was beautiful, despite the circumstances."

"Circumstances?"

"Theirs was an arranged marriage," Yuri explained. "Aphrodite was a gift to Hephaestus."

"A...*gift*."

Persephone cringed. How could a goddess—*any woman*—be presented as a *gift*?

"That is what Zeus likes to say," Hecate said. "But when she was born—a siren of beauty and temptation—Zeus was approached by several gods for her hand in marriage. Ares, Poseidon, even Hermes fell prey to her charms, though he will deny it. Zeus rarely makes a decision without consulting his oracle, and when he asked about marriage to each of those gods, the oracle foretold war, so he wed her to Hephaestus."

Persephone frowned. "But Aphrodite seems so...fierce. Why would she allow Zeus to determine who she weds?"

"Aphrodite *wanted* to marry Hephaestus," Hecate said. "And even if she hadn't, she would not have had any choice. All Divine marriages must be approved by Zeus."

"What? Why? I thought Hera was the Goddess of Marriage."

"She is—and he involves her to a point, but he does not trust her. She would approve of a marriage if it meant an end to his reign as King of the Gods."

"I still don't understand. Why do we need approval to marry?"

"Marriage between gods is not like mortals—gods share power, and they have children. There are many factors Zeus must consider before he gives his blessing."

"Share...power?"

"Yes—though I doubt it will affect Hades at all. He already has influence over the Earth, but you—you will have control over shadow, over death."

Persephone shivered. The thought that she would

have to learn to control and harness more magic was a little overwhelming. She was just now mastering her own magic. Of course, that wouldn't be a problem if Zeus did not approve of her marriage. Why hadn't Hades told her about this?

"Is there a chance Zeus will disapprove?" she asked, worrying her bottom lip. If he did, what would Hades do?

Darling, I would burn this world for you.

The words trailed along her skin, whispering along her spine—a promise Hades had made and would deliver upon if forced.

"I cannot say for certain," Hecate said, and her evasive words made anxiety flare in Persephone's stomach—a constant static that sat in her heart and pumped through her veins. The goddess was rarely anything but direct.

Yuri elbowed Hecate. "I am sure Zeus will approve," she said. "What reasons could he possibly have for denying you happiness?"

Persephone could think of one—and that was her power. After she had lost control in the Forest of Despair and used Hades's own magic against him, Hecate had confessed a fear she'd harbored since their first meeting— that she would be more powerful than any other god. That power would either land her a spot among the Olympians or as their enemy. Which, she could not say.

Yuri seemed to tire of the conversation and changed the subject quickly.

"Let's start with color palettes!" she said, opening a large book on the table. Tufts of cloth stuck out from between the pages.

"What is this?" Persephone asked.

"It's…well, it's a book of wedding ideas."

"Where did you get it?"

"The girls and I made it," Yuri said.

Persephone raised a brow.

"When did you start it?"

The soul's cheeks turned pink, and she stammered, "A few months ago."

"Hmm."

Persephone had a feeling the souls had been collecting wedding-themed items since the night she almost drowned in the Styx, but she said nothing, listening as Yuri showed her a variety of color pairings.

"I'm thinking lilac and green," she said. "It will complement black, which we all know is the *only* color Hades will wear."

Persephone giggled. "Does his color choice annoy you?"

"You mean his lack of color? Just once I'd like to see him in white."

Hecate snorted but said nothing.

As Yuri continued going over other options, Persephone couldn't help thinking about Zeus and wondering why they were planning a wedding before knowing if her union with Hades was even permitted. *Perhaps your marriage has been blessed*, she argued. *Perhaps Hades asked before his proposals.* It would explain why she'd never heard of the antiquated caveat.

Still, she would be sure to ask him later…and she would be anxious until then.

Persephone approved of the color palette, and with that settled, Yuri moved on to the wedding dress.

"I had Alma draw up some designs," she said.

Persephone flipped through the pages. Each dress was heavily embellished with jewels or pearls and layers and layers of tulle. She might not have ever dreamed of her wedding, but she knew for certain these were not the dresses for her.

"What do you think?"

"They are beautiful sketches," she said.

"You don't like them," Yuri said instantly, frowning.

"It's not that…" Persephone said.

"It's that," Hecate interjected.

Persephone glared. "It's just that…I think I want something a little more…simple."

"But…you are to be a queen," Yuri argued.

"But I am still Persephone," she said. "And I'd like to be Persephone…for as long as I can."

Yuri opened her mouth to protest once more, but Hecate intervened. "I understand, my dear. Why don't I take care of coordinating the gown? Besides, it's not as though you won't have another chance to wear a ballgown."

The Goddess of Witchcraft looked pointedly at Yuri.

Persephone's brows knitted together. "What do you mean?"

"Oh, my dear—this is just the *first* wedding. You'll have a second, perhaps a third."

Persephone felt the color drain from her face. "A… *third*?"

This was another thing she had yet to learn.

Hecate explained. "One in the Underworld, one in the Upperworld, and one on Olympus."

"Why Olympus?"

"It's tradition."

"Tradition," Persephone echoed. Just as it was tradition for Zeus to approve marriages—and now she wondered, if Zeus didn't approve of their marriage, did that mean he did not approve of their relationship at all? Would he try to force them apart just as her mother had? She frowned. "I'm not so eager to follow tradition."

Hecate smiled. "Lucky for you, Hades isn't either."

They stayed for a while longer, discussing flowers and location. Yuri favored gardenias and hydrangeas while Persephone preferred anemone and narcissus. Yuri favored the ballroom for the ceremony while Persephone favored one of the gardens—perhaps beneath the purple wisteria in Hades's garden. By the end of it, Hecate was smiling.

"What?" Persephone asked, curious as to why the Goddess of Magic seemed so amused.

"Oh, nothing," she said. "It's just…despite stating otherwise, you seem to know exactly what you want out of this wedding."

Persephone smiled softly. "I just…picked things that reminded me of us."

After their meeting, Persephone retired to the baths where she soaked in the hot, lavender-infused water for close to an hour. She was exhausted. It was the kind of weariness that went bone deep, a result of her body fighting near-constant anxiety and crushing guilt. It did not help that she had awoken to nightmares of Pirithous. Even after she and Hades had returned from Tartarus, she'd been unable to sleep, lying wide awake beside the God of the Dead, reliving the torture she'd inflicted upon the demigod, wondering what her actions made her. Suddenly, her mother's words came to mind.

Daughter, even you cannot escape our corruption. It is what comes with power.

Was she a monster? Or just another god?

Persephone left the baths and returned to Hades's— *their*, she reminded herself—bedchamber. She intended to change and dine with the souls while she waited to confront Hades about Zeus, but when she saw the bed, her body felt heavy and all she wanted to do was rest. She collapsed atop the silk sheets, comfortable, weightless, safe.

When she opened her eyes, it was night. The room was full of firelight, and shadowy flames danced on the wall opposite her. She sat up and found Hades near the fireplace. He turned to face her, naked, his muscles haloed by flames—broad shoulders, flat abs, strong thighs. Her gaze trailed all parts of him—from his glittering eyes to his swollen cock. He was a work of art as much as he was a weapon.

He sipped the whiskey in his glass.

"You are awake," he said softly, then downed what remained of his drink, leaving the glass on the table near the fireplace to come to bed. As he sat beside her, he cupped her face and kissed her. When he pulled away, his thumb brushed her lips.

"How was your day?" he asked.

She pulled at her lip with her teeth as she answered, "Hard."

He frowned.

"Yours?" she asked.

"The same," he said, letting his hand fall from her face. "Lay with me."

"You don't have to ask," she whispered.

He parted her robe, which had already fallen open, exposing one of her breasts to his hungry eyes. The silky fabric slid down her arms, puddling around her waist. Hades bent, taking her nipples into his mouth, tongue shifting between teasing laps and sharp sucking. Persephone's fingers tangled into his hair, holding him in place as her head fell back, delighting in the feel of his mouth on her body. The longer he worked, the hotter she grew, and she found herself guiding one of Hades's hands between her thighs, to her molten center where she desired most to be filled.

He obliged, parting her slick flesh, and as he filled her, she blew out a breath that turned into a moan, which Hades captured as his mouth closed over hers. For a long moment, Persephone held Hades's wrist as his fingers worked, curling deep, touching familiar parts of her, but then her hand shifted to his cock, and as her fingers met the softness of his shaft, he groaned, breaking their kiss and leaving her body.

24

She growled, reaching for his hand again, but he just chuckled.

"Do you not trust me to bring you pleasure?" he asked.

"Eventually."

Hades narrowed his eyes. "Oh, darling. How you challenge me."

He shifted her body so that she was on her side, back to his chest. One of his arms cradled her neck while the other gripped her breasts, skimmed down her stomach to her thighs. He drew her legs apart, hooking one over his own, spreading her wide. His fingers circled her clit and threaded through her curls before dipping into her warmth again. She inhaled, arching against him, his hard cock grinding into her ass. Her head pressed into the crook of his shoulder, her legs opening wider, coaxing him deeper—and Hades's mouth descended on hers, savage in his wish to claim.

Her breath quickened, and her heels slipped on the bedding, unable to ground. She felt euphoric and alive, and she wanted more even as the first vibrating orgasm wrecked her body.

"Is this pleasure?" he asked.

She did not have time to answer. Even if he'd given her time, she did not think she had the ability to summon words between heavy breaths as the head of Hades's cock nestled against her entrance. She inhaled as he eased inside her, back arching, shoulders digging into his chest. When he was fully sheathed, his mouth touched her shoulder, teeth grazing skin, hand continuing to tease her clit until she moaned. It was a sound he had summoned from somewhere deep inside her.

"Is this pleasure?" he asked again as he moved, setting a slow rhythm that made her aware of everything—each increment of his cock as it reached deep, the slamming of his balls against her ass, the way each thrust stole the breath from her lungs.

"Is this pleasure?" he asked again.

She turned her head toward his, gripping the back of his neck. "It is ecstasy."

Their lips collided in a vicious kiss and there was no more talking, just gasps, desperate moans, and the slamming of bodies. The heat grew between them, until Persephone could feel the perspiration from their bodies mixing. Hades's pace quickened; one hand kept her leg curled around his own, and the other was at her throat, holding her jaw between his fingers with the lightest pressure—and he held her like that until they came.

Hades's head fell into the crook of her neck where he pressed kisses to her skin.

"Are you well?" he asked.

"Yes," she whispered.

She was more than well. Sex with Hades always went beyond her expectations, and every time she thought they'd reached their peak—*nothing can get better than this*—she was proven wrong. This instance had been no different, and she found herself wondering just how much experience the God of the Dead had—and why was he holding out?

Hades withdrew, and Persephone rolled to face him, studied his face, glistening after their lovemaking. He looked sleepy and content.

"Has Zeus approved of our marriage?"

Hades stilled, as if his heart had stopped beating and he had ceased breathing. She wasn't sure what he was reacting to—perhaps he realized he'd forgotten to talk to her about this, or he realized he'd been caught. After a moment, he relaxed, but a strange tension settled between them. It wasn't angry, but it wasn't the elation they usually reveled in after sex.

"He is aware of our engagement," he said.

"That is not what I asked."

She knew him well enough now—Hades never said

or offered more than was needed. He stared at her for a moment before answering, "He will not deny me."

"But he has not given you his blessing?"

She wanted him to say it, though she already knew the answer.

"No."

It was her turn to stare. Still, Hades remained silent.

"When were you going to tell me?" Persephone asked.

"I don't know." He paused and to her surprise added, "When I had no other choice."

"That is more than obvious." She glared.

"I was hoping to avoid it altogether," he said.

"Telling me?"

"No, Zeus's approval," Hades said. "He makes a spectacle of it."

"What do you mean?"

"He will summon us to Olympus for an engagement feast and festivities, and he will drag out his decision for days. I have no desire to be in attendance and no desire to have you suffer through it."

"And when will he do this?" Her voice was a breathless whisper.

"In a few weeks, I imagine," he said.

She stared at the ceiling, the colors swirling together as her vision clouded with tears. She wasn't sure why this made her so emotional. Maybe it was because she was afraid, or maybe because she was tired.

"Why wouldn't you tell me? If there is a chance we cannot be together, I have the right to know."

"Persephone," Hades whispered, rising to his elbow. He loomed over her, brushing at her tears. "No one will keep us apart—not the Fates, not your mother, and not Zeus."

"You are so certain, but even you will not challenge the Fates."

"Oh, darling, but I have told you before—for you, I would destroy this world."

She swallowed, watching him. "Perhaps that is what I fear the most."

He studied her a moment longer, thumb brushing her cheek before his lips touched hers, then kissed down her body, drinking deep between her thighs, and when he rose again, there were no other names upon her lips but Hades.

———

Later she woke again to find Hades returning to their room, fully dressed.

Her brows knitted together as she rose into a sitting position, eyes still heavy with sleep.

"What's wrong?"

The god grimaced, his gaze hard and a little unkind as he answered, "Adonis is dead. He's been murdered."

She blinked as a wave of shock shivered though her.

Persephone did not like Adonis. He had stolen her work and published it without her permission, he'd touched her even after she'd said no, and he'd threatened to expose her relationship with Hades if she didn't get him rehired at *New Athens News*. He deserved a lot, but he hadn't deserved to be murdered.

Hades crossed the room, returning to the bar where he poured himself a drink.

"Adonis. Murdered? How?"

"Horribly," Hades replied. "He was found in the alley-way outside La Rose."

It took Persephone a moment to think, her mind not quite able to catch up with the news. The last time she'd seen Adonis was in the Garden of the Gods. She'd turned his arms into literal, wooden limbs, and he'd groveled at her feet, begging to be returned to normal. She'd done so under the condition that if he touched another woman without consent, he would spend the rest of his days as a corpse flower.

She hadn't seen him since.

"Has he made it here…to the Underworld?"

"He has," Hades replied as he downed a glass of whiskey and poured another.

"Can you ask him what happened?"

"No. He…is in Elysium."

Which told Persephone that his death had to have been traumatic to warrant placement upon the healing fields.

Persephone watched as Hades threw back another drink. He only drank like this when he was anxious, and what worried her most was how upset he seemed about the death of a man he'd once called a parasite.

Whatever he'd seen had disturbed him.

"Do you think he was killed because of Aphrodite's favor?" Persephone asked.

It wasn't uncommon. Over the years, many mortals had been killed for that very reason, and Adonis was someone who flaunted his association with the Goddess of Love.

"It's likely," he said. "Whether it was because of jealousy or a hatred for the gods, I cannot say."

Dread pooled in her stomach.

"Are you suggesting he was killed by someone who had a vendetta against Aphrodite?"

"I think he was killed by several people," Hades said. "And that they hate all the Divine."

CHAPTER III
Aggression

Hades's words were still on her mind when she headed to work at the Coffee House the next morning. She hadn't been able to pry any more information out of him regarding Adonis's death. He'd only added that he believed the murder had been planned and executed with intention, a fact that made Persephone fear there would be more assaults.

Despite his brutal death, there was no mention of it in any newspaper. She imagined that was due to Hades's involvement in the investigation, but that also made her think he'd seen something he didn't want the public—or her—knowing.

She frowned. She knew Hades was trying to protect her, but if people were attacking favored mortals—or anyone associated with the gods—she needed to know. While the world at large did not know she was a goddess, her association with Hades made her and her friends potential targets too.

Persephone chose a shadowed corner in the coffee shop to set up and wait for Helen and Leuce. Since launching her own online community and blog, *The Advocate*, a few weeks ago, the three met weekly, and because they had no office, they chose various locations across New Athens—the Coffee House being one of their preferred haunts. The two were running behind, probably due to the weather, as New Athens was experiencing a cold front.

That was probably an understatement.

It was freezing and snow had been falling from the dreary sky off and on for almost a week. At first, it melted as soon as it touched the ground, but today it had begun to stick to the roads and sidewalks. Meteorologists were calling it the storm of the century. It was the only story in the news that rivaled Persephone and Hades's engagement announcement. Today, she found that they shared space on the front page of every news outlet—from *New Athens News* to the *Delphi Divine*, their headlines warred:

God of the Dead to Wed Mortal Journalist

and

Winter Storm Steals Summer Sun

A third headline caused knots to form in Persephone's stomach. It was an opinion column in the *Grecian Times*—a national newspaper and a rival of *New Athens News*.

Winter Weather Is Divine Punishment

It was clear that the author of the article was not a fan of the gods, probably an Impious. It began:

In a world ruled by gods, nothing is chance. The question remains—whose wrath are we facing and what is the cause? Another mortal who claimed to be more beautiful than any of the Divine? Or one who dared rebuke their advances?

It was neither. It was a real-life battle between Hades, Persephone, and her mother, Demeter, the Goddess of Harvest.

Persephone was not surprised that it had come to this. Demeter had done everything in her power to keep Persephone and Hades apart, and it had started from her birth. Locked away in a glass greenhouse, Demeter had fed her lies about the gods and their motives, in particular Hades, who she detested merely for the fact that the Fates had woven their threads together. When Persephone thought of how she used to be under her mother's strict rule, she felt sick—blind, self-righteous, wrong. She hadn't been a daughter at all but a prisoner, and in the end, it was all for nothing, because when Persephone met Hades, all bets were off and the only bargain that mattered was the one she was willing to make with her heart.

"Your latte, Persephone," Ariana, one of the baristas, said as she approached. Persephone had come to know almost everyone in the Coffee House, both due to her celebrity and her frequent visits.

"Thank you, Ariana."

The barista attended the College of Hygieia and was studying epidemiology. It was a challenging channel of study considering some diseases were god-made and only curable if they deemed them to be.

"I just wanted to say congratulations on your engagement to Lord Hades. You must be so excited."

Persephone smiled. It was a little hard for her to accept well wishes with Demeter's storm worsening outside. She couldn't help thinking that if mortals knew the reason for the sudden change in weather, they would not be so happy about their marriage. Still, she managed to respond. "I am, thank you."

"Have you chosen a date?"

"No, not yet."

"Do you think you'll be married here? I mean, in the Upperworld?"

Persephone took a deep breath. She didn't mean to be so frustrated by the woman's questions. She knew they stemmed from her excitement—and yet they only served to make her anxious.

"You know, we haven't even discussed it. We've been *very* busy."

"Of course," the barista said. "Well, I'll let you get back to work."

Persephone offered a half-hearted smile as the barista turned to leave. She took a sip of her latte before turning her attention to her tablet, opening an article Helen had sent her late last night for review. She couldn't quite describe how she felt when she read the title, but it was something akin to dread.

The Truth About Mortal Activist Group Triad

In the years since the Great Descent, mortals have been restless at the presence of gods on Earth. Since then, various groups have formed in opposition to their influence. Some choose to identify with the ideology of an Impious. These mortals do not pray or worship the gods, nor look to them for reprieve, preferring instead to avoid the Divine altogether. Some Impious prefer to take a passive role in the war against the gods.

Others take a more active role and have chosen to join Triad.

"Gods have a monopoly on everything—from the restaurant industry to clothing, even mining. It's impossible for mortals to compete," says an anonymous member of the organization. "What good is money to a god? It isn't as if they have to survive in our world."

It was an argument Persephone had heard before, and while she could not speak for other gods, she could defend Hades. The God of the Dead was the wealthiest of the Olympians, but his charitable contributions made a great impact on the mortal world.

Helen's article continued:

Triad stands for three mortal rights—fairness, free will, and freedom. Their objective is simple: remove the influence of gods from everyday life. They claim to have new leadership that encourages a more peaceful approach to their resistance to the gods as opposed to their previous antics, which included bombing several public gathering places and god-owned businesses.

There was no evidence to suggest Triad had been behind any recent attacks. In fact, the only thing they'd been connected to in the last five years was a protest that had sprung up in the streets of New Athens to object to the Panhellenic Games. Despite being viewed as an important cultural event to some Greeks, Triad abhorred the act of gods choosing heroes and pitting them against one another. It was a practice that inevitably led to death, and while Persephone had to agree that fighting to the death was archaic, it was the mortal's choice.

Gods, I'm starting to sound like Hades.

She read on:

Despite this claim of peace, there have been a reported 593 attacks against people with a public association with the gods in the last year. Those responsible say they are upholding Triad's newest mission by ushering in a rebirth. This growing death toll has gone unnoticed by god and mortal alike, overshadowed by news of a marriage, a winter storm, and Aphrodite's newest fashion line.

Perhaps the gods do not see Triad as a threat, but given their history, can they be trusted? As demonstrated, they are not the ones who will suffer if the so-called activist group decides to act. It will be innocent bystanders, and in a world where mortals outnumber gods, should we be asking what the Divine should do?

It was the last sentence that left Persephone with a sour taste in her mouth, especially on the heels of Adonis's death. Still, even given the truths Helen highlighted in her article, Persephone needed more. She wanted to hear from Triad's leadership—had they taken responsibility for those 593 attacks? If not, did they plan to condemn rogue actions? What were their plans for the future?

She was so focused on making notes, she didn't notice anyone approach until a voice startled her from her work.

"Are you Persephone Rosi?"

She jumped, head snapping to meet the gaze of a woman with large brown eyes and arched brows. Her face was heart-shaped and framed by thick, dark hair. She wore a black coat, trimmed with fur, and clutched a cup of steaming coffee between her hands.

Persephone smiled at her and answered, "I am."

She expected the woman to ask for a photo or an autograph, but instead, she took the lid off her coffee and poured it in her lap. Persephone jumped to her feet as the burn settled skin-deep and the whole shop went quiet.

For a moment, Persephone was stunned, silenced by the pain and her magic, which shook her bones, desperate to defend.

The woman turned, her task fulfilled, but instead of leaving, she came face-to-face with Zofie, an Amazon and Persephone's aegis.

She was beautiful—tall and olive-skinned, dark hair falling in a long braid down her back. When Persephone first met her, she'd been dressed in gold armor, but after a trip to Aphrodite's boutique, she'd come away with a modern wardrobe. Today, she wore a black jumper. The only item that didn't fit was a large sword she held and swung at her assaulter's head.

Screams erupted in the shop.

"Zofie!" Persephone cried, and the Amazon's blade halted a hair from the woman's neck. Zofie's eyes locked with Persephone's, her expression frustrated, as if she did not understand why she could not continue with her execution.

"Yes, my lady?"

"Put the sword away," Persephone ordered.

"But—" Zofie began to protest.

"*Now.*"

The command slipped between clenched teeth. That was all Persephone needed, Zofie spilling blood on her behalf. This would already make headlines—people were shamelessly filming and taking pictures. She made a note to inform Ilias of this incident; perhaps he could get ahead of the media.

The Amazon grumbled but obeyed, and her sword vanished from sight. Without the threat of bodily harm, the woman regained her composure and turned to Persephone again.

"*Lemming*," she hissed with more hatred in her eyes than Minthe or Demeter had ever possessed and stormed out of the Coffee House, signaling the pleasant chime of the bell on the door.

As soon as she was gone, Zofie spoke.

"One word, my lady. I'll slay her in the alley."

"No, Zofie. That's all we need, a murder on our hands."

"It's not murder," she argued. "It's retribution."

"I'm fine, Zofie."

Persephone turned to gather her things, conscious that people were still watching. She wished she had control over lightning like Zeus, because she would electrocute every device in this place just to teach them to mind their own business.

"But…she wounded you!" Zofie argued. "Lord Hades will not be pleased with me."

"You did your job, Zofie."

"If I had done my job, you would not be injured."

"You came as soon as you could," Persephone said. "And I am not injured. I'm fine."

She was lying, of course, mostly to protect Zofie. The Amazon was liable to attempt to resign again if she knew how much pain Persephone was in.

Who would have ever thought to use coffee as a weapon? Persephone thought. What a betrayal.

"Why did she attack you?"

Persephone frowned. She didn't know.

Lemming, the woman had called her—another word for a blind follower. Persephone knew the word, but she'd never been called one before.

"I don't know," she said and sighed. She met Zofie's gaze. "Call Ilias, and advise him of what happened. Perhaps he can get ahead of the media."

"Of course, my lady. Where are you going?"

"To find Hades," she said. And to assess the damage to

her legs. Her skin stung beneath her clothes. "The last time someone tried to hurt me, he tortured them."

She shrugged on her coat and sent Leuce and Helen a quick text, letting them know their morning meeting was canceled and she'd see them later tonight.

"I will see you at Sybil's?" she asked the Amazon.

"Yes, for the housewarming," Zofie said, and her brows pinched together. "Shall I bring wood?"

Persephone laughed. "No, Zofie. Bring…wine or food."

Persephone didn't know much about Zofie's upbringing, but it was evident that the island from which she originated did not evolve with modern society. When she'd asked Hecate about it, she'd said, *"That's how Ares prefers it."*

"Prefers…what?"

"The Amazons are his children, bred for war, not the world. He keeps them sequestered on the island of Terme so that they will never know anything but battle."

After learning this, Persephone wondered how Zofie had come to know Hades and became her aegis.

She focused on the Amazon again. "If you need ideas, just text Sybil and ask her what to bring. She'll help."

When Persephone stepped outside, the cold sliced into her, and it was worse where her clothing was wet, freezing her skin beneath. She made her way down the sidewalk, slick with water and gathering snow, rounding the corner of the building until she was out of sight of passersby before teleporting to the Underworld.

She appeared in her bedchamber, half expecting Hades to be there, waiting, frustrated, ready to inspect her for injury, but he had not arrived yet. She set her purse aside and shrugged out of her jacket, peeling off her faux leather leggings. She could still feel the residual sting where the hot coffee had sat against her skin. Luckily, the damage was minimal—her thighs were red and a little swollen, a hint of bubbled skin speckled across her legs. *Maybe running cold water over it would help*, she thought.

As she turned to enter the bathroom, she found her way blocked by Hades.

Persephone startled, her hands pressing to her heart, over her naked breast. The god stood with glittering eyes, smartly dressed in his tailored black suit. His hair was slick and tied into a perfect bun at the back of his head, not a wisp out of place. His chiseled jaw was close shaven and well manicured. He was immaculate and sexual, a presence that stole her breath and made her ache.

"Hades! You scared me."

His gaze dropped to her chest and he grinned, reaching for her hand.

"You should have known I would find you once you took your clothes off. It is a sixth sense."

As he bent to brush his lips along her knuckles, his eyes dipped lower, and a frown touched his mouth. He released her hand only to press his palm against her thigh. She shivered, his touch cool against the heat of the blisters.

"What is this?" His question was almost a hiss.

Apparently, word hadn't reached him yet.

"A woman poured coffee into my lap," Persephone explained.

"*Poured*?"

"If you are asking if it was intentional, the answer is yes."

Something dark flashed in Hades's eyes. It was the same look she'd seen last night when he'd brought news of Adonis's death. After a moment, he knelt before her. A wave of magic burst from his hands, settling into her skin until she no longer felt the pain of the burns or saw the scalding upon her skin. Despite being healed, Hades remained on his knees, hands drifting to the backs of her legs.

"Will you tell me who this woman was?" Hades asked, his lips grazing the inner part of her thigh.

"No," she said, inhaling sharply, her hands coming to rest on his shoulders.

"I cannot...persuade you?"

"Perhaps," she admitted, the word escaping on a breath. "But I do not know her name, so all your...*persuading* would be in vain."

"Nothing I do is in vain."

Hades's grip tightened on her, and his head dipped between her legs, his mouth closing over her clit. Persephone gasped, her fingers threading into his slick hair.

"*Hades—*"

"Don't make me stop," he said, his voice rough.

"You have thirty minutes," she said.

Hades paused, looking up at her from the ground.

Gods, he was beautiful and so fucking erotic. The heat in the bottom of her stomach melted her insides. She was wet for him. By the time he put his mouth on her, she would come—he wouldn't even need to coax an orgasm from her.

"Only thirty?"

"Do you need more?" she challenged.

He offered a wicked grin. "Darling, we both know I could make you come in five, but what if I'd like to take my time?"

"Later," she said. "We have a party to attend, and I still need to make cupcakes."

Hades frowned. "Is it not a mortal custom to be fashionably late?"

Persephone raised a brow. "Did Hermes tell you that?"

"Is he wrong?"

"I will not be late to Sybil's party, Hades. If you wish to please me, then you'll make me come and on time."

Hades smirked.

"As you wish, my darling."

CHAPTER IV
Never Have I Ever

Persephone manifested on the doorstep of Sybil's apartment with Hades.

A shiver shook her spine.

It was a combination of the cold and thoughts from the last hour spent with the God of the Dead on his knees. She should be used to Hades's wickedness, but he still found ways to surprise her—pleasuring her as she stood, one leg drawn over his shoulder. His tongue had tasted and teased, devoured and savored. She'd pressed into him, unable to keep her body from bearing down upon his mouth. She'd come, coaxed by a growl that erupted from deep in Hades's chest. She'd finished with enough time to make the cupcakes for Sybil's party.

Another shiver racked her body. The cold was piercing, like needles sinking into her skin. It was unnatural weather for August and nothing—not even the happiness Hades's love had inspired—could quell the dread she felt as the snow continued to fall.

It's the start of a war.

They were Hades's words, spoken the night he had

proposed, this time on a bent knee with a ring. It had been the best moment of her life but overshadowed by Demeter's magic. Suddenly, the tips of Persephone's fingers tingled with power, reacting to the sudden shiver of rage that shot up her back.

Hades's hand tightened around her waist.

"Are you well?" he asked, no doubt sensing the surge in her magic.

Persephone had not yet completely managed to keep her magic from reacting to her emotions.

"Persephone?"

Hades's voice drew her attention, and she realized she had not answered his earlier question. She tilted her head, meeting his dark gaze. Warmth blossomed in the pit of her stomach as her eyes fell to his lips and the inviting stubble on his jaw, recalling how it felt against her skin, a delicious friction that teased and taunted.

"I am well," she replied.

Hades raised a doubtful brow.

"I am," she said. "I was just thinking about my mother."

"Do not ruin your evening thinking of her, my darling."

"It is a little hard to ignore her given the weather, Hades."

He lifted his head and stared at the sky for a moment, his body going rigid beside hers, and she knew he was just as concerned, but she didn't ask for his thoughts on the matter. Tonight, she wanted to have fun, because something told her that beyond this night, nothing would be.

She knocked, but instead of seeing Sybil, a blond man answered the door. His hair fell in soft waves just above his shoulders. His eyes were hooded and blue and his jaw marked by stubble. He was handsome but a complete stranger.

Weird, Persephone thought. She was certain this was Sybil's apartment.

"Um, I think we might have the wrong—"

42

"Persephone, right?" the man asked.

She hesitated and Hades's arm tightened around her.

"Persephone!" Sybil popped up behind the man, ducked under his arm, and pulled her into a hug. "I'm so glad you're here!"

There was a note of relief in her voice. Sybil pulled away, and her eyes shifted to Hades.

"I'm glad you could come too, Hades." Sybil's voice was quiet and shy. Persephone was a little surprised, given that she was no stranger to the gods. She had served Apollo only months ago as his oracle…until he stripped her of her powers of prophecy after she refused to sleep with him. His behavior made him the subject of Persephone's article, but her decision to write about the God of the Sun had been a disaster.

It turned out he was beloved, and Persephone's article was seen as slander. Not only that, Hades had been furious—so furious that he had held Persephone prisoner in the Underworld until he could bargain with Apollo so the god would not seek revenge.

That experience had taught Persephone a lot of lessons, chiefly that the world was not ready to believe a woman in pain. It was one of the reasons she'd started *The Advocate*.

"I appreciate the invitation," Hades replied.

"Aren't you going to introduce me?" the blond stranger asked.

Persephone noted the way Sybil froze. It was only a second, as if she had forgotten the man was present, and a small, apologetic smile formed upon her face before she turned.

"Persephone, Hades, this is Ben."

"Hi," he said, extending his hand for them to shake. "I'm Sybil's boyfrie—"

"Friend. Ben is a friend," Sybil said quickly.

"Well, soon-to-be boyfriend," Ben said, grinning, but

the look Sybil gave her was desperate. Persephone's gaze slid from the oracle to the mortal as she accepted his clammy, outstretched hand.

"It's...*nice* to meet you."

Ben shifted toward Hades. The God of the Dead looked down at his hand. "You do not want to shake my hand, mortal."

Ben's eyes widened a little, and an awkward silence followed, but only for a beat before Ben's smile returned.

"Well, shall we go in?" he asked.

He stood aside, gesturing for everyone to enter. Persephone arched her brow at Hades as they stepped into the warm apartment. Hades had the ability to see to the soul, and Persephone wondered what he glimpsed when he looked at Ben, though she thought she could guess.

Serial killer.

"What?" Hades asked.

"You promised to behave," she said.

"It is not in my nature to appease mortals," Hades replied.

"But it is in your nature to appease me," Persephone said.

"Alas," he said, his voice low. "You are my greatest weakness."

The entrance of Sybil's apartment was a short hallway that led to a kitchen and a small living room. The space was mostly empty, save for a love seat and a television. While it was nowhere close to the extravagance she'd lived in with Apollo, it was quaint and cozy. It reminded Persephone of the apartment she's shared with Lexa for three years.

"Wine?" Sybil asked, and Persephone was glad for the distraction.

"Please," she said, tamping down the ache that had formed in her chest at the thought of her dead best friend.

"For you, Hades?"

"Whiskey…whatever you have is fine. Neat…please," he added as if it were an afterthought. Persephone grimaced, but at least he'd asked nicely.

"Neat?" Ben asked. "Real whiskey drinkers at least add water."

Persephone's heart pounded as she watched Hades's eyes connect with Ben's. "I add the blood of mortals."

"Of course, Hades," Sybil said quickly, plucking a bottle from the collection on the counter and handing it to him. "You'll probably need it."

"Thank you, Sybil," he said, quickly loosening the cap to drink.

She poured Persephone a glass of wine and slid it across the counter.

"So how did you meet Ben?" Persephone asked, picking up her wine.

Sybil started to respond when Ben jumped in.

"We met at Four Olives where I work," he said. "It was love at first sight for me."

Persephone choked on her drink, the wine burning the back of her throat as she spit it back into the glass. Her eyes connected with Sybil's, who looked mortified, but before either of them could speak, a knock sounded at the door.

"Thank the gods," Sybil said, practically racing to the entrance, leaving Persephone and Hades alone with the mortal.

"I know she isn't convinced yet," Ben said. "But it's only a matter of time."

"What makes you so sure?" Persephone countered.

His back straightened as he proclaimed, "I'm an oracle."

"Oh fuck," Hades grumbled.

Persephone elbowed him.

"If you'll excuse me," he said, leaving the kitchen with his bottle of whiskey.

Ben leaned across the bar. "I don't think he likes me."

"Whatever gave you that idea?" Persephone asked, her nose still burning.

Ben shrugged a shoulder. "It's…just a feeling."

There was a long, awkward silence that passed between them, and just when Persephone started to excuse herself to go in search of Hades, the so-called oracle spoke.

"You've lost," he said.

"Excuse me."

"Yes," he whispered, his eyes unfocused and glazed. "You have lost, and you will lose again."

Persephone's jaw clenched.

"The loss of one friend will lead you to lose many—and you, you will cease to shine, an ember taken by the night."

Her anger slowly dissipated, turning to disgust as she recognized his words.

"Why are you quoting *Leonidas*?"

The television show was popular and had been one of Lexa's favorites about a Spartan king and his war with the Persians. It was a drama full of love and lust and blood.

Ben blinked, his eyes coming into focus.

"What did you just say?" he asked, and Persephone rolled her eyes. She hated false prophets. They were dangerous and made a joke of the real practice of prophecy. She started to speak but was interrupted by Hermes's cry of excitement.

"Sephy!" The God of Mischief threw his arms around her neck, squeezing her. He inhaled deeply. "You smell like Hades…and sex."

She shoved against the god. "Stop being creepy, Hermes!"

The god chuckled and released her, his sparkling gaze shifting to Ben.

"Oh, and who is this?" His interest was evident in the peak of his voice.

"This is Ben. Sybil's…" She wasn't sure how to finish that sentence, but she didn't need to because no one was listening anyway. Ben was already grinning at the God of Mischief.

"Hermes, right?" he asked.

"So you've heard of me?"

Persephone rolled her eyes. He'd asked her the same thing when they'd first met. She had never asked why he said it, but she had a feeling it was to invite some kind of compliment considering everyone *had* heard of him.

She was not surprised when it backfired.

"Of course," Ben replied. "Are you still the Messenger of the Gods or do they use email?"

Persephone's brows rose and she pressed her lips together to keep from giggling.

Hermes narrowed his eyes.

"It's Lord Hermes to you," he said and twisted away, muttering to Sybil as he passed, "You can keep him."

The God of Thieves was not upset for long when he noticed Hades standing in Sybil's living room. "Well, well, well, look who decided to darken the corner—literally."

Hades did look out of place in Sybil's apartment, much like he had the night he had come to Persephone and Lexa's to make cookies. At least he'd tried to fit in that night, wearing a black shirt and sweats. Tonight, he insisted on wearing a suit.

"*What happened to those sweats you wore to my house?*" Persephone had asked before they left.

"*I…threw them out.*"

Her eyes widened.

"*Why?*"

Hades shrugged. "*I did not think there would be a time when I would need them again.*"

She raised a brow. "*Do you mean to say you never thought you would hang out with my friends again?*"

"*No.*" He looked down at his suit. "*Do I not meet your expectations?*"

She had giggled then. "*No, by far, you exceed them.*"

He'd grinned then, and she thought her heart might beat right out of her chest. There was nothing as beautiful as Hades when he smiled.

Another knock announced the arrival of more guests— this time, Helen. She wore a long, beige coat with a fur collar that she slipped off and folded over her arm. Beneath the jacket was a long-sleeved white shirt and a camel-colored skirt with leggings. Her long hair was curled and fell in honey-colored waves over her shoulders. She'd brought wine and handed it to Sybil with a kiss on the cheek.

The two had not known each other long, but like everyone in Persephone's circle, they'd become fast friends.

"This weather," Helen said. "It's almost…unnatural."

"Yes," Persephone said, quiet, a wave of guilt slamming into her. "It's awful."

Another knock sent Sybil to the door, and she came back with Leuce and Zofie in tow. The two were now roommates, and Persephone had yet to decide if it was actually a good idea. Leuce had only recently returned to the mortal world after having been a tree for centuries, and Zofie had no real understanding of the humans, having been raised among female warriors. Still, the two were learning, from simple things like how to use the crosswalk and order food to more difficult aspects of mortal life like socializing and self-control.

Leuce was a naiad—a water nymph. She had white hair and lashes and pale skin that made her blue eyes look as bright as the sun. When Persephone had first met her, she was combative, and her pretty features were severe and angled. Over time, though, she had gotten to know the nymph, and her attitude toward her softened, despite the fact that she had been Hades's lover. Unlike Minthe, however, Persephone was certain there was no affection left between the two—a fact that made taking her under her wing a far easier decision. Tonight, she wore a simple, light blue dress that made her look like an ice queen.

When Zofie entered the apartment, she was smiling, only to falter when she noticed Hades standing in Sybil's living room.

"My lord!" she exclaimed and bowed quickly.

"You don't have to do that here, Zofie," Persephone said.

"But…he is the Lord of the Underworld."

"We're all aware," Hermes said. "Look at him—he's the only goth in the room."

Hades glared.

"Since everyone's here, let's play a game!" Hermes said.

"What's the game?" Helen asked. "Poker?"

"No!" everyone said in unison, eyes shifting to Hades, who glared as if he wished to incinerate them. Persephone could just imagine the amount of work she was going to have to put in later to make up for his suffering.

"Let's play Never Have I Ever!" Hermes said. He reached over the breakfast bar to the kitchen counter, clasping several bottles of various liquors between his fingers. "With shots!"

"Okay, but I don't have shot glasses," Sybil said.

"Then you're all going to have to pick something to gulp," Hermes said.

"Oh gods," Persephone mumbled.

"What's Never Have I Ever?" Zofie asked.

"Exactly what it sounds like," Hermes said as he set the bottles on the coffee table. "You make a statement about something you've never done, and if anyone has done it, they have to take a shot."

Everyone filed into the living room. Hermes sat on one

side of the couch while Ben had taken up the other—until he noticed Sybil settling on the ground beside Persephone. Then he abandoned the spot to squeeze beside her. It was awkward to watch, and Persephone averted her eyes, finding Hades staring. He stood across from her, not quite part of the circle they had formed. She wondered if he would find a reason not to play this game—and she couldn't deny that part of her wanted to see how he would respond to every single one of these statements.

She also dreaded it.

"Me first!" Hermes says. "Never have I ever...had sex with Hades."

Persephone's gaze was murderous—she knew because she could feel the frustration eating away the glamour she used to dim the color of her irises.

"*Hermes*," she gritted his name from between her teeth.

"What?" he whined. "This game is difficult for someone my age. I've done *everything*." Then Leuce cleared her throat, and his eyes widened as he realized what he had done. "Oh," he said. "*Oh*."

Persephone liked Leuce, but that did not mean she liked being reminded of her past with Hades. She made a point not to look at Leuce as she drank from a bottle of Fireball.

Ben went next. "Never have I ever stalked an ex-girlfriend."

There was a collective awkwardness that followed the false prophet's statement. Was he trying to prove he wasn't a creep?

No one drank.

Sybil was next.

"Never have I ever...fallen in love at first sight." It was a jab at Ben, who did not seem to notice—or perhaps he didn't care, so confident in his abilities as an oracle, he took a shot.

Next was Helen. "Never have I ever...had a threesome."

To no one's surprise, Hermes took a shot, but so did

Hades, and something about it made the color drain from Persephone's face. Perhaps it was the way he did it—eyes lowered, lashes fanning his cheeks, as if he did not wish to know that she saw him. Still, she tried to rationalize that they had discussed this before. Hades would not apologize for living before her, and she understood that. She *expected* Hades, God of the Dead, to have had many, varied sexual experiences—and yet she still felt jealous.

Finally, Hades lifted his eyes to hers. They were dark, a hint of fire igniting the irises like a sliver of a moon. It was an expression she knew well, not a warning so much as a plea—*I love you, I am with you now. Nothing else matters.*

She knew that—believed it with all her heart—but as the game continued, the instances where she was able to take a shot were few and far between—and nothing compared to Hades.

"Never have I ever...eaten food off someone's naked body," Ben said but added with a direct look at Sybil, "but I'd like to."

Hades drank and Persephone wanted to vomit.

"Never have I ever...had sex in the kitchen," Helen said. Hades drank.

"Never have I ever had sex in public," Sybil said. Hades drank.

"Never have I ever faked an orgasm," said Helen.

Persephone wasn't sure what came over her, but at that statement, she tipped her drink back and swallowed a gulp of wine. As she set the glass down, Hades raised a brow and his eyes darkened. She could feel his energy against her own, demanding. He was eager to have her speak—to taste her skin and confirm she had lied.

She didn't expect Hades to challenge her in front of everyone.

"If that is true, I will happily rectify the situation."

"Oh," Hermes teased. "Someone's getting fucked tonight."

"Shut up, Hermes."

"What? You're just lucky he didn't carry you away to the Underworld the moment you lifted that glass."

It still wasn't out of the realm of possibility with the way Hades was looking at her. He had questions and he wanted answers.

"Let's play another game," Persephone suggested.

"But I like this one," Hermes whined. "It was just getting *good*."

She gave him a scathing look.

"Besides, you know Hades is just making a list of all the ways he wants to f—"

"Enough, Hermes!" Persephone got to her feet and made her way down the hallway to the bathroom. She closed the door and sank against it. Her eyes fluttered closed, and she exhaled—it was a failed attempt to release the strange feeling that had been building inside her. She couldn't describe it, but it felt thick and heavy.

Then the air stirred, and she tensed, feeling Hades's body cage her own. His cheek touched hers, and his breath tickled her ear as he spoke.

"You had to know your actions would ignite me." His voice was raw and rough, and it made the bottom of her stomach tighten. His body was rigid, a force barely contained. "When have I left you wanting?"

She swallowed hard and knew he wanted the truth.

"Will you not answer?"

He lifted his hand to her throat—not squeezing but forcing her gaze to his.

"I'd really have rather not found out about your sexual exploits via a game in front of my friends," she said.

"So you thought it better to reveal that I had not satisfied you in the same manner?"

Persephone looked away. Hades's hand was still at her throat, and then he leaned forward, his tongue pressed lightly against her ear.

"Shall I leave no doubt in their minds that I can make you come?"

He lifted her skirt and tore at her lace underwear.

"Hades! We are guests here!"

"Your point?" he asked as he lifted her off the floor, leveraging her weight against the door. His movements were controlled but rough—a peek at the violence awake beneath his skin.

"It's rude to have sex in someone's bathroom."

Hades licked across her mouth before his tongue parted her lips and her protests were drowned as he kissed her hard—to the point where she couldn't breathe.

Why did I provoke him? Because I wanted this, she thought. *I needed this.*

She'd wanted to anger him, to feel him rage against her skin until she no longer remembered a past where she did not exist with him.

Her sex clenched as she felt the head of Hades's cock graze her opening, and in the next second, he was fully sheathed. Persephone's head rolled, and a sound escaped her lips, raw and unabashed, as a wave of pleasure welled inside her.

Then there was a knock on the door.

"I hate to interrupt whatever's going on in there," Hermes said. "But I think you two will want to see this."

"Not now," Hades growled, his head resting in the crook of Persephone's neck. His body was hard and rigid. She recognized it for what it was—an attempt at self-control.

It was a trait she wished he'd abandon.

She turned her head toward his, tongue grazing his ear, then her teeth. Hades inhaled; his hands squeezed her ass.

"Okay, first, it's rude to have sex in other people's bathrooms," Hermes said. "Second, it's about the weather."

Hades groaned and then growled. "A *moment*, Hermes."

"How long is a moment?" he asked.

"*Hermes*," Hades warned.

"Okay, okay."

Once they were alone, Hades left her. She felt his absence immediately—an ache that grew.

"Fuck," he said under his breath as he restored his appearance.

"I'm sorry," Persephone said.

Hades's brows furrowed. "Why are you apologizing?"

She opened her mouth to explain—maybe for her jealousy or because they'd had to stop, or because of the storm—she really didn't know. She closed her mouth, and Hades leaned toward her.

"I am not upset with you," he said and kissed her. "But your mother will regret the interruption."

Persephone wondered what he meant, but she didn't question him as they left the bathroom. From the hallway, she could hear the television blaring.

"A severe ice storm warning has been issued for the whole of New Greece."

"What's going on?"

"It's started to sleet," Helen said. She was at the window, the curtains parted.

Persephone approached. She could hear the faint tap of ice as it hit the window. She grimaced. She'd known the weather would get worse, but she hadn't expected it to happen so soon.

"This is a god," Ben said. "A god cursing us!"

Persephone met Hades's gaze. A tense silence filled the room.

The mortal turned to Hades, demanding. "Do you deny it?"

"It is not wise to jump to conclusions, mortal," Hades replied.

"I'm not jumping to conclusions. I have foreseen this! The gods will rain terror down upon us. There will be despair and destruction."

The oracle's words settled in the bottom of Persephone's stomach like a stone, cold and heavy. Despite the fact that she thought he was insane, she could not deny that what he spoke was completely possible.

"Careful with your words, oracle." It was Hermes who spoke this time. It was unnerving, seeing him so severe, so offended, and the tone of his voice sent shivers down Persephone's spine.

Ben's accusations were serious, and it was possible his prediction would incur the wrath of the gods.

"I am only speaking—"

"What you hear," Sybil finished. "Which may or may not be the word of a god, and judging by the fact that you have no patron, I'm guessing you're being fed prophecies from an impious entity. If you had training, you would know that."

Persephone looked from Sybil to Ben. She didn't know what an impious entity was, but Sybil knew what she was talking about. She had been trained for this.

"And what is so bad about an impious entity? Sometimes they are the only truth tellers."

"I think you should leave," Sybil said.

A tense silence followed as Ben seemed to register Sybil's words.

"You want me to...*leave*?"

"She didn't stutter," Hermes shot back.

"But—"

"You must have forgotten the way out the door," Hermes said. "I'll show you out."

"Sybil—" Ben tried to plead, but in the next second, he vanished. All eyes turned to Hermes.

"That wasn't me," the god said.

Their gazes moved to Hades, but he remained silent, and though no one asked, Persephone wondered where he'd deposited the mortal.

"I think we all should go," Persephone said, though what she really wanted was to be alone with Hades to ask questions. "This storm is only going to get worse the longer we stay."

Everyone was in agreement.

"Hades, I'd like to make sure Helen, Leuce, and Zofie get home safe."

He nodded. "I'll call Antoni."

As the women fetched their jackets, Persephone pulled Sybil aside.

"Are you alright? Ben is—"

"An idiot," Sybil said. "I'm so sorry if he offended you or the others."

"Don't worry...but at the rate he is going, I'm sure he'll incur the wrath of some god."

They did not have to wait for Antoni long. The cyclops pulled up in a sleek limo, and they filed inside—Hades and Persephone on one side, Leuce, Zofie, and Helen on the other.

"Did anyone else really hate that Ben guy?" Leuce asked.

"Sybil should keep a blade beneath her bed in case he comes back," Zofie said.

"Or she could just lock her door," Helen suggested.

"Locks can be picked," Zofie said. "A blade is better."

The cabin fell silent, except for the tapping of ice on the windows.

They dropped Leuce and Zofie off first. Once they had left the cabin, the darkness seemed to swallow Helen, whose petite frame was lost in the fur of her coat. She stared out at the night, her pretty face illuminated now and then by the streetlights.

After a moment, she spoke. "Do you think Ben is right? That this is the work of the gods?"

Persephone tensed and looked at the mortal, whose eyes had drifted to Hades—wide and innocent. It was strange to hear that question with no venom behind the words.

"We'll find out soon enough," Hades replied.

The limo came to a stop, and as Antoni opened the door, cold air filled the cabin. Persephone shivered, and Hades's arm tightened around her.

"Thank you for the ride," Helen said as she left.

Once they were on the road again, Persephone spoke.

"Does she really think a storm will keep us apart?"

The way Hades's jaw ticked told her everything she needed to know—*yes*.

"Have you ever seen snow, Persephone?" Hades asked, and she did not like the tone of his voice.

She hesitated. "From afar."

On the caps of mountains, but since she had moved to New Athens, never.

Hades met her gaze, his eyes glittering; he looked menacing and angry.

"What is going through your mind?" she asked quietly.

His lashes lowered, casting shadows on his cheeks. "She will do this until the gods have no choice but to intervene."

"And what happens then?"

Hades did not reply, and Persephone didn't force a conversation, because in truth, she was too afraid, and she thought she knew the answer.

War.

CHAPTER V
A Touch of Ancient Magic

"Antoni," Hades said not long after they dropped Helen off. "Please see that Lady Persephone returns safely to Nevernight."

"What?"

The word was barely out of her mouth before Hades gripped her head and kissed her. He made love to her mouth, parting her lips to thrust his tongue inside. The bottom of her stomach grew taut with anticipation, her thoughts turning from her mother's wrath to the promise Hades had made in Sybil's bathroom. She still felt the empty ache of their unfinished coupling, and she desperately wanted to lose herself in him tonight, but instead of giving her release, he drew away. Her lips felt swollen and raw.

More, Hades. Now. She wanted to scream at him because her body ached so badly.

And he knew it.

"Do not fret, my darling. You shall come for me tonight."

Antoni coughed, and it sounded like he was trying to cover a laugh.

In the next second, Hades's magic flared, smelling of spice and ash, and he was gone.

Persephone let out a long breath and then met Antoni's gaze in the rearview mirror.

"Where did he go?"

"I do not know, my lady," he answered, and she heard what he didn't say—*even if I did, I have been ordered to take you home.* Persephone suddenly knew what she would ask of Hecate at their next training session—how to follow someone when they teleported.

Antoni let Persephone out at the front of Nevernight. Despite the awful cold and stream of ice falling from the sky, mortals still stood in line, desperate to hold on to their chance to see the inside of Hades's infamous club. She was met by Mekonnen, an ogre and one of Hades's bouncers, as she exited the vehicle. He held an umbrella over her head and walked with her to the door.

"Good evening, Persephone," he said.

She grinned. "Hello, Mekonnen. How are you?"

"Well," he replied.

She was relieved when he didn't comment on the weather. Mekonnen held the door open, and she entered the club. She ascended the stairs to the floor, packed with mortals and immortals alike. She did not always walk the floor; sometimes she would teleport as soon as she set foot inside, but more and more, she was trying to grow comfortable with the kind of power that came with being engaged to Hades.

Which meant that this club, it was hers.

Sometimes she wished she could walk unseen among the crowds like Hades, observing and listening, uninterrupted, but she did not think that power would manifest among her skill set.

Persephone cut across the floor of Nevernight, passing

packed lounges, the backlit bar, and the sunken dance floor, where flushed bodies pulsed beneath red laser light. As she moved, she knew others watched. Even if they did not look at her, they whispered, and while she did not know what they said, she could guess. There was no shortage of rumors, no shortage of body language experts analyzing her every move, no shortage of "close friends" releasing details about her life in the Underworld, her struggles with grief, the challenges of planning a wedding, and while there was only a thread of truth to any of those articles, it was how the world formed their opinion of her.

Persephone knew words were both ally and enemy, but she always thought she would be behind sensational journalism, not the other way around.

She was just grateful that no one approached her. Not that she minded most of the time, but tonight she was feeling less trusting. Perhaps it had something to do with today's coffee incident. Still, she knew that one of the reasons people kept their distance was that she was being guarded. Adrian and Ezio, two of several ogres Hades employed as bouncers and bodyguards, flanked her from a distance. If anyone approached, they would converge.

Sometimes, though, even they weren't intimidating enough to deter desperate mortals.

"Persephone!" a female voice rang out, barely audible over the clamor of the crowd. Persephone was used to people calling her name, and she was getting better at not letting it halt her stride, but this woman pushed through the crowd and, just as she made it to the stairs, cut her off.

"Persephone!" The dark-haired woman said her name, out of breath from chasing her across the club. She was dressed in pink, and her chest heaved as she reached for her arm. Persephone jerked away, and suddenly, Adrian and Ezio stood between her and the mortal woman.

"Persephone," she said her name again. "Please. I beg you! Hear me out!"

"Come, my lady," Adrian implored, while Ezio maintained a barrier between her and the woman.

"A moment, Adrian," Persephone said and placed her hand upon Ezio's arm as she moved to stand beside him. "Are you asking for my help?"

"Yes! Oh, Persephone—"

"She is the future wife and queen of Lord Hades," said Adrian. "You will address her as such."

The woman's eyes widened. Not too long ago, Persephone would have cringed hearing Adrian's correction, but the times where she asked others to call her only by her name were fewer and fewer.

"I'm so sorry, so sorry!"

Persephone felt herself growing impatient.

"Whatever your issue, it must not be as pressing considering it is taking you forever to get to the point."

Gods, she really was starting to sound like Hades.

"Please, my lady—I implore you. I wish to bargain with Lord Hades. You must ask him to see me immediately."

Persephone ground her teeth together. So the woman was not asking for *her* help—she wished for her to beg Hades for his. She tilted her head, narrowing her eyes, attempting to place a cap on her anger.

"Perhaps I can help you," Persephone suggested.

The woman laughed, as if her suggestion was ludicrous. If Persephone were being honest, the reaction hurt. She realized this mortal did not know she was a goddess, but it was another reminder of the worth that was placed upon divinity.

Persephone's lips flattened. "Rejecting my help is effectively rejecting Hades."

She started up the stairs again, and the woman attempted

to lunge toward her, but Ezio placed his arm between them, preventing the woman from touching her.

"Wait, please." The woman's tone became desperate. "I did not mean to offend. It's just…how can you help me? You are mortal."

Persephone paused and glanced at the woman. "If what you are asking for requires the aid of a god, it is likely you shouldn't be asking for it at all."

"That is easy for you to say," the woman retorted angrily. "A woman who may ask anything of her lover, a god."

Persephone glared. This woman was like anyone else who wrote articles or whispered about her. She had created her own narrative around Persephone's life. She did not know how she had begged Hades for his aid, how he had refused, how she had fucked up and bargained with Apollo when she should have stopped interfering.

She looked up at Ezio.

"See her out," Persephone said and turned to head up the stairs with Adrian.

"Wait! No! Please!"

The woman's pleas erupted like the sound of fireworks inside the club, and slowly, the roar of the crowd turned quiet as they watched Ezio drag the woman from the club. Persephone ignored the attention and continued upstairs to Hades's office. By the time she was behind the gilded doors, frustration flooded her veins. A pain pricked her forearm that she recognized as her magic attempting to manifest physically—usually in the form of a vine or leaves or flowers sprouting from her skin.

The mortal had triggered her.

She took a breath to ease her anger until the prick of pain dissipated.

What is the opinion of the world anyway? Her bitter thought quickly turned into something far more painful as she realized why she had become so angry—the woman had essentially told her that she had nothing of value to offer, with the exception of her connection to Hades.

Persephone had struggled before with feeling like an object—a possession owned by Hades, often unnamed in articles where their relationship took center stage. She was *Hades's lover* or *the mortal*.

What would it take for the Upperworld to see her as the Underworld did? Hades's equal.

Persephone sighed and teleported to Hecate's grove, only to find the goddess engaged in battle with a tiny, fluffy black puppy that had the hem of her crimson gown clasped between its teeth.

"Nefeli! Release me at once!" Hecate shouted.

The pup growled and pulled harder.

Persephone giggled, her earlier frustrations suddenly gone, replaced by amusement at seeing the Goddess of Witchcraft gripping her skirts in an attempt to free herself from such a small, delicate creature.

"Persephone, don't just stand there! Save me from this... monster!"

"Oh, Hecate." Persephone bent to scoop up the ball of fur. "She is not a monster."

She held Nefeli aloft. She had small ears, a pointed nose, and expressive—almost human—eyes.

"She is a villain!" The goddess inspected her dress, full of tiny holes. Then she placed her hands on her hips, narrowing her eyes. "After everything I did."

"Where did you find her?" Persephone asked.

"I—" Hecate hesitated, and her hands dropped from her sides. "I...well...I made her."

Persephone's brows drew together, and she shifted the puppy so that she held her in the crook of her arm. "You... *made* her?"

"It's not as bad as it sounds," Hecate said.

When she offered no explanation, Persephone spoke. "Hecate, please don't tell me this was a human."

It wouldn't be the first time. Hecate had turned a witch named Gale into a polecat she now kept as a pet in the Underworld.

"Okay, then I won't," she replied.

"Hecate," Persephone chided. "You didn't—why? Because she annoyed you?"

"No, no, no," she said. "Though…that is debatable. I turned her into a dog because of her grief."

"*Why*?"

"Because she was going insane, and I thought she would rather be a dog than a mortal who had lost."

Persephone opened her mouth and then closed it. "Hecate, you can't just turn her into a dog without her permission. No wonder she attacked your skirts."

The goddess crossed her arms. "She gave me permission. She looked up at me from the ground and begged me to take her pain away."

"I am sure she did not mean for you to turn her into a dog."

Hecate shrugged. "A lesson for all mortals—if you are going to beg a god for help, be specific."

Persephone offered a pointed look.

"Besides, I needed a new grim. Hecuba is tired."

"A grim?"

"Oh yes," Hecate said with a devious smirk. "It's just an old tradition I began centuries ago. Before I take a mortal's life, I send a grim to torture them for weeks before their timely end."

"But…how are you able to take lives, Hecate?"

"I am assigned as their Fate," she explained.

Persephone shivered. She had never borne witness to the goddess's vengeance but knew that Hecate was known as the Lady of Tartarus for her unique approach to punishment, which usually involved poison. Persephone could only imagine the hell any mortal would go through with Hecate assigned as the cause of their death.

"But enough about me and this mongrel. You came to see me?"

Hecate's question pulled the smile from Persephone's face as she was reminded of the reason she had sought the goddess. Despite her earlier frustration, she no longer felt anger so much as disappointment.

"I just…wondered if we could practice."

Hecate narrowed her eyes. "I might not be Hades, but I know when you aren't telling the truth. Come—out with it."

Persephone sighed and told Hecate about the woman in the club. The goddess listened and, after a moment, asked, "What did you think you could have offered the woman?"

Persephone opened her mouth to speak but hesitated.

"I…don't know," she admitted. She didn't even know what the woman had wanted—though she could guess. It hadn't taken Persephone long to realize that mortals rarely asked for anything but time, health, wealth, or love. None of which Persephone could grant, not as the Goddess of Spring, much less as a goddess just learning her powers.

"I see where your mind is going," Hecate said. "I did not mean to make you feel lesser, but you have answered my question all the same."

Persephone's eyes widened slightly. "How?"

"You are thinking like a mortal," Hecate said. "What could I have possibly offered?"

"What could I have offered, Hecate? A wilted rose? The sun on a cold day?"

"You mock yourself and yet your mother terrorizes the

Upperworld with snow and ice. The sun is just what the mortal world needs."

Persephone frowned. The idea of attempting to counter her mother's magic was overwhelming. Again, Hecate stopped her.

"Coming from the woman who used Hades's magic against him."

Persephone narrowed her eyes. "Hecate, have you been hiding that you can read my mind?"

"Hiding implies that I willfully misled you," Hecate replied.

Persephone raised a brow.

"But yes, of course I can read minds," Hecate answered, and then, as if it would explain everything, she added, "I am a goddess and a witch."

"*Great.*" Persephone rolled her eyes.

"Don't worry," Hecate said. "I'm used to tuning out, especially when you're thinking about Hades."

The goddess scrunched her nose and Persephone groaned.

"My point is, Persephone, there will come a time when you can no longer masquerade as a mortal."

A frown pulled at Persephone's lips, but even she was beginning to wonder how long she would be able to keep up this charade, especially with her mother's magic running rampant in the Upperworld.

"It was noble, to want to be known for your work, but you are more than Persephone, a journalist. You are Persephone, Goddess of Spring, future Queen of the Underworld. You have so much more to offer than words."

She thought of something Lexa had told her about what it meant to be a goddess. *You are kind and compassionate and you fight for your beliefs, but mostly, you fight for people.*

Persephone took a deep breath.

"And what am I supposed to do? Announce my divinity to the world?"

"Oh, my dear, do not worry about how the world will come to know you."

Persephone shivered, and while part of her wanted to know what Hecate meant, another part of her didn't.

"Come. You wanted to practice."

The goddess sat on the grass and patted the spot beside her. Persephone sighed, knowing Hecate intended for her to meditate. She did not like meditating, but she had been working on drawing upon her magic, and while she was getting better, it was usually via Hades's instruction she was most successful.

She took her place beside Hecate, releasing Nefeli to wander in the surrounding meadow. Hecate began, coaching her to close her eyes as she narrated how Persephone should think of her magic—as a well or pool that she could draw from anytime.

"Imagine the pool—glistening, cool."

The problem was Persephone didn't think of her magic as a pool at all—it was darkness, shadow. It wasn't cool; it was fire. It wasn't calm; it was furious. It had been locked away so long, freedom had made it feral. When she got close, it gnashed, sprouted, drew blood. It was the opposite of peace—the opposite of meditation.

While she sat with her eyes closed, she felt magic stir around her—it was Hecate's—a heavy and ancient power that smelled like a fine wine, aged and sharp, and felt like dread. Persephone's eyes flew open only to find that the small, fluffy dog from earlier had transformed into a massive hellhound. She was no longer cute but fierce. Her eyes glowed red, her teeth were long and sharp, and her jowls dripped, salivating with hunger.

Nefeli growled, and Persephone's eyes darted to Hecate, who had moved to hover behind her new grim.

"Hecate—" Persephone's voice took on an edge of warning.

"Yes, my lady?"

"Don't *my lady* me," she snapped. "What are you doing?"

"We're practicing."

"This isn't practice!"

"It is. You must be prepared for the unexpected. Not all are as they appear, Persephone."

"I think I get it. The dog isn't cute."

A deadly growl erupted from Nefeli's throat. She inched toward Persephone like a predator cornering its prey, pinning her against the ground.

"Did she insult you, my sweet?" Hecate asked, her voice sweet but chiding.

Persephone glared at the goddess as she encouraged the hound she'd decried earlier.

"If you want her to yield, use your magic," Hecate said.

Persephone's eyes widened. What magic was she supposed to use to call off a hound? "*Hecate*—"

The goddess sighed. "Nefeli!"

As Hecate said the hound's name, her ears went back, and for a brief moment, Persephone thought that she was going to call off the dog.

Instead, Hecate said, "*Attack.*"

Persephone's eyes widened, and in the next second, she teleported, landing in the grass beside the Aleyonia Ocean. She'd only been here once, on a night when she'd wandered from Hades's palace and gotten lost. She rose onto her hands and knees, realizing that she'd missed falling from the cliffside by an inch. Her limbs shook as she settled into the grass, drawing her knees to her chest. She sat for a long while, letting the salty wind dry the tears that streaked her face, replaying what had happened in the meadow.

Teleporting had felt like her only option as soon as Hecate had given her orders, and while she was now safe, she also felt like she'd failed. She did not blame Hecate. She knew what the goddess was trying to teach her. She had to think faster. As soon as she had felt Hecate's magic surround her, she should have been on alert. Instead, she'd grown too comfortable—so comfortable she had not taken her instruction seriously.

She would not make the same mistake a second time—because eventually, there would be no room for second chances.

CHAPTER VI
A Treat

Persephone paced her bedchamber.

Hades had not returned since leaving her in the limo, and while she wasn't anxious about his absence, she *was* nervous about trying to sleep without him. Each time she looked at their bed, she felt dread. At least when Hades was here, she knew he would guard her sleep and wake her from her nightmares if Pirithous decided to show.

She paused in front of the fireplace, and her eyes fell to Hades's decanter of whiskey. Curious, she picked it up, studying the amber liquid. Through the crystal, it glittered like citrine gems. Once, she'd asked Hades why he preferred whiskey as his drink of choice.

"*It's healthy,*" he'd said.

She'd snorted.

"*It is,*" he'd argued. "*It helps me relax.*"

"*But you drink it constantly,*" she pointed out.

He'd shrugged then. "*I like to feel relaxed constantly.*"

If it helped Hades relax, maybe it would help her.

She pulled the cap free and took a drink. It was

surprisingly...sweet. It reminded her of vanilla and caramel, two ingredients she had a lot of experience with. She took another drink, detecting a hint of spice similar to Hades's smell. She liked it. Tucking the bottle against her breasts, she left the bedroom and wandered into the kitchen, flipping on the lights, which seemed far too bright after walking through the shadowed halls of the palace.

She was becoming more familiar with Milan's kitchen, and surprisingly, the cook was happy to share the space, most likely because Persephone could teach him more modern recipes. In particular, he was eager to learn how to make cakes.

"*You know,*" Persephone had said one afternoon as she taught him how to decorate sugar cookies. "*I'm sure there are plenty of celebrated chefs in Asphodel. Have you ever thought of bringing them into your kitchen?*"

"*I never had any reason to,*" Milan said. "*My lord is a creature of habit. He has eaten the same thing for eternity—no wish for variety or...flavor.*"

That sounded like Hades.

"*I am sure he will be open to trying a few new dishes.*"

"*If the suggestion comes from your lips, I have no doubt he will bend to your will.*"

Milan was not wrong. Persephone understood the power she wielded over Hades. He would do anything for her.

Burn the world for her.

Those words shuddered through her, their truth ringing deep, and she wondered as the snow and ice coated the earth above if Hades would hold true to his words.

She sighed and focused on her task. She decided that what she needed other than whiskey was brownies. She set to work, locating ingredients, bowls, and measuring cups. She started by melting butter, then mixed it with sugar. She took pleasure in beating the eggs, which was a good thing because she didn't want to take her frustration out on the actual batter—over beating wouldn't give her the texture she wanted. After the eggs, she added vanilla, flour, and cocoa powder. Once the batter was mixed, she poured it into a pan, smoothing the blunt end of her spoon over the top before sampling.

"Hmm," she sighed at the flavor upon her tongue—warm and sweet.

"How does it taste?"

The sound of Hades's voice was followed by his presence as he manifested behind her. Persephone turned her head toward him—she could feel his breath on her cheek as she answered.

"Divine."

She turned to him and dragged her finger along the spoon, gathering enough batter for him.

"Taste," she whispered as her fingers parted his lips.

It took no coaxing—Hades's tongue glided along her finger, the pressure of his mouth increasing as he sucked away what remained of the batter. When he released her, he made a deep sound in the back of his throat and his voice rumbled as he spoke.

"Exquisite," he said. "But I have tasted divinity and there is nothing sweeter."

His words tightened her chest and made the space they shared feel even smaller. They stared at one another for a moment, simmering in the heat they shared until Persephone turned away, returning the spoon to the bowl.

"Where were you?" she asked, picking up the pan of brownies and sliding them into the oven. An overwhelming wave of heat hit her face as she opened the door.

"I had business," Hades replied, evasive as ever.

Persephone let the oven door slam and turned to him. "Business? At this hour?"

She wasn't even sure of the time, but she knew it was early morning.

He offered a menacing smile and inclined his head. "I make bargains with monsters, Persephone." He glanced at the bowl on the counter. "And you, apparently, bake."

She frowned.

"You couldn't sleep?" he asked.

"I didn't try."

It was Hades's turn to frown, and then his eyes shifted. "Is that my whiskey?"

Persephone followed his gaze to where she'd left the crystal container.

"Was," she replied.

Then she felt Hades's hand on her chin as he turned her face to his and pressed his lips to hers, lightly at first and then harder, moving closer, sealing the space between them.

"I ache for you," he said against her mouth. His hands skimmed down her body, one hand squeezed her ass, and the other pressed against the silk of her dressing gown to stroke her damp center through the fabric. Persephone groaned, her fingers digging into his shirt as heat blossomed in the bottom of her stomach, melting between her thighs. Every part of her felt sensitive and swollen.

Hades broke the kiss and Persephone hissed as he moved to press his erection into the warmth of her body.

"Let's play a game," he said.

"I think I am done with games for the night," she said, breathless.

"Just one," he said, kissing her jaw, and reached for the batter-covered spoon she'd dropped into the mixing bowl earlier.

Her brows furrowed as she watched him, curious.

"Never have I ever," he said, trailing the back of the spoon across her chest. The batter was cold, and she shivered.

"Hades—"

"Shh," he said, smirking, and traced the spoon over her lips. She started to lick the batter away. "Stop."

She froze, his eyes heated.

"That's for me."

She swallowed hard.

"Never have I ever wanted anyone but you."

"Never? Even before you knew I existed?" she challenged.

"Yes," he said, and he licked her lips before parting her mouth. He tasted like fudge and whiskey and he smelled like spice—a blend of cloves and geraniums and wood. His lips drifted to her jaw, and her lips were left swollen from his kiss. He spoke against her skin, the words vibrating in the bottom of her stomach. "Before you, I only knew loneliness, even in a room full of people—it was an ache, sharp and cold and constant, and I was desperate to fill it."

"And now?" she breathed.

Hades chuckled. "Now I ache to fill you."

His tongue touched her chest as he licked away the batter on her skin, and his hands came to rest on her breasts, fingers teasing her nipples through her nightdress. Persephone gasped, her fingers fumbling with the buttons of his shirt, but Hades had other ideas as he lifted her onto the edge of the island, settling between her legs. He was so close, she couldn't continue undressing him.

"Tell me about tonight," he said, hands trailing her thighs lightly, teasing her entrance. She felt so uncomfortably empty.

"I don't want to talk about tonight," she said, reaching for his wrist, attempting to draw him inside her.

"I do," he said, still circling her, sending a pleasurable thrill up her spine like a lightning strike. "You were upset."

"I feel…stupid," she said.

"Never," he breathed as a finger curled inside her. Hades's arm kept her head from falling back, their eyes held as he begged. "Tell me."

"I was jealous," she said between her teeth, the ugly feeling tearing through her just as powerful as the pleasure he was giving her now. "That you had shared so much with so many before me, and I know you cannot help it and that you have lived so long…but I…"

Her words were swallowed by an overwhelming sensation—a wave of pleasure that rattled her brain and stole her words. She could barely breathe and Hades chased that feeling, fingers spiraling deeper, thumb brushing lightly over her clit.

"I'd have had you from the beginning," Hades said, his tone low, grating, sensual. "But the Fates are cruel."

"I was only given to punish," she said.

"No, you are pleasure. My pleasure."

He kissed her mouth again as his fingers continued to work and their breaths mingled, coming faster until Hades pressed his palm to her chest and guided her onto her back. He stared down at her as he spoke.

"It is you now, you forever."

As he bent, coaxing her legs wide, tongue tasting her swollen center, she arched off the granite counter upon which he feasted. His fingers and tongue moved faster, chasing her orgasm with each breathy moan, but before she could come, he stopped, straightened, and pulled her off the counter.

"What are you doing?" she asked as her feet touched the ground. There was something dark in his gaze and it was erotic and violent, and Persephone wanted to challenge it, to bring it to life.

"When I'm finished, the next time we play that damned game, you'll walk away so drunk, I'll have to carry you home."

"So what? You intend to fuck me in all the ways I haven't been fucked tonight?"

He laughed. "Technically, it's morning."

"I have to go to work soon."

"Pity," he said and spun her around, and with his hand on her neck, he pushed her forward until her face touched the granite countertop. He kicked her legs apart and entered her from behind, sinking deep. The hand that had grasped her neck moved to her mouth and he parted her lips. She sucked on his fingers, tasting the metallic of her come on his skin.

Persephone reached to grip the edge of the counter as Hades pumped into her, but as soon as he started, he lifted her off the counter. A guttural sound escaped her mouth as she moved with him still inside her, his cock touching a different, more sensitive place as her back met his chest.

"I haven't forgotten your earlier claim." His voice was gravelly against her ear. He was referring to the game they'd played at Sybil's, when she'd claimed to have faked an orgasm.

"I lied," she groaned, trying to move against him, but Hades would not budge.

"I know," he said, and his teeth grazed her shoulder. "And I intend to discourage such lies. I will fuck you to the point that you are desperate for release—over and over again so that when you finally do come, you won't even remember your name."

The promise in his voice excited her.

"You think you'll be able to stop?" she asked. "To deprive yourself of the satisfaction of my orgasm?"

Hades smirked. "If it means hearing you beg for me, darling—yes."

He craned her neck and devoured her mouth. His tongue twined with hers, sweeping and sliding, coaxing her mouth so wide, her jaw hurt. She could not even kiss him back. This one was his and she could only cling to him. When he released her, it was to turn her around, lift her leg, and enter her again. The angle let them remain close, and he covered her mouth with his, kissing her so hard, she couldn't take in air. When his lips left hers, it was to trail kisses and teeth over her neck, pausing to suck the sensitive skin until it bruised beneath his touch. When she could no longer hold herself up, he pressed her into the wall, thrusting harder, faster.

She watched his face, eyes wild and unfocused, a sheen of sweat beading across his face—until she could no longer focus on anything but the feel of him and the pleasure he wrung from within her.

"I love you," he said. "I have only ever loved you."

"I know," she whispered.

"Do you?" he questioned her through his teeth, but not from anger. He was straining, the veins in his neck popped, and his face was flushed.

"I know," she repeated. "I love you. I just want everything. I want more. I want all of you."

"You have it," he promised and kissed her again, their bodies slick and sticky. His hands moved, one pressed against the wall behind her, the other clenching her ass so tight, she knew it would bruise. Her chest felt tight, taut with the air she couldn't release.

Then, suddenly, he tore away with a curse, teeth grazing her lips. Her guttural cry was from frustration. He really meant to torture her—but then he pulled out completely and set her on her feet, adjusting their clothes before Hermes appeared in the kitchen.

Suddenly Persephone understood Hades's haste.

It would be the second time the God of Mischief had interrupted them. Hades's expression was murderous, but one look at Hermes silenced their frustration. The golden god appeared stricken, pale.

"Hades, Persephone—Aphrodite has asked for your presence. Immediately."

Persephone's first thought was that this must be about Adonis—but why did Hermes look so concerned? Something wasn't adding up.

"At this hour?" Hades's arm tightened around Persephone.

"Hades," Hermes said, his face ashen. "It's...not good."

"Where?" Hades asked.

"Her home."

There were no more questions—just the smell of sharp winter air and ash as they teleported.

CHAPTER VII
A Touch of Terror

They appeared in a large room that Persephone thought must be a study. The light was muted, making the walls look dark teal in color. Chestnut-colored bookcases lined with leather-bound tomes boxed in a desk of the same color. Thick frames of antique gold hung on the wall, encasing paintings depicting naked nymphs, winged cherubs, and lovers beneath trees. The opposite wall was all windows, bare, leaving them exposed to the freezing night.

The decor was not at all like Aphrodite's—no plush rugs, crystals, or pearls—and for a moment, Persephone thought they had arrived at the wrong location, but her eyes soon found the Goddess of Love sitting on the edge of a chaise in the center of the room. She was dressed in a light-blue silk nightgown and sheer robe. Her body was twisted toward a woman who lay draped beside her.

Persephone did not recognize her but thought she had hints of Aphrodite's features—in the curve of her lips, the arch of her brow, the tilt of her nose. She was pale, battered, and beaten. Her hands, which lay curled upon her rising stomach, were bloodied, nails broken and jagged.

But what caused Persephone's stomach to coil were the goddess's horns. Two bits of mutilated bone protruded from her muddy and knotted honey-colored hair. A small dog with dirty white fur was curled up tightly beside her, shivering.

This was not at all what Persephone had expected. This goddess had fought for her life, and if Persephone had not been able to sense life, she would have thought the goddess was dead because her breathing was so shallow.

"Oh my gods." Persephone's hands went to her mouth, and something thick and sour gathered in the back of her throat. She rushed to them and knelt, taking Aphrodite's hand in hers.

The goddess of love looked at Persephone, her eyes red and face splotchy. It was hard to see her so emotional. Aphrodite usually tried her best to repress her feelings. The most she conveyed was anger, and if that began to melt her frigid exterior, she shut down, but this—this had destroyed her defenses. Whoever this goddess was, she was important to her.

"What happened?" Hades asked the question, filling the room with a dark tension that seemed to curl into her lungs and steal her breath. There was an edge to his voice, a shudder of violence, and it trickled down her spine.

"We don't know for certain," a voice answered, startling Persephone. She realized Hades hadn't been talking to Aphrodite or Hermes but another—a man who loomed in the corner near the doors. It was as if he were prepared to make a quick exit, except that he also looked at ease, leaning against the wall, thick arms crossed over his chest. He was nearly equal in size to Hades, but he did not dress like any god she had ever seen. He wore a beige, threadbare tunic and a pair of trousers that came to his calves. Despite his simplicity in clothing, his blond beard and hair were well-manicured and almost silky in appearance.

She thought she could guess who this was as her gaze dropped to his feet, where a gold prosthetic leg peeked out from his pant leg. This was Hephaestus, God of Fire and Aphrodite's absent husband—or so the rumors said.

But if he was absent, what was he doing here now?

Hephaestus continued speaking, his voice like a match struck in silence.

"We believe she was walking her dog, Opal, when she was attacked and had just enough strength to teleport here. When she arrived, she was not conscious, and we have not been able to rouse her."

"Whoever did this will suffer," said Hermes.

It was strange to see the usually gleeful god so serious.

Persephone looked from Hermes to Hades, then to Hephaestus, noting their fierce gazes. She turned to the woman lying on the chaise and asked, "Who is she?"

This time, Aphrodite spoke, her voice thick with emotion.

"My sister, Harmonia."

Harmonia, Goddess of Harmony—she was the least combative of the gods, not even an Olympian. Persephone had never met her, nor had she realized her connection to Aphrodite.

She turned to Hades. "Can you heal her?"

He had healed her multiple times, but her wounds had never been anything like this. Still, he was the God of the Dead and had the ability to bring them back to life. Surely this wasn't beyond his abilities?

Still, he shook his head, a grim expression on his face.

"No, for this, we will need Apollo."

"I never thought those words would come out of your

mouth," Apollo said, appearing suddenly. He was dressed archaically, in a gold breastplate, a leather linothorax, and sandals with straps that wrapped around his strong calves. A gold cape hung off one shoulder, and some of his dark curls stuck to his sweaty forehead. Persephone thought that he must have been practicing, perhaps for the Panhellenic Games.

He was smirking, his dimples on full display, until his gaze fell upon Harmonia, and then his expression morphed into something fierce. It was almost frightening, how serious he could become in seconds, much like his brother Hermes.

"What happened?" he demanded, moving to kneel beside the chaise, and Persephone couldn't help detecting that the god smelled...different. His usual scent of laurel—sweet and earthy—was overpowered by something spicier, like cloves. She might not have noticed as much, but he had wedged himself between her and Aphrodite to reach for Harmonia.

"We do not know," Hermes said.

"That's why we summoned you," Hades replied, his voice dripping with disdain.

"I...don't understand," Persephone said. "How would Apollo know what happened to Harmonia?"

The god grinned again, his horror momentarily forgotten as he bragged, "As I heal, I can view memories. I should be able to tap into her injuries and discover how she received them...and from who."

Persephone stood and retreated a step, watching as Apollo worked, and she was surprised by how gentle he treated the goddess.

"Sweet Harmonia," he said quietly, placing his palm upon her forehead, brushing at her tangled hair. "Who did this to you?"

As he spoke, his body began to glow, and soon that glow was transferred to Harmonia. Apollo's eyes fluttered closed, and Persephone watched as his face contorted—brows furrowing, body spasming—and she realized that he was experiencing her pain. Apollo's breath grew ragged the longer he worked. It wasn't until his nose began to bleed that she started to worry.

"Apollo, stop!"

Persephone pushed him away. He fell back, his hand going to his nose where crimson now dripped to his lips. As he pulled his fingers away, he seemed confused by the effects of his healing.

"Are you okay?" she asked.

Apollo looked up at her, his violet eyes tired. Still, he smiled.

"Aw, Seph," he said. "You really do care."

She frowned.

"Why isn't she waking up?" Aphrodite asked, drawing their attention back to Harmonia, who had not stirred.

"I don't know," he admitted. "I healed her as much as I could. The rest…is up to her."

Persephone felt the color drain from her face. She thought about Lexa in limbo, choosing between returning or staying in the Underworld.

"Hades?" Persephone asked.

"I do not see her lifeline ending," he answered, and she got the feeling he was only answering her unspoken question for her sake, not Aphrodite's. "The more pressing question is what you saw as you healed her, Apollo."

He winced like he had a headache. "Nothing," he said. "Nothing that will help us anyway."

"So you couldn't view her memories?" Hermes asked.

"Not much. They were dark and hazy, a trauma response, I think. She's probably trying to suppress them, which means we may not have any more clarity when she wakes. Her attackers wore masks—white ones with gaping mouths."

"But how did they manage to harm her at all?" Aphrodite

asked. "Harmonia is the Goddess of Harmony. She should have been able to influence these...*vagrants* and calm them."

That was true. Even if her aggressor had managed to land a surprise blow, Harmonia should have been able to stop any further attack.

"They must have found a way to subdue her power," Hermes said.

All the gods exchanged a look. Even Hephaestus seemed concerned, uncrossing his arms to step out of the shadow just an inch.

"But how?" Persephone asked.

"Anything is possible," Apollo said. "Relics cause problems all the time."

Persephone had learned about relics while she was in college. They were any item imbued with the power of the gods—swords, shields, spears, fabrics, jewels—basically anything a god had owned or gifted to one of their favored. The items were usually scavenged from battlefields or graves. Some ended up in museums, others in the hands of people who intended to use them for their own disastrous gain.

"Hades?" She called his name because she could tell his mind was working, turning over possibilities as they spoke.

After a moment, he replied, "It could be a relic or perhaps a god eager for power."

She noted that his gaze was on Hephaestus. The blacksmith had created many things over the centuries—shields and chariots, swords and thrones, animatronics and humans. "Any ideas, Hephaestus?"

He shook his head, his expression grim as his gray eyes fell upon his wife and sister-in-law.

"I would need to know more."

Persephone got the sense that wasn't exactly true. Still, she understood wanting more information than what Apollo had been able to give.

"Let her rest, and when she wakes, give her ambrosia and honey," Apollo said, rising to his feet. Persephone rose with him and steadied him as he stumbled, placing his hand to his head.

"Are you sure you're okay?"

"Yeah," he breathed, then he laughed. "Stay alert, Seph. I'll summon you soon."

Then he vanished. Persephone met Hades's dark gaze, and while he seemed focused upon her for a moment, he quickly shifted to Aphrodite.

"Why summon us?"

Persephone winced at Hades's tone—it was void of emotion, but she thought she knew why. This made him uneasy like it made her uneasy, and if she had to guess, he was probably imagining her on that chaise beaten and bruised, not Harmonia.

Aphrodite's back straightened and she looked at Hades.

"I summoned Persephone, not you," she replied briskly, glaring at Hermes.

"What?" he countered. "You know Hades wouldn't let her come alone!"

"Me?" Persephone asked, eyes widened in surprise. "Why?"

"I would like you to investigate Adonis's and Harmonia's attacks," Aphrodite said.

"No," Hades said evenly.

The goddesses glared at him.

"You are asking my fiancée to put herself in the path of these mortals who hurt your sister. Why would I say yes?"

"She asked me, not you," Persephone pointed out. Although Hades had a point. If Adonis and Harmonia were attacked for their connection to the Divine, they would not hesitate to hurt her based on the mere fact that she was to marry the God of the Dead. "Still, why me? Why not ask Helios for assistance?"

"Helios is an asshole," Aphrodite spat. "He feels he owes us nothing because he fought for us during the Titanomachy. I'd rather fuck his cows than ask for his assistance. No, he would not give me what I want."

"And what do you want?" Persephone asked.

"Names, Persephone," Aphrodite answered. "I want the name of every person who laid a hand on my sister."

Persephone noted that Aphrodite didn't mention Adonis. Still, a cold dread swept through Persephone as she realized what the goddess was after—revenge.

"I cannot promise you names, Aphrodite. You know I can't."

"You can," Aphrodite said. "But you won't because of him."

She narrowed her gaze upon Hades.

"You are not the Goddess of Divine Retribution, Aphrodite," Hades replied.

"Then promise me you will send Nemesis to enact my revenge."

"I will make no such promise," Hades said simply.

They were getting nowhere—and then Hephaestus spoke.

"Whoever hurt the mortal and Harmonia has an agenda," he said. "Harming those who assaulted them will not lead us to the greater purpose. You might also, inadvertently, prove their cause."

Aphrodite glared, her eyes flashing with something that looked more like hurt than anger.

"If that's the case, I can see the value of Persephone investigating Harmonia's assault. She fits in—as a mortal and a journalist. Given her record of slander against gods, they may even think they can trust her, or at least turn her to their cause. In either case, it would be a better way to understand our enemy, make a plan, and act."

It was Hades's turn to glare at him, but Hephaestus's words made Persephone hopeful, and she turned to Hades.

"I would do nothing without your knowledge," Persephone assured Hades. "And I will have Zofie."

Hades stared at her for a long moment. He was stiff, everything in him hated this, but then he answered, "We will discuss the terms."

Persephone preened—that wasn't a no.

He continued, "But for now, you need rest."

She felt his magic rising to teleport, adding before they vanished, "Summon us once Harmonia wakes."

————

When they appeared in the Underworld, they faced each other. A long silence stretched where neither of them said a word. Persephone didn't think it was because they lacked anything to say but because they were both exhausted, and the weight of having to see Harmonia—one of their own—beaten near death was heavy. Persephone did not know whether she should scream or sob or collapse.

"You will keep me informed of every step you take, every bit of information you glean on this case. You will teleport to work. If you leave for any reason, I have to know. You will take Zofie *everywhere*." As he spoke, he closed the gap between them. "And, Persephone, if I say no…"

He did not finish the sentence because he didn't need to. She knew what he meant.

If he said no, he meant it, and she knew if she disobeyed, there would be no coming back, so she nodded.

"Okay."

He let out a breath and secured his hand behind her neck, pressing their foreheads together.

"If anything happened to you—"

"Hades," she whispered, wrapping her hands around his wrists. She wanted to meet his gaze, but he wouldn't release his hold on her neck. Still, she spoke. "I'm here. I am safe. You will not let anything happen to me."

"But I did," he answered.

Without explaining, she knew he was talking about Pirithous.

"Hades——"

"I do not wish to discuss it," he said and released her, taking a step back. Apparently, he didn't wish to touch her either. "You need rest."

She watched him for a moment, that same strange silence stretching between them. She didn't like it and she wanted to call him out on it, but she also didn't want to push him. He'd already said he didn't wish to talk, and he was right——she was tired.

She retreated to the bathroom where she showered. She needed the privacy, the heat, the mindless noise of the water pounding against the tile. She focused on these things as long as she could, avoiding thinking about Adonis, Harmonia, and Aphrodite.

Had it only been hours since they had been in the kitchen together? They'd been on the cusp of making love on every surface. She could still feel the emptiness Hades had carved inside her. Twice he had taken her today and twice he had stopped, albeit not by choice. She was wound tight and needy, though it seemed selfish to ask for sex given tonight's events.

Even so, he'd all but rejected her earlier——both her words and her body.

It was as if he wanted no part of her tonight.

Even knowing that wasn't true, an ache still formed in her chest at the thought, and she sat on the floor of the shower, knees drawn to her chest until the water ran cold.

Rising from the shower, she changed into a billowy

shirt and returned to the bedroom where she found Hades standing before the fire, still clothed.

She frowned.

"Are you coming to bed?"

He turned toward her and set his drink aside before approaching. He took her face between his hands as he spoke.

"I will join you shortly."

He stared at her for a moment, and when he leaned forward, she parted her mouth, anticipating his kiss—except he pressed his lips to her forehead.

A mix of emotions flooded her—disappointment and embarrassment warred. What was going on in Hades's head? Whatever it was, it felt like he was punishing her. She stared at him, swallowing what she wanted to say—the accusations she wanted to throw—and whispered good night before crawling beneath the cool covers, too tired to think long about Hades's avoidant kiss, and fell into a deep sleep.

———

She woke later to find Hades sitting on the bed, his bare back to her, feet planted on the floor.

Well, she thought, *he has made progress coming to bed at least.*

She reached for him; her hand splayed across the hard muscles of his back.

"Are you well?" she whispered.

He turned and looked at her, then shifted completely, his naked body stretching until his mouth lined up with hers, but instead of kissing her, he brushed his thumb tenderly over her cheek.

"I am well," he said and straightened. "Sleep. I will be here when you wake."

But those words did not bring her comfort, and instead of listening, she sat up and rolled onto her knees.

"What if I don't want to sleep?"

She straddled him, her arms going around his neck while his hands settled on her waist.

"What's wrong?" she asked. "You did not kiss me earlier and you will not lay with me now."

She felt his hands flex against her sides.

"I cannot sleep," he said. "Because I cannot stop my mind."

"I can help you," she whispered.

He smiled a little, but it was sad, and when he said nothing more, she spoke.

"And…why won't you kiss me."

"Because there is rage inside my body, and to indulge in you…well, I am not certain what kind of release I would find."

"Are you angry with me?" she asked, her fingers twining into his hair.

"No, but I am afraid that I have agreed to something that will only hurt you, and already I cannot forgive myself."

"Hades," she whispered his name, his fears hurting her heart. She wanted to tell him that it wasn't just his decision, it had been hers too, but she knew she could not give him comfort. This was a god who had lived for centuries, a god who knew the world unlike she did, a god who had reason to believe as he did, and she could not argue with that.

She leaned closer; her breath caressed his lips. The tension between their bodies was electric.

"Indulge in me," she whispered. "I can handle you."

He crushed her to him, thrusting his tongue into her mouth, kissing her until she couldn't breathe, until her eyes watered and her chest hurt, and just when she thought she couldn't handle it anymore, he broke from her.

As she drew in ragged breaths, his hands skimmed under her nightshirt, guiding the fabric over her head. When she was naked, his hands pressed into every part of her—her back and breasts and ass—and he kissed her mouth and sucked her neck and nipples. The sweet sensation and biting pleasure had her dragging her nails down his back, and then he entered her—slipping one finger inside, then the other, working her so fast and so hard, she didn't recognize the sounds coming out of her mouth.

"Please," she chanted. "Please, please, please."

"Please what?" he asked.

Her answer was guttural cry of release. She wasn't recovered when he deposited her on the bed, and her legs were so numb, they hung open, ready for him. Hades sat back on his heels before her, stroking himself.

"Can you handle me?" he asked.

"Yes," she breathed. In the next second, he grasped her ass, tilted her hips, and slammed into her, moving at a pace that spoke of his desperation to come. Once again, his hands were everywhere—gripping her thighs, kneading her breasts. Now and then, he bent to taste her tongue or lick the sweat from her skin, and when they came, Persephone was sure everyone in the Underworld heard their cries of ecstasy.

Hades collapsed upon her, ragged and wet and heavy.

Persephone wrapped her legs around him, and her hands moved to his hair, smoothing it from his face. When she caught her breath, she spoke, her throat aching from the cries Hades had torn from her throat.

"You're mine. Of course I can handle you."

It was what she'd wanted to say earlier when he'd asked, but she hadn't had enough air to do so. Hades pulled away to look at her, his gaze penetrating her, straight to the soul.

This, she thought, was the most vulnerable they'd ever been with one another.

"I never thought I'd thank the Fates for anything they gave me, but you—you were worth all of it."

"All of what?"

"The suffering."

CHAPTER VIII
A Concession

Persephone woke in a panic.

It wasn't spurred by a dream but by the feeling that she had overslept. She shot up from bed, her gaze falling to Hades, who stood before the fireplace. After the intensity with which he'd made love to her last night, she had expected him to be asleep beside her. Finding him awake and fully dressed made her chest feel a little hollow.

Still, he was beautiful and there was something different in his expression, a vulnerability that came with the words he'd spoken last night.

He was afraid.

And he had every right to be, because someone out there had incapacitated a god.

She knew that fear was not for himself, though. It was for her, and all she could think was that perhaps if she were stronger, if she could call upon her power like Hades, he wouldn't have to worry.

"Did you sleep at all?" she asked.

"No."

She frowned. She had not heard him stir. Had he risen shortly after she had fallen asleep?

"Nightmare?" he asked.

"No. I...thought I overslept."

"Hmm."

He threw back his drink and set it aside, approaching her. She craned her neck, holding his gaze, as he brushed her cheek with his fingers.

"Why didn't you sleep?" she asked.

"I didn't feel like sleeping," he said.

She arched a brow. "I thought you would be exhausted."

He chuckled and spoke gently. "I didn't say I wasn't tired."

His thumb lingered on her mouth, and Persephone drew it between her lips, sucking hard. Hades inhaled, nostrils flaring, and his other hand tangled into her hair at the base of her neck.

It was a sign—a hint—that he had not fully released the darkness he tried to keep at bay last night, or perhaps he had refilled his well as she slept. Either way, she saw the same hint of violence, the same need for unabashed passion as last night.

His eyes were on her lips, and the tension between them dampened the space between her legs.

"Why are you holding back?" she whispered.

"Oh, darling, if you only knew."

"I'd like to." She let the sheet drop from around her breasts.

There was a beat of silence, a moment when Hades was still as stone, but he did not bite. Instead, he swallowed hard and said, "I will keep that in mind. For now, I'd like you to get dressed. I have a surprise for you."

"What could be more of a surprise than what's going on in that head of yours?"

He offered a breathy laugh and kissed her nose. "Dress. I will wait for you."

Persephone tracked him as he headed for the doors, calling out to him as he reached them.

"You don't have to wait outside."

"Yes, I do."

She didn't question him—just let him slip out as she left the bed and dressed for the day. On a typical August day, she'd wear a summer dress to work, something bright and patterned, but her mother's storm raging above called for warmer clothes. She picked a long sleeve black shirt, gray skirt, and tights. She paired it with heels and her warmest woolen jacket. When she stepped into the hallway, Hades was waiting, frowning.

"What?" she asked, looking down at her outfit.

"I'm trying to assess how long it will take me to undress you."

"Isn't that why you stepped out of the room?" she asked.

The corner of his mouth lifted. "I'm merely planning ahead."

She warmed—was he making a promise to deliver on his earlier thoughts? He held out his hand for her to take and then pulled her flush against him before his magic surrounded them.

They manifested in what appeared to be a waiting room. There was an emerald couch over which two modern art prints hung and a gold and glass coffee table. The floor was white marble, and a wall of glass overlooked a familiar street. She recognized it was Konstantine Street—the same one she'd walked down with Lexa when she'd first visited Alexandria Tower.

A rush of emotion burned her eyes at the thought of her best friend. She cleared her throat and asked, "Why are we at Alexandria Tower?"

The tower was another building owned by Hades out of which the Cypress Foundation, Hades's philanthropic business, operated. Persephone had learned from Lexa that Hades had multiple charities—ones that supported animals and women and those who had lost. She remembered feeling embarrassed that she had not known of his multiple endeavors, and when she'd confronted him, he'd explained that he had been so used to existing alone, he never thought to speak about how he was involved in the Upperworld.

Later, she discovered his world extended beyond the Underworld and his philanthropy to the underbelly of New Greece. She was well aware she did not understand the gravity of what Hades controlled, and that thought made her shiver.

"I would like for you to office here," Hades said.

Persephone turned to look at him, eyes wide.

"Is this because of yesterday?"

"That is one reason," Hades replied and continued. "It will also be convenient. I'd like your input as we continue the Halcyon Project, and I imagine your work with *The Advocate* will lead to other ideas."

She lifted a brow. "Are you asking me to work with Katerina?"

Katerina was the director of the Cypress Foundation and worked with Sybil on the Halcyon Project, a state-of-the-art rehabilitation center that would offer free care to mortals. Not long ago, they'd announced a therapy garden that would be dedicated to Lexa, who had worked on the plan before her death.

"Yes," he said. "You are to be queen of my realm and empire. It's only fitting that this foundation begins to benefit your passions as well."

Persephone said nothing and turned in a circle, assessing the space from a new perspective. There were four doors— two on either side of the waiting area. One led to a conference room, the other three to smaller offices. They were bare except for simple desks, but as she observed, she started to imagine operating in this place.

"You are opposed?" he asked.

"No," she said. Her thoughts were just spiraling.

She thought of something Hades had said: *It is only a matter of time before someone with a vendetta against me tries to harm you.* They were words Persephone had hardly believed at the time, mostly because she hadn't wanted to—but since then, she'd seen the truth over and over again, from Kal to Pirithous to the angry woman who had poured coffee on her.

Now there was another potential threat—Adonis and Harmonia's unknown attackers.

She would be insane not to take Hades up on his offer.

"Thank you. I can't wait to tell Helen and Leuce."

The corner of Hades's lip lifted, and he reached to brush her cheek.

"Selfishly, I will be glad to have you close."

"You rarely work here," Persephone pointed out.

"As of today, this is my favorite office."

She tried not to smile, narrowing her eyes upon the god, her future husband. "Lord Hades, I must inform you that I am here to work."

"Of course," he said. "But you will need breaks and lunch, and I look forward to filling that time."

"Isn't the point of a break not to do anything?"

"I didn't say I'd make you work."

His hands tightened on her waist. It was a familiar pressure, one that was usually followed by a kiss, but as he started to pull her forward, someone cleared their throat, and Persephone turned to find Katerina.

"My Lady Persephone!" She grinned, offering a cute curtsy. She was dressed in yellow silk and khaki slacks. Her tight curls created a halo around her head.

"Katerina," Persephone said and smiled. "A pleasure."

"I apologize for the intrusion," Katerina said. "As soon as I heard Hades had arrived, I knew I would have to catch him before he vanished."

Persephone glanced up at Hades, who was now looking at Katerina. The expression on his face made her curious. He seemed calm enough on the surface, but there was a slight tightening of his lips that made her wonder just what Katerina had to share with the God of the Dead.

"I will be along shortly, Katerina."

"Of course." The mortal's gaze slipped to Persephone. "We're honored to have you here, my lady."

She left after that, and Persephone peered up at Hades.

"What was that about?"

"I will tell you later," he said.

She raised a challenging brow. "Just as you were going to tell me where you had been the other night?"

"I told you I was bargaining with monsters."

"A non-answer if there ever was one," she commented.

Hades frowned. "I do not wish to keep things from you. I just do not know what to burden you with in your grief."

Persephone opened her mouth and then closed it. "I am not angry with you. I was joking, mostly."

Hades offered a breathy laugh. "Mostly."

He was stroking her cheek again, and his gaze was tender.

"We'll talk tonight," he promised.

She thought he would kiss her, but instead he withdrew his touch and left the floor. Persephone stood there for a second, lost in a haze of desire, and suddenly all she wanted to do was follow him and challenge him to take her in his glass office before all of creation as he'd once promised. He wouldn't hesitate—he was just as insatiable as she—and if she weren't more careful with her thoughts and actions, there would be no talking tonight as he promised.

She sighed and withdrew her phone, sending a quick text to Leuce and Helen, letting them know to meet her at Alexandria Tower instead of their usual spot. Persephone had to admit, she was relieved that she would be able to work without the public watching her every move.

She roamed the room again, soaking in the reality that she had a new space for her business, mentally preparing for how she would arrange the space and her new office.

She ended up by the windows. Being on the third floor meant she had a stunning view of New Athens, shrouded in heavy clouds, mist, and snow. Plows and salt trucks were working to clear the roads; all the while, more snow and ice fell. Even the window was pebbled with ice. She thought of Hecate's words. *Your mother terrorizes the Upperworld with snow and ice. The sun is just what the mortal world needs.*

She placed her hand upon the glass.

There was a part of her that knew she could combat her mother because she had before. She'd sent Demeter to her knees in Hades's court, and the Goddess of Harvest, ancient and powerful, had not risen against her power. Still, another part of her feared that had been a result of Demeter being less powerful in Hades's realm.

You used Hades's powers against him, she reminded herself, and it had been terrifying. Her insides shook in the aftermath, and she had felt exhausted in the weeks following, sleeping when she wasn't working. She knew it was a sign that she was not yet strong enough to wield that kind of power. She was going to have to build up endurance, and the only way to do that was to practice more.

She shifted her gaze as a droplet of water skidded down the windowpane. She moved her hand, and beneath it, the ice had begun to melt. She pressed her fingers together, trying to decide if it was her power or her touch that had heated the glass. Her skin was not any warmer than usual, but her magic was on guard and alert. She could feel it, like highly sensitive nerves reacting to her frustration.

But that was the problem.

She had to start using power intentionally.

Placing her hand upon the window once more, she focused on the energy in her palm, warm and electric. Soon, the ice began to melt again. She watched beads of water trail down the glass, and all she could think was that this was a parlor trick. It was nothing compared to the magic she would need to bring down Demeter's eternal winter.

She let her hand fall, and as she did, the beads of water froze in place.

"Persephone?"

She turned to find Sybil standing in the door of the office.

"Sybil," she said, smiling. They hugged.

"Is it true? You will be working here?" Sybil asked.

"Hades has asked that I use this space as my office, and I have to admit, I'm more than happy to accept."

She would be safe here, but more importantly, Leuce and Helen would be safe.

"How are you?" Persephone asked. "Has Ben bothered you?"

Sybil gave her a dark look and huffed. "I am so sorry about him, Persephone. I didn't know he was so…"

"Weird?"

"I think I'm going to have to change my number."

"I would offer to threaten him—or have Hades do it—but he did not seem to fear the gods."

"I think he is too self-centered to fear the gods," Sybil said.

"I'm sorry, Sybil."

She shrugged. "That's what I get for trying to rebound," she joked. Still, Persephone frowned. Sybil was referring to her short-lived relationship with Aro. The mortal had been a long-time friend of Sybil's, and it had seemed like a good match, but for whatever reason, Aro had just wanted to remain friends.

"I think I'm more upset that I will never be able to go into Four Olives again. That was one of my favorite lunch spots."

"Guess there's always delivery," Persephone said.

"Yes, but he's likely to show up with my order, and I really do not want him to know where I work."

"Based on his creep factor, I'd say he already knows where you work."

Sybil offered Persephone a dull look. "Thanks, friend."

Persephone grinned. "Don't worry. I don't think he could get past Ivy."

Ivy was the receptionist for Alexandria Tower. She was a dryad—a woodland nymph. She was organized and regimented. No one went beyond her desk who was not invited.

"Let's have lunch soon," Sybil said, offering another hug before returning to work.

Persephone wasn't left alone long before Leuce and Helen arrived. Helen squealed at the news of their new office space, and the two ran around the floor in a flurry, checking out the offices, arguing over which desk they would take, and discussing decor. Persephone wandered into the first office on the left, shed her jacket, and pulled out her laptop.

As she sat, there was a knock at the door. Looking up, she found Helen waiting in the doorway.

"Hey, did you have a chance to read my article?"

"Yes. Have a seat," Persephone said.

"You didn't like it," Helen said immediately, stepping farther into the office.

"It isn't that, Helen. You have some valid points, but... this is a dangerous article."

Helen's brows knitted together. "How is it dangerous?"

"You comment on the gods," Persephone said and quoted, *"In a world where mortals outnumber gods, should we be asking what the Divine should do?"*

"I am not asking for anything less than you did when you wrote about Hades," Helen argued.

"Helen—"

"Fine. I'll take the sentence out," Helen said, her tone clipped, her frustration obvious. It gave Persephone pause—she'd never witnessed this behavior from her before. In all the time she had worked with her at *New Athens News* and since launching *The Advocate*, Helen had been cheerful and enthusiastic. Then again, Persephone had never critiqued her work before.

Despite her reaction, Persephone felt relieved that she'd agreed to delete her commentary on the gods.

"I also want you to find someone in Triad's leadership to interview."

Helen's lips flattened. "You don't think I tried? No one returned my emails. These people don't want to be known."

"Email isn't the only way to track down a source, Helen. If you want it bad enough, you'll do the footwork."

Helen's blue eyes sparked. "And how do you suggest tracking down the secret leadership of a terrorist organization?"

Persephone shrugged a shoulder. "I'd pretend I was one of them."

"You want me to pretend I'm a member of Triad?"

"You want to break a story? You want to be the first to reveal the higher ranks of New Greece's most dangerous terrorist organization? This is what it will take. In the end, it's entirely up to you. What do you want?"

Helen was silent, staring at Persephone. After a long moment, she asked, "And what if they find out what I'm doing?"

Persephone stiffened but answered. "I can protect you."

"You mean Hades can."

"No," she said. "I mean that I will protect you."

Helen left and Persephone's shoulders sagged. Why had her conversation with Helen felt like a standoff? She definitely expected Helen to be a little more receptive to her feedback, and the fact that she hadn't was surprising. It felt contrary to the person she thought Helen was—but perhaps she didn't know the girl at all.

All of a sudden, magic curled around her, straightening her spine, and the familiar scent of laurel permeated the air.

"Fuck," Persephone said right before she vanished from sight.

CHAPTER IX
The Palaestra of Delphi

She would never get used to being stolen away by another god's magic, save Hades. She didn't like the feel of it, the way it cradled her, caressed her skin, invaded her senses, but at least she knew who was doing it based on the scent of the magic.

"Apollo," she growled.

The cold hit her instantly as she manifested at the center of a long, rectangular courtyard surrounded by a roofed porch. The snow falling from the sky was minimal—a few flurries swirling in the air—but the earth at her feet was wet and muddy. She scanned her environment, attempting to figure out exactly where she was, but froze as a well-muscled, naked man stumbled backward, like he'd been pushed.

Her eyes widened, heart hammering. *Move*, she told herself, but for some reason, her feet wouldn't go. Then she was yanked by her arm, crashing into a hard, leather-clad chest. Persephone planted her hands and pushed, but whoever held her released her quickly. She staggered back, and her eyes slowly made their way up the colossal frame of a man. From his strong calves wrapped with the leather straps of his sandals to his leather linothorax to his round, white-irised eyes. They were probably the most stunning part about him—and the most unnerving. His jaw was strong, his face handsome and framed by inky curls. The man was a warrior, a hoplite, if she had to guess judging by his outfit.

Persephone started to thank the man for helping her when she heard a loud thud behind her. She whirled to find the naked man had rolled onto his stomach while another naked man had his hands cupped beneath his chin, his head pulled back.

"Do you yield?" yelled the man.

The other man growled, an angry sound that came from deep in his chest.

Beside her, the man who had saved her chuckled.

She looked at him.

"Where am I?" she asked.

The man did not seem to hear her, so she asked again.

"Do you know where I am?"

Again, he did not seem to hear. This time, she stepped in front of him. His gaze fell, meeting hers.

"Can you tell me where I am?"

His brows knitted together, and he looked around. Maybe he was confused by her question. After a moment, he stuck out his hand, as if asking for hers. Hesitantly, she obliged and he flipped it, tracing letters into her palm.

D-E-L-P-H-I, he spelled, and then P-A-L-A-E-S-T-R-A.

A palaestra was a training center, primarily used for wrestling.

The Palaestra of Delphi.

She was in Delphi.

"Apollo," she gritted out, frustrated that the God of

the Sun had brought her here with absolutely no notice. Despite his warning last night at Aphrodite's, she thought he'd at least visit before whisking her away to some unknown engagement.

Then she looked up into the man's haunting, white eyes.

"You are deaf?" she asked.

He nodded.

"But you read lips," she said.

He nodded again.

"Thank you for saving me earlier."

He brought his flat palm to his lips and moved it in a forward motion, speaking, "You're welcome."

His speech was slightly distorted, almost guttural.

She smiled just as a voice rang out that made her cringe.

"There you are, sugar dumplin'!"

Persephone whirled to find the God of the Sun striding toward them. He looked luminous, especially in the gloom of the day. He wore a similar outfit to the enormous man behind her, but his breastplate was gold and laurel leaves twined through his dark hair. Despite the exuberant tone of his voice, he seemed almost frustrated, his jaw tight, his eyes an unnatural shade of purple.

"Apollo," she gritted out as he took hold of her arm.

"Don't like that one, either, huh?" he asked.

"We talked about nicknames."

"I know but I thought you might…warm to it." She glared and Apollo sighed. "Fine. Let's go, Seph!"

"Apollo," she warned, planting her feet. "Let go of my arm."

He whirled to face her, eyes aglow. Something was definitely off.

"Bargain," he snapped, as if that word would convince her to let him push her around.

"The word you are looking for is *please*."

They glared at one another, and then all of a sudden, she felt a presence behind her. She tilted her head back and found the massive man who had helped her earlier. He hovered, glaring at Apollo, thick arms crossed over his chest.

"Are you challenging me, mortal?" Apollo's eyes narrowed. Persephone could feel his magic gather.

"You will not fight him," Persephone said, glaring at him pointedly.

Apollo chuckled. "Fight? There would be no fight. This one couldn't take me in battle."

"I'll fight for you, my lord." Another voice joined the fray, and they all turned to see the naked men who had been wrestling earlier. They'd stopped and now stood bare and muddy, completely oblivious to the cold—or too numb. The one speaking had been the one with the advantage earlier. He was handsome, with large brown eyes, a mass of short, curly hair, and a beard.

"There's no need," Persephone said.

"I do not answer to you, woman."

For the briefest second, Persephone saw fury flash in Apollo's eyes.

"This woman is Hades's betrothed, the future Queen of the Underworld. Kneel before her or face my wrath."

The man's eyes widened before he dropped to his knee, followed by his opponent and the deaf man, her new friend. When she looked at the God of the Sun, he was smiling.

"See what your title does to men, Persephone?"

She sighed. "I should have left this bargain when I had the chance."

She pushed past Apollo and headed for the cover of the porch. She didn't know where she was going, but it was cold, and she was angry.

"You don't even know where you're going, Seph," Apollo said, jogging to catch up.

"As far away from your dick-measuring contest as possible," she replied.

"You act like that was my fault," he said. "You were the one who didn't come when I asked."

"You didn't ask. You *commanded*. We talked about this."

Apollo was silent as he walked beside her. After a moment, he started to make what sounded like hissing sounds. "I'm...s-s—"

Persephone slowed as Apollo struggled beside her. He tried again.

"I'm sor—"

His mouth quivered, as if the words made him want to vomit.

"I'm *sorry*," he finally managed, shuddering.

"Is your brain hemorrhaging?" Persephone asked.

"This might surprise you, but apologizing isn't my thing," Apollo said, glaring.

"I am astonished. I would have never guessed."

"You know, you could acknowledge how difficult that was for me. Isn't that what friends are for?"

"Oh, we're friends now? Because it sure didn't feel like we were friends earlier."

Apollo frowned.

"I...didn't mean to upset you," Apollo said. "I was... frustrated."

"I noticed. Why?"

"I got...distracted while bringing you here," he admitted. "I thought...I lost you."

Persephone's brows furrowed. "Why were you distracted?"

Apollo started to open his mouth and then closed it. "The snow started falling again."

At the mention of snow, she turned in the direction he was gazing. The flurries swirled, thicker now, and her stomach knotted.

"Can we please agree that you will not teleport my entire being without permission?"

"Does Hades need permission?"

Again, she glared.

"How else am I supposed to summon you?"

"Like normal people do."

"I am not people."

"Apollo—"

They'd been together for seconds and she had already warned him twice.

"Fine," he sighed, folding his arms over his chest as he pursed his lips.

"Why did you bring me here?" Persephone asked.

"I wanted to introduce you to my hero," he said. "But you already met him."

"The big one?" she asked, thinking he meant the deaf man, and was surprised when Apollo's features hardened.

"No, that is my hero's opponent, Ajax. *My* hero is Hector, He Who Holds Everything Together."

She expected him to look a little prouder of that fact, but as he continued to speak, she understood his frustration.

"The one who insulted you."

"Hmm, where did you find him?"

"Delos," he said. "He is a decorated hero but arrogant. It will be the death of him."

"And yet you give him your favor?"

"Delos is where my mother took refuge to give birth to me and Artemis," he said. "Those are my people, and he protected them. I owe him favor."

They cast their gazes toward the field where several men lingered, all naked. She noted Hector, whose eyes were narrowed, expression mocking. She followed his gaze and saw that he stared at Ajax, who was in the middle of removing his clothes. Persephone averted her eyes. She knew it was traditional for Greeks to participate in most sports naked—with the exception of chariot races—but did they really need to practice that way too?

"Hades is not going to be happy when he finds out how I spent my day," she mused.

She expected Apollo to make a sarcastic reply, but all he said was, "Hmm."

When she looked at him, his gaze was fixed to Ajax, eyes burning. She knew that look, even in someone else's eyes, because it was the way Hades looked at her. She elbowed Apollo.

"I thought Hector was your hero," Persephone said.

"He is."

"Then why are you staring at Ajax?"

A muscle feathered in Apollo's jaw.

"It would be foolish of me not to watch my hero's opponent."

"When he's undressing?" she asked, raising a brow.

Apollo sneered. "I don't like you."

She cackled, but her amusement was short-lived when she heard something that darkened her spirits.

"Look at him—dressed like a warrior and can't hear a thing," one of the men on the field said. He stood beside another, arms crossed, nodding toward Ajax. "What a joke."

Persephone's fists clenched, and she looked to Apollo, whose face remained emotionless.

"I don't trust him," said another. "What if he's fooling us all? Perhaps he's pretending he is deaf so we will let down our guard or go easy on him?"

"He's a favor fuck," a woman added. "Poseidon's if I've heard correctly."

They all laughed but Persephone was appalled. She looked at Apollo.

"Will you let them continue to speak like this?"

"They are not my heroes," he said.

"They might not be your heroes, but you are chancellor of the games. Do you not set the standard for their behavior?" She paused. "Or is this the standard?"

Apollo's gaze was murderous, but their attention returned to the field as Hector bent to pick up a wooden staff.

"Apollo." Persephone's voice rose in pitch.

Hector reared back, his strength evident in the bulge of his muscles, and threw the staff toward Ajax. Persephone watched in horror as the staff flew through the air, straight for Ajax's head, but then the mortal turned in time and caught the staff with one hand. He stared at it for a second before his cold gaze fell upon Hector and those who had stood aside during the attempted assault. Their smirks faded into gaping mouths, just as Persephone's was now.

Ajax broke the staff across his knee and discarded the pieces. Hector smiled.

"So your reflexes are good—but how are you in the pit?"

In the next second, he charged Ajax. Together, they fell into the mud, water sloshing everywhere, spraying the faces of those closest. Apollo drew closer to the edge of the portico as the two wrestled—except they weren't exactly wrestling, they were fighting. For a moment, Hector seemed to have the upper hand, pummeling Ajax's face after he landed on his back, but Ajax quickly took charge, capturing Hector's fist between his hands and throwing him off as if he weighed nothing. The two got to their feet, circling each other, their expressions full of rage.

Hector rushed at Ajax, who bent, punching him in the stomach. Then he lifted Hector off his feet and flipped him onto his back.

"They hate each other," Persephone said.

"They are opponents," Apollo replied, but Persephone

was not so sure. Hector laughed and joked with the other heroes; it was Ajax he treated differently. She wondered briefly if it was because he was different—deaf—or perhaps it was jealousy. Ajax was strong and capable despite his hearing. Still, Persephone felt as though she knew this rage—she had felt it in the Forest of Despair.

Her gaze returned to Hector, who moaned on the frozen ground.

As quick as their fight had begun, it was over. Ajax did not stand over Hector to gloat, but he did turn and glare at Apollo before gathering his clothes and leaving the courtyard.

Persephone's brows drew together as she looked from the mortal's retreating form to the God of the Sun.

"Aren't you going to check on your hero?" she asked.

"No. It is Hector's punishment for his hubris," Apollo said. "Perhaps this will humble him before he faces Ajax in the Panhellenic Games."

"Will you still host the games in this weather?"

"If men and women cannot fight in a little snow, then they do not belong in the games."

"It's not just about the competitors, Apollo. What about the spectators? Travel is dangerous in this weather."

"If you are so worried, then maybe you should talk to your mother."

Persephone dropped her gaze, frowning. "So you know?"

"We all know," Apollo said. "It's not like Demeter hasn't done this before. It's just a matter of when Zeus will intervene."

Persephone's stomach soured.

"Will she listen to Zeus? If he tells her to stop?"

"She will," Apollo replied. "Or there will be war."

They left the field and Apollo gave Persephone a tour of

the Palaestra of Delphi. It was a beautiful facility with several rooms for bathing, sports, and equipment that branched off from the portico surrounding the field. There were a few indoor training fields and a large open stadium for chariot practices. She looked out over the field now from a private suite that included a bar, large televisions mounted to the walls, and leather seats that faced a panel of windows. Persephone was just happy to be inside where it was warm.

"This place is amazing," she said.

There was something even more impressive about chariot races and stadiums. Persephone had only ever seen them on television, but being here in person gave her an idea of just how monumental they were.

"I'm glad you like it," said Apollo. "I am...very proud of it."

Persephone didn't think she'd ever heard Apollo say something like that.

There was silence as she stared at the center of the track where a low wall called a spina ran down the oblong track. Several statues decorated it, including a gold one of Apollo, but there were also Artemis and a woman she did not recognize.

"Who is the third statue?" she asked.

"My mother, Leto," Apollo said. "She risked her life to give birth to my sister and I, so we protected her."

Persephone knew that Hera had Leto pursued relentlessly before and after she'd given birth to her divine twins, jealous of Zeus's infidelity. She also knew what Apollo meant by *protect*—he and his sister had slaughtered mortal and creature alike. Persephone's mouth tightened at the thought.

"I'd like you to attend the first of the games with me," Apollo said. "It's a chariot race."

"Are you asking or telling?" Persephone said.

"Asking," Apollo replied. "Unless you say no."

"And here I thought you were changing," she replied mildly.

"Baby steps, sugar tits."

"If Hades manifests to kill you, I'm not intervening."

"What? It's not like I know what they taste like from experience!"

"The simple fact that we are having this conversation is enough to send Hades into a rage."

"Maybe you should tell him toxic masculinity isn't attractive."

Persephone rolled her eyes and countered, "He doesn't trust you."

"But he should trust you."

"He does. He also knows how many times I told you not to call me names." She gave him a challenging look.

Apollo pouted and folded his arms over his chest. "I'm just having fun."

"I thought we were having fun!"

The God of the Sun brightened. "You were having fun?"

She sighed loudly. "You make me regret keeping up my end of this bargain."

He grinned. "Lesson number two, Sephy. When a god gives you an out, take it."

"And what's lesson number one?"

"Never accept a bargain from a god."

"If those are lessons, no one's listening."

"Of course not. Gods and mortals always want what they can't have."

"Including you?" she asked, glancing at him.

He seemed to sober then, a grimace marring his perfect face.

"Me more than anyone," Apollo replied.

CHAPTER X
A Walk in the Park

Apollo returned Persephone to Alexandria Tower without warning. Her only indication he was about to act was the smell of his magic.

"Apollo!" she growled, but her frustration was lost as the floor seemed to go out from beneath her feet. Her stomach lurched, the world flashed, and when it cleared, she found Hades sitting behind her desk in her new office.

"Hi," she said.

"Hi," his voice rumbled—a low growl—and her brows furrowed.

He did not sound pleased, but he seemed comfortable, eased back in her chair, a finger pressed against his mouth, legs spread wide, and she had the thought that she would fit snugly in the gap between his thighs.

"Are you well?" she asked.

"Harmonia is awake," he said.

Persephone's heart rose into her throat.

"How is she?" Her words came in a rush.

"We're about to find out," he said and rose to his feet,

coming around the desk. "Did you enjoy your time with Apollo?"

Persephone wasn't surprised that Hades knew where she'd gone; he could probably smell Apollo's magic. Still, she frowned, knowing Hades was not happy—and yet there was nothing he could do. She and Apollo were bound by a bargain she'd insisted on fulfilling when he'd attempted to release her from the contract—something Hades had not at all been excited to learn.

Still, Persephone stood by her decision. The last thing Apollo needed was to feel abandoned.

"On a numeric scale?" she asked. "I'd give it about a six."

Hades lifted a brow. It was as if he wanted to be amused, but his irritation was winning.

"I'm sorry you are not pleased."

"I am not displeased with you," he answered. "I'd just rather Apollo not cart you off to Delphi during your mother's tantrum and while Adonis and Harmonia's attackers are still out there."

"Did you…follow me?"

The thought didn't upset her—in fact, she wished Hades could trace her location more often. There were times when he was not able to find her. Somehow—and she wasn't sure exactly how—she blocked his ability to sense and trace her magic. It had happened a few times—once when she had gotten lost in the Underworld, again when Apollo had stolen her away for a ridiculous musical competition, and finally when Pirithous had kidnapped her. Each instance was more dangerous than the last.

Hades's eyes fell, and he lifted her hand so that her ring was on full display, the gems glinting under the light, the centers to several delicately crafted flowers.

"These stones—tourmaline and dioptase—give off a

unique energy, your energy. As long as you wear this, I can find you anywhere."

Persephone wasn't surprised by that ability; Hades was the God of Precious Metals.

"It wasn't…intentional," Hades added. "I didn't set out to…put a tracker on you."

"I believe you," she said. "It's…comforting."

Hades stared at her and then brushed his lips along her fingers. His breath was warm against her cold skin.

"Come. Aphrodite is waiting," he said, and they vanished.

They appeared outside a mansion composed of white stucco and glass. The front door was wood and had a long, elegant handle. A window beside it allowed Persephone to look in and see a staircase. She would have never guessed that the study she had been in last night belonged to this house. That room was traditional and warm, while this was modern and sleek.

Persephone shivered, hugging herself as the wind whipped around them, smelling of salt and stinging cold. Demeter's winter had not neglected the islands around New Greece either, it seemed.

"Can't we just teleport inside like last time?" Persephone asked, her teeth chattering.

"We could," he answered. "If we had been invited."

"What do you mean? Didn't Aphrodite let you know Harmonia was awake?"

Hades did not reply immediately.

"Hades," Persephone warned.

"She sent Hermes for you," Hades replied. "He found me instead."

They stared at one another. Persephone wasn't sure

what to say. Aphrodite was trying to go behind Hades's back, and while Persephone wondered what the Goddess of Love hoped to accomplish sans Hades, she also wondered if Hades realized she wouldn't have come without him.

"You won't do this without me," he said.

She had her answer. It was a blow—a pain she hadn't anticipated. He didn't trust her, not with this anyway, and while she recognized she didn't have the best track record for obeying, this was different—*she* was different. Her eyes stung and she swallowed a lump in her throat as she turned her head almost mechanically to face the entrance.

"Persephone—"

But whatever Hades was about to say was lost as the door opened. A woman answered—except Persephone did not think she was a woman at all. She looked alive enough—rosy cheeks and glassy eyes—but Persephone could not sense any kind of actual life—no fluttering heartbeat or warmth.

She must be an animatronic, Persephone thought, one of Hephaestus's creations.

"Welcome." Her tone was soft, breathy—it reminded Persephone of Aphrodite's voice, only slightly strained. "My lord and lady are not expecting guests. State your names please."

Persephone started to open her mouth, but Hades breezed past the woman—robot—whatever she was—and entered the home.

"Excuse me!" she called after Hades. "You are entering the private residence of Lord and Lady Hephaestus!"

"I am Lady Persephone," she said. "That is Lord Hades."

The God of the Dead turned to her. "Come, Persephone."

She folded her arms over her chest and glared. "You could show some courtesy. You *weren't* invited, remember?"

Hades's mouth tightened.

The animatronic was silent, and Persephone wondered for a moment if she had broken it, but her face changed, lighting up as if she were excited or pleased, and she said, "Lady Persephone, you are most welcome. Please, follow me."

The woman turned and started toward an open living area. As she passed Hades, she added, "Lord Hades, you are most unwelcome."

He rolled his eyes but fell into step beside Persephone. Heat unfurled in her chest as he grasped her hand. She tried to pull free, but he held tight, and she relented. Despite how angry she was with him, it helped that he wanted to touch her.

Aphrodite's home was what she expected—luxurious, open, romantic—and then there were elements that weren't at all what she imagined—modern lines, metal art, and polished wood. It was a fusion of the Goddess of Love and the God of Fire, and yet from what she had heard and seen of the two, it surprised her that their distinct differences meshed so well—and so obviously—in their home. She'd expected them to live separately and for that to be obvious.

They were led down a hallway. On one side were windows, on the other canvases sprayed with blush pink and gold. Persephone kept her gaze on the art, unwilling to look out upon the garden opposite and see all Aphrodite's tropical plants weighed down with snow.

The maid paused to open the door and announced them as she entered. "My Lady Aphrodite, Lady Harmonia—Lady Persephone and Lord Hades are here to see you."

They stepped into a library, and while it had the same floor-to-ceiling windows on the wall opposite her, it somehow seemed warmer. Perhaps it was all the mahogany bookcases, lined with leather-bound and gold-embossed books, or the lamps that cast an amber glow upon the walls.

Aphrodite and Harmonia sat side by side on a settee uphol-stered in rich velvet the color of the cold ocean outside. In front of them was a tray with a steaming pot of tea, mugs, and small sandwiches.

Persephone couldn't look away from Harmonia. The blond goddess was a beauty just like her sister. She appeared more youthful, her face less angled, and her expressions softer. Apollo's magic had done a lot to heal the cuts and bruises that had marred her skin last night, but it was evident she had been through trauma. It haunted her eyes and the energy around her. She sat as if she feared she might break—or perhaps as if she trusted no one, even though she was safe. Curled up on her lap was Opal, who was freshly bathed, her fur white as snow once more.

Persephone tried not to stare at Harmonia's horns—or what was left of them anyway. The white bone looked wrong jutting out of her silklike hair.

Would they grow back, she wondered. Could they be restored with magic? She did not know because she'd never known anyone to get close enough to a god or goddess to dehorn them. She would have to ask Hades later.

"Thank you, Lucy," Aphrodite said, and the anima-tronic bowed before departing. The goddess's eyes shifted to Persephone and then to Hades. "I see Hermes failed to follow instructions," she commented briskly.

"You can thank Apollo for that," Persephone said.

"Persephone and I are doing this together, Aphrodite," Hades said.

There was silence.

"Persephone," Aphrodite said. "Please, have a seat."

Persephone took a chair opposite the two goddesses. Aphrodite continued as if Hades were not darkening the room, though he came to stand behind Persephone.

"Tea?" she offered.

"Yes." Persephone's voice was soft. She wanted something warm to break the chill in her bones.

Aphrodite poured tea and slid the cup and saucer toward her.

"Sugar?"

"No, thank you," Persephone said, taking a sip of the bitter drink.

"Cucumber sandwich?"

It was strange to watch Aphrodite play hostess, and Persephone got the impression she was being so courteous because of the role she wanted her to fill in finding Harmonia's attackers.

"No, thank you," Persephone said.

Silence followed, and it was Harmonia who broke it with a soft clearing of her throat.

"I suppose you are here to speak with me," she said. Her voice was low and soothing, and she spoke carefully but lyrically.

Persephone hesitated, her eyes shifting to Aphrodite for a second. "If you are feeling well enough. We need to know what happened last night."

She couldn't tell how Harmonia felt about taking them through the trauma of her encounter with her attackers. Harmonia didn't flinch or blink. It was as if she were locking up all her emotions in an effort to communicate with them.

"Where shall I start?" she asked and looked to Hades.

"Where were you when you were attacked?" he asked.

"I was in Concorida Park," she said.

Concorida Park was in New Athens. It was large and had many wooded paths.

"In the snow?" Persephone asked.

Harmonia offered a small smile. "I go for a walk there every afternoon with Opal," she said. The fluffy white dog in her lap grunted. "We took our usual route. I didn't sense anything untoward—no violence or animosity before they attacked."

The fact that Harmonia walked through the park often and took the same route probably meant that someone knew her routine and planned the attack. The snow also ensured few witnesses.

"How did it happen?" Hades asked. "What do you remember first?"

"Something heavy consumed me," she answered. "Whatever it was took me to the ground. I could not move, and I could not summon my power."

There was a long stretch of silence, and then Harmonia began again.

"It was easy for them after that—they came out of the woods, masked. What I remember most was the pain in my back—a knee settled on my spine as someone took my horns and sawed them off."

"No one came to your aid?" Persephone asked.

"There was no one," Harmonia said and shook her head. "Only these people who hate me for being something I cannot help."

"After they took your horns, what did they do?" Hades asked. The question was careful but almost made Persephone cringe.

"They kicked and punched and spit upon me," Harmonia answered.

"Did they say anything while they…attacked you?"

"They said all sorts of things," she said. "Broken things." She paused for a moment, her lashes gathering with tears. "They used words like whore and bitch and abomination, and they sometimes strung them together into a question like where is your power now? It was as if they thought I was a goddess of battle, as if I had done some sort of wrong against them. All I could think is that I could have brought them peace and instead they brought me agony."

Persephone did not know what to say; perhaps that was because there was nothing to say. She had no ability to understand the people who had hurt Harmonia or their motive. It was hate, pure and simple. Hate for what she was and nothing more.

"Is there anything else you remember? Anything that you can recall now that would help us find these people?" Hades continued. Then he added gently, "Take your time."

Harmonia thought, and after a moment, she started to shake her head. "They used the word *lemming*," she said. "They said you and your lemmings are all headed toward destruction when the rebirth begins."

"*Lemming*," Persephone repeated and looked up at Hades. "That is what the woman at the Coffee House called me."

She'd also heard the word rebirth before, in the article Helen had written about Triad. Were these masked attackers members? Or just rogue supporters?

Harmonia was quiet and lifted her slender, shaking hand to touch the broken horns at the front of her head.

"Why do you think they did it?" she whispered.

"To prove a point," Hades replied.

"What is the point, Hades?" Aphrodite asked, the anger evident in her voice.

"That gods are expendable."

Expendable.

Disposable.

Useless.

"And they wanted proof," he added. "It won't be long before news of your attack spreads, whether we want it to or not."

"Are you not the god of threats and violence?" Aphrodite asked. "Use your seedy underbelly to get ahead of this."

"You forget, Aphrodite, that we must discover who they are first. By that time, word will have already spread, if not among the masses, among those who wish to see us fall."

Persephone found herself thinking of Sybil—what would the oracle do in a time like this? It was a PR nightmare, but worse, it communicated that the gods were fallible—that they could, potentially, be defeated—and the last time mortals had fought against the gods, the world had drowned in their blood.

"But we must let it go for now," he said.

"Why? Do you wish for this to happen again?" Aphrodite demanded. "It has already happened twice!"

The words were an insult to Hades—and Persephone—who only wished to help.

"Aphrodite," Persephone spoke her name, her tone warning.

"I understand what Lord Hades is saying," Harmonia interrupted. "Someone is bound to let their knowledge of my ordeal slip, and when they do, you will be ready…won't you, Hades?"

Persephone looked from Harmonia to the God of the Dead, who nodded.

"Yes," he said. "We will be ready."

CHAPTER XI
A Touch of a Nightmare

Persephone and Hades left the island of Lemnos and returned to the Underworld. When they appeared in his bedchamber, Hades grasped her shoulders and crushed her against him as he took her mouth against his, kissing her as if he were claiming her soul. For a moment, she was stunned. She'd had it in her head that they'd return and argue. Hades knew she was angry with him, and he did not like to let it simmer. She gave way to the feel of his lips, the thrust of his tongue, the smell of ash and pine clinging to his skin. He shifted his arm, cradling her head in the bend of his elbow while the other went to her face. With a final sweep of his tongue across her lips, he pulled away.

Her eyes fluttered open to find Hades gazing at her tenderly, as if he were realizing his love for her all over again.

"What was that for?" she asked, breathless.

"You defended me to Aphrodite," he said.

Persephone opened her mouth to speak but had no words. She'd snapped at the Goddess of Love because her words had been cruel, and Hades was not deserving of her censure. It hurt her to think she'd once done the same.

"I am thankful," he added.

She smiled up at him, and her gaze lowered to his lips before his brows knitted together over his hardening, dark eyes.

"I hurt your feelings," he said, frowning.

His words were an arrow to her chest, stealing her smile as she recalled what had made her ache outside Aphrodite's home. She looked away for a moment, her thoughts a little chaotic, but she thought it was best to just be direct. She met his gaze.

"Do you trust me?" she asked.

Hades's eyes widened.

"Persephone—"

"Whatever you're about to do, stop," Hecate said, appearing in the room, her hand covering her eyes.

The two turned to look at her. She was dressed more formally than usual, wearing robes the color of midnight roses and her hair in braids.

"Shall we undress before she opens her eyes?" Hades asked, gazing down at Persephone.

Hecate dropped her hand and glared. "The souls are waiting. You two are late!"

"Late for what?" Persephone asked.

"Your engagement party!" They exchanged a look as Hecate reached for Persephone's hand and dragged her toward the door. "Come. We don't have much time to get you ready."

"And me?" Hades said. "What shall I wear to this party?"

Hecate looked over her shoulder.

"You only have two outfits, Hades. Choose one."

Then they were out the door, heading down the marble hall toward the queen's suite where Persephone usually prepared for events. Once inside, Hecate summoned her magic. The smell of it made Persephone stiffen, perhaps because the last time Hecate had used it in Persephone's presence, she'd ordered her grim to attack. It was the smell that triggered her—blackberry and incense—and the feel—something old and ancient and dark—but when it touched her, it was a caress, a faint prodding that felt like silk unfurling over skin. She relaxed beneath it, closing her eyes and letting it take hold, tangling around her body and in her hair. It wasn't long after that Hecate spoke.

"Perfect," she said, and Persephone opened her eyes to find the Goddess of Magic smiling.

"No lampades this time?"

"Unfortunately, we do not have time for leisure," Hecate said. "Come—look at my handiwork."

The goddess turned Persephone to face the mirror, and she released a breath. She wore a dusty pink gown with a fitted bodice and a skirt made of tulle. It was simple and beautiful. In the process of using her magic, Hecate had stripped away Persephone's glamour, and she stood in her Divine form; slender white horns twisted from her head, and white camellia flowers formed a crown at their base. Her hair curled down her back, all varying tones of gold. Her eyes—bottle green and gleaming—made her look wild, untamed, menacing.

She'd always known there was darkness inside her. Hecate and Hades had both seen it when she could only feel it.

Now she saw it too.

There is darkness within you. Anger, fear, resentment. If you do not free yourself first, no one else can.

She met Hecate's gaze in the mirror, and the witch offered a gentle smile. She'd heard her thoughts.

"This darkness is not the same. This darkness is toil and trauma, grief and loss. It is the darkness that will make you Queen of the Underworld."

Then Hecate leaned forward, holding Persephone's lithe

shoulders between her hands, settling her chin upon her shoulder.

"Look long at yourself, my love, but do not fear the change."

Persephone stared for a moment longer and found that she wasn't afraid of the person staring back at her. In fact, she liked her despite the pain and the grief. She was broken and somehow better for it.

"Come." Hecate slid her fingers through Persephone's and teleported.

They appeared in the middle of Asphodel, beneath an ethereal canopy of lights and glimmering white cloth. Lanterns and bouquets of white and blush roses, delphiniums, stock, and hydrangeas flanked either side of the road. There were candles in every window and tables outside each home crowded with an array of food, all various specialties of the souls who resided inside. The smells were varied and mouth-watering. The souls themselves were out in droves, all well dressed and gleeful.

"Lady Persephone has arrived!" Hecate announced, and after they bowed, they cheered, approaching her to hold her hand or clutch her dress.

"We are so excited, Lady Persephone!"

"Congratulations, Lady Persephone!"

"We cannot wait to call you queen!"

She smiled and laughed with them until Yuri approached, throwing her arms around Persephone.

"What do you think?" Yuri asked, smiling so wide, Persephone was certain she hadn't seen the soul this happy since meeting her.

"It is truly beautiful, Yuri," Persephone said. "You outdid yourself."

"If you think this is beautiful, you have to see the meadow!"

Yuri took Persephone's hand and guided her down the long road, past homes and flowers and lanterns to the emerald green of the Asphodel meadow. From the center of town, she'd seen orbs of light in the distance, but now that she approached, she saw what they really were. The lampades hovered a few feet from the ground, their unearthly light illuminating the whole, narcissus-covered meadow where white blankets were arranged. Each space had a picnic basket decorated with the white delphiniums from the bouquets she'd seen in town.

"Oh, Yuri, it's perfect," Persephone said.

"I thought of it because you like picnics," Yuri said, and beside her, Hecate snorted.

Persephone arched a brow at the goddess. "What? I do like picnics."

"You like picnics alone. With Hades. You like Hades," Hecate said.

"So? This is my engagement party."

Hecate threw her head back, laughing.

"Do you like it?" Yuri asked. She seemed to take Hecate's words to mean Persephone might not like the decor.

"I love it, Yuri. Thank you so much."

The soul beamed. "Come! We have so much planned—dancing and games and feasts!"

They returned to the crowded center of town, and Persephone found herself marveling at the diversity of the souls—there were people here from all walks of life, and she wanted to learn from each. They were all dressed differently, had different skin tones and accents, cooked different food and made different tea, had different customs and beliefs. They'd lived different lives, some without advancement and others with, some only a few years and others long lives—and yet here they were, at the end of all things, sharing their eternity with no hint of anger or animosity.

"Look who's arrived—and in new robes too," Hecate said, pulling Persephone out of her thoughts. She turned, eyes connecting with Hades's as he manifested at the end of the road—the entrance to Asphodel. His presence halted her steps and made her heart drum painfully in her chest.

He was stunning, a King of Darkness, cloaked in shadow. His robes were the color of midnight, trimmed in silver and draped over only one shoulder, leaving part of his muscled chest and bicep exposed. She tracked his bronzed skin, the contours and the veins that trailed up his arm and disappeared beneath his long, silken hair. This time, he wore half of it up, and his black horns were crowned with iron spikes.

Standing on opposite ends of the road, Persephone was struck by how similar they were—not in appearance but something deeper, something that threaded through their hearts and bones and souls. They'd begun in two very different worlds but wanted the same thing in the end—acceptance and love and solace—and they'd found it in each other's eyes and arms and mouths.

This is power, she thought as her body flushed and fluttered with a chaotic tangle of emotion—the passion and pain of loving someone more than the air in her lungs and the glimmer of stars in the night sky.

"Lord Hades!" A chorus of voices rang out as several children rushed toward him, hugging his legs. Others hung back, too shy to approach. "Play with us!"

He grinned and it hit her hard in the chest, the laugh that followed shaking her lungs. He bent and swept a small girl named Lily into his arms.

"What shall we play?" he asked.

There were several voices all at once.

"Hide-and-seek!"

"Blindman's bluff!"

"Ostrakinda!"

It was strange, almost heart-wrenching, to hear their requests, mostly because Persephone could tell how long they'd been in the Underworld by their choices.

"Well, I suppose it's just a matter of which we shall play first," Hades replied.

Then he looked up and met Persephone's gaze. That smile—the one that made her heart stir because it was so rare and yet so genuine—remained in place.

With his gaze came many others. Some of the children who had been too shy to approach Hades came to her, taking each of her hands.

"Lady Persephone, please play!"

"Of course," she laughed. "Hecate? Yuri?"

"No," Hecate said. "But I shall watch and drink wine from the sidelines."

They moved to an open space close to the picnic area Yuri and the souls had arranged and played most of the games the children had suggested hide-and-seek, which was far too easy for Hades as he liked to turn invisible just as he was about to be found, which meant by the time they moved on to playing blindman's bluff, Persephone had declared that Hades could not be it, as he would use his powers to find them on the field. Their final game was ostrakinda, an ancient Greek game where they split into teams—one representing night and one representing day—which corresponded with the white and black colors on a shell that was tossed into the air. Depending on which side turned upward, one team would chase the other.

Persephone had never played the game before, but it was simple enough. The biggest challenge would be escaping Hades—because as he stood opposite her on team night, she knew he had his sights set upon her.

Between them, a boy named Elias held a giant shell in his hand. He bent his knees and jumped, sending it flipping into the air. It landed with a thud in the grass, white side up, and there was chaos as the children dispersed. For a second, Persephone and Hades remained in place, eyes locked. Then a predatory grin crossed the god's face, and the Goddess of Spring whirled. As she did, she felt Hades's finger's ghost across her arm—he'd already been so close to capturing her.

She sprinted. The grass was cool beneath her feet, and her hair breezed behind her. She felt free and reckless as she turned to glance over her shoulder at Hades, who was gaining on her, and she suddenly recalled that she had not felt this way since before Lexa's accident. The thought faltered her steps, and she came to a stop altogether, her high crushed beneath the weight of guilt.

How could she have forgotten? Her face heated and a thickness gathered in her throat that brought tears to her eyes.

Hades came to her side. Recognizing something was wrong, he asked, "Are you well?"

It took her a moment to answer—a moment where she worked to swallow the tears gathering behind her eyes and suppress the tremble in her throat.

"I just remembered that Lexa was not here." She looked at Hades. "How could I have forgotten?"

Hades's expression was grim, his eyes pained.

"Oh, darling," he said and pressed his lips to her forehead. It was enough because it was comfort. He took her hand and led her to the picnic area, where the souls had now gathered to feast. Yuri showed them where they were to sit—at the very edge of the field upon a blanket that was weighted down with the same lanterns and bouquets that decorated the road. The basket was full of foods and wineskins, offering a sampling of the culture in Asphodel.

They feasted, and the meadow was full of happy chatter, laughter, and the delighted screams of children. Persephone watched the scene, her heart full. These were her people, but most importantly, they were her friends. The urge to protect and provide for them was almost primal. It was that impulse that surprised her, but it was also how she knew she wanted to be Queen of the Underworld—because taking on that title meant something far more than royalty. It was responsibility. It was caring. It was making this realm an even better, more comforting space.

"What are you thinking?" Hades asked.

She glanced at him and then at her hands. She held a wheat roll and had been breaking off pieces; her lap was covered in crumbs. She set it aside and brushed them away.

"I was just thinking about becoming queen," she said.

Hades offered a small smile. "And are you happy?"

"Yes," she said. "Of course. I was just thinking of how it will be. What we will do together. If, that is, Zeus approves."

Hades's lips thinned. "Just keep planning, darling."

She did not ask him any more questions about Zeus because she knew what he would say—*we will marry despite Zeus*—and she believed him.

"I would like to speak about earlier," Hades said. "Before we were interrupted, you asked if I trusted you."

She could tell by his expression that her question had hurt his feelings. She hesitated to speak, searching for the words to explain herself.

"You did not think I'd come to you when Hermes summoned me to Lemnos," she said. "Tell me, truthfully."

Hades clenched his jaw before answering, "I did not."

Persephone frowned.

"But I was more concerned about Aphrodite. I know what she wants from you. I worry you will try to investigate and identify Adonis and Harmonia's attackers on your own. It isn't because I don't trust you but because I know you. You want to make the world safe again, fix what is broken."

"I told you I wouldn't do anything without your knowledge," Persephone said. "I meant it."

Persephone wanted to find Adonis and Harmonia's attackers as much as Hades and Aphrodite, but that did not mean she was going to be rash. She'd learned a lot from her mistakes. Not to mention seeing Harmonia and how she'd suffered gave her even more pause. This threat was obviously different. Gods with control of their powers weren't able to fight it, which meant she'd have an even harder time.

"I am sorry," he said.

"You once said words had no meaning," she answered. "Let our actions speak next time."

She would show Hades she meant what she said, and she could only hope he'd do the same.

———

Later, after the souls had retreated to their homes for the night, they remained in the meadow. Hades rested on his back, his head in Persephone's lap. She played with his hair, smoothing her fingers through it as it spilled over her thigh and into the grass. His eyes were closed, his thick lashes grazing the high points of his cheek. He had faint lines around his eyes that deepened when he smiled. If there were any around his mouth, she could not see for the stubble on his face.

Gods did not age beyond a certain point in their lifetime. It was different for everyone, which was why none of them looked the same, and probably a decision made by the Fates. Hades looked as though he had matured into his late thirties.

"Hades." She said his name and then quieted, hesitating.

"Hmm?" He looked up at her and she held his gaze.

"What did you trade for your ability to have children?"

He stiffened and shifted his eyes to the sky. It was something she'd been thinking about since playing in the meadow. One day, after they'd greeted souls at the gates of the Underworld, Hades admitted that he could not give her children because he'd bargained away the ability. She did not know the details, and in that moment, she'd been more concerned about easing his anxiety. He'd seemed to think that this admission would mean the end of their relationship.

But Persephone was not sure she wanted children, and she was no closer to making that decision now even though she asked.

"I gave a mortal woman divinity," he answered.

The words made her throat feel tight, and her fingers stalled as they threaded through his hair. After a moment, she asked, "Did you love her?"

Hades offered a humorless chuckle. "No. I wish I could claim it was out of love or even compassion," he answered. "But...I wanted to claim a favor from a god, and so I bargained with the Fates."

"And they asked for your...*our*...children?"

This time, Hades rolled into a sitting position, twisting to face her, eyes roaming her face.

"What are you thinking?"

She shook her head. "Nothing. I just...am *trying* to understand Fate."

Hades smiled wryly. "Fate does not make sense. That is why it is so easy to blame."

The corners of her lips turned upward, but only for a moment as she looked away. Her thoughts were muddled as she tried to sort out how exactly Hades's bargain made her feel.

He reached to brush his fingers along her cheek.

"If I had known—if I'd been given any inkling—I would have never—"

"It's alright, Hades," Persephone interrupted. "I did not ask to cause you grief."

"You did not cause me grief," he answered. "I think back on that moment often, reflect upon the ease with which I gave up something I would come to wish for, but that is the consequence of bargaining with the Fates. Inevitably, you will always desire what they take. One day, I think, you will come to resent me for my actions."

"I do not, and I will not," Persephone said, and she believed that despite a strange feeling knotting her chest. "Can you not forgive yourself as easily as you have forgiven me? We have all made mistakes, Hades."

He stared at her for a moment and then kissed her, guiding her backward to the pillowy ground. She relaxed beneath his weight and let him devour her mouth with slow, heated strokes. She drew her knees up, caging him between her thighs as she sought his hard length beneath his robes. Once she had him in hand, Hades pulled back to position himself against her heat. She arched against the feel of him thrusting into her. He settled there for a moment, buried deep and filling, kissing her once more before setting a languid pace. Their breaths were slow to quicken, their moans soft, their words whispered, and beneath the starry Underworld sky, they found release and refuge in each other's arms.

———

"Persephone." The voice was melodic—a soft whisper across skin.

Her breath caught in her throat as hands drifted up her calves. Her fingers fisted in the silk sheets and her back arched, restless, her body still half-buried in sleep.

"You will like it," he whispered, his lips brushing her lower abdomen. She twisted and wriggled beneath the breathy touch.

"Open for me," the voice coaxed. The words were a

request, but the hands that forced her knees apart were a command.

She wrenched her eyes open, recognizing the sunken face and bleeding eyes staring into hers.

"Pirithous," she said, hating the way the name sounded and felt in her mouth—a horrible curse that didn't deserve the breath it took to speak. She screamed, and his bony hand clamped down upon her mouth. He shifted so that he straddled her, his thighs pressing into her body tight.

"Shh, shh, shh, shh, shh!" he cooed, his face bent close to hers, his dark hair caressing her cheek. "I'm not going to hurt you. I will make everything better. You'll see."

She clawed at him, and yet he did not seem to notice.

When he pulled his hand away, she could no longer make sound—he had stolen her voice. Her eyes widened and tears spilled down the sides of her face. This was another one of the demigod's powers.

He offered a horrible grin that seemed to tear across his face.

"There," he said. "I like you better this way. Like this, I can still hear you moan."

There was a sour taste in the back of her mouth, and as Pirithous slipped down her body to settle between her thighs, she began to kick and thrash. Her knee rose, hitting Pirithous in the face, and as he fell back, she lurched into a sitting position.

She scurried back, kicking against the mattress until she was pressed into the headboard. Her body felt hot and cold at the same time, her clothes soaked through with sweat. For a moment, she stared blindly into the darkness, her breath ragged—then she noticed a shadow move toward her and she screamed.

"No!" She jerked back, head thudding against the headboard painfully as vines split her skin, sending a bone-shattering pain throughout her whole body. She screamed, the sound piercing even to her own ears.

"Persephone." Hades's voice cut through the darkness—and then the hearth blazed to life, flooding the room with light, illuminating the mess she had made of her body and the bed. There was blood everywhere, and thick vines protruded from her arms and shoulders and legs, flaying her skin. When she saw them, she began to sob.

"Look at me," Hades snapped, and the sound of his voice made her flinch. She met his gaze, her face stained with salty tears.

There was something in his eyes, a glint of panic she had never seen before. It was as if, for a moment, he did not know what to do. He grasped the thorns and they dissolved into dust and ash, then his hands were on her skin, sending warmth and healing through her body. The flesh she had mangled with her magic fused together into a pink puckered line until it smoothed. When he was finished, he stood.

"I will take you to the baths," he said. "Can I...hold you?"

She swallowed thickly and nodded. He scooped her up gingerly and left the bloodied bed.

They did not speak as Hades wandered down the corridor. The smell of lavender and sea salt was comforting. Instead of taking her to the main pool, Hades navigated along a separate path, down a hall with walls that glistened. As he eased her to her feet, she found that they had come to a smaller room with a round pool. The air was warmer here and the light easier on her tired eyes.

"Can I undress you?" he asked.

She nodded, and yet it took him a moment to move, to slip his fingers under the straps of her bloodied gown and draw it down her arms. His robes followed. He stared at her for a moment and then reached to brush a piece of her hair over her shoulder, and she shivered.

"Do you know the difference?" he asked. "Between my touch and his?"

She swallowed and answered honestly. "When I am awake."

He paused a long moment before asking, "Can I touch you now?"

"You don't have to ask," she answered, and Hades's jaw tightened.

"I wish to," he said. "In case you aren't ready."

She nodded, and he scooped her up and entered the pool, holding her against him. The blood upon her skin colored the water crimson as it danced away in ribbons. He did not ask about her nightmare, and she didn't speak until the tension in his body had lessened.

"I don't understand why I dream about him," she whispered. Hades stared down at her, frowning. "Sometimes I think back to that day and remember how afraid I was, and other times I think I should not be so affected. Others—"

"You cannot compare trauma, Persephone." Hades's tone was gentle but firm.

"I just feel like I should have known," she said. "I should have never—"

"Persephone," Hades said, his voice gentle, and yet there was an edge beneath it, a frustration that made her eyes burn. "How could you have known? Pirithous presented himself as a friend. He played upon your kindness and compassion. The only person who is wrong here was Pirithous."

Her mouth began to quiver, and she covered her eyes with her hands. Her body shook hard, and Hades shifted, holding her against his bare skin, her head tucked beneath his chin. She was not sure how long she cried, but they remained in the pool until she was finished. They dressed and returned to bed where Hades poured two glasses of whiskey. He handed one to Persephone.

"Drink," he said.

She accepted and downed the alcohol.

"Do you wish to sleep?" he asked.

She shook her head.

"Come sit with me," he said and took a seat beside the fire. He guided her into his lap, and she rested her head against his chest, comforted by the heat at her back and the smell of Hades's skin.

Sometime later, Persephone felt Hades's magic stir the air. She opened her eyes, realizing she had fallen asleep and now lay in bed. She rolled and rose into a sitting position, startling when she saw Hades. There was something completely feral about him—as if he'd been able to drown his humanity in the depths of his darkness and all that remained was a monster.

This is a battle god, she thought.

"You went to Tartarus," she said, her voice low.

Hades did not speak.

She did not need to ask what he'd done there. He'd gone to torture Pirithous, and the evidence was all over his face—streaked with blood.

Again, Hades was silent.

After a moment, Persephone rose and approached him, placing a hand on his face. Despite the wild look in his eyes, he leaned into her touch.

"Are you well?" she whispered.

"No," he replied.

Her hand dropped, slipping around his waist. It took Hades a moment, but he finally moved, arms wrapping around her, holding her tight against him. After a moment, he spoke, and his voice sounded a little more normal, a little warmer.

"Ilias and Zofie found the woman who assaulted you," he said.

"Zofie?" Persephone asked, drawing back.

"She has been helping Ilias," he answered.

Persephone was curious about exactly what Hades meant by that, but it was a conversation for another time.

"Where is the woman?"

"She is being held at Iniquity," he answered.

"Will you take me to her?"

"I'd rather you sleep."

"I do not want to sleep."

Hades frowned. "Even if I stay?"

"There are people out there attacking goddesses," Persephone said. "I'd rather hear what she has to say."

Hades cupped her jaw and then threaded his fingers through her hair, grimacing. She knew he was worried, wondering if she could handle this confrontation so soon after the horror of her nightmare.

"I'm okay, Hades," she whispered. "You will be with me."

That only seemed to make him frown more. Still, he finally answered.

"Then we will do as you wish."

CHAPTER XII
A Touch of Enlightenment

Persephone had not returned to Iniquity since the first time she'd visited. She'd come with the hope of saving Lexa and had left with nothing but the knowledge that she did not know Hades or his empire very well.

The club was a speakeasy-style accessed by members with a password. This space was neutral territory, and behind these walls, deals were made with balance in mind. After learning about the evil Hades was willing to let exist in the world, Persephone often found herself wondering the same—what malevolence would she allow if the results brought peace, if they prevented war, for instance?

They manifested in a room that looked similar to the one where she'd met Kal Stavros, the owner of Epik Communications, a Magi and a mortal who had offered to save Lexa in exchange for Hades and Persephone's story. She hadn't had a chance to refuse before Hades arrived and ended the bargain, permanently scarring Kal's face.

The accused sat beneath a circular pool of light. Her long, dark hair was silky and straight. She kept her head pressed against the back of the chair. A black snake slithered slowly around her neck while two others made their way around her arms; another six slinked in a circle around her feet. Her hatred was palpable as she glared at them, her mouth set in a hard line.

Persephone inched forward until she stood at the edge of the light.

"I do not need to tell you why you are here," she said.

The woman glared, and when she spoke, her voice was clear, not a hint of fear or even rage. Her calm put Persephone on edge. "Will you kill me?"

"I am not the Goddess of Retribution," Persephone said.

"You did not answer my question."

"I am not the one being questioned."

The woman stared.

"What's your name?" Persephone asked.

The woman lifted her chin and replied, "Lara."

"Lara, why did you attack me in the Coffee House?"

"Because you were there," she answered, nonchalant. "And I wanted you to hurt."

The words, while not surprising, still stung.

"Why?"

Lara did not reply immediately, and Persephone watched as the snake paused its slithering to lift its head from her neck to hiss, exposing venomous fangs. Lara jerked, squeezing her eyes shut, preparing for the bite.

"Not yet," Persephone said, and the snake stilled. Lara looked at the goddess. "I asked you a question."

This time, as the woman answered, tears rolled down her face.

"Because you represent everything that is wrong with this world," she seethed. "You think you stand for justice because you wrote some angry words in a newspaper, but they mean nothing! Your actions are by far more telling—you, like so many, have merely fallen into the same trap. You are a sheep, corralled by Olympian glamour."

Persephone stared at the woman, knowing her anger had grown from something—a seed that had been planted and nurtured by hate—so she asked, "What happened to you?"

Something haunting bled into Lara's eyes. It was an expression that was hard to explain, but when Persephone saw it, she knew it for what it was—trauma.

"I was raped," Lara hissed in a barely there whisper. "By Zeus."

Her admission came as a shock despite Zeus being known for this behavior—a fact that should not be fact at all. Power had given Zeus, and so many others like him, a ticket to abuse for no other reason except that they were male and in a position of authority.

It was wrong and the behavior was at the core of their society. Even among the goddesses, who were equal or, in some cases, more powerful, assault was used as a means of control and oppression. Hera was a prime example—deceived and raped by Zeus, she was so ashamed, she agreed to marry him. As his queen, even her role as Goddess of Marriage had become Zeus's.

Beside Persephone, Hades stiffened. She glanced at the God of the Dead, whose jaw ticked. She knew Hades punished those who committed crimes against women and children severely—was he motivated by his brother's actions? Had he ever punished Zeus?

"I'm sorry this happened to you," Persephone said.

She stepped toward Lara, and the snakes that had kept her firmly in her seat vanished into tendrils of smoke.

"*Don't,*" Lara snapped. "I do not want your pity."

Persephone halted. "I am not offering pity," she replied. "But I would like to help you."

"How can you help me?" Lara seethed.

The question hurt—it felt the same as when the woman had approached her in Nevernight and rebuked her. Still, she had to do something. She had never experienced the extent of Lara's nightmare, but even then, Pirithous haunted her in a way she never imagined.

"I know you did not do anything to deserve what happened to you," Persephone said.

"Your words mean nothing while gods are still able to hurt," Lara offered in a painful whisper.

Persephone could not speak because there was nothing to say. She could argue that not all gods were the same, but those words were not right for this time—and Lara was right. What did it matter that not all gods were the same when the ones who hurt went unpunished?

It was then that Persephone remembered something her mother had said.

Consequences for gods? No, Daughter, there are none.

The words made her sick, and she clenched her fists against them, swearing that one day, things would be different.

"How would you have Zeus punished?" Hades asked.

Both Persephone and Lara looked at him, surprised. Was he asking because he planned to do something about this? Persephone's gaze shifted to Lara as she spoke.

"I would have him torn apart limb by limb and his body burned. I would have his soul fracture into millions of pieces until nothing was left but the whisper of his screams echoing in the wind."

"And *you* think you can bring that justice?" Hades's voice was low, a deadly challenge, and Persephone realized that while she'd been here to sympathize, he was here to get to something else—her loyalty.

Lara glared. "Not me. Gods," she said. "New ones."

Her eyes took on a glassy, almost hopeful look, as if she

were imagining what it would be like—a world with new gods.

"It will be a rebirth," she whispered.

Rebirth. Lemming. They were words Persephone had heard before, and they made her think that Lara was connected to the same people who had attacked Harmonia and perhaps Adonis, and it sounded like they were desperate to usher in a new era of gods by any means possible.

"No," Hades said. His voice seemed to thread through her, throwing her out of the strange possession she had been under. "It will be a *massacre*—and it will not be us who dies. It will be *you*."

Persephone looked at Hades and took his hand.

"What happened to you was horrible," Persephone said. "And you are right that Zeus should be punished. Will you not let us help you?"

"There is no hope for me."

"There is always hope," Persephone said. "It is all we have."

There was a beat of silence, and then Hades spoke, "Ilias, take Miss Sotir to Hemlock Grove. She will be safe there."

The woman stiffened. "So you will imprison me?"

"No," Hades said. "Hemlock Grove is a safe house. The goddess Hecate runs the facility for abused women and children. She will want to hear your story if you wish to tell her. Beyond that, you may do as you please."

———

Persephone was exhausted, and an ache was forming behind her eyes, spreading to her temples. She could count the days she'd slept through the night in the last three weeks on one hand. She cupped her coffee between her hands and sipped, her thoughts turning to Hades. Her heart clenched tight every time she thought of how he'd found her, broken and bleeding in their bed, his eyes full of panic and pain. She'd wanted to comfort him, but the only words she could find were ones to question her own sanity and perception of reality.

That had only seemed to irritate him.

She shivered, suddenly recalling the way her skin split as her magic roared to life, the way Hades had looked when he'd asked if she knew the difference between his touch and Pirithous's, how she'd cried in his arms until she fell asleep, waking later to find him returning to their room, face splattered with blood. The Persephone who had unknowingly invited the God of the Dead to play cards would have been fearful, disgusted, but she was no longer that goddess. She had been deceived and betrayed and broken, and she saw Pirithous's end as judgment and justice—even more so now that she'd heard Lara's story.

She could hardly blame Lara for the attack. She'd channeled her pain in the only way that made sense to her. Surely Zeus saw that his actions were making organizations like Triad stronger?

Persephone's office phone rang, startling her, sounding louder than usual. Maybe it was because she was sleep deprived, but she snatched it from its cradle quickly, mostly to silence the sound, and then remembered she needed to answer.

"Yes?" Her greeting came out more like a hiss, and she followed quickly with something a little more professional. "Can I help you?"

"Lady Persephone, I am sorry to bother you," Ivy said on the other end. "I have Lady Harmonia here. She says she does not have an appointment with you. Should I send her up?"

Harmonia was here to visit? That surprised her. She hadn't expected to see her so soon after her ordeal. More importantly, she hadn't expected Aphrodite to let her out of her sight.

"Yes, of course. Please, send her up."

Persephone stood, smoothing out her jumper and hair. She felt self-conscious today, having had no time to get ready when she and Hades returned home from Iniquity. She'd thrown on the most comfortable work outfit she owned and wrangled her hair into a braid that was not at all interested in remaining a braid.

She stepped into the waiting area, which had been redecorated to fit Persephone's style. A couch with modern lines sat against the wall. A set of colorful floral portraits hung above it, while two spacious sapphire chairs sat opposite. A glass table separated the two, and a vase of white narcissus sat at its center.

The funny thing about how it had been decorated was that Persephone had not asked or given any direction. She'd just returned to work the day after Hades had gifted her the space to find everything arranged. When she'd asked him about it, he blamed it on Ivy.

"She cannot stand empty space," he said. "You gave her an excuse to decorate. She will be forever in your debt."

"You're the one who let me office here," Persephone replied. "She should be in your debt."

"She already is."

Persephone hadn't asked for clarification. Whatever deal was between him and Ivy was working in both of their favors.

Her attention turned to the elevator, which dinged as it hit her floor. As it opened, she could hear Ivy speaking to Harmonia.

"Lord Hades keeps us busy. Most recently, he purchased several acres in preparation for his plans to start a horse rescue and rehabilitation ranch..."

Persephone raised a brow. That was new information. She made a mental note to ask him about that later, but for now, she focused on smiling as Ivy and Harmonia left the elevator.

The Goddess of Harmony looked very different from when last Persephone saw her, for which she was relieved. No longer bruised and broken, she appeared healed, at least outwardly. She wore a top with bell sleeves, skinny jeans, and boots. Her long blond hair was curled and fell in waves over her shoulders. A large bag hung on her shoulder, and Persephone noticed Opal's small face poking out from inside.

When Harmonia saw Persephone, she smiled.

"Good morning, Lady Persephone," Ivy said, inclining her head.

"Good morning, Ivy," she replied. "Good morning, Harmonia. I did not expect you."

The goddess blushed. "I'm so sorry. If this is a bad time, I can come back."

"Of course not. I am glad you are here," Persephone said.

"Can I get either of you anything? Coffee? Tea, perhaps?" Ivy asked, ever the hostess.

"Coffee for me," Persephone said. "You, Harmonia?"

"The same."

"Of course! I will be right back."

The two watched until Ivy disappeared down the hall, then Harmonia turned to Persephone, smiling softly.

"She is very kind," Harmonia said.

"Yes, I adore her," Persephone said and then gestured to her. "You look well."

"I am better," Harmonia answered, though Persephone saw a flash of unease in her eyes. She recognized it the same as she recognized in herself—a monster that dwelled beneath the surface. It would have her looking over her shoulder for months, years—maybe forever.

"Come. Have a seat in my office," Persephone said, directing her inside and closing the door.

They took a seat on the couch, and Harmonia picked Opal up from her bag, settling the dog in her lap.

"I did not expect you to be out and about so quickly." Persephone said.

"What else am I to do?" Harmonia asked. "Hide until they are all found? I do not think that is possible."

"I am sure Aphrodite would disagree."

Especially since Adonis had been murdered.

Harmonia offered a faint smile. "I am sure she would. It is actually Aphrodite I came to speak to you about."

Persephone raised her brows. "Oh?"

Her eyes fell to Harmonia's hands, which raked through Opal's long hair nervously.

"I believe my sister was the intended target of my attackers," Harmonia said.

"What makes you so sure?"

"They said so," she answered.

The bottom dropped out of Persephone's stomach.

"Are you worried Aphrodite will come to harm?"

"No," Harmonia said. "I worry that the intention of these people is to prove just how vengeful the Olympians can be, and I fear they targeted my sister."

"Why start with her? There are other gods far more temperamental."

"I do not know," Harmonia admitted. "But I cannot help thinking that another god—an Olympian—helped them attack me."

"Why do you say that?"

"I recognized the weapon they used to restrain me—the feel of it anyway. It was a net, similar to one Hephaestus made, but the magic was not his."

"Whose magic was it?"

Harmonia started to speak when there was a knock at the door and Ivy entered.

"Just bringing your coffee," she said, setting a tray on the coffee table.

"Thank you, Ivy," Persephone replied.

"Anything for you, my dear. Call if you need me!"

Alone again, Persephone poured each of them a cup of coffee, and as she handed Harmonia her cup and saucer, she asked, "Whose magic?"

"Your mother's."

"My...*mother's*?" Persephone sat with that information for a beat. She did not question how Harmonia knew who she was; she was certain Aphrodite disclosed that information. "What did it smell like? The magic?"

"Unmistakable," Harmonia replied. "It was warm like the sun on a spring afternoon. It smelled like golden wheat and the sweetness of ripened fruit."

Persephone did not respond.

"I did not wish to tell you in front of my sister," Harmonia explained. "There is a chance I could be wrong...especially if the weapon they have was created from relic magic."

That was a possibility.

"But you sensed no other magic?"

Harmonia frowned and offered a quiet, "No."

"But...why?" Persephone asked aloud. "Why would she help these people so intent on hurting gods?"

"Perhaps because they've hurt her," Harmonia supplied, and then she explained, "Perhaps she targeted Aphrodite because she is one of the reasons you and Hades met."

Something akin to shock settled upon Persephone's shoulders. She had never considered that her mother would hurt those who supported her and Hades's relationship—especially via a group of mortals who hated the gods. It did not make sense, unless they were missing something.

"If these mortals hate gods, why would they accept help from one?"

"Mortals are still powerless," Harmonia said. "And it would not be the first time something like this has happened. Throughout every Divine war, gods have taken the side of their would-be enemy. Hecate is an example—a Titan who fought alongside the Olympians."

That was true—and Hecate was not the only god to choose the Olympians. Helios had been another, and as Persephone was often reminded, he used his allegiance as a reason to avoid helping the gods in any capacity.

"I'm so sorry."

Persephone's brows knitted together as she met Harmonia's gaze. "Why are you sorry? You were the one who suffered."

"Because it is not in my nature to add to your pain," she said.

"This isn't your fault."

"Nor is it yours," Harmonia said as if reading her mind, and then the goddess offered as an explanation, "I can see your aura turning red with shame and green with guilt. Do not blame yourself for your mother's actions. You did not ask her to seek vengeance."

"It is not so easy," Persephone replied. "When so many suffer as a result of my decision to marry Hades."

"Is it because you chose to marry Hades or something far deeper?"

Persephone looked at Harmonia questioningly.

"At the root of Demeter's anger is a multitude of fears. She is afraid of being alone, and she likes to feel needed."

It was true.

Demeter liked to be the savior, which was why it had taken her so long to disclose the mysteries of her cult, which included gardening. It gave her a sense of power and need when the world begged for food and water.

"Will you tell Aphrodite of your suspicions? That she was the intended target of your attack?"

"No," Harmonia said. "Because she will only feel guilty. Besides, you'd have no chance at handling this situation quietly once Hephaestus found out. He would set the world on fire for her."

Persephone smiled at those words. She'd heard the same thing from Hades, and suddenly she felt like she understood the love the God of Fire possessed for the Goddess of Love.

"He really cares for her."

"Yes," Harmonia answered. "I see it in their colors every day, but it is a dark love they possess for one another, hindered by shared pain and misunderstanding. One day, I think they will come to accept one another." Harmonia looked at her watch. "I must return to Lemnos before Aphrodite comes looking for me."

Opal grunted as Harmonia picked her up and returned her to the bag.

"Of course," Persephone said, standing with the goddess.

As she opened the door, she found Sybil on the other side preparing to knock. The oracle dropped her hand and offered a smile that quickly faded when her eyes shifted to Harmonia, her expression becoming troubled.

Strange, Persephone thought.

"Sybil, this is Harmonia," Persephone said. Perhaps she did not recognize the goddess, though that did not make sense with her background as an oracle.

"It's...very nice to meet you," Sybil said, though she seemed distracted.

Harmonia extended her hand. "A pleasure, Sybil." She paused. "You are an oracle."

"Was," Sybil said, almost breathlessly.

"You will always be an oracle, even if you do not work for the Divine," Harmonia said. "It is your gift."

There was a strange tension that filled the space between the three. Perhaps it was because of how Sybil's job as an oracle had ended. It had been heartbreaking for her, to see something she'd worked so hard for crumble within seconds.

"I was coming to see if you were ready for lunch," Sybil said.

"Perfect timing," Harmonia said. "I was just leaving. Persephone, if you need anything, please reach out. Sybil, it was nice meeting you."

Harmonia left, and Sybil turned to watch her go.

"What was that about?" Persephone asked once she was out of sight.

"What?" the oracle asked, brows drawing together.

"Something's off. What did you see when you looked at Harmonia? I saw your expression change."

"Nothing," Sybil said quickly. "Let's eat. I'm starving."

CHAPTER XIII
A Perfect Storm

Persephone, Sybil, and Zofie walked down the street to Ambrosia & Nectar for lunch, grateful for the warmth once they were inside. Despite not being far from Alexandria Tower, the café had felt miles away as they managed to walk through tall snow drifts, all while being pelted by snow and ice. The snowplows could not keep up—though they were still trying.

They took their seats, and Persephone helped Zofie navigate the menu, informing her of her favorite dishes.

"I want to try everything," the Amazon said. If it were any other person, Persephone would assume she was joking, but she knew if she did not stop the Amazon, she'd try to do exactly that.

"You will have time to try everything eventually," Persephone promised.

They ordered and while they waited for their food, Zofie instructed Sybil on how to disarm an intruder, specifically, in the event that Ben returned to her apartment.

"If he attacks with a blade, catch it in a parry and spin."

She demonstrated the movement with a flick of the wrist, and Persephone was glad that Zofie had not manifested her actual blade. "If he thrusts at you, parry his blade down."

"Zofie," Sybil said. "Has anyone told you that people do not fight with swords anymore?"

The Amazon looked affronted. "My sisters and I always fight with a blade!"

Persephone tried not to laugh. "Okay, what if no swords are involved? Just hand-to-hand combat?"

"Go for the nose," Zofie said, a malicious glint in her eyes.

Their conversation continued like that even after their food arrived. Persephone sat in relative silence, lost in her own thoughts, trying to piece things together.

One issue was that she didn't have enough information on Adonis's death, but perhaps they'd sought to draw Aphrodite out with his murder. But why try to enrage an Olympian other than to create unrest? Wasn't Demeter's snowstorm doing that enough? Still, if Harmonia's assumption was correct, who would Demeter go after next? There were a number of gods and goddesses who supported her—Hecate, Apollo, though arguably reluctant, then there was...

"Hermes," Sybil said. "What are you doing here?"

Persephone blinked and met the god's gold gaze. He looked like he'd just come from tennis practice, dressed in white pants and a light blue polo. He slid into the booth beside Persephone, scooting her along the vinyl with little effort.

"Eating lunch with my besties," he answered. "What does it look like?"

"It looks like you're crashing our lunch," Persephone said.

"Well, it's not like *you* were chatting it up," he said, reaching for Persephone's fork and digging into her untouched food, popping a bite into his mouth. As he chewed, he spoke, looking at Persephone.

"I bet I can guess what you were thinking," he said. "Reliving a night of mind-blowing sex with Hades."

"Gross," Zofie said.

Sybil giggled.

But Persephone wished that *was* the case. She'd take that over thinking of her mother—or her actual night with Hades, which had only been full of blood and tears.

She managed to roll her eyes and lie. "Actually, I'm thinking about the wedding."

Hermes brightened. "Tell me you've picked a date!"

"Well, no," she said, pursing her lips. "I was actually thinking about...eloping."

It was an idea that had crossed her mind multiple times since Hades had proposed, and given the drama that surrounded their engagement, it was looking like the best option. Did anyone really need to know they were married anyway?

"Eloping?" Hermes repeated, as if he did not know what the word meant. "Why would you elope?"

"I mean, there's a lot of unrest between mortals and gods right now, and a public wedding would just enrage my mother more."

She was now thinking that if her mother was involved in the attack on Harmonia, things may just escalate with a wedding.

"And a private one wouldn't?" Hermes challenged, brow raised.

"I do not understand this wedding," Zofie said. "Why do you need to marry? You love Hades, do you not? Is that not enough?"

Loving Hades *was* enough—but his proposal was the promise of something more. A commitment to a life they would share and cultivate together. She wanted that.

"If I was marrying Hades," Hermes said, scooping up

another bite of Persephone's food, "I'd want a televised wedding so everyone knew that piece of ass was mine."

"Sounds like you thought a lot about marrying Hades," Sybil observed.

"Apparently there's no need to plan anything until Zeus approves our marriage anyway," Persephone said, glaring at Hermes.

"Why are you looking at me like I should have told you?" Hermes asked defensively. "Everyone knows that."

"In case you've forgotten, I grew up in a glass house with my narcissistic mother," Persephone retorted.

"How could I forget?" Hermes asked. "When there's a raging ice storm outside to remind me?"

Sybil elbowed the god.

"Ouch!" He glared at her. "Watch it, oracle."

Persephone's gaze broke from Hermes, falling to her hands in her lap.

"This isn't your fault, Persephone," Sybil said.

"It feels like it."

"You want to marry the love of your life," she said. "There's nothing wrong with that."

"Except that…everyone seems to disapprove. If it isn't my mother, it's the world, or Zeus." Persephone paused. "Maybe we should have waited on the engagement. It's not like we aren't going to be together forever."

"Then you allow others to determine how you live," Sybil said. "And there is nothing fair about that."

It wasn't fair, but Persephone had learned a good deal about fairness in the time since meeting Hades. In fact, the lesson had come from Sybil herself.

Right, wrong, fair, unfair—it's not really the world we live in, Persephone. The gods punish.

She was starting to understand why the Impious grew in ranks, why some had become organized and formed Triad, why they wished for the gods to have less influence over their lives.

"That isn't good," Sybil said, nodding at a television in the corner where the news streamed.

Impious Gather to Protest Winter Weather

Persephone wanted to sink into herself.

She caught part of what the anchor was saying.

"*This uncharacteristic weather has many believing a god or goddess may be on a quest for vengeance. Both the Impious and the Faithful are calling for an end in two very different ways.*"

Persephone looked away, and yet she could not escape the broadcast, the words still reaching and ringing in her ears.

"*Why is it mortals suffer every time a god has a mood swing? Why should we worship such gods?*"

"I understand the Impious less and less," said Hermes.

Persephone looked at him. "What do you mean?"

"When they began, they were angry with us for being distant and careless, as if they wanted our presence. Now they seem to think they can do without us."

"Can they?" Persephone asked, because she truly did not know.

"I suppose that depends. Would Helios still provide the sun? Or Selene the moon? Despite how mortals perceive the world, we are the reason for its existence—we can make and unmake it."

"Yes, but…if they did provide the sun and moon and all the power to maintain the world. If the gods…took a step back from mortal society…what would happen?"

Hermes blinked. "I…do not know."

It was clear he'd never considered that before.

The truth was the gods would never be able to completely release their hold on the world, because it would end, but could they strike a balance? And what did that look like exactly?

"Excuse me—" A man approached their table, cellphone in hand. He was middle-aged and wore gray slacks and a white shirt.

Hermes whipped his head around.

"No," he said, and the mortal's mouth snapped close. "Leave."

The man twisted away and wandered off in a daze.

"That was rude," Persephone said.

"Well, you are anything but a blushing bride today," he argued. "I doubt you wanted to pose for a picture with some weirdo." Then his expression softened. "Besides, you look sad."

Persephone frowned, which didn't help her case. "I'm just…distracted," she mumbled.

Hermes surprised her by reaching out and placing his hand atop her own. "It's okay to be sad, Sephy."

She hadn't really thought much about what she was feeling. Instead, she'd focused on staying busy, creating new habits to replace the old ones that reminded her that Lexa was not here anymore.

"We better get back," she said, once again choosing action over feeling.

———

Hermes left them outside Ambrosia & Nectar, giving each of them a peck on the cheek, even Zofie, who was too shocked to react at first, then she tried to shank him. Persephone took hold of her wrist, but instead of scolding Zofie, she glared at Hermes.

"Ask next time you decide to kiss someone," she said.

For a moment, his eyes widened, and then he looked genuinely remorseful. "I'm sorry, Zofie."

The Amazon sulked, arms crossed over her chest.

"Well, I'm off," he said. "I have a date with a goat man. Let's go out soon."

Once he vanished, Persephone, Sybil, and Zofie exchanged a look.

"Goat man?" they all asked in unison.

Persephone and Sybil returned to work, leaving Zofie to patrol. Each time Persephone arrived or returned from an outing, the Amazon made rounds outside and inside Alexandria Tower. What she did after, Persephone did not know. Though, she had to admit, she was glad that Hades had assigned Zofie to work with Ilias. It gave her the chance to do more task-based work and socialize.

Gods knew the Amazon needed that.

Ivy greeted them as they entered the building, heading to the elevator.

"Hermes is right," Sybil said. "We should go out soon."

Persephone knew what Sybil was thinking—they hadn't been anywhere since Lexa died. She frowned at the thought.

"Yeah," she said, distracted. "We should."

"You can say no," Sybil said, and Persephone met her gaze. "If you're not up for it yet. We all would understand, you know?"

Persephone swallowed thickly.

"Thank you, Sybil," she whispered.

They embraced, and Persephone rested her head on Sybil's shoulder until they came to her floor, but as they stepped off the elevator, they found Leuce and Helen standing beside each other, staring out the windowed walls at a jumble of flashing red and blue lights in the distance. Despite the heavy fog and wintery mix, Persephone knew that the highway was in the distance and that something horrible had happened.

"Oh, my gods," Persephone whispered, coming to stand beside Leuce and Helen.

The television blared suddenly, and the three turned to find that Sybil had turned on the news. A banner ran across the bottom of the screen, announcing the horror they could see in the distance:

Multiple Wrecks Reported on the A2 Motorway

"...the accidents are believed to be caused by slick roadways and heavy snow. No word on the number of fatalities, but it has been reported that several are injured."

Images and video of the crash moved in the background. Persephone watched in shock as car after car came upon the wreck, unaware due to the heavy mist, and with no ability to brake in time or gain traction on the slick road, plowed into vehicle after vehicle.

"How horrible," Helen said just as they witnessed a large tractor trailer slide into the back of a car, sending it flying into the air. "How could that person survive?"

They couldn't—and there was no safe way to escape the wreck. Leaving the car meant the possibility of slipping on ice or being hit by another vehicle in the lineup; staying meant hoping that the next person didn't hit too hard.

Persephone stared, a lump forming in her throat. This was what she dreaded—that Demeter would take her anger out on humanity, not only because she couldn't get her way but because she knew it was the best way to get to Persephone.

"Why parade as a mortal? You are a goddess."

"I am more like them than you."

"You are not, and once they discover who you really are, they will shun you for pretending you were one of them."

"Your mother is insane," Leuce said under her breath.

Persephone did not need to be told—she knew well enough.

She turned from the television and walked blindly toward her office. Once inside, she picked up the phone and dialed Ilias.

"Lady Persephone," he answered.

"Where is Hades?" she asked.

He must have sensed the distress in her voice, because he did not hesitate to tell her.

"He is at Iniquity, my lady."

"Thank you."

Her hands were shaking so badly, she barely managed to hang up the phone before vanishing, appearing in Hades's office. From here, he spied on those who used his club while they sat in the bar below, drinking and smoking and playing cards. Today, however, she found he was not alone. A man she did not know stood opposite Hades's desk in a navy-blue suit despite the fact that there were two empty chairs waiting. If Persephone had to guess, the man had not been invited to sit.

As soon as she arrived, their voices halted, and Hades's hot gaze turned to her.

"Darling," Hades said with a nod of his head. There was no hint of surprise in his voice, and yet she knew by his expression he worried at her sudden appearance.

Then the man turned to look at her. He was handsome and most definitely a demigod—those bright aqua eyes gave his parentage away immediately, a son of Poseidon. He had brown skin and short dark hair and stubble covering his jaw. She had never seen him before.

"So you are the lovely Lady Persephone," he said. His eyes dipped, appraising, and she felt disgust immediately.

"Theseus, I think you should leave," Hades said, and the demigod's gaze left hers, almost reluctant. Persephone shuddered noticeably, disturbed by his presence.

"Of course," he said. "I am late for a meeting anyway."

He nodded toward Hades and turned to exit, pausing in front of Persephone.

"Pleased to make your acquaintance, my lady," he said and held out his hand. She glanced at it and then met his gaze. In truth, she did not wish to take his hand, so she said nothing at all, but instead of being offended, the man grinned and let his hand fall.

"You are probably right not to shake my hand. Have a good day, my lady."

He brushed past her, and she watched until he had left the office, not really trusting to give him her back. Once he was gone, Hades spoke.

"Are you well?"

She turned to find that Hades had moved silently across the room toward her.

"Do you know that man?" Persephone asked.

"As well as I know any enemy," Hades replied.

"Enemy?"

He nodded toward the closed door where the demigod had disappeared.

"That man is the leader of Triad," he replied.

She had questions, so many of them, but when Hades's hand touched her chin, tears came to her eyes.

"Tell me," he said.

"The news," she whispered. "There's been a horrible accident."

He didn't seem surprised, and Persephone wondered if he'd already sensed the death.

"Come," he said. "We will greet them at the gates."

CHAPTER XIV
The Temple of Sangri

Persephone had often come to the pier to greet new souls who crossed the River Styx on Charon's ferry, but this time, Hades teleported to the opposite side of the shore—to the gates of the Underworld. It was cold here, as if the air from the Upperworld were seeping through the ground, but she hardly noticed, because seeing the gates in person left her breathless.

They were as tall as the mountains they were built into and made of black iron. The bottom of the gates had been crafted into a line of narcissus, and from them sprouted spiraling vines decorated with flora and pomegranates. Their raised edges glinted gold beneath the muted sky, which extended over their heads but disappeared into a strange and terrifying darkness around them. Beyond the gates was a great elm. Persephone could feel its age, even from this distance. It was as old as Hades and its roots went deep, its limbs heavy with orbs of bright, bluish light.

"What clings to that tree?" she asked Hades.

"Dreams," he replied, looking at her. "Those who enter the Underworld must leave them behind."

There was a certain sadness that overtook her at the

thought, but she also understood—there was no room for dreams in the Underworld, because life here meant existing without burden, without challenge. Life here meant rest.

"Must all souls walk through these gates?" Her voice was quiet because, for some reason, this space felt sacred.

"Yes," Hades answered. "It is the journey they must take to accept their death. Believe it or not, it was once more frightening than this."

Persephone's gaze met his. "I did not mean that it was frightening."

He offered a small smile and touched her lips with his finger. "And yet you tremble."

"I tremble because it is cold," she said. "Not out of fear. It is very beautiful here, but it is also...overwhelming. I can feel your power here, stronger than anywhere else in the Underworld."

"Perhaps that is because this is the oldest part of the Underworld," he said.

A cloak appeared in Hades's hands, and he shrugged it around Persephone's shoulders.

"Better?" he asked.

"Yes," she whispered.

In the next second, both Hermes and Thanatos appeared. Their wings were wrapped around them like cloaks, then they unfolded, expanding and stretching, nearly filling the space in which they stood to reveal a handful of souls. There were about twenty in total, all various ages, ranging from what Persephone guessed was a five-year-old to a sixty-year-old. The five-year-old arrived with her father, the sixty-year-old with his wife.

Thanatos swept into a bow.

"Lord Hades, Lady Persephone," he said. "We...will return."

"There are more?" Persephone asked, her eyes wide, staring at the God of Death.

He nodded grimly.

"It's alright, Sephy," Hermes said. "Just focus on making them feel welcome."

The two gods vanished, and as they did, the father of the five-year-old fell to his knees.

"Please," he begged. "Take me but do not take my daughter! She is too young!"

"You have arrived at the gates of the Underworld," Hades replied. "I am afraid I cannot change your Fate."

Before, Persephone might have found Hades's words to be callous, but they were the truth.

She did not think it was possible for the man to look any paler, but he managed it and screamed, "You are a liar! You are the God of the Dead! You can change her Fate!"

Persephone took a step forward. She felt as if she were shielding Hades from this man's rage.

"Lord Hades may be God of the Dead, but he is not the weaver of your thread," she said. "Do not fear, mortal father, and be brave for your daughter. Your existence here will be peaceful."

She turned her attention to the daughter then and knelt before her. She was adorable, small with blond, curly pigtails and dimples.

"Hi," she said quietly. "My name is Persephone. What's your name?"

"Lola," the girl replied.

"Lola," she said with a smile. "I am glad you are here and with your father too. That is lucky."

So many children came to the Underworld without their parents only to be adopted by other souls and reunited with their loved ones years later. If these were the circumstances these two would suffer, she was glad they were together.

"Would you like to see some magic?" she asked.

The girl nodded.

Persephone hoped this worked as she scooped up a handful of the black dirt at her feet. She envisioned a white anemone—and watched as it effortlessly materialized in her palm. She blew out a breath, thankful, and Lola's face lit up as Persephone threaded the flower into her hair.

"You are very brave," she said. "Will you be brave for your father too?"

The girl nodded, and Persephone straightened, taking a step back. Shortly after, more souls joined them, guided to the Underworld by Hermes and reaped by Thanatos. Before their work was finished, the small space was crowded with one hundred and thirty people and one dog, whose owner had also made it into the afterlife. Persephone greeted many of them, and Hades followed suit. There were children and teens, young adults and older ones. Some were fearful and others were angry. Only a few were unafraid.

At some point, Hades's fingers slipped between hers and he gestured toward the gates, which were opening soundlessly to reveal the elm beyond in its fullness—beautiful and ancient and glowing.

"Welcome to the Underworld," he said.

Together, they led the souls through the gates and beneath the far-reaching limbs of the elm. As they walked, thousands of tiny orbs of light appeared and glowed, rising above their heads to settle on the leaves of the tree. The souls watched in wonder, not horror, not realizing that those small balls of light were the hopes and dreams they'd formed over a lifetime. Persephone felt immense sadness, watching it happen, but Hades squeezed her hand.

"Think of it as a release," he said. "They will no longer be burdened with regret."

She took some comfort in that, and as they left the shelter of the tree, they came to a lush strip of greenery and a pier that stretched over the black water of the Styx. The bank of the River of Woe was covered in white narcissus blooms. Returning from the other side was Charon, dressed in white robes that glowed like a torch against the muted gloom of the Underworld. His powerful arms rowed the boat to port, and he grinned.

"Welcome, welcome!" he said. "Come. Let's get you all home."

Persephone had never seen this process before, but she watched as Charon chose who was allowed into his boat. It was not even full when he decided that was enough.

"No more," he said. "I will return."

As he rowed away, Persephone looked to Hades. "Why did he not take more?"

"Remember when I said the souls made this journey to accept death?"

She nodded.

"Charon will not take them until they have."

Persephone's eyes widened. "What if they don't?"

"Most do," he said.

"And?" Persephone prodded. "What about the rest?"

"It is a case-by-case basis," he answered. "Some are allowed to see how the souls live in Asphodel. If that does not encourage them to adjust, they are sent to Elysium. Some must drink from the Lethe."

"And how often does that happen?"

"It is rare," he said. "But inevitably, in times like these, there is always someone who struggles."

She could imagine. None of these people woke up and expected to die today.

Charon returned a few more times, and by the end of it, the only two left were the man with the five-year-old daughter. Charon tried to take her, but the father protested vehemently, and Persephone did not blame him.

"We go together or not at all!"

Persephone looked from Charon to Hades and then to the man, who held his daughter in his arms. She clung to him too. As much as she had accepted her end, she did not want to leave her father either.

Persephone left Hades's side and approached the man.

"What are you afraid of?" she asked.

"I left my wife and son behind," he said.

She considered this news—but she knew that several of the souls who had already passed over the Styx had left loved ones behind. She also knew that there would be more like him. She could not make a promise to him she could not keep for everyone.

So instead, she asked, "And do you not trust, after all that you have seen here, that you will see them again?"

"But—"

"Your wife will have comfort," she said. "Because you are here with Lola, and she will wait to be reunited with you both here in the Underworld. In Asphodel. Do you not wish to make a space for them? To welcome them when they come?"

The man looked at Lola and hugged her to him, crying for a long time. They let him, and all the while, Persephone felt the heaviness of this task. She could not imagine how Thanatos, Charon, and the judges managed this every day.

After a while, the man composed himself and took a breath.

"Okay. I am ready."

Persephone turned to Charon, who smiled. "Then welcome to the Underworld," he said and helped the two onto the boat.

Hades and Persephone joined them.

The ride was quiet; the souls looked out over the water, their expressions somber. Hades's hold on Persephone's hand tightened, and she knew it was because he recognized the burden she carried—it was sadness and grief and despair—but her spirits were soon lifted when she spotted a group of souls from Asphodel on the opposite shore waiting to greet them.

"Look!" Lola exclaimed, pointing a tiny finger.

As Charon came to dock, Yuri and Ian helped them onto the crowded deck.

"Welcome," they said.

There was a flutter of activity as they were accepted into the throng. The souls had been perfecting their welcome party and had managed to turn it into more of a celebration, bringing music and baskets of food. Initially, she worried that Hades would disapprove, seeing as these souls had yet to be judged, but the god had felt this was an even better entry into his realm, for it would always be on the minds of those who ended up in Tartarus.

"They will reflect on this moment and mourn that they were not better in life."

Hades and Persephone stayed with Charon, watching as the souls took off down the stone pathway, through the Fields of Mourning. As they went, they danced and sang and cheered. It felt like a happier end to a dreadful day.

Beside them, Charon chuckled. "They certainly shall never forget their entrance into the Underworld."

Persephone looked at him. "Do you think it will overshadow the suddenness of their death?"

The daimon offered her a gentle smile. "I think your Underworld will more than make up for it, my lady."

With that, he pushed off the pier and started across the river again.

She turned to Hades.

"Is it still a fate woven by the Fates if it is caused by another god?"

She truly did not know.

"All fates are chosen by the Fates," Hades replied.

"Lachesis had probably allotted an amount of time to each of them that ended today, and Atropos chose the wreck as their manner of death. Your mother's storm provided the catalyst."

Persephone frowned, and Hades squeezed her hand again. "Let us leave this place. I have something to show you."

She let Hades teleport them but was surprised by where he brought her—to the Temple of Sangri. It was a large building made of marble and white stone. A set of steps made a steep climb toward the closed and gilded doors, which lay just behind a row of ancient Ionic columns with scrolls capped in gold. As decorative as they were, they were also practical, supporting a pediment detailed with Demeter's symbols—the cornucopia and wheat grains—which were also gold.

"Hades...why are we at my mother's temple?" Persephone asked.

"Visiting."

The God of the Dead kept her gaze, kissing her hand, then guided it to his arm as he started up the steps.

"I do not wish to visit," she said.

"Your mother wants to fuck with us," he said. "Then we shall fuck with her."

"Do you intend to burn her temple to the ground?" she asked.

"Oh, darling," Hades replied. "I am far too depraved for that."

They crested the steps, and she felt a surge of Hades's magic as the doors flew open. Several priests and priestesses dressed in white halted their meandering when they saw the God of the Dead entering, their eyes widening with fear.

"L-lord Hades—" One of the priests shook as he spoke his name.

"Leave," he commanded.

"You cannot enter the Temple of Demeter," a priestess dared to say. "This is a *sacred* space."

Hades ignored the woman.

"Leave," he said again. "Or be witness—and complicit—in the desecration of this temple."

Demeter's priests and priestesses fled, leaving them alone in the firelit room. The doors slammed, causing the shadows on the wall to shudder.

In the silence, Hades turned to her.

"Let me make love to you."

"In my mother's temple? Hades—"

He cut her off with a kiss that made her moan. It was delicious and deep, and desire curled into her stomach like claws.

"My mother will be furious," she said when he pulled away.

"*I'm furious*," he hissed as his hand dug into the base of her skull and his lips returned to hers. His other hand traveled down, over her ass and under her thigh, hooking her leg around his hip. His erection nestled against her aching core and she moaned. His lips moved to her jaw and then her ear as he breathed, "And you haven't said no."

She didn't want to say no. Today's events had left her wound up, restless, stressed. She needed release—she needed him.

He pulled away and they stared at one another for a moment before Persephone smoothed her hands over Hades's chest to his shoulders and helped him out of his jacket. As it fell away to the floor, her clothes followed. They undressed one another—a slow and languid process that involved a lot of kissing and licking and sucking—until they stood bare, and then Hades gathered her into his arms and carried her down the column-flanked aisle toward her mother's altar, which overflowed with cornucopias of fruit and sheafs of wheat. Two large, gold basins full of fire roared on either side, and the air here was hot, causing sweat to drip from their skin.

Hades knelt and laid her upon the tiled floor before shifting to settle between her legs. He stared down at her, his eyes like fire, roving every part of her body, and then he bent and licked her, his tongue warm against her center. When he pulled away, his lips glistened with her desire and he smiled wickedly.

"You are wet for me."

"Always," she whispered.

"Always," he repeated. "Even at the sight of me?"

She nodded and Hades licked his lips.

"Do you want to know how I feel when I see you?" he asked, bending to press a kiss to the inside of her knee.

She nodded.

"When I see you, I cannot help but think of you like this," he said, his voice a sultry whisper against her skin as his lips continued up her thigh. "Bare. Beautiful. Drenched."

Each of his words was punctuated with the swirl of his tongue against her skin, and her breath quickened the closer he got to her burning core.

"My cock is heavy for you," he said. "And I am desperate to fill you."

He stared up at her, his head hovering above the apex of her thighs, and she could feel his breath against her molten flesh. Her fingers curled into her palms, nails biting into her skin.

"Then why am I so empty?"

The corner of his mouth lifted, and then he descended, mouth covering her clit. She arched against him and her hands went to her breasts, drawing her nipples between her fingers. She moaned and met his fiery gaze. As soon as she did, he jerked on her hips, hands digging into her ass, and then he was inside her, fingers curling deep, stimulating a part of her that made her breath catch hard in her throat. The more she cried, the faster his tongue moved, the more his fingers coaxed, and when he broke free from her, his lips and fingers gleamed.

He let her relax upon the tile and crawled up her body, mouth descending upon hers. He tasted like her—tangy and salty—and as his tongue slid against hers, she reached between them, wrapping her hand around his hard cock, smoothing her thumb over the head, thick with need. Hades groaned.

"Do you wish to take me in your mouth?" he asked.

"Always," she said, sitting up.

He shuddered and closed his eyes. "That word."

"What's wrong with that word?"

"Nothing," he said and took her place upon the floor, one hand behind his head. "It's…perfect."

Persephone wrapped her hand around Hades's cock, licked him once, and then took him into her mouth. His hand tightened into her hair, and he hissed, thighs tightening around her bent knees. She kept her mouth concentrated on the soft tip for a long while, savoring each bead of moisture that rose to the surface, and then took him to the hilt. He let out a long breath and jackknifed into a sitting position, pulling her from his length and pressing his hot mouth to hers. He guided her to her back, moving to grasp his cock as he pressed it into her slick folds, teasing her entrance and her clit.

Persephone groaned and ground her heels into his ass.

"Now, Hades," she commanded. "You *promised*."

He offered a breathy laugh. "What did I promise, my darling?"

He bent to kiss her neck, and his teeth grazed her ear. She turned toward him, angrily, hoping to capture his lips, but he moved.

"To fill me," she breathed. "To fuck me."

"That was no promise," he said. "It was a vow."

And then he sheathed himself fully, settling deep, and for a moment, he rested against her, their slick bodies melding together. His lips touched her jaw, then her mouth, as he waited for her to relax beneath him.

"Let me make love to you," he said again and held her gaze as he shifted, rising onto his hands above her. He began to move, setting a pace that ensured she felt every part of his cock. She bent beneath him, her back coming off the floor. Hades sat back then, hands digging into her thighs as he angled her hips and plunged into her again and again, steady and agonizing.

She wanted it to last forever. She wanted to come. She wanted everything all at once.

Then he withdrew and bent his head between her thighs, mouth descending upon her once more before he shoved into her again, body hovering over hers, strong arms caging her in. She watched his face as he moved, eyes heavy-lidded, his jaw tense, lips parted. He bent now and then to kiss her—once, twice, a third time—before neither of them could keep their eyes open, until their heads rocked back, and they came.

After, they lay on the tiled floor, limbs tangled together.

"What is this I hear about a horse rescue?" she asked, her voice low. She was tired, and her body still shook from her release.

Hades did not react, his fingers continuing to thread through her hair. "I was going to tell you by showing you," he said. "Who told you?"

"No one told me," she replied. "I overheard."

"Hmm." He made the sound sleepily.

After a moment, she shifted so that her arms could rest on his chest, with her chin propped upon them.

"Harmonia visited today," she said.

"Oh?" He raised a dark brow, his eyes half-open.

"She thinks the weapon used to capture her was a net," she said. "And that it was made with my mother's magic."

Hades did not speak, did not move a single muscle in his face.

"Why would my mother help attack her own people?"

"It has happened every time new gods rise to power," Hades replied. He did not seem surprised at all.

"New gods or new power?" she asked.

"Perhaps both," he replied. "I suppose we will find out sooner or later."

Persephone was silent, considering Hades's words.

"What was Theseus doing in your office today?" she asked, suddenly curious. When she'd arrived, whatever conversation they'd been having hadn't seemed to be going well, based on the tension in the room.

"Trying to convince me he had nothing to do with your assault and the attack on Adonis or Harmonia."

"And did he?"

"I could not detect a lie," Hades admitted.

"But you still think he was responsible?"

A ghost of a smile touched his lips, like he was proud she could read him so well.

"I think his inaction makes him responsible," Hades said. "By now, he must know the names of her attackers, and yet he refused to divulge them."

"Don't you have methods for extracting information?" she asked, arching a brow.

Hades chuckled. "Eager for blood, darling?"

She frowned. "I just don't understand what power he has to keep that information."

"The same kind of power any man with a following has," Hades replied. "Hubris."

"Is that not a punishable offense in the eyes of a god?"

"Trust, darling, by the time Theseus comes to the Underworld, it will be I who escorts him straight to Tartarus."

CHAPTER XV
Becoming Power

The remainder of the week passed quickly with Persephone conducting her own research on Triad. She learned the organization had a faulty beginning, claiming that their leadership was decentralized. This led to several individuals conducting their own protests—some peaceful and others more violent. When Zeus had declared them a terrorist organization, as a result encouraging several Faithful mortals to seek and attack those associated with the group, they had temporarily disbanded only to reform a year later under new leadership.

That was five years ago.

Since then, there had been a few protests and more violent attacks, but Triad had never taken responsibility for those, claiming they were rogue Impious. Persephone thought back to what Hades had said about Theseus—that the leader of Triad claimed to have no involvement with Adonis's murder and Harmonia's attack. Could this be a case of the Impious striking out on their own with the help of Demeter?

She could not say. She only hoped it didn't take another attack to find out.

It was Saturday before Persephone made it to Hecate's cottage to train, and she'd done so without Hades's knowledge. He'd insisted she rest since sleep had evaded her most nights, but she knew after witnessing the horrible wreck that took so many lives in the Upperworld, training was a priority. Plus, she had some questions for the ancient goddess.

When she arrived, Hecate was at work inside her cottage, wrapping dried herbs with twine—thyme, rosemary, sage, and tarragon. There were several bundles, and the whole place smelled both sweet and bitter.

Persephone sat down to help, selecting stems from each pile before carefully tying the twine into a neat bow.

"What kinds of spells do you plan to cast with all this?" Persephone asked.

The corner of Hecate's lip lifted.

"None. These herbs are for cooking."

"Since when?" Persephone asked, but her question almost sounded like an accusation. She had never witnessed the goddess cook anything but poisons.

"I grow all kinds of herbs," Hecate said. "Some for my spells, some for Milan, and some for recreation."

Persephone arched a brow.

"Why does Milan need so much?"

"These herbs last for at least three years," Hecate said. "But I imagine he is preparing for the wedding feast."

Persephone froze. She hadn't even thought about food—and what about cake? Were these even things she should be thinking about given the events of the past week? She frowned, and tensions gathered between her brows.

"I did not mean to cause you stress," Hecate said.

"You didn't," Persephone said and paused. "Hecate, you sided with the Olympians during the Titanomachy, yes?"

"Why do you ask?"

Persephone flinched at the tone of her voice—it was cold, almost irate. Was this a topic the goddess preferred not to talk about?

Hecate continued wrapping bundles of herbs, eyes never leaving her task.

"I just...wondered why you did not side with the Titans," Persephone said. "Since you are one of them."

"Being one of them does not mean I agree with them," Hecate said, continuing to work, her hands moving fast. "Under the Titans, the world would not have evolved, and I believed the Olympians, though gods themselves, were far more human than the Titans."

Persephone grimaced. "I do not think my mother's reasons are so noble."

"What do you mean?"

Persephone explained what Harmonia had told her—that she'd sensed Demeter's magic in the park where she'd been attacked—and her suspicions that she might be working with Triad or rogue Impious.

She couldn't get Harmonia's words out of her head.

Warm like the sun on a spring afternoon, smelling of golden wheat and sweet, ripened fruit.

Demeter's magic had been all over the weapon—the net—that had ensnared Harmonia. It made sense, why the goddess could not summon her magic to calm her attackers. Harmonia was a lesser god. Against Demeter, she had little chance of overpowering an ancient Olympian.

When Persephone was finished with her explanation, Hecate did not seem surprised.

"She is not the first god to attempt to overthrow her kind, nor will she be the last," she replied.

It was the same thing Hades had said.

"You do not seem worried," Persephone observed.

"I only worry about what I can control," Hecate said. "Your mother's actions are her own. You cannot stop her from choosing this path, but you can fight her along the way."

Persephone met Hecate's gaze.

"How?"

The goddess stared and, after a moment, picked up a crude pair of scissors they'd used to cut herbs earlier. She placed them on the table before Persephone.

"You learn to heal yourself."

"Why? You said I should fight. Shouldn't I be practicing magic?"

"Healing is a necessary power to master before going up against any of the Divine. All gods have the ability to heal themselves to some extent. Today, we will discover yours."

All gods? Persephone had no idea. She'd thought up until this point, it was just a power possessed by a few.

Persephone stared at Hecate, and then her eyes dropped to the scissors.

"And what am I supposed to do with these?"

"You will cut yourself or I will do it for you."

There was a moment when she thought Hecate must be joking, but that quickly passed as she recalled how the Goddess of Witchcraft had ordered Nefeli to attack her. That night, she'd gone beyond teaching simple magic tricks. This was serious, and Hecate had proven she'd do whatever it took to ensure Persephone's power manifested.

Persephone picked up the scissors. "What am I supposed to do once I cut myself?"

"Do it and I'll tell you," Hecate replied.

Still, Persephone hesitated. She'd never intentionally hurt herself before, and the idea of doing so made her cringe.

Just pretend it's your magic, she thought, thinking back

to the other night when she'd dreamed Pirithous was in her room and thick branches had torn her arms and legs to pieces. *This is nothing compared to that.*

She held the scissors over her palm. In a flash, Hecate's hand reached out and drove downward. The ends of the scissors pierced through Persephone's hand and jammed into the table beneath.

At first, Persephone was so shocked she didn't react. Then Hecate pulled the blades from her hand, and with the blood came the pain. Persephone screamed, gripping the wrist of her injured hand as her magic welled to the surface, flooding her veins. This was the kind of magic that burst from her skin—the kind that had erupted the night she'd dreamed of Pirithous.

"Healing yourself is a form of defense," Hecate said calmly, as if she hadn't just stabbed her.

"What the fuck, Hecate?" Persephone demanded, her voice raw and raging. Her eyes burned with magic; she could feel it—a residual heat that made her eyes water.

"Your magic won't wake to heal a scratch," the goddess said.

"So you had to stab me?" Persephone demanded.

A horrible smile spread across the goddess's face. "You have to learn to summon your power without pain, fear, or anger. It must become second nature, and so we will use pain, fear, and anger to train."

Persephone ground her teeth, her magic burning her skin.

"Channel your magic, Persephone. What does it feel like to have Hades heal you?"

Persephone warred with her mind, caught between listening to Hecate and her anger, but the pain in her hand also drew her attention, and soon she focused on it and the memories of Hades's healing hands. It had been so effortless for him, a pulse of power that warmed the skin, like slipping into a hot spring.

"Good," she heard Hecate say, and when Persephone opened her eyes, she saw that her hand was healed. The only evidence that she'd been injured was the blood on the table.

"Again," the goddess said, picking up the scissors.

Persephone flinched and stood. "No."

Hecate stared, still holding the bloodied shears aloft. "What do you want, Persephone?"

"What does that have to do with stabbing myself?"

"Everything. Your magic is reactive, more than likely due to trauma, and while that is not your fault, we are running out of time. Do you think you can take four minutes to heal yourself on the battlefield?"

"This is not battle, Hecate."

"It soon will be—and where would you rather learn? So I ask you again. What do you want?"

She wanted…Hades. She wanted the Underworld, the Upperworld. She wanted…

"Everything," she said, breathless.

"Then fight for it," Hecate said.

Persephone extended her palm.

They practiced for over an hour. After the twentieth time, Persephone stopped flinching when the scissors speared her palm. It wasn't long after that she began to heal the wound before the blades even left her body. Directed by Hecate, she became familiar with the way her magic reacted to the intrusion, strongest upon impact, immediately heating her skin and raising the hair on the back of her neck.

"It is urging you to use it," Hecate said. "It wants to protect you."

Persephone had heard those words before, but now she

was starting to understand them and her magic. It wasn't some foreign thing that invaded her body. It was just as natural to her as her blood and bone.

"That's enough for today," Hecate said.

Persephone had lost count of the times she'd been stabbed. She felt tired but strangely aware. Like her body had become a viper, coiled and ready to strike. For once, since her powers had awakened, they did not feel so far away.

"Yes, my dear," Hecate hissed, and Persephone met the goddess's dark gaze. "You understand now because you can feel it. It isn't about summoning power. It is about becoming it."

Becoming power.

"How often can we train like this?" Persephone asked.

"As often as you'd like," Hecate said.

"Please, Hecate."

The goddess stretched out a hand and cupped her chin. For the first time since they'd started training today, her gaze turned gentle.

"As long as you remember that I love you," Hecate answered.

The words made Persephone's stomach clench; they were words full of dread and promise and fear. But those were feelings that existed outside this cottage too—in the Upperworld where her mother's magic raged and where Harmonia had been attacked. At least here with Hecate… she knew she'd be safe.

"Of course. How could I forget?"

Hecate offered a sad smile. "Oh, my dear. I can make you regret that we were ever friends."

———

Persephone considered heading to Elysium to visit Lexa, but after her session with Hecate, she felt particularly drained.

Instead, she returned to the palace. Cerberus, Typhon, and Orthrus walked dutifully beside her, and she got the sense they'd been ordered to escort her within the Underworld, more than likely due to her tendency to wander off and find trouble. Her suspicions were confirmed when, as soon as she stepped foot inside Hades's palace, the three Dobermans dispersed.

She wasn't upset by their presence or their escort, but it did make her look forward to a time when she needed it less. Once again, she thought of Hecate's words and wondered what exactly she was getting herself into by asking the goddess to train her as she'd done today.

"Oh, and Persephone," Hecate had said as she was leaving her cottage. "Do not tell Hades about today. I do not think I need to tell you that he would disapprove."

Those words weighed heavily upon her as she made her way to their bedchamber. She'd made a practice of being completely transparent with Hades, especially after losing Lexa. It took a lot of work considering she wasn't used to communicating at all. Growing up beneath her mother's thumb had taught her that expressing one's opinion or feelings drew attention and criticism. It was best to just stay silent—to exist as much in secret as possible to keep from punishment.

That was the way she'd lived for years, but after Lexa's death, she realized she couldn't do that anymore. More importantly, there was no need. Hades wanted to hear from her, wanted to understand her perspective—and she wanted the same from him.

She was still considering how to talk to him about Hecate's training methods when she entered the bedroom to find Hades occupying his usual space in front of the fire and another god she did not know. He was handsome and elegant—black skin, hair white and short, curling close to his head. He had wide, doe-like eyes and full lips. He wore white with gold accents—a belt about the waist and a layer of necklaces. His feet were bare, but that was probably because he did not need shoes—large, white wings sprouted from his back.

"Hello," she said, closing the door behind her. "Am I... interrupting something?"

She realized it was a strange question, but...the bedroom was also a strange place for Hades to conduct business.

The unknown god snorted.

"Persephone," Hades said, pulling one hand out of his pocket to gesture toward the god. "This is Hypnos, God of Sleep. He is Thanatos's brother. They are nothing alike."

Hypnos glared. "She would have figured that out on her own. You didn't have to tell her."

"I didn't want her to have the false impression that you would be as kind."

Persephone stared, a little surprised by how quickly the tone and atmosphere of the room had changed in the presence of these two.

"I am not unkind," Hypnos argued. "But I do not do well in the presence of idiots. You are not an idiot, are you, Lady Persephone?"

He was definitely not like Thanatos. This god felt more unpredictable. Perhaps it was because of the nature of sleep.

"N-no," she said, offering a hesitant answer.

"I have asked Hypnos here so that he may help you sleep," Hades said quickly.

"I am sure she's gathered that," Hypnos snapped.

"And you? Did you tell him that you do not sleep?"

Hypnos laughed—a deep sound that came from somewhere in his throat. "The God of the Dead admitting that he needs help? That is a pipe dream."

Up until now, Hades had remained unfazed by the grumpy god, but suddenly, his eyes darkened.

"This is about you," he returned, working to make his voice sound gentle and calm despite the fact that he gritted his teeth. "She hasn't been sleeping, and when she does, she wakes from nightmares. Sometimes covered in sweat, sometimes screaming."

"It's…nothing," Persephone tried to argue. She wasn't keen on going down this path—on reliving what she had experienced since the day Pirithous took her. "They're just nightmares."

"And you're just a glorified gardener," Hypnos replied.

"*Hypnos*," Hades let out a warning growl.

"No wonder you live outside the gates of the Underworld," Persephone muttered.

It was the first time Hypnos looked amused. "For your information, I live outside the gates because I am still a deity of the Upperworld, despite my sentence here."

"Your sentence?"

"It is my punishment to live beneath the world for putting Zeus to sleep," he said.

"Twice," Hades emphasized.

Hypnos glanced askance at the god; an angry brow arched.

"Twice? You didn't learn the first time?" Persephone asked.

Hades attempted to suppress a smirk.

"*I* learned, but it's hard to ignore a request from the Queen of the Gods. Rejecting Hera means living a hellish life, and nobody wants that, *right*, Hades?"

Hypnos's pointed question took the amusement out of Hades's gaze. Satisfied with his jab, the god returned his attention to Persephone.

"Tell me of these nightmares," Hypnos said. "I need details."

"Why must you hear about them?" Hades asked. "I told

you she was having trouble sleeping. Is that not enough to create a draught?"

"Enough, perhaps, but a draught will not solve the issue." Hypnos glared at Hades. "I am older than you, my lord—a primordial deity, remember? Let me do my job."

Hypnos returned his gaze to Persephone. "Well?" His voice was gruff, demanding, but she got the sense that if he did not wish to help her, he would have already left. "How often do you have them?"

"Not every night," she said.

"Is there a pattern? Do they come after a particularly stressful day?"

"I don't think so. That is part of the reason I do not want to go to sleep. I'm not sure what I'll find on the other side."

"These dreams...did they proceed something traumatic?"

Persephone nodded.

"What?"

"I was kidnapped," she said. "By a demigod. He was obsessed with me and...he wanted to rape me."

"Was he successful?"

Persephone flinched at Hypnos's direct question, and Hades growled.

"*Hypnos.*"

"Lord Hades," Hypnos snapped. "One more interruption and I will leave your company."

Persephone's eyes shifted to Hades, whose hand had sprouted lethal black spires.

"It's alright, Hades. I know he is trying to help."

The god smiled ruefully. "Listen to the woman. She appreciates the art of dream interpretation."

"No," Persephone said. "He was not successful, but when I dream, he seems to get closer and closer to...being successful."

She couldn't help it—she spared a glance at Hades as she spoke and saw that he was pale. Her chest felt tight. She hadn't thought about what this might do to him—perhaps she should have told him to leave. Though she doubted he would have listened.

"Dreams—nightmares—prepare us to survive," Hypnos said. "They bring our anxieties to life so we may fight them. You are no different, Goddess."

"But I survived," Persephone argued.

"Do you believe that you would survive if it happened again?"

She started to speak.

"Not in the same situation—a different one. One where perhaps a more powerful god abducted you."

She slammed her mouth shut.

"You do not need a draught," he said. "You need to consider how you will fight in your next dream. Change the ending, and the nightmares will cease."

The god stood then.

"And for the love of all gods and goddesses, go to fucking sleep."

With that, Hypnos vanished.

Persephone looked at Hades. "Well, he was pleasant."

Hades's expression told her everything she needed to know about what he thought of the God of Sleep. Then his eyes drifted down and narrowed.

"Why is there blood on your shirt?" he asked.

Persephone's eyes widened, and when she looked, she saw a crimson stain. She hadn't noticed it before leaving Hecate's cottage. She guessed this was the way to tell Hades about her afternoon training session.

"Oh...I was practicing with Hecate," she said.

"Practicing what?"

"Healing," she said.

Hades's brows drew together. "That is a lot of blood."

"Well...I couldn't exactly heal if I wasn't injured," she

explained, but she could tell by the look on Hades's face that was the wrong thing to say. He tilted his head to the side, mouth hardening.

"She is having you practice on yourself first?"

Persephone opened her mouth to speak, but there was nothing to say except, "Yes...why is that wrong?"

"You should be practicing on fucking...*flowers*. Not yourself. What did she have you do?"

"Does it matter? I healed myself. I did it." She was proud. "Besides, I don't have a lot of time. You know what happened to Adonis and saw what happened to Harmonia."

"You think I would let what happened to them happen to you?" he asked.

"That is not what I'm saying." She spoke carefully, knowing that her words mattered here—Hades already blamed himself for what happened with Pirithous. "I want to be able to protect myself."

Hades just stared, his eyes dipping to the blood, which caused her to cross her arms over her chest to hide it.

"I swear I'm fine," she said. "Kiss me if you think I'm lying."

His eyes returned to hers and he inched forward, his hand cupping her jaw. "I believe you, but I will kiss you anyway."

The lips pressed to hers sweetly—it was too short and too tame. When he pulled away, she stared up at him and asked, "Why didn't you tell me I had the ability to heal myself?"

"I figured at some point Hecate would teach you," he said. "Until then, it was my pleasure to heal you."

She flushed, not at any particular memory but at the sound of Hades's voice—a lover's voice, warm and hypnotic. Her eyes fell to his lips, luscious, alluring.

"What shall we do this evening, darling?" Hades asked.

A smile curved Persephone's lips as she answered, "I am eager for a game of cards."

CHAPTER XVI
Hide-and-Seek

"We play by my rules," Persephone said.

They sat across from each other before the fireplace in their bedroom, a table and deck of cards between them.

Hades raised a brow. "Your rules? How do they differ from the established rules?"

"There are no established rules," she said. "That's what makes this game so fun."

Hades frowned and she knew this was exactly the kind of game he hated. He needed structure, guidelines—*control.*

"Just listen. The goal is to collect every card in the deck," Persephone said. "Each of us will lay down a card at the same time. If the cards add up to ten or you lay down a ten, you slap the deck."

"You...*slap* the deck?" Hades asked.

"Yes."

"Why?"

"Because that is how you claim the cards."

He cleared his throat. "Go on."

"Outside the rule of tens, there is a rule for face cards," she explained.

She had to give it to Hades, he did make a show of interest in the rules of the game, more than likely because he was interested in the stakes. "Depending on the face card you draw, you have a certain number of chances to get another face card, or the player who laid down the first face card takes all the cards."

"Okay," he said very deliberately.

She continued. "And last, if you slap at the wrong time, then you have to put two cards at the bottom of the pile."

"Right," he said. "Of course. What is this game called again?"

"Egyptian Ratscrew," Persephone said.

"Why?"

She frowned. "I–I don't know. It just is."

Hades raised a brow. "Well, this should be fun. Let's get to the important part—stakes. What do you wish for if you obtain this…whole deck of cards first?"

Persephone considered this before saying, "I would like a weekend," she said. "Alone. With you."

Hades's lips quirked. "You are wagering for something I would gladly give—and have, many times."

"Not a weekend sequestered to your bedchamber," she said, rolling her eyes. "A weekend…on an island or in the mountains or in a cabin. A…*vacation*."

"Hmm. You aren't giving me a very good reason to win," he said.

Persephone smiled. "And you? What do you wish for?"

"A fantasy," he said. "Fulfilled."

"A…fantasy?"

"A sexual one."

It took everything in her not to stutter.

"Of course," she managed smoothly, taking a shallow breath. *Now who was making it hard to want to win?* She bit her lip. "Can I ask what this sexual fantasy entails?"

"No." His eyes sparkled with amusement. "Do you accept?"

"I accept," Persephone said, and as she spoke, she squeezed her thighs together, feeling a jolt of heat pool low in her stomach. She hoped she could focus enough on the game to actually attempt winning.

She cut the deck and gave each of them twenty-six cards. The first card she put down was a two of spades. Hades placed a queen of clubs.

"That means I have three chances to get another face card," she explained.

Her next card was a king.

"Now you have four chances to get a face card."

"Alright."

His first card was a five of diamonds, the next a three of clubs, the third a jack of hearts. Then it was Persephone's turn—luckily, she laid down another face card.

"Now you have one chance to draw a face card," she said.

What he drew was a ten of spades.

Lightning-fast, Hades's hand came down upon the deck with a loud bang.

Persephone flinched and stared at him in surprise. She hadn't expected him to move so fast—or to remember the rules so well.

"What?" he asked when he noticed her expression. "You said to slap."

"That wasn't a slap. That was more like a collision."

He smirked. "I just really want to win."

She raised a brow. "I thought you were intrigued by *my* wager."

"Yes, but I can make your wager come true at any point."

"And you do not think I can make your fantasy come true at any point?"

Hades's lips quirked. "Can you?"

They stared at one another for a heartbeat. The tension between them gathering rapidly, a storm on the horizon. Part of her wanted to discard the game completely just to embed his body into hers.

Then Hades spoke, his voice low and gruff. "Shall we continue?"

Their game progressed—a near-endless exchange of cards. At one point, Hades only had one card left—Persephone's victory was at hand. She was so excited, she could taste it.

"Do not look so smug, darling. I will come back with this card," he promised.

And when he laid the card down, it was a ten.

He slapped the deck and claimed the cards—a winner.

Persephone glared.

"You cheated!" she accused.

Hades chuckled. "A loser's claim."

"Careful, my lord—you may have won but I am responsible for the experience. You want it to be good, don't you?"

She wasn't even sure what he was going to ask for—a fantasy of some sort. What did he wish for? She thought of the time he'd threatened to take her in his glass office. Perhaps he had darker wishes—submission or bondage or roleplaying. She could barely breathe as she waited for him to speak—to instruct.

Then he stood, loosening his tie and cuff links. Persephone tilted her head back, gaze trailing the planes of his well-muscled physique.

"Ten seconds," he said.

Persephone's brows furrowed. She'd expected other words to come out of his mouth like...undress or maybe kneel.

"What?" Maybe she'd misheard him. There was no way she'd misread the tension in this room. Her gaze dipped to where his erection strained against his slacks.

She hadn't.

"You have ten seconds to hide. Then I will seek you out."

"Your fantasy is hide-and-seek?" she asked.

"No. My fantasy is the chase. I am going to hunt you, and when I find you, I will bury myself so far inside you, the only thing you'll be able to say is my name."

That seemed fair.

She feigned considering this proposition and said, "Will you use magic?"

His smile widened. "Oh, this will be much more fun with magic, darling."

She narrowed her eyes. "But this is your realm. You will know everywhere I go."

"Are you telling me you don't wish to be caught?"

It was her turn to smile. Without another word, she teleported and appeared in Hades's garden. She had landed in the open, upon the black stone path that wound through colorful flowers and dark trees. She darted into the foliage, ducking under curtains of wisteria and parting willow branches.

She felt Hades appear. He was heat, a flame that warmed her skin, and she was drawn to it like a moth. She pressed herself into the trunk of the willow, watching him through its graceful limbs.

He turned in her direction, taking deliberate but careful steps toward her.

"I've thought of you all day," he said, and a thrill went through her. She peeled herself away from the tree and wandered along the garden's edge. Hades continued following and talking.

"The way you taste, the feel of my cock slipping inside you, the way you moan as I fuck you."

Persephone came to the garden's wall, heart beating faster. She was trapped. She turned to find Hades blocking her way, his gaze hungry. He stuck one arm out and then the other, caging her between him. His breath caressed her lips as he spoke.

"I want to fuck you so hard, your screams reach the ears of the living."

Persephone's lips curled, and she leaned close, tongue flicking out to taste his lips before she asked breathlessly, "Why don't you?"

Then she vanished.

She appeared in Asphodel, at the center of their crowded streets. It was a market day, which meant the souls were out in droves, trading the goods they made in the comfort of their homes. The yeasty smell of bread, bitter teas, and sweet cinnamon wafted through the air.

"Lady Persephone!"

"My lady!"

"Persephone!"

The souls called and began to crowd her. The children were especially happy to see her and squeezed between the older souls to reach her, hugging her legs and grasping her hands.

"Come play with us, Persephone!"

"I'm so very sorry, everyone. I'm afraid I'm…in the middle of a game with Lord Hades."

"What kind of game?" one of the children asked.

"Can we play too?" another said.

She really should have kept her mouth shut, but when Hades arrived, the souls of Asphodel turned their attention to him.

"Hades!" the children cried and bounded toward him. The Lord of the Underworld caught one—the smallest child, Theo—and lifted him into the air. The child giggled and Hades smiled. It was a breathtaking smile, and it hit her heart like an arrow. Once again, she found herself thinking of Hades as a father.

She swallowed.

"Hades, play with us!" they cried.

"I'm afraid I have made a promise to Lady Persephone I must keep," he said. "But I will make a promise to you now—Lady Persephone and I will return to play as soon as possible."

He leveled his gaze with hers, and it was clear he was still intent upon his goal.

"We shall visit soon!" Persephone promised and vanished. Hades followed—she could feel his magic twining with hers, and when they appeared, it was in the Asphodel fields.

He kissed her, and for a brief moment, Persephone forgot that they were in the middle of a chase. It was rough and his tongue clashed with hers. He drank deep, as if he wished to consume her essence. Her fingers dug into his muscled arms as she held on, drowning in his power.

She managed to come to her senses and pull away. Hades looked surprised, and his eyes darkened. He gripped the front of her dress and dragged her against him, tearing the fabric in two so that it exposed her breasts. He took each one in his hand and covered them with his mouth, working her nipples with his hot tongue until they were taut. Then he kissed up her neck, his hands replacing his tongue as they pinched each tight bead.

Persephone's head fell back as she gasped, and Hades growled low in his throat. "Surrender."

Her head spun, surrounded by his scent. He had pulled away enough so she could see his face, and as she met his gaze, she answered. "No."

It was one of the most difficult things she'd ever done in her life.

Then she vanished.

This time, she appeared in Hades's cavernous throne

room. Despite having multiple windows, much of the room was left in darkness. She ascended to the throne and took a seat. The obsidian was slick and cold against her arms and back, and despite the fact that her dress was torn, she sat with her back straight, breasts exposed.

If Hades thought this was his win, he was mistaken.

When he materialized and saw her upon his throne, his eyes seemed to darken, and his lips curved into a seductive smile. He was ravenous, and his desire permeated the air. It smelled like spice and smoke, and she leaned toward him, wanting to taste it.

"My queen," he said and started toward her.

"Halt!" she commanded. To her surprise, Hades immediately obeyed, though it was clear he hadn't wanted to—his hands fisted, and his jaw tightened, his shoulders tense. Before he could protest, though, she gave another command. "Undress."

He watched her a moment, and his lips curled. "For someone who doesn't like titles, you sure are commanding."

She glared at him. "Must I repeat myself?"

Now Hades was smiling. He lifted his hand, and Persephone stopped him.

"Not with magic. The mortal way. Slowly."

"As you wish," he said.

Hades took his time unbuttoning his shirt and pants. He removed his shirt first, showing off his burnished skin and the muscles of his arms and stomach. Next, he slid out of his pants, revealing his thick and heavy erection.

By the time he was finished and stood naked before her, she sat on the edge of his throne, her hands gripping the arms. She considered reaching for him, wrapping her fingers around his cock, but refrained.

"And your hair," she said. "Take it down."

He reached up, massive muscles flexing, as he untied his

usually slicked-back hair. The long, dark locks fell around his shoulders in waves, making him look feral and untamed. It thrilled her.

But there was one more thing she wanted.

"Drop your glamour," she said.

The corners of his mouth lifted. "I will if you will."

She stared at him for a moment, then released her hold on her magic. It was like letting a heavy cloak drop from about her or shedding skin that had become taut and vaguely uncomfortable. Hades's eyes swept her whole body—from her slender, white horns that twisted out from a head of unruly, golden hair to her bare feet, dirty from running through the garden and Asphodel. It shouldn't feel so intimate, because the way he looked at her was familiar, but when his dark eyes met hers, she felt like she might implode from the intensity.

He dropped his glamour next. Persephone loved watching Hades transform. His magic evaporated like smoke, peeling from his body to reveal the ancient god beneath. Hades wasn't often in his Divine form, which was strange considering he encouraged Persephone to remain in hers. His horns were black, lethal, and yet graceful, having the same slender curves as a gazelle's. The dark of his eyes burned away to reveal electric-blue irises.

She stood then, studying him as intently as he was her, and approached.

"Don't move," she whispered.

She thought she heard him groan, but she couldn't be sure.

She placed her palm on his chest. His body was an inferno beneath her hand, as hot as the River Phlegethon. His skin was smooth and his muscles hard. She explored him—his abs and his sides, moving lower until her hand came into contact with his erection. When her fingers closed around him, Hades inhaled, his hands fisting so tight, she was sure he had pierced flesh.

She looked up at him, stroking him until a thick bead of come glistened at the tip of his cock. She removed it with her finger and brought it into her mouth. Hades watched like a predator. She was pushing his limits, but that was what she wanted.

She returned to his throne, never taking her eyes off him, the taste of him upon her lips, and said, "Come."

Now Hades grinned. "Only for you."

She considered vanishing again, but Hades was on her instantly. He shredded the rest of her clothes and picked her up from his throne by the waist. She had no desire to resist him. She melded with him—chest to chest, legs around his waist, soft skin to iron muscle.

Hades drove into her and a guttural cry escaped from deep inside each of them.

"I was beginning to think all you wanted to do was stare," he said against her skin.

She answered with a moan as he leveraged her weight and started to move in and out. Every slick inch of him filled her to bursting.

"I wanted you," she managed. "I wanted to fuck the moment we were alone."

Her voice was a whisper now, husky and thick with pleasure. Each time he thrust, she stopped speaking, reveling in the pleasure racking her body.

"And instead of fucking, you asked for a game. Why?"

"I like foreplay," she said, nibbling his ear.

Hades's chuckle turned into a growl and he kissed her hard, slamming into her for a few uncontrolled moments. Persephone's cries filled the throne room but softened when his momentum slowed. It was sweet torture—he was dragging her to the edge of a cliff, holding her over by a thread.

Hades was the ultimate addiction. He was a glorious high, an intoxicating bliss she wanted all the time.

"I hate waiting for you," she said.

"Then find me," Hades said, kissing down her neck.

"You are busy."

"Dreaming about being inside you," he said.

She managed a breathy laugh.

"I love that laugh," he said, kissing her.

"I love you," she said.

Something changed when she uttered those words. Hades met her gaze and held it as he seated himself on the edge of his throne. Persephone kept her legs wrapped around his waist.

"Say it again," he said.

She studied him for a moment and twisted his hair around her fingers. It would be her lifeline, because she knew by Hades's voice and the way he looked at her, she was about to be consumed.

"I love you, Hades," she said softly.

His smile was breathtaking, and he kissed her, helping her move up and down his shaft.

"I love you. You are perfection," he said, squeezing her bottom where he still held her. "You are my lover. You are my queen."

He leaned back and slipped his hand between them. A new sensation accosted her as he stroked her cleft. She groaned and took control, riding him harder, faster, feeling him deeper than ever before.

Hades responded, meeting her thrusts. The pounding of their bodies was vicious, and they came brutally. Persephone collapsed against him, their bodies slick and hot, as they struggled to catch their breath.

After a few moments, she felt Hades kiss her hair.

"Why is this the first time I am hearing about your fantasies?" she asked.

When he did not immediately respond, she looked at him.

"How do I verbalize such a thing?" he asked.

She shrugged. "I suppose you just...tell me what you want," she said. "Is that not what you would want from me?"

A smile pulled at his lips. "Yes," he answered. "So tell me, what is your fantasy?"

Persephone did not expect that question, and despite the fact that she lay in her lover's arms, naked and covered in sweat from lovemaking, she blushed.

"I...do not think I have one," she said.

"You'll forgive me if I do not believe you," he said.

"No," she said. "I won't. It is in your nature to detect lies."

Hades offered a small laugh and then, "But what will it take? To learn of your fantasies?"

Persephone did not respond immediately as she traced her finger along his well-muscled chest.

"One day...I want you...to restrain me," she said.

She noted how hard Hades swallowed, but he did not laugh, and for that, she was grateful.

"I will always do as you ask," he said.

They were silent for a long moment, then Persephone spoke.

"And you?" Her voice was quiet. "What other fantasies live in that head of yours?"

Hades chuckled, his arms tightening around her slick body.

"Darling, every time I fuck you, it's a fantasy."

CHAPTER XVII
A Touch of Shadow

Persephone headed to work early Monday morning. She had received an email from Helen late last night asking for a meeting first thing. She had an update on Triad and their leadership, and Persephone was eager to find out what she'd learned. On the way, she opened her tablet to catch up on the news. The first headline that drew her attention was the largest, and it was located under a banner that read breaking news.

> **An individual identifying themselves as a member of the Rebirth Movement, a sect of impious mortals, claim they have successfully dehorned a goddess.**

Dread pooled in Persephone's stomach but also hope. Hades had suspected this news would come out eventually. This was their chance to track the culprits who had hurt and mutilated Harmonia and possibly murdered Adonis.

Upon reading the article, she was a little surprised to find there wasn't much information, and even the author sounded skeptical of the report. It seemed they had received a call from an individual who told them of the incident—but without any details. They'd stated the group had managed to "subdue a goddess" and "cut off her horns."

> When asked for proof of the incident, the caller stated, "The world will have proof when we wear the horns of the gods to the battlefield."
>
> Whether this report is factual remains to be seen, but one thing is clear, the Rebirth is a violent entity—the worst kind, because they believe they are actually fighting for the greater good.
>
> "We are a shield for those who no longer wish to be ruled by the gods. We will cut the threads that bind us to fate, free those under the spell of their divinity. We are freedom."

It was a promise and a declaration of war.

"My lady?" Antoni's voice was a soft rumble. She looked up, meeting his gaze in the rearview mirror. "Are you alright?"

"Yes," she answered. "I was just reading something... disturbing."

Antoni's brow dipped. "Is there anything I can do?"

"No, Antoni, but thank you," Persephone said. As she started to store her tablet, Antoni moved to exit the vehicle. "Don't, Antoni. It's too cold."

"Allow me to help you to the door. The sidewalk and steps are slick."

"Even more reason for you to stay," she answered.

"If you insist," he finally relented. "I will see you this evening."

"Of course. Have a good day, Antoni."

"And you, my lady."

Persephone did not know what sort of errands or tasks Antoni had outside of taking her to work. Once, when the giant had come to get her, he had come from picking up dry cleaning, though when asked if it was for Hades, he'd said no. Another time, he'd had a case of red wines that, he had explained, was an order for Milan. Whatever it was, though, he always seemed perfectly happy to execute.

She left the warm comfort of the back seat of the Lexus and entered the frigid daytime air. The sidewalk was slick, but a layer of salt and sand made it easier to stabilize. Once inside, she greeted Ivy, accepted her coffee with a grateful nod, and entered the elevator. On the way up, she held the cup to her cheeks and nose until they were warm and kept her jacket on even after she entered her office. Was she imagining things? It definitely felt colder in here. Persephone knew this weather could lead to energy and power failures, and she had no doubt Demeter would continue to that point. In fact, she wouldn't be surprised if that was her mother's next method of killing—freezing people to death.

There was a knock at her door, and Persephone looked up, meeting Helen's gaze. She was dressed in a black knitted top and a black-and-white plaid skirt. She wore thick stockings and knee-high boots to keep warm, and her blond hair was twisted into an updo. A pair of pearl earrings completed the look. Despite the fact that Helen always looked chic, Persephone thought she looked a little more dressed up than usual.

"You look very beautiful," Persephone said.

"Thank you," Helen said, her cheeks coloring. "I...am meeting someone for lunch."

"Oh?" Persephone raised a brow. "Anyone I know?"

"I don't think so. At least not yet."

Persephone took that to mean Helen hoped to introduce her to this mystery person. Still, she didn't press. Helen had arrived for their meeting, and as much as Persephone enjoyed the company of both her and Leuce, she liked to keep things as professional as possible at work.

After a beat of silence, Persephone gestured to the couch in front of her desk.

"Have a seat," she said. "I believe you had something to share."

"Yes," Helen said, sitting. "I wanted to discuss my article with you. I'm taking it in a new direction."

"Go on," Persephone encouraged, curious. She took up her pen, ready to take notes.

Helen hesitated.

"I did what you suggested," she began, and something about those words made Persephone's stomach turn. "I reached out to members of Triad and managed to land an interview with one of their leaders—a high lord."

"A *high* lord?"

"They...have a kind of hierarchy," Helen explained. "It's to protect those who cannot protect themselves."

"You mean those with power are at the top," Persephone said.

"*Real* power," Helen said, as if Persephone did not know what real power was.

"You mean like the gods?"

"Yes and no," she said. "They have the power of the gods, but they use it to protect. They answer prayers, Persephone. They *listen*."

"Helen," Persephone said, dropping her pen. "You are misguided."

"I'm not. I have seen it."

"You've seen it," Persephone stated flatly. "What have you seen? Give me an example."

"I have been to their meetings and heard testimony," Helen said. Persephone made a mental note to come back to what Helen had just disclosed—meetings? What meetings?

The mortal continued. "This man had cancer. He prayed to Apollo, offered sacrifices, even showed up at one of his performances and begged for his help. No answer—not a word. He came to Triad, and one of the high lords *healed* him."

Persephone stiffened hearing this story. It sounded all too familiar.

"Have you ever stopped to consider why the gods may not have answered those prayers?"

"Yes! And the answer is always why? Why should we suffer illness and disease and death when the gods exist in perpetual health and immortality?"

Persephone did not have an answer for that, because even she did not know, except that after losing Lexa, she had to believe that every fiber woven into the tapestry of the world served a greater purpose. Perhaps it was that sometimes a friend must die for a goddess to rise.

She stared at Helen, wondering what had lured her to the side of Triad so quickly.

"Seriously, Persephone. I thought you would understand after what happened to Lexa."

"*Do not* say her name," Persephone said, her voice shaking.

"If given the chance, would you not have had her live forever?"

"What I want does not matter. You speak of things you know nothing of. It is one thing to proclaim the gods should be held accountable for their actions—that, certainly, is true. It is another thing to actively disturb the balance of the world."

And Persephone had learned the consequences of those actions the hard way.

Helen rolled her eyes. "You have been brainwashed—too much time spent on Hades's dick."

"That is not appropriate," Persephone snapped and stood. "If this is the intended direction of your article, I will not approve it for publication."

Helen lifted her chin, defiance flashing in her eyes.

"You don't have to," she said, a smug tone in her voice. "I'll take it to Demetri."

"Do it," Persephone said. "But you will regret it."

"Is that a threat?" Helen asked.

"That depends," Persephone said. "Are you afraid?"

She noted the doubt that flashed in Helen's eyes. Persephone picked up her phone and chose Ivy's direct line.

"Lady Persephone?"

"Ivy. Please summon Zofie."

As she hung up, Helen spoke.

"*You're* afraid. Afraid you'll lose your status when Hades falls."

Persephone placed her hands flat on the table and leaned forward, ensuring that the glamour that kept the true fire of her eyes hidden melted away as she leveled her gaze with Helen's.

"Now *that* felt like a threat," Persephone said, her voice quiet. "Was it a threat?"

Helen's eyes went wide, and before the mortal could speak, there was a knock at the door. Neither of them moved, both held in place by the tension in the room. Persephone recognized it as her magic—it made the air feel heavy and electric.

Another knock and the door opened. Zofie stood in the threshold, her dark hair in her usual braid. She was dressed in a black tunic, pants, and boots. She looked unassuming, not at all the warrior she was raised to be.

"My lady, you needed my assistance?"

"Yes, Zofie. Please escort Helen from the premises. She is to speak to no one as she leaves the building."

"I need to pack my office," Helen argued.

Persephone didn't look at her, keeping her gaze on her aegis.

"Zofie, see that Helen only collects her personal belongings from her office."

"As you wish, my lady," Zofie said, bowing her head. She turned to Helen. "Go."

Helen took a step toward the door but turned back to Persephone.

"A new era is coming, Persephone. I thought you were smart enough to be at the forefront. I guess I was wrong."

Without warning, Zofie pushed Helen out the door, causing her to stumble forward. The mortal caught herself before spinning to face Zofie.

"How dare you!" Helen snarled.

Zofie drew a dagger from a hidden sheath beneath her tunic. It glinted beneath the fluorescent lights in the waiting area.

"Lady Persephone didn't say you had to leave the building walking. *Go.*"

When they were gone, Persephone collapsed into her chair, feeling exhausted. She couldn't quite wrap her mind around the conversation she'd just had with Helen. She definitely had not expected her to change her perspective on Triad after such a short investigation. Then again, she did not know much about Helen outside of her work ethic, which had always appeared dedicated and enthusiastic.

And those qualities she hadn't lost but applied elsewhere.

Perhaps there was something else at work that Persephone could not see, something in Helen's personal life that made siding with Triad the better option.

Feeling frustrated, Persephone left her floor for Hades's office. When she arrived, it was empty, and everything looked untouched. The desk was clear except for a vase of white narcissus and a picture frame. The narcissus were refreshed daily by Ivy, who, being a dryad, had a special talent for keeping flowers alive longer than usual.

Even in his absence, being in a space that smelled like him calmed her nerves, so she lingered, walking to the window to stare out at the wintery day. Below, she saw Helen waiting on the icy sidewalk, her arms crossed tightly over her chest as she shivered noticeably. After a moment, a black limo arrived.

Persephone's brows lowered, wondering who'd sent it for her. Helen usually took public transportation to and from work. Perhaps she was more tangled in Triad than Persephone thought. The driver was no help. He left the comfort of his cabin dressed in a suit and no identifying markings. He opened the door, and Helen slid inside before the vehicle crept down the road.

Suddenly, Hades manifested behind Persephone, standing close. She expected him to place his hands around her waist; instead, he caged her with them, palms pressed flat to the window.

"Careful," Persephone said. "Ivy will scold you for smudging the glass."

"Do you think she will have an opinion if I fuck you against it?"

Persephone turned to face him, and the teasing light in his eyes dimmed.

"What's wrong?"

She told him everything, including what she considered to be Helen's threat—*when Hades falls*. Slowly, he peeled his hands from the window, and they settled at his sides. His brows lowered, his lips twisting into a grimace.

"Are you afraid for me?"

"Yes. Yes, you idiot. Look at what those people did to Harmonia!"

"Persephone—"

"Hades," Persephone cut him off. "Do not diminish my fear of losing you. It's just as valid."

His features softened. "I'm sorry."

"I know you are powerful," she said. "But...I cannot

help thinking that Triad is trying to bring about another Titanomachy."

She hated to say it—hated to unearth what had caused such unrest within Hades—but she needed to speak the words, say them aloud. She thought that once they were in the air between them, they would sound ridiculous, completely improbable.

But they didn't.

Because she was certain the primordial gods and the Titans had felt untouchable, and they had still fallen.

Hades placed his hands on either side of Persephone's face.

"I cannot promise we will not have war a thousand times over during our lifetime," he said. "But I will promise that I will never leave you willingly."

"Can you promise to never leave at all?"

He offered a small, sad smile and then kissed her. His hands twined into her hair and then glided to her back and hips, exploring. She wanted this more than she wanted to think about how he hadn't answered her question, so she rubbed his cock through his pants, eliciting a growl from somewhere deep in his throat. In response, he gripped her hips, grinding into her, but Persephone pushed against his chest and met his gaze.

"Let me have this," she said.

"What do you want?" he asked.

She took his hands and led him behind his desk, where she pushed him into his chair and knelt before him. Poised between his thighs, she released the button of his slacks and unzipped them, his jutting sex rising, thick and hard, from the fabric.

She held his gaze as she wrapped her hand around the base of his cock, stroking him, increasing the pressure as she moved toward his head. If his gaze were fire, she would have burned happily beneath it. She smiled as he ground his teeth, and his fingers turned white as he held on to the arms of his chair. Then she bent, drawing her tongue along his crown. He tasted bitter and warm and smelled like spice.

A soft groan escaped his mouth, and then words.

"Yes," he said. "This. I dream of this."

She had questions—what had he dreamed, exactly? Her mouth? This act, performed like this? In his open office? But she asked none of them and continued, spurred by his breathing, which pitched unevenly, ragged and labored.

"Lord Hades," Ivy's voice entered the fray, and she felt Hades tense, his posture changing as he stiffened and sat up straighter. Her presence didn't keep Persephone from continuing; she worked harder, lavishing every sensitive dip and arch of his cock with her tongue.

"Why are you sitting?"

Ivy sounded perplexed, and Persephone laughed despite Hades's cock filling her mouth. His reaction was immediate. He twined one of his hands into her hair.

"I'm working," he said.

"There's nothing on your desk," Ivy said.

"It's…coming," he said, his fingers digging into her scalp.

"Right, well, when you have a moment—"

"Leave, Ivy. Now."

Persephone heard nothing else from her. She assumed she was gone when Hades placed another hand on her face. For a moment, her eyes met his as he spoke.

"Take all of me," he said and thrust into her mouth.

He went deep and her eyes watered, her throat full of him—but she wanted to be this for him.

"Yes," he hissed. "Like that."

He pumped into her and she choked but he stayed there, rigid in her mouth until he came, her throat thick with his come. She swallowed hard, feeling the burn of it in her nose.

When he pulled out, she took in ragged breaths, her forehead resting against his knee. Hades's hand smoothed her hair.

"Are you well?" he asked.

She looked up at him. "Yes. Tired."

He brushed her lips with the tips of his fingers. "Tonight, I will make you come just as hard."

"In your mouth or around your cock?"

He smiled at her question and replied, "Both."

Hades restored his appearance and helped Persephone to her feet.

"I know you are having a hard day," he said. "I hate to leave, but I came to tell you I will be meeting with Zeus."

"Why?"

She could think of two reasons.

"I think you know," he said. "I hope to secure Zeus's approval for our marriage."

"Will you confront him about Lara?"

"Hecate already has," Hades said. "It will take a good two years before his balls grow back."

Persephone's eyes widened.

"She…castrated him?"

"Yes," Hades said. "And if I know Hecate, it was bloody and painful."

"What good is his punishment if he can just regenerate?"

"It is a power that cannot be taken away, I am afraid. But at least for a little while, he will be…*less*…of a problem."

"Unless he denies our marriage," Persephone said.

"There is that," he agreed.

She wanted him to reassure her, to say that would not happen, that Zeus would not dare. Hades seemed to sense her unease. He secured his hands behind her neck and brought his forehead against hers.

"Trust, darling, I will let no one—not king or god or mortal—stand in the way of making you my wife."

Persephone returned to her floor and found Sybil, Leuce, and Zofie at Helen's desk. It was adjacent to Persephone's and decorated simplistically—with marble and gold accents.

"What's going on?"

"Zofie filled us in on Helen," Leuce said. "So I thought I'd go through her things."

"Because…?"

"Because she's been hiding things," the nymph said.

"How do you know?"

"I have been watching her," she said. "She would take phone calls out of the office. I thought it was weird, so I followed her one day."

"And?"

"And she was meeting some guy who kept glorifying Triad…and himself," she said. "I think they're sleeping together."

"What did he look like?"

"A demigod," she said, and her lips twisted into a look of disgust. "A son of Poseidon if I had to guess. It's in the eyes."

Theseus, Persephone thought.

"When were you going to tell me?"

"Today," Leuce said. "That's why Helen went to you this morning—she wanted to get to you first."

Persephone lowered her gaze to Helen's desk. It was neat and organized. She had varying research stored in file folders and labeled in clean handwriting.

Sybil was looking through a small, black book.

"What's that?" Persephone asked.

"Notes," the oracle said. "Just trying to see if she left anything useful."

"I say we burn her things," Zofie said. "Leave no trace of her treason."

"I wouldn't call her a traitor," Persephone said and searched for the words—confused, foolish, delusional all came to mind.

"She's a climber," Sybil said. "She's searching for an opportunity that will get her to the top fast. It's why she left *New Athens News* with you. She thought she could ride to the top with you."

"Did you see that in her colors?"

"Red, yellow, orange, a touch of green for jealousy."

"You knew all that by looking at her and you didn't warn us?" Leuce countered.

Sybil looked up from the black book. "I saw ambition when I looked at her. It can be a positive or negative trait. I didn't know how she was going to use it."

"I don't think any of us did," Persephone said.

"Sephy, it's lunch time!"

Hermes appeared beside her suddenly, singing. She jumped, not expecting him so soon, but as her eyes darted to the clock, she saw it was almost noon. Time had gotten away from her.

"It'll be a few minutes, Hermes—what are you wearing?"

It looked like a romper and was army green in color.

He shoved his hands in his pockets and twisted.

"You don't like it? I call it my lounge suit."

"And…you're going to lunch in it?"

Hermes glared. "Just say you don't like it, Sephy. You won't hurt my feelings, and yes, I fully intend to go to lunch in my lounge suit."

"Um, Persephone," Sybil said. "I think you should take a look at this."

"Oh no, you don't!" Hermes wrapped a hand around Persephone's arm to hold her in place.

"Hermes, let go of me."

He pursed his lips. "But…I'm hungry!"

She glared and he released her, grumbling. "Fine."

The oracle handed over the open book. On one of the pages, Helen had drawn a triangle and then scribbled in a date, address, and time. The date was today, the time, eight this evening.

"Leuce—can you look into this?"

"Wait. Let me see," Hermes said.

"I thought you were hungry," Persephone shot back.

"Stop reminding me," Hermes said through his teeth and snatched the black book from her hands.

He spent a minute studying the page and then said, "That is the address for Club Aphrodisia."

"Does that…belong to Aphrodite?"

"No, a mortal owns it," he said. "He calls himself Master."

Sybil and Leuce giggled.

"What kind of club is it?" Persephone asked, though she thought she could guess.

"A sex club," he said. "Uh, not that I have been."

Persephone raised a brow.

"You mean to say Helen has a meeting at a sex club?" Leuce asked.

"Maybe she's kinky," Hermes said with a shrug. "Who are we to judge others' sexual preferences?"

Persephone frowned. "I think we should check it out."

Hermes laughed. "You think Hades is going to let you go to a sex club?"

"I'll make him come."

"I'm sure you will, Sephy, but not there."

Persephone gave him a scathing look. "If you aren't going to be helpful, you can eat lunch alone."

"I'm just saying Hades would totally kill the vibe. If we're going to go, he can't come."

"Then you tell him," she said. "I won't go without his knowledge."

"Uh, no. He'll make me swear an oath that I'll protect you with my life."

"Won't you?" she asked.

Hermes opened his mouth to speak and then paused, his gaze softening. "Of course I'd protect you."

Persephone offered a small smile.

"We can go," Leuce suggested. "Sybil and I."

"No," Persephone said. "Not alone and not without me."

This felt personal, not only because it involved Helen—a woman she'd thought of as a friend and employee—but because she feared her friends could become targets too. If this meeting was about the future of Triad and their plans, she needed to be there.

She looked at Hermes. "Prepare to take that oath, Hermes, and protect me with your life."

Hades reluctantly agreed to let Persephone go to Club Aphrodisia but had done as Hermes predicted and made the god swear an oath to protect her.

"What does that even mean?" Persephone had asked when he'd returned later to inform her that he'd gained Hades's permission.

"Don't worry about it, Sephy. I got this," he'd said. "Wear something sexy!"

Persephone shook her head and tried not to laugh as the god departed in a hurry.

After work, she returned to the Underworld. Before getting ready for the night's investigation, she teleported to Elysium. It had been a while since she'd visited Lexa, and she found that what she wanted most after what happened with Helen was her best friend.

She took her time wandering through the golden fields, speckled with gloriously lush trees with wild and deep roots.

Now and then, poppies shot from the ground, mingling with the grass. Once, before Thanatos had allowed Persephone to approach Lexa, she had asked the God of Death about the sporadic poppies.

"They are eternal resting places," he had replied.

"You mean..."

"When a soul no longer wishes to exist in the Upperworld or the Underworld, they are released into the earth."

He went on to explain that the energy from their souls often acted like magic. "From it, poppies and pomegranates spring."

She'd had more questions—when does a soul decide it no longer wants to exist? Of course, she was thinking of Lexa when she had asked, but Thanatos's reply was not what she expected.

"Sometimes they do not get to choose. Sometimes they come to us so broken, to continue would be torture."

It was then Persephone had understood she had been lucky with Lexa. At least she had only had to drink from the Lethe. Apparently, there were worse fates.

As Persephone crested one of many hills, she paused, looking for the familiar dark curls of Adonis, but did not find him. It was possible she wouldn't even recognize him here. Even Lexa, while familiar, looked different, and it had been months since she'd last laid eyes upon the favorited mortal. Even if she saw him, it wasn't like she could approach. Elysium was for healing. Souls here did not receive visitors; they didn't even socialize among themselves.

Lexa was the exception, and Persephone had a suspicion Hades had something to do with that, though she'd never asked.

She stood a while longer, gaze lingering upon the fields, before continuing on to find Lexa.

She took her time, enjoying the peace that came with

being in this part of the Underworld. Here it was easy to forget about the threat of her mother, Triad, and Helen's sudden change in behavior. It was like this environment forced those thoughts away, making them harder to reach for, and she always had the sense that if she stayed here long enough, she'd forget to leave.

There was another hill, and as she descended into a low valley with more trees where Lexa tended to stay most often, her gaze snagged on a pair of souls sitting beneath one of the trees. They were shoulder to shoulder, heads inclined, and she almost looked away, feeling as though she was intruding upon an intimate moment. Except that she soon realized that she was staring at Thanatos and Lexa. Beside one another, they were opposites, Thanatos with his white hair, a flame against Lexa's midnight locks. The only thing they shared were brilliant blue eyes and apparently breath and space, Persephone thought mildly.

She wondered what she should do—turn around and come back later? Duck and watch from afar? Approach and force them apart? She didn't get the chance to decide, however, because Thanatos's eyes locked upon her, and he was quick to jump to his feet, putting distance between him and Lexa, who frowned when she saw Persephone.

Feeling awkward and uncertain, she ambled down the hill toward them. She hesitated when she saw Thanatos approaching while Lexa remained beneath the tree, head tilted back, her eyes closed.

"You're not here at your usual time," Thanatos observed.

"No," she agreed but did not apologize. Elysium might be watched over by him, but Hades was king. "I have somewhere to go tonight. I thought I'd come to see Lexa early."

"She is tired," he said.

"She was just talking to you," Persephone pointed out and narrowed her gaze.

"I understand you miss her," Thanatos said. "But your visits will not produce the results you want."

She reared back as if he had slapped her. Thanatos's features changed, his eyes widened slightly, and he took a step toward her, as if realizing the pain his words had caused.

"Persephone—"

"Don't," she said, taking a step back.

She didn't need to be reminded that Lexa would never be the same. She mourned that fact every day, wrestled with the guilt that this was her fault.

"I didn't mean to hurt you."

"But you did," she said and vanished.

Since she could not visit Lexa in the Underworld, Persephone teleported to Ionia Cemetery, to her grave. It was still new—a barren mound with a headstone that read *beloved daughter, taken too soon*. Those words gripped her heart for two reasons—because it did feel as though Lexa had been taken too soon, but also because Persephone knew they were wrong. In the end, dying was Lexa's choice.

I accomplished what I needed to, she'd said, right before she walked off with Thanatos to drink from the Lethe, and things would never be the same again.

It was the first time Persephone had come here since Lexa's funeral. She took a quivering breath as she knelt beside the grave. It was dusted with snow, and as her palm touched the cold earth, a carpet of white anemone sprouted from the dirt. This magic was easy to release because the emotion behind it was so raw, so painful, it practically poured out of her skin.

She spent some time brushing snow from the flowers and from the headstone.

"You don't know how much I miss you."

She spoke to the grave, to the headstone, to the body buried six feet below. They were words she could not say to the soul in the Underworld because they were words she would not understand. It was why she was here—to talk to her best friend.

She sat on the ground, the cold seeping through her clothes and into her skin. She sighed, resting her head against the stone at her back and looking up at the sky—flurries of snow melted on her skin.

"I'm getting married, Lex," she said. "I said yes."

She laughed a little. She could practically hear Lexa screaming as she jumped in the air and threw her arms around her neck, and as happy as that thought made her, it also crushed her.

"I have never been so happy," she said. "Or so sad."

She was quiet for a long time, letting silent tears stream down her face.

"Sephy?"

She looked up to find Hermes standing a few feet away, looking like gold fire amid the snow.

"Hermes, what are you doing here?"

"I think you can guess," he said, running his fingers through his blond hair as he took a seat beside her. He was dressed casually, in a long-sleeved shirt and dark jeans.

"No jumper this time?"

"That is only for very special occasions."

They smiled at one another, and Persephone wiped at her eyes, lashes still damp from crying.

"Did you know that I lost a son?" he said after a long moment.

Persephone gazed at him, only viewing the profile of his beautiful face—but she could tell by the deep gold of his eyes and the set of his jaw, this topic of conversation was difficult for him.

"No," she whispered. "I'm so sorry."

"You know of him," Hermes said. "His name was Pan, the God of the Wild—of Shepherds and Flocks. He died many years ago and I still grieve him. Some days it's like it happened yesterday."

She knew what questions others would ask—how did he die? But that was not a question she wanted to ask because it was one she did not like to answer, so instead, she said, "Tell me about him."

A smile curved his lips.

"You would have liked him," he said, nudging her with his shoulder. "He was like me—handsome and hilarious. He loved music. Did you know he invented the pipe? He challenged Apollo to a competition once." Hermes paused to laugh. "He lost, of course. He was just...fun."

He continued, telling stories of Pan—his great and not so great loves, his adventures, and finally his death.

"His death was sudden. One moment, he existed, and then he didn't, and I heard of his passing upon the wind—through shouts from mortals and mourners. I did not believe it, so I went to Hades, who told me the truth. The Fates had cut his thread."

"I am so sorry, Hermes."

He smiled, though sad. "Death is," he said. "Even for gods."

At those words, the cold shivered through her, too deep to ignore.

"We should go," he said, rising to his feet, he held out his hand. "We are due at Club Aphrodisia, and I know you aren't wearing *that*."

She managed to laugh as he helped her to her feet, and before they vanished to go their separate ways, Hermes met her gaze.

"No one ever said you had to pretend everything was okay," Hermes said. "Grief means we loved fiercely...and if that is all anyone ever has to say about either one of us in the end, I think we lived our best lives."

CHAPTER XVIII
Club Aphrodisia

Persephone stood bundled in her warmest jacket, still freezing as they exited the back of Hades's limo. Beneath her coat, she wore a thin, black gown that showed more skin than was appropriate for this kind of weather. A deep V-neck exposed the swell of her breasts while high front slits showed off her thighs. She had a hard time deciding if Hades would approve of the dress, but she imagined he would be just as conflicted if he saw her—torn between frustration and a deep desire to fuck her.

Sybil also wore black, though her dress was shorter and looked more like lingerie. It reminded Persephone of something Aphrodite would wear. Leuce dressed in a red see-through top and tight jeans while it appeared Zofie had raided her armoire, wearing a black steel-boned corset that showed off her elegant frame and dark pants. Surprisingly, Hermes wore a more tame outfit—a white V-neck and gray jacket with dark jeans. Secretly, Persephone had hoped he'd show up in his jumper.

"Enjoy your evening," said Antoni as he returned to the driver's seat.

"I'll call when we're ready," Persephone promised.

"I don't see a sex club," said Leuce, looking at the buildings lining the sidewalk.

She was right—there was no sign for Club Aphrodisia. There was a restaurant, a bar, and an empty building.

"It's around the back," Hermes said.

They followed him down the dark alleyway, which had been shoveled and sanded, making the walk easier than Persephone had expected.

The club was discreet and there was no signage—just an entry where a pool of yellow light spilled over a set of emerald doors where two bouncers stood. They checked their identification and held the doors open for them. Inside, they were greeted by a man dressed in an impeccable black suit.

"Ah, Master Hermes," said the attendant. "Welcome."

"Sebastian," the God of Trickery greeted.

The man's eyes shifted to Persephone, Sybil, Leuce, and Zofie.

"You've brought guests. Women." Sebastian seemed surprised, raising his brows.

Hermes cleared his throat. "Yes. These are my friends. You have heard of the Lady Persephone. She is soon to marry Hades."

"Of course," Sebastian said. "How could I be so blind to your beauty. I did not know that Lord Hades shared."

"He doesn't," Persephone said.

Hermes cleared his throat. "And these are her friends— Sybil, Leuce, and Zofie."

"We are truly honored. I hope you find your time here pleasurable. Follow me."

Sebastian led them upstairs, and as Persephone followed beside Hermes, she elbowed him.

"Never been here before, huh?"

223

"Only a couple times," he said.

Persephone eyed him. "Only twice and you are so well known?"

He grinned. "What can I say? My skills are legendary."

Persephone rolled her eyes and elbowed him harder.

"Ouch!" He rubbed his side. "What? I've had a lot of practice!"

She shook her head, and while part of her wanted to laugh, another part of her was reminded of her conversation with Hades shortly after their game of Never Have I Ever. She was still learning. Sometimes she wondered if she gave Hades exactly what he needed, especially after the way he'd taken control in his office earlier today. He'd been rough and unapologetic while he'd thrust into her mouth. It wasn't the first time they'd had rough sex or the first time she sensed he needed something more than their standard experience. Perhaps this club would give her some ideas.

As they reached the top of the steps, they found themselves in a dark hallway. Persephone reached out her hand to hold the wall for support and found that it was soft—velvet. They passed a number of doors, all with names like Carnal, Passion, Lust before coming to one called Craving.

Inside, the suite was lit with muted blue lights, which cast most of the place in darkness. There were two large black leather couches that looked more like beds and a bench with restraints. A paddle lay atop. Persephone kept her coat on as she approached the balcony, where red light streamed from the ceiling, bathing the floor in shadowy crimson.

Below, there were several beds, large couches, benches, and two cages. There were people everywhere. Some wore masks and some did not. Some engaged in sex of all kinds—oral and otherwise. Some sat on couches and in chairs, chatting and watching. There was also a dance floor, though small; a few people swayed there while they touched and explored. It was all sort of quiet and not at all like Persephone had imagined.

She supposed what she *had* imagined was more like the sex she had with Hades, but what she shared with him was far more intense. It wasn't about sharing—not like this place.

Still, it was slow and kind and respectful. A woman was being spanked by a man while she gave another man a blow job. Several couples were having sex, their faces contorted in pleasure. Another woman was restrained while a man pleasured her. For a long moment, Persephone was drawn to their play in particular. She couldn't decide why she was fascinated but she realized it was because she'd always thought of restraints as one thing—a loss of control—but this looked different. Sensual and teasing and loving. It looked like trust.

She started to feel warm all over and cleared her throat, a deep ache settling in. She'd given Hades what she'd considered her best work earlier in the day. Their encounter had been hot and heavy, and her need was desperate. She curled her fingers around the balcony's ledge.

"So what do you think?" Hermes asked, sidling up alongside her.

"It's…different," she said, searching for the right words.

"Not as seedy as you thought?" he asked, quirking a brow.

"No," she said. "It's…actually kind of…tame."

Even with a community vibrator.

"See anything you'd like to try?"

Persephone stared.

"I mean with Hades," he added.

She rolled her eyes and changed the subject.

"Where do you think this meeting is taking place?" Persephone asked.

"I suppose it depends on the kind of meeting she's having," Hermes said.

Sybil, Leuce, and Zofie joined them at the balcony.

Leuce offered a small laugh. "I guess some things never change."

Persephone assumed the nymph was referring to the fact that ancient Greek society was hypersexualized, and in truth, their views of sex hadn't changed all that much. Even in their modern society, prostitution was legal.

"Quick, cover your eyes, Zofie," Leuce joked.

"Why?" the Amazon asked. "I am familiar with sex."

Everyone stared, surprised.

"What?" she asked, sounding exasperated. "I may not know modern society, but sex is not modern."

Hermes chuckled and Sybil smirked.

"*You've* had sex?" Leuce asked.

Zofie rolled her eyes. "Of course."

"But...we played Never Have I Ever," Leuce said. "And you didn't drink! Not *once!*"

Zofie was quiet for a long moment and then said, "I think I misunderstood the game."

They laughed and watched for a while, commenting on various acts and positions. Couples mingled, trading and engaging in different types of sex, but over time, Persephone noticed a few leaving the floor—one by one, moving into the darkness.

She stiffened.

"Where do you think they're going?" Sybil asked.

"I don't know," Persephone answered.

"Shall we investigate?" Hermes asked.

"Someone needs to stay and watch for Helen," Persephone said. "Sybil, Leuce—will you watch for her and text when she arrives?"

"Of course," Sybil said.

"Zofie, I need you to stay here with them."

"My orders are to protect you, my lady."

"Actually, I swore an oath to protect her tonight," said Hermes. "You will forgive me for not trusting anyone else to do so."

The Amazon glared at Hermes and started to protest when Persephone interrupted.

"Zofie, this is important. I am ordering you to protect my friends. If Helen is here with Triad and she recognizes any of us, we're in trouble."

"Very well, my lady," she said, still glaring at Hermes.

Persephone shed her jacket and the two left the suite, placing cloth masks over their faces before heading to the floor of the club. Hermes paused in the darkness of the stairwell.

"Do as I do," he said and drew her arm through his as they wandered onto the floor. They took their time, strolling around beds of tangled limbs and couches with men and women lost in the throes of passion. What struck her was how quiet it was here—even with music and moaning.

One couple smiled at them—the man was poised between his partner's legs.

"Would you like to join?" he asked.

"We're more than happy to watch," said Hermes.

They didn't seem upset as the man went down on the woman. Persephone averted her eyes, feeling strange standing in the center of this room, watching people freely engage in sex so openly. She was not sure she could do this, was not sure she would feel comfortable with people watching her or Hades. She was possessive—he was possessive. It would not end well.

Soon, they moved into the darkness, navigating down a hallway where a man stood.

"My lady," he said.

She stiffened at the title but realized as Hermes released her arm he was there to help her down the steps. She accepted his hand and walked ahead of Hermes into a circular, crowded room, lined all around with columns and recessed archways. It was a theater but built more like an amphitheater. The stage sat at the lowest point of the room, and at its center was a goddess.

She was being restrained, her arms and legs pulled tight across a black bench. She was not conscious, and there was blood dripping from a wound at her head.

Persephone froze for a moment; a cold trickle of fear shivered down her spine. She did not recognize the goddess, but she sensed that she was still alive. Bystanders booed her and threw things at her, while others chanted *cut her horns* over and over.

"That is Tyche," Hermes said.

Persephone jumped. She hadn't felt the god approach, but now that he was near, her anxiety lessened a bit.

"Tyche," Persephone whispered back. "The Goddess of Fortune and Prosperity?"

"The only one," he replied, his voice grim. She looked at him, noting the tightening of his jaw and the hardening of his eyes.

"What are we going to do?" Persephone asked.

They had to help her.

"We wait," Hermes said. "We do not know who or what is on their side."

Persephone felt dread at that comment—an overwhelming force that pulled her into a fast current. She thought of the weapon that had taken Harmonia down and her mother, whose magic had powered it. What would they face here?

She studied the large crowd but did not find Helen among them.

More people joined until the room was packed and hot. The mask stuck to Persephone's skin, uncomfortable and wet. With more people came more anger and taunting.

There was violence in the air, and she pressed closer to Hermes, feeling more and more uncomfortable. The god tightened his hold on her, which was less comforting than it should have been, because she knew Hermes too was tense.

Sudden applause drew their attention to the stage, where a man stood. He was dressed in a navy suit, tailored to his large body. He had wavy blond hair and eyes so bright and blue, she could see their sparkle, even from a distance.

Demigod, she thought.

"That is Okeanos," Hermes said.

"Who is Okeanos?"

"He is a son of Zeus," Hermes said. "He has a twin, Sandros. They are not usually far from each other."

Persephone watched Okeanos as he circled Tyche like a predator, a look of disgust upon his face. He stopped at her head and took hold of one of her horns, breaking it effortlessly. The snap made bile rise in Persephone's throat but drew cheers from the crowd. After he had broken the second horn from her head, he held them aloft like a trophy while the crowd hailed him like some hero from ancient times.

Then he tossed them aside as if they were nothing—as if he had not just mutilated the goddess restrained upon the table.

"The Olympians make a mockery of power!" he shouted. "They parade around, celebrities more obsessed with their image and their wealth and hurting mortals than granting your *desperate* prayers."

The crowd roared in agreement.

"It is a tale older than time. Gods outlive their usefulness to the world and must be replaced by new ones, those who understand it and see its potential. We are those gods. It is time to take back our world."

More cheers.

Persephone felt sick. It was the narrative she'd expected and the one Helen had perpetuated. These demigods really wanted to overthrow the Olympians. The problem was these people—Adonis, Harmonia, Tyche—were not Olympians. They were innocent. What was the point of hurting them?

Movement from Tyche drew Okeanos's attention. The demigod continued to speak as he approached the goddess.

"We will have a rebirth! A new world where your prayers are answered, where the gods intercede only when asked, where they heal and do not hurt, but the price is dire."

He picked up a blade that must have been sitting above Tyche's head. It gleamed, sharp and dangerous.

"Are you willing to pay it?" he asked, and the crowd responded with a resounding yes.

Just then, Persephone smelled her mother's magic. It drew her attention and sent her heart racing. For a moment, she felt panic, her breath came in short gasps, and her vision blurred, but as quickly as she felt the magic, it was gone, and when her eyes returned to the stage, Okeanos was lifting the blade.

"No!" Persephone cried and flung out her hands. Just as several heads moved in her direction, they froze—except Okeanos, whose gaze narrowed upon her.

Fuck.

Demigods may not be as powerful as other gods, but it was impossible to know what magic they were born with, and it looked like Okeanos could control time. Without a word, he flung out his hand and sent a bolt of lightning barreling toward her.

Persephone's eyes widened, and she dove to avoid the hit, but as she landed on the floor, someone materialized in front of her—a goddess.

"Aphrodite—"

The goddess flung out her arm, and in the next second,

Okeanos's body lurched, and his heart flew from his chest into Aphrodite's waiting hand. His eyes widened, and as he fell to his knees, Persephone lost her grip upon her magic, and the crowd was mobile once again.

There was a moment of heavy silence before the crowd realized what had happened.

"Gods! There are gods among us!" someone yelled.

Then chaos ensued—some screamed and fled while others peeled off their masks and searched for weapons within the theater.

"Hermes!" Persephone cried. "Get Tyche!"

The God of Mischief was gone in a flash, appearing on stage beside the motionless goddess. The crowd surged forward in an attempt to attack Hermes, but the god's eyes had begun to glow, and some faltered.

Persephone got to her feet.

"Aphrodite!"

The goddess did not seem to hear her, her attention on the still-beating heart in her hand, the blood seeping between her fingers. Then Persephone's eyes shifted as a mortal rushed the goddess, a long candlestick raised to strike.

"Aphrodite!"

Still, the goddess remained calm, almost passive as she turned her head in the direction of the mortal, threw out her hand, and sent him flying backward into the crowd, scattering bodies until he landed with a loud crack against the opposite wall.

Persephone expected the mortals to bolt, but instead, they rushed toward them.

A hand yanked her hair, pulling her head back, throat taut, and ripped off her mask. The movement was so violent, she was stunned, and it took her a moment to meet a familiar set of eyes.

"Jaison?"

She hadn't seen him since Lexa's funeral. He'd ceased all communication with her—now she knew why. His dark curls were longer and his face unshaven. He looked rough and angry.

"Well, well, well, the favor fuck has come to infiltrate our meeting."

"Jaison—" She said his name, reaching for his hand to lessen the pull he had on her head. She was surprised when the mortal released her, and she stumbled back only to be pushed hard by someone. As she lurched forward, she was shoved again. This time, she managed to stop herself before another person could touch her, but she was surrounded.

She met Jaison's eyes.

"Why?" she found herself asking.

"Isn't it obvious? Hades could have saved Lexa. *You* could have saved her."

"Don't you dare," Persephone said, her eyes watering, burning with fresh tears.

"If you had done it right the first time, she wouldn't have left. She wasn't the same when she came back."

"Because she wanted to die!" Persephone shouted. "She was tired, but you were too selfish to see that. I was too selfish."

"Do not pretend you care," he said. "If you did, you wouldn't marry Hades."

The circle tightened, and Persephone went rigid.

"Don't do this," she said. "You will regret it."

"We do not fear Hades," Jaison said.

"It isn't Hades you should fear," she said. "It's me."

He laughed—and the others joined in, but Persephone's anger was boiling over. A hand reached for her and she exploded—literally. Thorns burst from her arms and legs and palms. They shot out like blades and cut through the mortals surrounding her, skewering many of them—including

Jaison—at which ever level they stood, head or throat or chest or belly. She screamed at her anger, at the carnage, at the pain, but as it died, the thorns retracted, reeling into her body as if they were part of her. Still, she was left broken and bloody, her skin split.

She fell to her knees at the center of her massacre, leaning forward, breathing raggedly. She tasted blood.

Heal, she thought. *You have to heal*.

Then she felt Hades's unmistakable presence. She saw his shoes first, then her eyes made the slow climb up his body. When she saw his face, she saw a god—an ancient one full of rage and darkness and death.

It took Persephone a moment to realize why the room had gone so quiet—it was because everyone was dead. Had she done this? Or was this Hades's malice?

"*Hades.*" She tried to say his name, but the blood in her mouth was thick and she choked on the word, sending a spray of crimson onto his shoes. Her head spun, and she fell the rest of the way to the floor.

Hades bent and scooped her into his arms. She'd never seen him look this way—haunted, triggered—and she knew he was fighting something horrible and dark. She wanted to comfort him, and all she could think was that she hoped he knew how much she loved him.

Then everything went dark.

PART II

"Hateful to me as the gates of Hades is that man who hides one thing in his heart and speaks another."

—HOMER, *THE ILIAD*

CHAPTER XIX
The Island of Lampri

When Persephone woke, she was in an unfamiliar bed. Her tongue felt swollen, but she could breathe, her throat no longer thick with blood. She lifted her arms, her skin smooth and unmarred from the magic she'd used to defend herself in the basement of Club Aphrodisia. She was healed, and yet she couldn't help feeling like she'd failed because she hadn't been able to do it on her own.

She sat up, scanning the bright room for Hades. It did not take her long to find him. The balcony doors were open, letting in fresh, salty air that moved the gauzy curtains over the bed. Just outside, Hades sat. She slipped from the bed, wrapped the sheet around her body, and joined him.

He wore a black robe and leaned forward, elbows resting on his thighs, a glass of whiskey caught between his fingers. His features were severe, brows knitted together, jaw set tight. He seemed deep in thought, and she was a little afraid to disturb him, but she wanted to see his eyes.

"Hades," she whispered.

He looked at her, his gaze stormy, and she wondered what kind of battle he was fighting inside.

"Are you well?" she asked.

"No," he said, and the answer made her flinch. He took a drink from his glass, and his gaze returned to his feet. Hesitantly, she approached and reached to thread her fingers through his hair. It was wet and smelled strongly of spice. She took a deep breath, comforted by it.

"Hades," she said his name again. This time, it took him longer to raise his eyes to hers. "I love you."

She noticed how thickly he swallowed and averted his eyes. She sighed and reached for his glass, setting it on the table beside him. She managed to straddle him in the small chair, one knee on either side of his legs. She took his face between her hands and brushed her thumbs across his cheeks. He was so beautiful and so broken.

"Will you tell me how you're feeling?"

"I don't know that there is anything to say," he answered.

She studied him for a long moment. "Are you angry with me?"

"I am angry with myself for letting you go, for trusting another to take care of you."

"I ordered Hermes—"

"He swore an oath," he snarled, cutting her off. Persephone froze for a moment, taken off guard by Hades's anger. She hadn't been awake long enough to think through this. She'd just seen him and wanted him. She should have known he would take this personally. He blamed himself for Pirithous; he would blame himself for this too.

Still, she tried to explain.

"Hades." She placed her hands on his chest. "I...hurt myself. *I* failed. I couldn't heal."

Hades's jaw tightened.

"I'm okay," she said. "I'm here."

"Barely," he said through clenched teeth.

It was the first time she noticed Hades's hands weren't

on her. Instead, they gripped the arms of his chair. When she saw this, she slipped off his lap and took a step away, her back hitting the rail of the balcony.

"I don't know what to do," she said helplessly.

"You can stop," he said, his gaze full of rage. "You can decide not to get involved. You can stop trying to change people's minds and save a world. Let people make their decisions and face the consequences. It is how the world worked before you, and it is how the world will continue."

She pushed off the balcony, straightening beneath his angry words.

"This is different, Hades, and you know it. This is a group of people who have managed to capture and subdue *gods*."

"I know exactly what it is," he snarled. "I have lived through it before, and I can protect you from it."

"I didn't ask you to protect me from it," Persephone said, her voice rising.

"I can't lose you." He stood, caging her, his teeth bared. "I almost did, do you know that? Because I couldn't fucking get my mind right to heal you. I have held men and women and children to me as they bled like you bled. I have had my face sprayed with their blood. I have had them beg for their life—a life I could not extend or heal or gift because I cannot fight their fate. But you—you did not beg for life. You were not even desperate for it. *You were at peace*."

"Because I was thinking about you," she spat back at him. It was like he'd taken a knife to her chest. Her heart felt open and exposed, beating with all her pain and his. Hades froze. "I wasn't thinking about life or death or anything but how much I loved you, and I wanted to say it, but I couldn't..."

She stopped. She didn't need to explain further—Hades already knew why she hadn't been able to talk, and she didn't want to remind him of the horror he'd experienced while she lay unconscious and bleeding. His stare lingered on her face before his head fell into the crook of her neck and his body shook against hers. She said nothing as she felt hot tears soak through her skin. It was a long time before he composed himself, and when he pulled away, his eyes were dark and rimmed with red. She had never seen him like this before. This was his pain, real and raw.

She pressed her hand to his cheek. "Will you take me to bed?"

"I will take you here," he said and bent to kiss her. He tasted like salt and whiskey, and he spoke against her mouth. "And then I will take you on the bed and then in the shower and on the beach. I will take you on every surface of this house and every inch of this island."

His hands moved to her hips, and he drew her against him as he returned to the chair. She let the sheet drop from her body before straddling him. Hades's hands cupped her breasts and then he took her nipples into his mouth. Persephone threaded her fingers through his hair as he worked, her breath growing shallow, her body moving against his erection, which was still covered by the robes he wore. She grew frustrated, wanting to feel skin against skin, and parted them, exposing his chest and his engorged flesh. She moved against his warmth, the friction making her wetter.

Hades's hands moved to her ass, squeezing as she rocked against him, then his fingers slipped inside her and she shuddered. She spent a few minutes basking in the feel of him but soon desired more. She pulled him free and reached for his cock, guiding him inside her. She ground herself against him, feeling frenzied and desperate. The hair trailing from his stomach to his groin teased her clit. While she took control, Hades leaned back, his arms stretched over his head, gripping the top of the chair. He watched her face, eyes glittering, still full of shadow.

Soon his hands returned to her waist, and he helped

her move, grinding himself into her. The feel of him was a tonic she would take for the rest of her life. It brought life to her limbs and flame to her soul. His mouth moved over her shoulder, teeth grazing her skin. Their breaths mingled; their moans started to release in quick succession. Persephone felt the bottom of her stomach tighten, her muscles clenched around Hades's cock, and his hot release poured into her.

She collapsed against him, breathing hard. After a long moment, she shifted, pressing a kiss to his chest before straightening with Hades still inside her. She grinned.

"Are you tired?"

"I have never felt more alive," he said, and it seemed that some of the darkness had dimmed from his eyes. She kissed him—long and slow, her tongue lapping at his until he was hard once more. She pulled away and rested her head against his chest, content to stay like this forever.

"Where are we?" she asked, her voice was quiet.

"We are on the island of Lampri," he answered. "Our island."

"Our?"

"I've had it," he said. "But I rarely come. After I found you in the club, I did not wish to go to the Underworld. I did not wish to be anywhere but alone. So I came here."

There was another long stretch of silence.

"Do you know if Tyche survived?"

It was then Hades's hands tightened around her.

"No," he said. "She did not."

―――――

Later, Hades gave Persephone her phone, which allowed her to check in with Sybil, Leuce, and Zofie. They'd created a group text to tell her they loved her. Her eyes watered at their sweet messages. She let her know she was okay and asked after them.

We're fine. Zofie made sure we got home safe, said Sybil and she explained what happened upstairs. *We knew something was wrong when people came out of the shadows screaming that a god was attacking people. We didn't know if it was Hermes or...Hades.*

But it had been neither.

It had been Aphrodite.

It had been her. Suddenly, she recalled the carnage she'd caused. How many people had she killed?

She set the phone aside, and when Hades entered the bedroom, he paused.

"What's wrong?"

"How many people did I kill?" she whispered.

Hades paused and then asked, "What do you remember?"

"Hades—"

"Will it help to know?" he asked.

She opened her mouth to speak but did not know how to answer.

"Think on it," he said. "I say this as a god who knows the answer."

After, they walked along the beach. It was strange seeing Hades in such a bright place, dressed down in nothing but a cloth wrapped around his waist. His skin was burnished beneath the sun, turning a golden bronze. She couldn't look away.

"Why are you staring?" he asked.

"Does it upset you?" she asked, frowning.

"No," he said, matter-of-fact. "It makes me want to fuck."

She grinned.

When they reached the shore, she ran into the ocean, squealing with delight as the water rushed upon her, soaking the bottom of her white dress. She turned to find Hades wading toward her.

"How long has it been?" she asked Hades. "Since you have visited the ocean?"

"For fun?" he asked. "I hardly know."

"Then we will make this memorable," she said, hoisting herself up his body, fingers digging into his broad, muscled shoulders as she wrapped her legs around his waist. His cock settled against her, and her teeth grazed his bottom lip.

"I love you," she whispered.

Their mouths and bodies fused together. Her blood pounded, scattering her thoughts. Their hands skated across each other's skin, enjoying the feel of one another. When Hades's fingers tightened on her bottom, grinding into her with a desperate ferocity she wanted to match, they broke from one another, lips throbbing.

"I want to show you something," he said.

She raised a brow, her lust dwarfing any other thoughts. "Is it your cock?"

He chuckled. "Don't worry, my darling. I'll give you what you want, but not here."

They left the water and Hades guided her down the beach toward a grove of tropical plants and trees. Beyond them was a path that became rocky as it neared an open cave. Just inside was a set of steps that spiraled down into a grotto. The water was the color of hundreds of shimmering sapphires. Above them, the roof had collapsed, allowing for a stream of warm sunlight to filter in, hitting the water. Lush greenery grew within the walls of the cave, spilling down over the roughened surface.

Persephone stared, awed by how beautiful it was.

"Do you like it?" he asked.

"It is beautiful."

Hades grinned and started down another set of steps that led to the water. He shed the covering at his waist and stood naked, turning to face her. As she approached him, Hades stepped off the edge, sinking into the deep pool. She watched him surface some distance from the shore.

His eyes glistened, dark and reverent.

"Will you join me?"

She pulled the thin dress over her head, discarding it beside her as she dove into the water. Hades caught her around the waist, pressing his lips to hers as they surfaced. Floating in the grotto, he made love to her mouth as she reached between them, guiding his cock between her legs so she could feel him there. Her breath caught as his lips left her mouth, trailing her jaw.

"I will build temples in honor of our love, and I will worship you until the end of the world. There is nothing I wouldn't sacrifice for you." He drew away to look at her, eyes like shimmering stars. "Do you understand that?"

"Yes," she said, tightening her hold around him. "I will give you everything you ever wanted, even things you thought you would live without."

Their mouths collided again, and Hades gripped her, guiding them backward toward a dip in the rock wall where a trickling waterfall kept a larger cave obscured. He lifted her from the water and walked into it, guiding her against the wall of the cavern. One arm stretched up, and the other found purchase beside her head. She held his smoldering gaze.

"There is something dark that lives inside me," he said. "You have seen it. You recognize it now, don't you?"

She nodded.

"It wants you in ways that would scare you."

Was he telling this to scare her? Because it had the opposite effect, sending a thrilled shiver down her spine.

"Tell me."

"That part of me wants you praying for my cock. Writhing beneath me as I pound into you. Begging for my come to fill you."

Persephone kept her hands pressed into the wall, her

nails scraping at the rock behind her. She stared up at him through her lashes, feeling both shy and daring.

"How do you prefer to receive prayer, my lord?"

"On your knees," he said.

She watched him as she knelt, level with his erection. Hades gathered her hair into one hand, twining it around his fists until her scalp pricked with pain.

"Suck me," he ordered, and she obeyed.

She took him into her mouth, lavishing his crown with her tongue, sucking the tip until she tasted his come. Hades groaned, his hand tightening in her hair, bringing tears to her eyes, but she continued, wanting to play with the darkness surfacing in the bite of his hold. When he started to thrust into her mouth, all she could do was receive, a vessel for his pleasure. Both his hands cupped her head, his muscles bulged, his breath ragged. She thought he would come, but he withdrew suddenly, dragging her to her feet roughly, molding his mouth to hers. She widened her stance as he guided his cock between her legs, teasing her opening, slick with need for him.

"Hades—" Her voice came out strangled—a plea he answered by gripping her hips and slamming into her. While he leveraged her against the wall, another hand came to rest upon her neck, his face pressed against her own as he moved. Each thrust drew a desperate moan from her throat, and her fingers bit into his shoulders, scraping down his skin. Hades's mouth returned to hers, tongue tasting, teeth scraping. He kissed and moved with a ferocity she hadn't felt before, and it drew filthy words and sounds from her mouth she'd never said or heard before.

"I want to feel your release," she said, arching her back, her shoulder blades cutting into the rock. "I want your come inside me." Her breath caught in her throat. "I want to feel it drip down my thighs." Her heels dug into his ass.

"I want to be so full of you, I only taste you for days." Her mouth closed over his earlobe, and she sucked hard.

As she spoke, Hades continued to thrust; his mouth moved to her neck where he sucked her skin and bit her hard. She cried out at the sweet sting as the vibration of her first orgasm began to rock through her. It continued, not peaking, just lasted on and on until her whole body shook, and when Hades groaned, offering a feral growl, she felt the heat of his release inside her.

They stayed plastered against one another for a while, until Hades peeled himself away and lifted her into his arms, teleporting to the bedroom, where he laid her down upon the bed. She expected him to stretch out beside her, but instead, he knelt between her legs and kissed up her thighs until his mouth covered her clit, his tongue sweetly devouring her swollen skin.

"Hades," she whispered his name again and again. Her hands dove into his hair and then fell into the sheets beneath her, twisting as another climax tore through her, and when she came down from the high, Hades finally rested beside her.

Exhausted, she fell into a deep sleep.

Later she woke, finding Hades asleep beside her. He lay on his stomach, his fingers threaded through hers. He looked peaceful, the tendrils of darkness that had clung to him hours earlier banished by slumber. She watched him for a while and then disentangled herself from his grasp, pulling on a robe and slipping outside. She leaned against the balcony rail, watching the night. It was peaceful here, untouched by her mother's destruction.

And it felt wrong to be here, wrong to feel so happy when such chaos reigned.

"Why do you frown?" Hades asked.

His voice startled her, and she turned to find him in the doorway, his naked body wreathed in light from the bedroom.

Heat blossomed low in her belly as her eyes fell to his erect flesh and she thought of how he had looked at her in the grotto, the erotic words he'd spoken, the restraint he'd broken.

She swallowed and shook the thoughts from her head.

"You know we cannot stay here," Persephone said. "Not with what we left behind."

"One more night," Hades said—pleaded.

"What if that's too late?"

Hades did not speak. He left his place in the doorway and came to her, cupping her face, eyes searching.

"Can I not convince you to stay here?" he asked. "You would be safe, and I would return to you every free moment."

Her hands closed over his forearms.

"Hades," she whispered. "You know I won't. What kind of queen would I be if I abandoned my people?"

His lips tilted upward, but his gaze was sad. "You are Queen of the Dead, not Queen of the Living."

"The living eventually become ours, Hades. What good are we if we desert them in life?"

Hades sighed and rested his forehead against hers.

"I wish that you were as selfish as me," he said.

"You are not selfish," she said. "You would leave me here to help them, remember?"

His gaze fell to her lips and he kissed her. His hands slid to her waist, dipping beneath her robe, reaching to cup her hot center.

Persephone gasped, his name on her lips.

"Hades," she breathed against his lips.

"If not another night, then at least another hour," he said.

How could she say no?

Her arms closed around his neck as he lifted her onto the edge of the balcony, fingers dipping into her slick flesh long enough to elicit a moan. When he withdrew, her nails bit into his skin and Hades chuckled.

"You were wrong," he said, bringing his fingers to his mouth. "I am selfish."

She watched him, a carnal hunger erupting inside her. As he sucked on his flesh, she spread her legs wider, inviting him to return.

"Only an hour," she reminded Hades.

His smile was barely there, and just as he moved to join them once again, he growled, pulling Persephone from the balcony's ledge onto the ground.

"Fuck," he spat. "*Hermes.*"

"I'd love to join you," said the god, appearing on the balcony only a few steps away. "Another time, perhaps."

Persephone turned away to fasten her robe, and when she looked back, she saw that the god's chiseled face was marred with a large gash that ran from the bottom of his eye to his lip.

Her eyes widened.

"Hermes, what happened to your face?"

He smiled, his eyes gentle despite his answer. "I broke an oath."

Persephone's lips parted, and her gaze returned to Hades, who did not look at her, too angry and focused upon the God of Mischief.

"What do you want, Hermes? We were about to return."

"How long is 'about to'?" he asked, but the smirk he offered was humorless, and Persephone found that she did not like the melancholy clinging to him. Was this his grief at losing Tyche or something else?

"Hermes—" Hades began.

"Zeus has summoned both of you to Olympus," Hermes interrupted. "He has called Council. They wish to discuss your separation."

CHAPTER XX
A Council of Olympians

"Our separation?" Persephone repeated, looking to Hades. "Are there not more pressing issues? Like Triad murdering a goddess and attacking another?"

"I only gave you one reason Zeus called Council," Hermes said. "That does not mean we will not discuss other concerns."

"I will be along shortly, Hermes," Hades said, having made no attempt to cover himself.

Hermes nodded, and then he looked at Persephone.

"See you later, Sephy," he said, winking. He vanished, and she thought that perhaps he was trying to soften the guilt she felt at seeing his face scarred.

Persephone turned to Hades. "Did you do that to Hermes's face?"

His jaw tightened. "You ask and yet you know."

"You didn't have—"

"I did." He cut her off. "His punishment could have been worse. Some of our laws are sacred, Persephone, and before you feel guilt for what happened to Hermes's face, remember that he knew the consequences even if you did not."

His words felt like a reprimand. She averted her eyes and said quietly, "I didn't know."

Hades sighed, sounding frustrated, but he took her hand, tugging her to him.

"I'm sorry," he said, pressing a palm against her cheek. "I meant to comfort you."

"I know," she said. "It must be trying...to constantly have to teach me."

"I never tire of teaching," he said, his voice quiet. "My frustration comes from another place."

"Perhaps I can help...if you told me more," she offered.

Hades held her gaze, considering before he spoke.

"I worry my words will come out wrong and that you will find my motives barbaric."

She frowned. She was not surprised he felt this way. She'd called him the worst sort of god. She'd assumed his bargains with mortals were merely for his amusement, not real attempts at saving souls.

"I'm sorry," she said. "I think I gave you this fear when we met."

"No," he said. "It was there before you, but it only mattered when I met you."

"I understand Hermes's punishment," she said. "I am comforted."

Despite her words, she felt his expression remained uncertain, guarded. Still, he leaned forward and pressed his lips to her forehead. She closed her eyes against his kiss, feeling the warmth of it through her body. She met his gaze as he pulled away.

"Would you like to accompany me to Council?" he asked.

Her eyes widened. "You are serious?"

He offered a small smile. "I have conditions," he said. "But if the Olympians are to discuss us, it is only fair you are present."

She grinned.

"Come. We must prepare," he said, and she felt the brush of his magic as they teleported.

She'd expected to appear in their bedroom so they could dress, but instead, Hades had brought them to a room full of weapons.

"Is this…"

"An arsenal," Hades said.

The room was round, the floor black marble like the rest of the castle. Most of the walls were fixed with what looked like bookcases, only they held a variety of weapons—blades and spears, javelins and slings, bows and arrows. There were modern weapons too—guns and grenades and other artillery. There were also shields, helmets, chain mail, and leather breastplates on display, but what drew her attention was the piece at the center of the room—a display of Hades's armor. It looked both threatening and deadly. Sharp metal spikes covered the shoulders, arms, and legs. A black cape hung over the left shoulder, and a dark helm rested at its feet.

Persephone approached and brushed her fingers along the cold metal of the helmet. She tried to imagine Hades dressed in this. He was already large and imposing—this would make him…monstrous.

"How long has it been?" she asked quietly. "Since you wore this?"

"A while," he answered. "I do not need it unless I am fighting gods."

"Or against a weapon that can kill you," she said.

Hades did not respond. He reached around her and picked up the helm.

"This is the Helm of Darkness," he said. "It grants its wearer the ability to become invisible. It was made for me by the cyclopes during the Titanomachy."

She knew of the three weapons—Hades's helm, Zeus's lightning bolt, and Poseidon's trident. There were always turning points during battle—a time when the tide changes for better or worse for either side. These weapons had changed fate for the Olympians and allowed them to defeat the Titans.

Seeing the helm made Persephone feel dread. She suspected Triad wished for war. Would she see Hades clad in this armor soon?

"Why do you need this helm?" she asked. "One of your powers is invisibility."

"Invisibility is a power I gained over time as I became stronger," he said, then he offered a wry smile. "Outside of that, I prefer to protect my head during battle."

He thought he was funny, but Persephone frowned as he handed the helm to her. She held it between her hands, staring at the scratches and small dents upon its surface. She always imagined no one getting close enough to Hades to hurt him during battle, but the marks on this helm reminded her otherwise.

"I want you to wear this while at Council," he said.

Persephone lifted her head. "Why?"

"Council is for Olympians," he said. "And I am not eager to introduce you to either of my brothers, especially under these circumstances. You will not like everything that is said."

"Are you worried my mouth will sabotage our engagement?" she asked, raising a brow.

Hades grinned, and it was refreshing considering he'd been so serious the past few days since her injuries in Club Aphrodisia.

"Oh darling, I have faith your mouth will only improve it."

They stared at one another for a long moment before her gaze dipped, trailing over his muscles to his still erect cock.

"Are you going to Council naked, my lord? If so, I *insist* on watching."

"If you keep staring at me like that, we will not go to Council at all," he said, and with a flick of his wrist, they were both dressed in black—Hades in his suit and Persephone in a sheath dress. It made her wonder how the other gods dressed to attend Council. Would they wear the finery of ancient gods?

Hades held out his hand.

"Ready?"

Truly, she wasn't certain, but she was comforted by Hades and his helm. This would be one of the last times she ever had time to consider if she was ready. There would come a point when there was no time, when everything depended upon quick action.

She placed her fingers into his palm, still cradling the helm, and they teleported.

They landed in shadow, her back to a large column, and when she looked to the side, she could see more curving off to the left and right. Persephone could hear voices— booming and frustrated.

"This storm must end, Zeus! My cult begs for relief."

Persephone did not know who spoke, but she guessed it was Hestia judging by the still-gentle tone.

"I am not eager to see the storm go," Zeus said. "The mortals have grown too bold and need to be taught a lesson. Perhaps freezing to death will remind them who rules their world."

Persephone met Hades's gaze. Zeus's words were an issue. They were why Harmonia had been attacked and why Tyche had died. It was behavior mortals were growing tired of, and they were rebelling.

Hades placed his finger to his lips, took the helm from her, and placed it upon her head. She did not feel any different once it was on, except it was heavy and did not sit on her head properly. Hades's lips brushed against her knuckles before he let her go. He moved through the darkness undetected. She only knew when he appeared before the Olympians because he spoke—his voice dark, dripping with disdain.

"You will be reminding them of nothing save their hatred for you—for all of us," Hades said, responding to Zeus's earlier statement.

"Hades." His name came out as a growl from Zeus's mouth.

Persephone crept along the outside of the columns. Beyond them, she could see the backs of a set of thrones and the fronts of three others—Poseidon, Aphrodite, and Hermes. Each throne represented a piece of the gods. For Poseidon, it was a trident, for Aphrodite, a pink shell, for Hermes, his herald's wand.

Her gaze lingered longest on Aphrodite, recalling how she'd stood with Okeanos's heart in her hand, unfazed by the savagery of her magic. Would she face consequences for killing one of Zeus's sons? Persephone did not know the rules of the Olympians, but she thought the goddess must have justified herself to the God of Thunder, because she sat here among the twelve as if nothing had occurred.

Persephone crept closer until she touched the edge of one of the thrones—one she guessed belonged to Apollo, as golden rays shot out from the very top.

"From what I understand, Hades, the storm is your fault. Couldn't keep your dick out of Demeter's daughter."

"Shut up, Ares," Hermes said.

Persephone noted the darkness shadowing the god's eyes and the set of his jaw, which made his cheekbones look sharp.

"Why should he? He speaks the truth," a voice said from the right—Persephone thought it sounded like Artemis.

"You could have fucked a million other women, but you chose to stay with one, and the daughter of a goddess who hates you more than she loves humanity," Ares continued.

"That pussy must be gold," Poseidon mused.

Persephone felt something sour in the back of her throat and then a dark sense of dread as Hades's magic flared, strong and vibrant.

"I will personally cut the thread of any god who dares to speak another word about Persephone."

"You wouldn't dare." Persephone recognized Hera's voice. "The consequences of killing a god outside of the Fates' will are dire. You could lose your dear goddess."

A tense silence followed as Persephone tried to imagine the look upon Hades's face. It probably communicated something along the lines of *try me*.

"The fact remains that the snowstorm is causing great harm." Athena's silky voice, calming and commanding, entered the fray.

"Then we must discuss solutions to ending her rage," said Hades.

"Nothing will convince her to end her assault except the separation of you from her daughter," said Hera.

While that was true, it also implied there were no other ways to end Demeter's wrath.

"That is out of the question."

"Does the girl even wish to be with you?" Hera challenged. "Is it not true you trapped her in a contract to force her to spend time with you?"

Persephone's fingers rolled into fists.

"She is a *woman*," Hermes said. "And she loves Hades. I have seen it."

"So we should sacrifice the lives of thousands for the true love of two gods?" Artemis said. "Ridiculous."

"I did not come here so that Council could discuss my love life," Hades said.

"No, but unfortunately for you," said Zeus, "your love life is wreaking havoc upon the world."

"So is your dick," Hades said. "And no one's ever called Council about that."

"Speaking of dicks and the problems they cause," Hermes interjected. "Is no one going to speak about the trouble your offspring are causing? Tyche is dead. Someone is attacking us...*succeeding* in killing us...and you want to bicker about Hades's love life?"

Persephone couldn't help smiling at Hermes's words, but it didn't take long for the other gods to steal it away.

"We'll have nothing to worry about if Demeter's storm continues," said Artemis. "Mortals will be frozen to the ground. It will be Pompeii all over again."

"You think Demeter's wrath is the worst that could happen?" Hades asked, his tone menacing. "You do not know mine."

It was a threat, one Persephone knew would take the conversation nowhere. Hades had asked her not to reveal herself, but the fact was, these gods were having a conversation about her—her thoughts, her feelings, her choice—and they were making no progress toward what really mattered, and that was whatever Demeter was planning with Triad. She left the spot beside Apollo's throne and made her way around the arc. When she came to the edge—where Ares sat—she took off Hades's helm and set it aside. Shaking off her glamour, she stepped into the center of the arc and was suddenly surrounded by eleven Olympians.

Her gaze connected with Hades's and held. He sat rigidly, his hands curled around the edges of his throne. Beneath his gaze, she was able to straighten her shoulders and lift her chin. She had no idea how she looked to these ancient gods, probably young and inexperienced, but at least they would see her and know her and, by the end of this, respect her.

"Hades." She spoke his name, and it seemed to calm him. She offered him a small smile before her attention was drawn to Zeus, whose voice seemed to rumble deep beneath her feet.

"Well, well, well. Demeter's daughter."

"I am," she said, disliking how the God of Thunder's eyes

gleamed when they were upon her. She'd seen the king many times; an imposing and large figure, his body filled his throne. Despite being younger than his two brothers, his hair had a silver tone to it that made him look older. She did not know why—perhaps he felt it gave him more authority or he'd bargained away some of his youth in exchange for power. Beside him was Hera, who looked upon her with judgment. Her face, beautiful and noble, was carved and cynical.

She glanced to her left, finding Athena's passive, golden face, her mother's empty throne, and then Apollo and Artemis. Apollo inclined his head a fraction. It was the only acknowledgment she received—there was no light in his eyes or tilt to his lips. She tried not to let his mood disrupt her as she looked to her right, where she found Poseidon staring openly and hungrily. Then Hermes, Hestia, Aphrodite, and Ares.

Hermes smiled, his eyes gentle.

"You have caused a lot of problems," Zeus said, drawing her reluctant attention. She met his lackluster gaze.

"I think you mean my mother has caused a lot of problems," Persephone said. "And yet you seem intent upon punishing Hades."

"I merely seek to solve a problem in the simplest way possible."

"That might be true if Demeter were only responsible for a storm," Persephone said. "But I have reason to believe she is working with the demigods."

There was a beat of silence. "What reasons?"

"I was there the night Tyche died," Persephone said. "My mother was there. I felt her magic."

"Perhaps she was there to retrieve you," Hera suggested. "As is her right by Divine law. She is your mother."

"Since we are basing our decisions on archaic laws, then I must disagree," Persephone said.

Hera's gaze hardened, and Persephone got the distinct impression she did not like being challenged. "On what grounds?"

"Hades and I fuck," Persephone stated. "By Divine law, we are married."

Hermes choked on a laugh, but everyone else remained quiet. She looked to Zeus. As much as she hated it, he was the one she needed to convince.

"It was my mother's magic that kept Tyche restrained," Persephone said.

The god stared at her for a beat and then looked to Hermes for confirmation.

"Is this true, Hermes?"

Her fingers curled into fists.

"Persephone would never lie," he replied.

"Triad is a true enemy," Persephone said. "You have reason to fear them."

There were a few laughs, and Persephone glared around her. "Did you not just hear what I said?"

"Harmonia and Tyche are goddesses, yes, but they are not Olympians," said Poseidon.

"I'm sure the Titans thought the same of you," she shot back. "Besides, Demeter *is* an Olympian."

"She would not be the first who attempted—and failed—to overthrow me," Zeus said, and she noted how he glanced both to his left and right. Despite how the Olympians sat—in this circle, unified—they were divided. There was hatred here, and it permeated the air like smog.

"This is different," Persephone said. "You have a world ready to shift their alliance to a group of people they believe are more mortal than god, and my mother's storm will force the decision."

"So we return to the real issue," Hera said. "You."

Persephone glared; her jaw tightened.

"If you return me to my mother, I will become a real issue," Persephone said. "I will be the reason for your misery, for your despair, for your ruination. I promise you will taste my venom."

No one laughed. No one spoke. There was only silence. She glanced at Hades, whose gaze burned into hers. She did not sense that he was disappointed with her, but he was on edge. Poised. Ready to act if necessary.

"You speak on what we will *not* do," Zeus said. "But what would you *have* us do? When the world suffers beneath a storm of your mother's creation?"

"Were you not ready to watch the world suffer minutes ago?" Persephone countered. It was not what she wished for, of course. It was the last thing she wanted, but she felt as though these gods were seconds away from sending her back to her mother, and Persephone would not go. She would have Hades. She would have the world—one way or the other.

"Are you suggesting we allow it to continue?" Hestia asked.

"I'm suggesting you punish the source of the storm," she said.

"You forget. No one has been able to locate Demeter."

"Is there no god here who is all-seeing?"

There was laughter.

"You speak of Helios," said Artemis. "He will not help us. He will not help you, because you love Hades and Hades stole his cattle."

Still, Persephone stared at Zeus, despite the other replies.

"Are you not King of Gods? Is Helios not here by your grace?"

"Helios is the God of the Sun," Hera said. "His role is important—more important than a minor goddess's obsessive love."

"If he were so great, could he not melt the snowstorm that ravages the earth?"

"Enough!" Zeus's voice echoed in the chamber, his eyes gleaming as they fell upon her. Persephone felt her insides shake. She did not like Zeus's gaze, did not like whatever thoughts were churning inside his head. Still, when he spoke, she was pleased by his words.

"You have given us much to consider, goddess. We will search for Demeter—all of us. If she is in league with Triad, let her admit it and face punishment. Until that point, however, I will defer judgment on your wedding to Hades a little while longer."

Hera glared at her husband, clearly unsatisfied with this choice.

"Thank you, Lord Zeus," Persephone said, bowing her head.

She hated speaking the words or thinking too long upon why he'd made this decision. She had a feeling he hoped to somehow gain her favor.

Persephone's eyes shifted to Hades as Zeus continued.

"On this night, we will say goodbye to Tyche."

One by one, the gods vanished from the room.

"See you later, Sephy!" Hermes said.

Hades left his throne, and Persephone spoke as he approached.

"I'm sorry. I know you asked that I stay hidden, but I couldn't. Not when they wished—"

He silenced her with a kiss. It seared her lips and her mouth, and when he pulled away, he held her face.

"You were wonderful," he said. "Truly."

Her eyes watered. "I thought they would take me from you."

"Never," he whispered, and he spoke the word over and over again like a prayer—a desperate plea—until she almost believed it.

CHAPTER XXI
A Touch of Fear

The pyre upon which Tyche rested was beautiful—marble, set with emeralds and rubies and dusted with gold. Upon it were stacks of wood, and atop that, Tyche herself. Her face and limbs were pale white, bathed in moonlight. Her body was draped in black silk. Her hair, as dark as midnight, spilled over the edge of the pyre.

The gods stood several feet away in an arc while other residents of Olympus gathered behind them. There were no words spoken as Hephaestus lit the pyre with his magic. The flames were small at first but consumed quickly, and Persephone couldn't look away.

My mother has done this, she thought.

Her eyes watered as the air filled with smoke. The sprigs of lavender and rosemary meant to help cover the smell could not mask the overwhelming scent of burning flesh. Hades's arms tightened around her waist.

"Tyche's death was not your fault," he said. She felt the vibration of his voice against her back. She did not feel at fault, but she did wonder who would be next? How soon until her mother and Triad struck again?

"Where do gods go when they die?" Persephone asked.

"They come to me, powerless," he said. "And I give them a role in the Underworld."

"What kind of role?"

Persephone was curious, given the bargains he made with mortals.

"It depends on what challenged them in their life as a god. Tyche, though, she always wanted to be a mother. So I will gift her with the Children's Garden."

Something thick gathered in her throat, and it took her several moments to swallow it down.

"Will we be able to speak with her? About the way she died?"

Persephone hated to ask, but she wanted to know Tyche's story just as they knew Harmonia's.

"Not immediately," he answered. "But within the week."

Persephone did not relish the idea of asking Tyche to relive her death, especially once she was in the Underworld. It was supposed to be a space of renewal and healing, but they could not fight this enemy if they did not know what they were dealing with.

Her gaze lingered on the flames consuming the goddess until they dwindled and nothing but the bright, blurred image of embers remained.

It was late when Persephone woke. The hazy light of the Underworld filtered in through the windows. She rolled, surprised to find Hades lying beside her.

"You're awake," he murmured. He lay on his side, hair down, eyes shadowed.

"Yes," she whispered. "Have you slept?"

"I have been awake for a while."

It was his way of answering no.

Hades brushed her lips with his fingers. "It is a blessing to watch you sleep."

With so much happening, Persephone hadn't thought much about her nightmares. Since Hades had brought Hypnos to visit her, they'd remained at bay, though Persephone doubted that had much to do with the God of Sleep and more to do with the fact that she had been healing from severe injuries.

They stared at one another for a long moment, and then Persephone let her head fall to Hades's chest. He was warm and she could feel and hear his heart beating against her ear—a steady rhythm that kept pace for her.

"Did Tyche make it across the river?" Persephone asked.

"Yes, Hecate was there to greet her. They are very good friends."

That was comforting. Hades's thumb brushed lightly up and down her lower back. His hands were warm, and the movement lulled her, making her eyes heavy with sleep.

"I would like to train with you today," Hades said after a moment.

"I would like that," she said. She had trained with Hades before and always learned something. He was gentle and patient in his instruction, and it inevitably resulted in sex.

"I don't think you will," Hades said.

Persephone pushed away just enough to meet his gaze.

"Why do you say that?"

His gaze bore into hers. A darkness lingered there as deep and as ancient as his magic.

"Just remember that I love you."

———

Persephone felt a deep sense of dread as she stood opposite Hades at the center of her grove. It was the way he was looking at her—as if he'd buried all his warmth. He was dressed in a short, black chiton that showed off his power-ful arms and thighs. Her gaze drifted over his skin, the rise and fall of his muscles, and when she found her way back to his eyes, a deep ache settled in her chest. He stared back, emotionless, when desire would normally ignite his eyes.

Then he spoke, his voice low and gruff, shivering down her spine.

"I will not watch you bleed again," he said.

"Teach me," she breathed.

She'd requested the same of him the night they'd met, when she had invited him to her table to play cards. Then, she hadn't understood what she was really asking. She wasn't sure she understood now, but the difference was this god loved her.

"You love me," she whispered.

"I do."

But the truth of it wasn't written on his face. He looked severe, the hollows of his cheeks deep and shadowed. Then the air around them changed, growing heavy and charged. She had felt this before, in the Forest of Despair when Hades's magic had risen to challenge her own. It raised the hair upon her arms and made her heartbeat feel sluggish in her chest.

Then everything went silent.

Persephone hadn't even noticed the noise before; she just knew there was an absence of it now. She glanced at the silvery trees that surrounded them, at the dark canopy overhead—and then she noticed movement to her left and right. Before she had time to react, something shadowy passed through her, shaking her very bones, jarring her soul. It wasn't exactly painful, but it did steal her breath. She fell to her knees, her stomach churning. She wanted to vomit.

What the fuck.

"Shadow-wraiths are death and shadow magic," Hades said, matter-of-fact. "They are attempting to reap your soul."

Persephone struggled to catch her breath, lifting her eyes to meet Hades's. His expression sent a strange current of fear through her, and the most unnerving part about the feeling was that she had never feared him before.

"Are you…*trying* to kill me?"

Hades's cold laugh chilled her to the bone.

"Shadow-wraiths cannot claim your soul unless your thread has been cut, but they can make you violently ill."

Persephone swallowed, still tasting the sour film at the back of her throat as she rose to her feet on shaking legs.

"If you were fighting any other Olympian—*any enemy*—they would have never let you up."

"How do I fight when I do not know what power you will use against me?"

"You will never know," he said.

She stared at him for a beat, and then something emerged from the earth beneath her feet—a clawed, black hand. It closed around her ankle and jerked. She fell forward as it pulled, dragging her into the pit from which it had emerged. She shoved her hands out to break her fall and felt a sharp pain in her wrist as she landed.

"Hades!" Persephone cried, clawing at the dirt in an effort to anchor herself, her heart racing with fear and adrenaline. She rolled and sat up as quickly as possible, her hands going for the strange claw that held her ankle like a vice, but when she tried to pry it away, sharp thorns jutted from it, piercing her skin.

Persephone jerked back, growling before summoning a huge thorn from her skin and stabbing the creature that held her. Black blood oozed from it, but it let go and disappeared into the Earth. Before she could turn, another shadow passed through her. This time, she arched, screaming as she fell to the ground. On the floor of the grove, she struggled to breathe, and her vision blurred.

"Better," she heard Hades say. "But you gave me your back."

He loomed over her, a true God of the Dead, a shadow darkening her vision.

She hated feeling like he was the enemy. She turned her head so he couldn't see the tears threatening, her fingers curled into fists. Thorns sprouted from the Earth, but Hades vanished before they had a chance to entangle him. She rolled onto her hands and knees and found him across the clearing.

"Your hand gave away your intentions. Summon your magic with your mind—without movement."

"I thought you said you would teach me," she said, her voice quivering.

"I am teaching you," he said. "This is what will become of you if you face a god in battle. You must be prepared for anything, for everything."

Persephone stared down at her hands. They were bloodied and dirty, and she had only been training five minutes, but in that time, Hades had succeeded in illustrating just how ill equipped she was to handle any kind of battle. She remembered Hecate's speech—*Mark my words, Persephone. You will become one of the most powerful goddesses of our time.* She laughed humorlessly. How was she supposed to become that powerful, that controlled when faced with gods who had spent lifetimes honing their power?

Except that she had possessed such power. In the Forest of Despair. She had used Hades's power against him, and it had felt cruel and agonizing, and it tasted like sorrow— bitter and acrid.

"Up, Persephone. No other god would have waited."

I will coax the darkness from you he'd whispered before he had explored her body for the first time, and right now, those words dug into her, unraveling threads of darkness. She stood, shaking. Not from the battering her body had taken but from frustration, from anger.

The earth began to shake, and pieces of rock rose from the ground. In response, Hades's magic surrounded her—an army of smoke and shadow. It should feel wrong, contrary to her own magic, but Hades had never been the enemy.

Except right now, she reminded herself. *Right now, he is.*

As the rock and pieces of earth rose, Hades's shadows did too, barreling toward her. She watched them, focused on them, forced them to slow, and held out her hand—not to stop the magic but to harness it. The magic seeped into her skin. It was a strange feeling, tangible, as it twined with her blood, and when she opened her hand, black claws protruded from the tips of her fingers.

Hades smiled.

"Good," he said.

And then Persephone hit her knees.

Her chest felt as though it had imploded—all her breath stolen by whatever invisible force had hit her. As she struck the ground, every fear she'd possessed over her short life was suddenly clawing its way from her throat.

All of a sudden, Demeter stood before her.

"Mother—"

She yanked Persephone up by her wrist. It was still sore from her fall earlier, and the jerk sent a sharper pain through her.

Crying out, Demeter laughed.

"Kore," she said, and Persephone winced at the name. "I knew this day would come."

Persephone struggled to free herself, to grasp her power, but it would not rise to her call.

"You will be mine. Forever."

"But the Fates—"

"Have unraveled your destiny," Demeter said and teleported. The smell of Demeter's magic made Persephone want to vomit. She manifested inside the walls of a glass box.

Outside was Demeter. Persephone charged the glass, hitting and kicking, screaming at the top of her lungs.

"I hate you! I hate you!"

"Perhaps now," Demeter said. "But in a millennium, you will have only me. Enjoy watching your world die."

Everything went dark, and suddenly, Persephone was surrounded by images. All around her were screens upon which the lives of her friends and enemies played out, passing by as she remained the same within her prison. Even Lexa had a space—a stagnant image of her weather-worn headstone. She watched as the lives of Sybil, Hermes, Leuce, Apollo, and more continued without her. Sybil thrived and died, Hermes and Apollo spiraled, and Leuce returned to Hades—her lover, her true soul mate—who welcomed her to his bed. She watched as he found solace in the body of another—in Leuce, who was left, and other women she did not recognize. They came, a revolving door, and Hades emptied himself in each, breathing hard in the crooks of their necks until he was left spent and still alone.

Persephone's fingers dug into the palms of her hands; her throat bled as she screamed at him and cursed him.

You said you would burn this world for me, and yet it lives, and it thrives, and you exist within it—without me.

She took her anger out upon the walls, but even her rage wasn't strong enough to summon her power. As she stood there, watching Hades's world continue without her, she swore she would end it. She would end him.

"Persephone."

Her name—the way it was spoken, a soft, breathless whisper—drew her attention down, and she met Hades's gaze. Suddenly, the world was different, as if she had escaped her cage and now stood at the center of a burning battle-field. On the ground at her feet lay Hades, eyes glassy, the crease of his lips full of blood and spilling down his face.

Persephone fell to her knees.

"Hades." Her voice was different, strained. She brushed his hair from his face, and despite the blood, he smiled at her.

"I thought…I thought I'd never see you again."

"I'm here," she whispered.

He lifted a hand and brushed a finger along her cheek. She inhaled, closing her eyes, until his touch fell away, and when she opened them, she found that he had closed his.

"Hades!" She placed her hands upon his face, and his eyes opened into slits.

"Hmm?"

"Stay with me," she begged.

"I cannot," he said.

"What do you mean you can't?" she said. "You can heal yourself. Heal!"

His eyes were open wider now and his expression sad.

"Persephone," he said. "It's over."

"No," she said, shaking her head. She threaded her fingers through his matted hair and smoothed her hands over his chest.

Hades's hands clamped down upon hers. "Persephone, look at me," he commanded. It was the strongest his voice had sounded since she'd found him lying here. "You were my only love—my heart and my soul. My world began and ended with you, my sun, stars, and sky. I will never forget you but I will forgive you."

Tears burned her eyes and thickened in her throat.

"Forgive me?"

It was like those words made her more aware of her surroundings and the horror around her. She suddenly realized where she was and remembered the events that had preceded this—she was in the Underworld, and it burned. There was nothing left of the lush and elegant beauty Hades had created—not the gardens or the village of Asphodel, not even the palace loomed upon the horizon. In their place were fire and thorns—they were thick and spiraling, gathering debris like a needle through thread—and it was one of those branches that had pierced Hades through the stomach.

"No!"

She tried to command the branch to vanish, and when that didn't work, she tried to break it, but her hands slipped on Hades's blood.

"No, please. Hades, I didn't mean—"

"I know," he said, quiet. "I love you."

"Don't," she begged, tears streamed down her face. Her throat hurt, and her chest hurt. "You said you wouldn't leave. You *promised*."

But Hades did not move again, and Persephone's screams filled the silence as her pain manifested into darkness.

Later, she woke surrounded by the familiar scent of spice and ash, her body cradled gently against a hard chest. She opened her eyes and found herself within Hades's arms. The shock of seeing him well and unharmed made her skin feel too tight and tingly.

"You did well," he said.

His words only served to summon a fresh wave of emotion. Her lips quivered and she covered her face as she began to cry.

"It's okay," Hades said. His arms tightened around her, and his lips pressed into her hair. "I'm here."

She only sobbed harder. She worked to collect herself, to rein in her emotion, because she needed distance from him and this space where she had witnessed horror that had felt so real.

She struggled free of his grasp.

"Persephone—"

She got to her feet and turned on him. He sat on the

ground, looking much the same as when they started, completely unchanged by what had occurred, and that only served to anger her more.

"That was cruel." Her throat hurt as she spoke, rasped and ruined. "Whatever that was, it was cruel."

"It was necessary," Hades said. "You must learn—"

"You could have warned me," she said. "Do you even know what I saw?"

His jaw tightened and she knew he did.

"What if the roles had been reversed?"

His eyes went flat.

"They have been reversed," he said.

She flinched. "Was that some kind of punishment?"

"Persephone—" He tried to reach for her, but she took a step away.

"Don't." She put her hands up to stop him. "I need time. Alone."

"I don't want you to go," he said.

She didn't know what to say, so she shrugged. "I don't think it's your choice."

She vanished, but not before hearing Hades utter a low and guttural growl.

CHAPTER XXII
A Touch of Regret

Persephone appeared in a bathroom. As she landed, she went to her knees and vomited into the toilet. She wasn't there long when she heard her name.

"Persephone?" Sybil's confused voice came from nearby, and the goddess looked up to find the oracle in the doorway, a knife in hand. "Oh my gods, what happened?"

She came farther into the room, and Persephone put up her hand to stop her from approaching.

"It's okay. I'm okay," she said, heaving once again.

There were a few long seconds when she couldn't speak, and Sybil approached, drawing her tangled hair away from her face and placing a cool cloth against her forehead. When the nausea passed, Persephone sat back against the tub, her body sagging with exhaustion. Sybil took a seat nearby. Persephone had no idea what she must look like, but if her hands were any sort of indication, it must be bad. They were dirty and bruised, her nails torn and bloodied, and there was a soreness in her wrist that reminded her of her earlier fall.

"Will you tell me what happened?" Sybil asked.

"It's a long story," Persephone answered, but really, she didn't want to think about it right now, because she wasn't sure she could keep from getting sick, and she had nothing left to throw up. Just thinking of having to recall details made her stomach churn.

"I have time," Sybil said.

Movement came from the door, and for a heartbeat, Persephone thought Hades might have followed her to Sybil's, but instead she found a familiar face staring back.

"Harmonia?" Persephone asked, her brows knitting together. "What are you doing here?"

Harmonia smiled, holding Opal in her arms. "Hanging out," she said. "Are you alright?"

"I will be," Persephone replied and then looked at Sybil. "Can I...take a bath?"

"Of course," Sybil said. "I'll...get you some clothes."

Persephone waited to move until Sybil returned. She placed a set of clothes on the countertop near the sink along with a towel and washcloth.

"Thanks, Sybil," Persephone whispered.

The oracle hesitated in the doorway, frowning.

"Are you sure you're okay, Persephone?"

"I will be," she said and then smiled faintly. "Promise."

"I'll make you some tea," Sybil said before closing the door.

Persephone rose and started the faucet, letting it run hot until the steam wafted in the air and fogged the mirror. She peeled off her clothes and lowered herself into the waiting water. Completely immersed, she closed her eyes and focused on healing everything that ached—her scratched throat, bruised body, and sprained wrist. Once she felt a little more whole, she drew her knees to her chest and buried her face into her arms and sobbed until the water was cold. After, she rose, dried off, and dressed.

She found Sybil in the living room alone, a cup of

tea waiting. The oracle sat cross-legged on the couch with the television on, but Persephone didn't recognize the program, and Sybil didn't seem to be paying attention either. She had a deck of oracle cards in hand and was shuffling them.

"Where is Harmonia?" Persephone asked.

"She left," Sybil said.

"Oh," Persephone said, taking a seat beside Sybil. "I hope she didn't leave because of me."

She couldn't help feeling like she had interrupted something, though she supposed she really had. She'd come to Sybil's because it was the only place she felt she could go—and she knew it would be safe.

"Of course not," Sybil replied. "She left because Aphrodite would come looking for her."

"She is very protective of her sister," Persephone said. "I...did not know you two were friends."

"We connected shortly after we met outside your office," Sybil said.

There was a long pause; the sound of Sybil's shuffling continued a little while longer until she stopped and looked at Persephone.

"Do you want to tell me what happened?"

Persephone sat quietly before taking a sip of tea and setting it aside.

"Everything is falling apart," she whispered.

"Oh, Persephone," Sybil said. "Everything is coming together."

At her words, Persephone lay her head in Sybil's lap and cried.

———

Persephone woke later to Sybil's alarm. She'd fallen asleep on the couch without returning to the Underworld. She rose to get ready, borrowing Sybil's clothes—a pair of thick tights, a skirt, and a button-up.

"We were supposed to visit the construction site for the Halcyon Project today but had to reschedule because of the weather," Sybil said as she poured Persephone a cup of coffee.

Persephone frowned. She hoped Zeus kept his word and truly searched for Demeter. Better yet, she hoped the Olympians could convince her to cease her attack.

"It's not your fault, you know," Sybil said.

"It is," Persephone said. "I am sure you saw this coming before it even happened."

The oracle shook her head. "No, I would only be able to see what my god wanted me to see," she answered. "But you are not in control of your mother's actions."

"Then why do I feel so responsible?"

"Because she is hurting people and blaming you," Sybil said. "And she is wrong to do so."

Demeter may be wrong, but the burden was still heavy. Persephone thought of the people who had died in that terrible crash on the highway. She would never forget receiving so many souls into the Underworld at once, or how she'd watched as their dreams left them as they passed beneath the elm, or the guilt that could still cling to a soul even after they passed through the gates. She knew it would not be the last time something like that happened, though she'd prefer her mother not be responsible.

Persephone sighed and took a drink of her coffee, setting it aside as they left Sybil's apartment. They decided to walk the short distance to Alexandria Tower in the cold. Persephone considered teleporting, but part of her wanted to experience what her mother's magic was doing firsthand. She sought to feed her anger and frustration—and it worked. The walk was miserable—snow and ice hit their faces, and their feet slid on snow, compacted on the sidewalk. Ice broke apart from towering high-rises and skyscrapers, crashing to the ground with enough impact to injure or damage.

By the time they made it up the icy steps and into the tower, they were frozen.

"Good morning, my lady!" Ivy said, coming around her desk, a coffee in each hand. "Good morning, Miss Kyros."

She handed the cups to each of them.

"Ivy, are you a magician?" Persephone asked as she took a sip of coffee, letting the steam warm her nose.

"I'm always prepared, my lady," Ivy answered.

Sybil started up the stairs, and as Persephone began to follow, Ivy spoke.

"My lady, I'm not sure you've had a chance to read the papers this morning, but I think you'll want to start with *New Athens News*."

Dread settled in Persephone's stomach.

"It's not good," Ivy said as her mossy eyes met Persephone's. "I didn't think it would be."

Persephone headed upstairs to her office. After she was settled, she pulled up the news. The bold headline read:

Meet Theseus, the Demigod Leader of Triad

The article was written by Helen and began by giving an overview of Theseus—she called him a son of Poseidon, charming and well-educated. The description made Persephone feel nauseous considering she'd met the demigod and he'd made her uneasy.

The article continued:

Theseus joined Triad after witnessing several men get away with murder, despite their crimes being witnessed by mortals and divine alike.

"I still remember their names," says Theseus.

"Epidaurus, Sinis, Sciron. They were thieves and murderers, and they were allowed to continue their crime sprees despite the prayers of locals. I was tired of watching the world worship gods for their beauty and power rather than their actions."

Theseus added:

"Gods do not think in terms of good and bad—justice or injustice. I'll give you an example. Hades, God of the Underworld, allows criminals to continue breaking the law so long as they serve him."

Persephone's teeth clenched tight, her fingers digging into the screen of her tablet. While not completely untrue, Theseus's statement was misleading. Persephone had learned upon her first visit to Iniquity that Hades was heavily involved in the criminal underworld of New Greece. He had a network of criminals at his beck and call, and they all paid a debt to continue their business in the form of a charity. Persephone did not know the extent of Hades's reach, but from what little she knew, he ruled it.

Persephone read on:

Soon, Theseus, the son of an Olympian, found himself leading Triad down a new path—a peaceful path.

"I was horrified at the early history of Triad. The bombs and the shootings. It was barbaric. Besides, why not let the gods speak for themselves? I knew it wouldn't take long for one—or many—to execute their wrath upon the world. I was right."

In a fit of anger, Persephone threw her tablet. It landed with a crash against the wall and then shattered on the floor.

There was silence and then the door opened. Leuce poked her head in.

"Are you okay?"

As the nymph entered, the door hit the tablet she'd thrown. Leuce paused, staring down at it, and then picked it up.

"Helen make you angry?" she asked.

"It's intentional," Persephone said. "She is antagonizing me just as Triad attempts to antagonize the gods."

"You aren't wrong," Leuce said, setting the broken tablet on Persephone's desk. "Helen does not even know what she believes—she is merely a follower. Somehow, she thought that path lay with Theseus. I have no doubt she will come to regret that decision."

She would—Persephone would see to that.

"Shall I order you a new tablet?"

"Please," Persephone said.

"Of course."

Leuce left, and as she closed the door behind her, Hades appeared in front of it, manifesting in coils of dark smoke. He was exhausted, his face drawn with shadows that told her he had not slept last night. A pang of guilt hit her square in the chest. He'd probably stayed up agonizing over his actions and her words.

"Do you need something?" she asked.

Hades reached behind him and turned the lock into place.

"We need to talk," he said.

Persephone pushed away from her desk but remained seated.

"Talk," she said.

He approached, massive frame practically filling the room, body rigid, and she thought he must be angry with her, which made her frustrated. It was he who had taken their training too far, and yet even she realized the value of what Hades had been teaching—no other god would have been merciful.

Hades knelt before her and his hands spread out over her knees.

"I am sorry," he said, holding her gaze. "I went too far."

Persephone swallowed and looked away. It was hard to hold his gaze given that all she could recall right now was how he'd looked in death.

"You never told me you had the power to summon fears," she said, her voice quiet.

"Was there ever a time to speak of it?"

There wasn't—she knew that. Still, it was part of her desire to know everything about him—the powers he possessed, the charities he maintained, the deals he made.

When she didn't respond, Hades spoke. "If you will let me, I'd like to train you differently," he said. "I'll leave the magic to Hecate, and instead I will help you study the powers of the gods."

Persephone's brows rose. "You would do that?"

"I would do anything if it meant protecting you," he said. "And since you will not agree to being locked away in the Underworld, this is the alternative."

She smiled at him.

"I'm sorry I left," she said.

"I do not blame you," he said. "It is not very different from what I did when I took you to Lampri. Sometimes, it's very hard to exist in the place where you experience terror."

Persephone swallowed hard. That was exactly what it had been, and it had all felt so real.

"Are you angry with me?" Hades whispered.

Persephone looked at him again. "No. I know what you were trying to do."

"I would like to tell you that I will protect you from everyone and everything," he said. "And I would. I would keep you safe forever within the walls of my realm, but I know what you wish is to protect yourself."

She nodded, and within his gaze, she saw the conflict of his soul. He would have to let her hurt so that she could be powerful.

"Thank you," she whispered.

He smiled faintly, and then her eyes shifted to the copy of *New Athens News* on her desk, darkening.

"I assume you have already read this," she said.

"Ilias sent it this morning," Hades said. "Theseus is playing with fire and he knows it."

"Do you think Zeus will act?"

Last time Zeus had spoken out against Triad, many Faithful mortals had organized to hunt down its members. The problem was, not every person who identified as Impious was a member of Triad. Still, they were slain.

"I do not know," he admitted. "I do not think my brother sees Triad as a threat. He does, however, see your mother's association as dangerous, which is why he shifted his focus to her."

"What will become of her if Zeus can find her?"

"If she ceases her attack upon the Upperworld? Probably nothing."

Again, she heard Demeter's voice.

Consequences for gods? No, Daughter, there are none.

"You mean she will get away with the murder of Tyche?"

Hades did not speak.

"She must be punished, Hades."

"She will be," he replied. "Eventually."

"Not only in Tartarus, Hades."

"In time, Persephone," Hades said gently, and his touch shifted from her knees to her hands, which she had curled into tight fists. "No one—not the gods, certainly not me—will keep you from retribution."

There was silence, and then Hades rose.

"Come," he said, slipping his fingers between hers and drawing her to her feet.

Her brows drew together. "Where are we going?"

"I just wanted to kiss you," he said, bringing his mouth to hers. His magic surfaced, and she felt the familiar pull of teleportation. When they drew apart, they stood in the middle of a clearing in the Upperworld. It was covered in snow and surrounded by thick trees, bent with ice. Still, it was beautiful. When she turned, she found a building—Halcyon. It was still under construction, just a skeleton of the structure it would become, but it was clear it would be magnificent.

"Oh," Persephone breathed.

"I cannot wait for you to see it in the spring," he said. "You will love the gardens."

"I love it all," she said. "I love it now."

She looked at Hades then, at the snow in his hair and on his lashes.

"I love you."

Hades kissed her before guiding her through the labyrinth that would be Halcyon. The walls were up, the drywall in place. He named each room as if he knew the layout by heart—reception and dining, community and residents' rooms, and spaces for various types of therapy. Finally, they came to a space on the top floor after climbing several sets of stairs. It was a large room that overlooked the garden that would be dedicated to Lexa. In the distance, all the way around the room, Persephone could see the misty skyline of New Athens.

It was breathtaking.

"What room is this?" she asked.

"Your office," Hades said.

"Mine? But I—"

"I have an office at every business I own. Why shouldn't you?" he said. "And even if you do not work here often, we'll put it to use."

Persephone laughed, and Hades smiled in return. They stared at one another for a moment. There was a tension between them she wanted to mend. It did not come from their anger or their distance but from something far more primal. She felt it within her—a pull tied so deep, it made her bones ache.

She shivered.

"We should return," Hades said.

Still neither of them moved.

"Hades," Persephone whispered his name, an invitation. In the next second, their mouths collided. Hades pressed into her, his erection hard between her hips as she hit the wall. His hands curled around her wrists as he pinned them beside her head.

"I need you," he breathed, kissing down her jaw and neck. His hands moved, fingers pressing firmly into her ass, bunching her skirt. Persephone's breath came fast, fingers fumbling for the buttons of his shirt. She wanted to feel the heat of his skin against hers.

"Stop that!"

Apollo appeared only a few feet away. He looked annoyed, as if he were the one who was interrupted. He was dressed casually, in jeans and a white tunic-style shirt that had a laced V-neck. His curls were unruly and fell playfully against his forehead.

"Go away, Apollo," Hades growled, still working his way down Persephone's neck to her collarbone.

"Hades." Her fingers tightened around the lapels of his jacket.

"No can do, Lord of the Underworld," Apollo said. "We have an event."

Hades sighed—which sounded more like a growl—and pried himself from Persephone. She worked to catch her breath and straightened her skirt and blouse.

"What do you mean we have an event?" she asked.

"Today's the first of the Panhellenic Games," he said.

She'd completely forgotten about the games. The chariot races were tonight.

"That isn't until tonight," she argued.

"So? I need you now."

"For what?"

"Does it matter?" he asked. "We have a—"

"Don't," Hades snapped, and Apollo shut his mouth. "She asked you a question, Apollo. Answer it."

Persephone looked at Hades, surprised by his comment.

The god narrowed his violet eyes, crossing his arms over his chest. "I fucked up. I need your help," he admitted, glaring away from them.

"You needed help and yet you wish to command it from her?"

"Hades—"

"He demands your attention, Persephone, and has your friendship only because of a bargain, and when you needed him before all those Olympians, he was silent."

"That's enough, Hades," Persephone said.

She did not fault Apollo for not speaking up at Council—what was there to say?

"Apollo is my friend, bargain or not. I will speak to him about what bothers me."

Hades stared at her for a moment and then kissed her again—deeply and far longer than appropriate with an audience. When he pulled away, he said, "I will join you at the games later."

When he vanished, she turned to Apollo.

"He really doesn't like you."

He rolled his eyes.

"That's nothing new. Come on. I need a drink."

CHAPTER XXIII
A Lover's Quarrel

"Vodka?" Apollo asked as he poured himself a glass. **He** stood on the other side of the island in his pristine kitchen. Persephone had only been to Apollo's penthouse once, when she was helping Sybil move. It was a modern space with large windows and a monochrome color scheme. If she didn't know how regimented Apollo was, she'd assume no one lived here, but the god was known for discipline, and that extended to his surroundings. He kept everything perfectly organized and clean—even his stainless-steel appliances were unmarred, a feat that deserved an award.

"It's ten in the morning, Apollo," Persephone pointed out, sitting at the breakfast bar opposite him.

"Your point?"

She sighed. "No, Apollo. I don't want vodka."

He shrugged.

"Suit yourself," he said, downing the glass.

"You're an alcoholic."

"Hades is an alcoholic," Apollo said.

He wasn't wrong.

"So you need my advice?" Persephone asked, changing the subject.

Apollo poured another drink and consumed it. She watched him, waiting, noting how much he looked like Hermes in this moment. It was in the set of his jaw and the puckering of his brows—they could not deny their shared blood.

"I fucked up," he admitted at last.

"I figured," she said mildly, maintaining his gaze even as he narrowed his violet eyes in annoyance.

"Rude," he shot back.

Persephone sighed. "Apollo, just tell me what happened." She knew he was stalling, and she wanted him to spit it out before he polished off that bottle of vodka, not that it would faze him much. She just wanted him to hurry this along before she decided *she* needed a drink.

"I kissed Hector."

Persephone blinked, a little shocked by his admission. "I thought you liked Ajax."

"How did you know about Ajax?"

"At the palaestra, you kept looking at him," she said. She didn't mention that he had smelled different when he'd come to Aphrodite's. Some other scent had been mixed into his magic, and she'd recognized it as Ajax's when he'd helped her in the field.

Apollo frowned.

"Why did you kiss Hector?"

He scrubbed his face with his hands. "I don't know," he moaned. "I was angry with Ajax, and Hector was there, and I thought…why not…*see* what this is about…and then Ajax walked in."

"Oh, Apollo."

She could see his misery—it was so blatant within his gaze, it hurt her heart.

"I don't even know why I care. I swore I would never do this again."

"Do what again?"

"This! *Love!*"

Suddenly she understood. Apollo was referring to Hyacinth, the Spartan prince he'd fallen for ages ago. The mortal had died in a horrible accident. Later, Apollo went to Hades and begged the God of the Dead to throw him in Tartarus so that he would not have to live in a world without his love, but Hades refused, and Apollo sought revenge in the arms of Leuce.

"Apollo…"

"Don't…pity me."

"I'm not. I don't," she said. "But Hyacinth's death wasn't your fault."

"Yes, it was," he said. "I was not the only god who loved Hyacinth, and when he chose me, Zephyrus, the God of the West Wind, grew jealous. It was his wind that changed the trajectory of my throw, his wind that resulted in the death of Hyacinth."

"Then his death is Zephyrus's fault," Persephone said.

Apollo shook his head. "You do not understand. Even now, I see it happening with Ajax. Hector grows jealous every day. The fight he picked with Ajax at the palaestra was not the first."

"What if Ajax likes you?" Persephone asked. "What if he's willing to fight for you? Will you decide not to pursue him out of fear?"

"It is not *fear*—" Apollo started and then looked away angrily.

"Then what is it?"

"I don't want to fuck this up. I'm not…a *good* person now. What happens when I lose again? Do I become…evil then?"

"Apollo," Persephone said as gently as she could. "If you

are worried that you will become evil, then you have more humanity than you think."

He gave her a look that begged to differ.

"You should talk to Ajax," she said, and though she offered the advice, she knew how hard it was to communicate. It had been her greatest challenge when it came to her relationship with Hades. In part, she blamed her mother. Over the years, Persephone had become accustomed to staying quiet, even when she had an opinion or a desire, fearing the consequences, namely her mother's scorn. Hades was the first person who welcomed her insight, and she had to admit, it was still hard to believe that he actually wanted to know what she thought.

"He doesn't *want* me."

"You don't know that."

"I do because he said so!"

Persephone just stared at the god. A deep frown pulled at his mouth, and his eyes held a pain she could only compare to what she'd felt when she'd been in the Forest of Despair.

"What exactly did he say?" she asked.

He sighed, clearly frustrated. "We were kissing, and everything was great, and then he pushed me away and said...*I can't do this* and left."

Persephone lifted a brow—he was definitely leaving something out.

"You're *sure* that's what he said?"

"Yes," Apollo hissed. "He might be deaf, but he can definitely speak, Persephone."

"That doesn't mean he doesn't want you," Persephone said.

"What else is it supposed to mean?"

"You were supposed to...*I don't know*...chase him!"

"The last time I chased someone, they begged to be turned into a tree."

"This is different!" Persephone said, frustrated. She paused a moment and then sighed. "Did Ajax kiss you back?"

A pink tint made its way to Apollo's cheeks, and Persephone had to bite her cheek to keep from giggling. It was strange to see the egotistical God of Music embarrassed.

"Yes, he kissed me back, which is why I don't understand...how...how could he not want me?"

"He didn't say he didn't want you. He said he couldn't do this, which could have meant anything. It could have meant he couldn't do this right now. You don't know until you ask."

"Well, now I can't ask because I kissed Hector."

"That's exactly why you need to talk to him!" Persephone argued. "Would you have Ajax think you do not care for him?"

"Why should I care what he thinks?"

She recognized his response as a defense mechanism—anytime something didn't go his way, he immediately decided it wasn't worth his time or energy.

"Apollo, you are an idiot."

He glared. "You're supposed to be my friend."

"If you're looking for someone to praise your every decision, turn to your worshippers. Friends tell you the truth."

He didn't look at her, choosing instead to glare at the wall, so she continued.

"Talk to Ajax, Apollo, and Hector."

"Hector? *Why*?"

"Because you owe him an explanation too," she said. "You kissed him, which means now he has reason to believe there's more between you than before."

The god frowned, and after a moment, he mumbled, "I said I'd never do this again."

"You cannot help how you feel."

"I *knew* better," he argued. "I am not *good* for anyone, Seph."

She sat there, shaking her head, feeling defeated for him.

"Hyacinth didn't think that," she said, her voice quiet. "I'm betting Ajax doesn't either."

The God of Music scoffed. "What do you know? You're only here because of a bargain, and you're only in that bargain because you refused to communicate with Hades."

Persephone's lips flattened, and her chest ached at Apollo's words. She knew that well enough. She was reminded of it often—every time she wanted to call and talk to Lexa or go to lunch with her best friend, every time she entered Elysium. She managed to blink enough to keep her tears at bay and cleared her throat.

"A decision I will regret for the rest of my life."

She gave no clarification before she vanished from Apollo's sight.

CHAPTER XXIV
The Chariot Races

Persephone arrived at Talaria Stadium with Sybil, Leuce, and Zofie. From the outside, the arena looked more like a marble building with stacked columns and archways of reflective windows. On a normal August day, they would mirror the beauty of the setting sun. Instead, they were packed with ice. Despite the weather, people were everywhere, making their way through the snow toward one of many entrances around the stadium.

"It says here there are eight heroes competing," said Leuce, looking at her phone. The glow made her white eyes spark. "Three women and five men."

"There should be more women," Zofie said, who sat beside Leuce and still towered over them. "We handle pain far better."

They laughed.

"Does Hades have a hero in the games, Persephone?" Sybil asked. Her hair was pulled back into a curled ponytail, and she'd changed into something a little less formal after work, now sporting jeans and a pink New Athens University hoodie.

"Not that I'm aware," Persephone said. Hades had never

chosen a hero—not in the games and not in battle—though he had resurrected them.

"Chariot races were never my favorite," Leuce said, wrinkling her nose. She was probably recalling something from her life in the ancient world.

"Why?" Persephone asked.

"Because they're bloody. Why do you think they begin the games with them?"

"To weed out competitors," Zofie said, a menacing gleam in her eyes.

That filled Persephone with a sense of dread, and she worried for the competitors, in particular Ajax. She knew he was skilled, but if anything happened to him, Apollo would be devastated.

"Do not worry," Sybil said. "They train for this."

"Training means nothing when it comes to animals," said Zofie.

Antoni pulled around to the back of the stadium and parked at a private entrance where only a handful of people lingered. They left the comfort of the limo and stepped into the chill evening. Persephone had chosen to wear a white dress, a black blazer, and thick black stockings. Still, the wind cut through them. Once inside, they were led into an elevator, to the top floor, where they were taken to a private suite. It was a modern, monochrome space with a bar, black leather couches, and large televisions on display in every corner of the room, playing footage from previous games and interviews with heroes. A platform of seats were positioned near a large floor-to-ceiling window that overlooked the arena, which looked exactly like the practice area at the Palaestra of Delphi.

"This is nice," said Leuce, approaching the windows.

"Can we not sit closer?" Zofie asked.

"I do not wish to eat dirt, Zofie," said Leuce. "Or die. Have you not seen how those chariots crash?"

Persephone's eyes shifted to Sybil, wondering if she would be comfortable here given that the space was so reminiscent of Apollo, but the oracle smiled.

"I am well, Persephone," she said.

The four ordered drinks from the bar.

"Whiskey, please," Persephone said. "Neat."

"*Whiskey*?" Leuce asked, raising a brow. "Aren't you a wino?"

Persephone shrugged. "I tried some of Hades's whiskey the other night and I liked it."

Their orders came, and Persephone sipped her drink, enjoying the flavor and the smell, and it made her wish Hades was here already.

"Sephy!"

She spun, finding Hermes approaching, dressed in a white blazer, slacks, and a light blue shirt. He looked comfortable and handsome.

"Hermes! I did not know you would be in this suite!"

"Looks like it's you, me, some Olympians, and any playthings they choose to bring," he said, and Persephone's eyes widened. "You're sharing, Sephy!"

She almost groaned. The last thing she wanted to do was be in the same room with Zeus, Poseidon, Hera, and Ares. Suddenly, Zofie's idea of sitting on the frontlines, despite its dangers, sounded like the better option.

Persephone took a bigger drink.

Soon, gods began to arrive with their favored in tow, and the room grew warm and fragrant with magic. The first to arrive was Artemis—beautiful and athletic, she wore a short dress and her hair slicked back into a tight, straight ponytail. As she entered, she halted, frowning at Hermes and then at Persephone.

"It's you," she said.

"She has a name, Artemis," said Hermes. "Play nice."

"I am playing nice," she said, but her approach was predatory. "I find you intriguing, goddess."

"*Persephone*," Hermes said. "Her name is Persephone."

"Still determined to marry Hades and let the world die?" Artemis asked.

Persephone cocked her head to the side and asked, "Aren't you the Goddess of the Hunt?"

Artemis lifted her chin. "What does that have to do with anything?"

"I would think you could use your exceptional tracking abilities to locate my mother instead of insulting me."

Artemis's lips flattened. "You have an insufferable mouth, goddess."

Persephone's lips curled. "I think that is the only thing you and Hades would agree on."

Artemis rolled her eyes and stalked away.

"Ignore her," said Hermes. "She has a stick up her vagina."

Persephone looked at the god. "It's ass, Hermes. Stick up her ass."

He shrugged. "They're close."

She tried not to laugh.

More people arrived. Zeus came with Hera and Poseidon with a beautiful ocean nymph who sported blue hair. Hades's brothers smiled at her, but only Zeus spoke. He made her uncomfortable, and she found herself tensing at his approach.

"You look well, Lady Persephone."

"Thank you," she said, though the words felt awkward and insincere.

"I trust Hades will be along shortly," he said.

"Yes. We look forward to an update on your progress toward finding my mother and ending the storm," she said.

Zeus's face hardened, and then he gave a curt nod. "Of course."

As he walked away, she got the impression he had not

thought twice about the mortals on Earth while he lounged upon Olympus.

Aphrodite and Harmonia arrived a while later. It was Harmonia Persephone noticed first, as the goddess made a straight path toward their group, smiling as she stood close to Sybil.

"It's good to see you, Harmonia. How are you?"

"I am well," she said and smiled. "I'm sorry I had to leave…"

She let her voice trail away as Aphrodite joined them.

"Persephone," she said and nodded to the others. "Everyone…else."

There was a beat of silence that followed her approach. Usually, Persephone was quick to begin a conversation, but all she could think of was what Aphrodite had looked like in the basement of Club Aphrodisia—bloodied, holding a demi-god's heart in her hand. She wondered how the goddess had found out about the rally. Was she satisfied with the blood-shed? They were questions that would have to wait, as a loud burst of music and cheers interrupted their mingling.

"Oh, the games are starting!" Zofie said.

They took their seats, and Persephone was relieved when Hermes dropped into the one to her right—Sybil was on the left. They watched as the opening ceremony began below. The first announcement was for Apollo—the chancellor of the games—who was carried out upon a litter—or an open chair—which was hoisted by four very strong men with oiled and bare chests. They wore white tunics, gold cuffs, and laurel leaves in their hair—the same outfit Apollo sported. He grinned and waved at the crowd, no sign of his agony present. He was followed by a group of women who danced and threw petals upon the ground.

They made a lap around the field and then returned to the stadium.

"Will Apollo sit with us?" Persephone asked.

"No, he has his own box," Hermes said.

After, the gods' heroes marched into the center of the field below as they and their sponsoring god were announced. She recognized several who had trained at the palaestra, including Hector and Ajax.

"Do you have a hero in the games?" she asked Hermes.

"I do," he said. "Third from the left. His name is Aesop."

Persephone found him in the lineup—a strong yet lean man with sandy blond hair.

"You don't seem particularly excited," Persephone pointed out.

He shrugged. "He has gifts, but he is not strong like Ajax or forceful like Hector. Those two are the real competition."

There were others too—Damon, who belonged to Aphrodite, and Castor, who belonged to Hera. Anastasia to Ares, Demi to Artemis, and Cynisca to Athena. As they marched onto the field, they flexed their muscles in a posing routine that made the crowd cheer louder.

"Ladies and gentlemen, gods and goddesses, Royal Divine among us—give another round of applause for our New Greece heroes!"

Persephone leaned toward Hermes and spoke over the roar of the crowd.

"You said Hector was forceful," Persephone said. "What does that mean?"

"You'll see."

At the sound of a trumpet, she sat forward, and eight chariots emerged from the shadows of the stadium, each drawn by four powerful horses. They were mighty steeds, their coats silken and of varying colors. Their hooves pounded the earth as they converged upon the track, sending up dust and clumps of dirt as their handlers—the heroes—urged them on.

"How does this work?" she asked Hermes, her heart already racing from the thrill.

"The charioteers must make twelve laps around the hippodrome. They will keep count there," he said, pointing to a mechanical system at the center of the arena—a series of dolphin statues that would nose-dive once the first lap had been conquered.

"Why do they use such an ancient form of score-keeping?" she asked.

He shrugged. "We pick and choose what we wish to keep from antiquity, Sephy. Haven't you noticed?"

While they spoke, her eyes remained on the field, watching the race—a battle between beast and man to be the first to the turning post. There was so much dust, so much speed, so much power, it had to be dangerous.

Just as that thought crossed Persephone's mind, one of the chariots flipped.

Her shocked inhale caught in her throat as the chariot landed and shattered, the broken body of Castor crushed beneath, but what made her blood run colder still was the laugh that escaped both Zeus and Poseidon at the mortal's immediate death.

"No victory for you, eh, Hera?" Zeus taunted.

Persephone glanced at Hermes, who quickly reached for her hand and squeezed.

"It is a game to them, Sephy."

She bit her lip hard, recalling why Triad protested the games—this was what they objected to. There was more movement on the field as a group of people ran onto the track to remove the debris from the broken chariot, wrangle the horses, and carry away the body.

"Why aren't they stopping?" Persephone asked. "That man…Castor…he's dead."

"It is the nature of the game," Hermes said.

Not long after the first accident, there was another.

Two chariots collided in a tangle of horses and reins. Aesop was thrown from his chariot while Demi's leg was crushed beneath hers—her screams reached them from the floor. Still, they were both alive.

Persephone was torn between continuing to watch and fleeing this place entirely, but she stayed because Ajax was still in the race and in the lead—beside Hector. The wheels of their two chariots were inches from one another, their horses charging on. Of the two, Hector seemed the most desperate, urging his steeds on with the use of his whip— lashing over and over until he used it on Ajax.

"He can't do that." Persephone leaned forward, looking to Hermes. "Can he?"

The God of Mischief shrugged. "There aren't really rules. Is it fair? No."

She suddenly understood what Hermes meant when he'd described Hector as forceful.

Her attention returned to the track.

Hector continued to lash Ajax until he managed to latch on to the whip and jerk it from Hector's grasp—but Hector's cheating came with a price, as his chariot strayed too close to the wall, hitting with such force, it broke into pieces and sent him flying. Persephone did not even see where the mortal landed. She was too focused on Apollo, who had appeared on the field just as Ajax finished his final lap, winning the race.

Ajax drew his chariot to a stop, his wide smile on display for the crowd. As he dismounted, Apollo approached and hesitantly reached out, touching the mortal's bloodied face where the whip had split his skin. Then, all of a sudden, the two kissed. Ajax cradled Apollo's face between his hands, his mouth devouring, his body overpowering. Their display of affection was met with cheers—even from Hermes.

"Yes! Get it, Brother!"

Persephone tried not to laugh.

When the crowd began to boo, Apollo spun to find Hector rising from the dust, cradling his arm against his chest. He spat blood, a gush of crimson coming from his nose and mouth, hatred gleaming in his eyes.

It was then Persephone noticed something strange—a group of spectators breaking from their place among the crowd and making their way down the stadium steps.

"Hermes...who are those people?"

Just as she posed the question, Ajax seemed to take note, and in the next second, he was drawing Apollo behind him as shots rang out and screams filled the air.

"Get down!" Sybil shouted, but Persephone could only watch the horror as Ajax pushed Apollo to the ground, taking bullet after bullet.

"No!" Persephone's scream was raw and painful, scraping against her throat as she stood and slammed on the window.

"Persephone!" Hermes reached for her. "We have to go!"

Apollo screamed beneath Ajax's convulsing body. Finally, he managed to roll, and the bullets that raced toward them stopped midair, dropping to the ground.

"There are others here who will fight," Hermes argued. "But not you."

Hermes had his hand wrapped around her upper arm as he dragged her away from the window. Then, there was a terrible sound—a cracking that sounded like Zeus's magic escaping from the clouds—except it wasn't. Part of the stadium had exploded.

"Get the mortals out!" someone commanded, and there was a sudden rush of magic. Persephone watched as Harmonia vanished with Sybil and Leuce. Zofie stood, hand outstretched toward Persephone.

"Go!" Hermes pushed her toward the Amazon.

Then there was another deafening explosion, and

Persephone found herself floating through the air, landing hard at the center of the track amid flying debris and dust. As she hit, there was a sharp pain in her ribs, and it felt as though her breath had been sucked out of her body. She rolled onto her back, gasping for air, just as a shadow loomed overhead.

A mortal man holding a rock aloft.

Persephone screamed, her magic stirring, and from the ground, great thorns rose, piercing the man. He dropped the stone, run through with the vine, blood dripping from his mouth.

She rolled and crawled away, getting to her feet amid the chaos of desperate screams and death. People lay motionless while others climbed over the bodies to escape the ruined arena. There were hundreds of these masked attackers, and even as the gods descended, they continued to take aim. She did not understand this but knew it for what it was—hate.

Magic ignited the air in a stream of bright light— lightning bolts struck, and energy pulsed. Artemis unleashed a spray of deadly arrows while Athena ran others through with a spear and Ares with a sword. Zofie fought too, having landed across the arena. A streak of blood ran from her head down her face, but her blade was drawn, and she was nimble, quick, and dangerous.

It was bloodshed. It was a battle.

"Persephone!" Her name tore from Apollo's mouth. She whirled, but it was too late. A bullet struck her shoulder.

"No!" Apollo's eyes glowed as he ran toward her.

She staggered a couple of steps, shocked, the left side of her body numb. She managed to look down, and as she saw the blood seeping into the white fabric of her dress, she began to fall, but before she could land in the dirt, strong arms surrounded her. The catch jarred her, and she gave a guttural cry.

"I've got you," Hades said. She stared into his dark, stormy eyes for only a second before he teleported.

CHAPTER XXV
Monsters

When they appeared in the Underworld, within the walls of Hades's bedchamber, a hot pain settled deep in her bones, radiating from her shoulder. Persephone moaned, forcing herself to breathe through the pain as Hades settled her upon the bed. He started to ease her arm out of her blazer and then tore her dress for access to the wound, and as his fingers brushed it, she inhaled sharply between her teeth.

"Wh-what are you doing?" she said between her teeth.

"I need to see if the bullet left your body," Hades said.

"Let me heal it."

"Persephone—"

"I have to try," she snapped. "Hades—"

He curled his hands into fists and stepped back, rubbing his forehead with bloodied fingers.

"Do it, Persephone," he growled.

She closed her eyes against his frustration, knowing that his panic was winning. He'd never wanted to see her bleed again, and here they were. She drew in deep breath after deep breath until a calmness overtook her and she was able to focus on the fiery pain emanating from her wounded shoulder. This time, she just wanted the heat to end, so she imagined that the magic she used to soothe it was cool and crisp—a kiss of frost in early spring.

"*Now*," she heard Hades's low growl.

But Persephone knew her magic was working—the wound throbbed as it healed.

Finally, Hades let out a low breath and Persephone opened her eyes, staring down at her exposed shoulder to see that the skin was slightly pink and puckered, but the wound was healed.

"I did it," she said and smiled as she looked at Hades.

"You did," he said, his eyes moving from her wound to her gaze, and she got the sense that he didn't quite believe her.

"What are you thinking?" she asked, her voice quiet.

"Nothing you wish to know," he said.

She believed it.

Finally, he approached.

"Let's clean you up."

Once again, Hades gathered her to his chest and took her into the bathroom. When her feet touched the floor, she reached to brush loose tendrils of hair from Hades's face. Her blood was still smeared on his skin.

"Are you well?"

Instead of answering, he turned on the shower, letting the water grow hot.

He took her hand and kissed her palm before reaching behind her and unzipping her ruined dress, guiding it down over her breasts and hips until it puddled on the floor. Her bra followed, his touch lingering on her breasts, then her waist, then her thighs as he slid her panties down her legs, pausing as he knelt on the floor to gaze up at her.

"Hades," she whispered his name, and then his lips touched her skin as he kissed a fiery path back up her body.

Her hands tangled into his hair as he paused to tease each of her nipples before his mouth devoured hers.

When her fingers tangled into his jacket, she pulled away.

"Shall I undress you?" she asked, eager to have his skin against hers.

"If you wish," he said.

She reached for the buttons on his shirt, but a sharp pain in her shoulder made her wince and she dropped her arm. Hades frowned.

"Let me," he said, making quick work of the buttons, shedding his jacket, shirt, and slacks. When he was naked, he gripped her sides and drew her to him, his arms wrapping tightly around her. His mouth slanted against hers and she opened for him. The feel of him inside her in any way was like injecting magic into her veins—it made her feel wild and passionate. Except that soon, she felt real magic— healing magic—as Hades's palm came to rest upon her.

She broke the kiss and looked down at her shoulder. Where she had left a scar, there was now smooth skin.

"Was I not good enough?" she asked.

It wasn't exactly the question she intended to ask, and she knew once the words were out of her mouth that they hurt Hades, but it was all she could think to say, because this kind of magic was important to her and she wanted to master it.

"Of course you are good enough, Persephone," Hades said, and he brought his hands to her jaw, sliding his fingers into her hair. "I am overprotective and fearful for you, and perhaps selfishly, I wish to remove anything that reminds me of my failure to protect you."

"Hades, you did not fail," she said.

"We will agree to disagree," he said.

"If I am enough, then you are enough."

He did not speak, and she moved her hands up his chest, twining her arms around his neck.

"I am sorry. I never wanted to see you suffer again, not like you did in the days following Tyche's death."

"You have nothing to be sorry for," he said and kissed her.

This time, he guided her into the shower. They stood outside the spray as he reached for the soap and wet a cloth. He started with her shoulder, gently washing the blood away. He moved to her breasts, groping and squeezing, his slick hands teasing each one before moving on to her stomach and sides, her thighs and her calves. On his knees before her, he gave an order.

"Turn."

She obeyed the command, placing her hands flat on the wall as he made his way back up her body. He spent time washing between her thighs, fingers teasing her flesh. By the time he rose to his feet, she was flustered, and though his erection swelled between them, he did not move to take her. Instead, he stared at her intently and said, "I love you."

"I love you too," she said, and there was something in this moment, in the exchange of words that brought tears to her eyes. "More than anything."

They weren't powerful enough words, but she couldn't find the ones she needed, the ones she wanted. The ones that conveyed just how much her blood and bone, heart and soul ached for him.

"Persephone," Hades whispered her name, brushing a stray tear from her face. He gathered her into his arms and carried her out of the shower. They were not even dry as he settled beside the fire. Cradled against his chest, they sat in silence as the events of the evening rushed back into their reality.

Talaria Stadium had been the perfect space for an attack. The distraction of the chariot races, the added drama between Apollo, Ajax, and Hector. No one suspected a thing.

"All those people," she whispered. "Gone."

She wondered how many had died, then the guilt settled upon her as she realized she should have been at the gates to greet them, to calm them.

Hades's arms tightened around her. "You will not be able to console everyone who makes their way to the gates unexpectedly, Persephone. Those deaths are far too numerous. Take comfort. The souls of Asphodel are there, and they will represent you well."

"They represent you too, Hades," she said.

Then she considered something—the innocent weren't the only ones to die tonight. Among them were those who had started the violence.

"What about the attackers who died tonight?"

She met Hades's gaze. She couldn't tell what he was thinking, but he answered her question without hesitating.

"They await punishment in Tartarus." He paused, then asked, "Do you wish to go?"

A smile tugged at her lips. It wasn't in anticipation but in response to his question. Weeks ago, he would have never suggested a trip to the chamber of torture he used to punish souls, and yet now, he did so without faltering.

"Yes," she answered. "I wish to go."

————

They arrived in a part of Tartarus Persephone had never visited before. It was a cavernous hall, each side of it flanked with massive obsidian columns. It took her a moment to realize that each set of columns was blocked by a gate. They were in a dungeon. The air here was thick, heavy with an ancient power. She tipped her head back, searching for the source of the magic.

"There are monsters here," said Hades, as if to explain.

"What...kind of monsters?" she asked.

"Many," he said, looking slightly amused. "Some are

here because they were slain. Some are here because they were captured. Come."

He took her hand and led her past many darkened cells. As they went, she heard hissing and growls and a horrible wailing. Persephone looked to Hades for an explanation.

"The harpies," Hades said. "Aello, Ocypete, and Celaeno—they get restless, especially when the world is chaos."

"Why?"

"Because they sense evil and wish to punish," he said.

They passed many more, including a creature who was half woman, half snake. Graceful fingers wrapped tight around the bars of her cell as her head came into view. She was beautiful; her hair was long and fell over her shoulders in red waves, curtaining her bare breasts.

"Hades," she hissed, her slitted eyes gleaming.

"Lamia," he said in acknowledgment.

"Lamia?" Persephone asked. "The child killer?"

The monster hissed at her words, but Hades answered. "The very one."

Lamia was the daughter of Poseidon and a queen. Her affair with Zeus led to Hera cursing her to lose any child she birthed, and eventually, she went mad, stealing babies from their mothers only to feast upon their flesh. Her story was horrifying, especially given that Lamia had gone from desiring a child above all else to consuming them.

They continued farther until they came to the end of the passage where a gate kept a massive dragon-like creature imprisoned. It had seven snake-like heads, scales, and webbed fins along its neck. They hissed, baring fangs that dripped a black liquid into a pool that came up to their large, bulbous belly. In that water were several souls whose faces were burned beyond recognition.

"What is this?" she asked.

"That is the Hydra," Hades said. "Its blood, venom, and breath are poisonous."

Persephone stared.

"And the mortals in the pool? What did they do?"

"They are the terrorists who attacked the stadium," he said.

"Is this their punishment?"

"No," Hades said. "Think of this as their holding cell."

Persephone let Hades's words settle between them. That meant there was no reprieve when the judges assigned a soul's fate to Tartarus. Their punishment began immediately, and these burns, the venom eating through their skin straight to bone, were only the beginning.

"And how will you punish them?" she asked, tilting her head to meet his gaze. Hades stared down at her.

"Perhaps…you would like to decide?"

Again, she found herself smirking despite the horror of their conversation. Hades was asking her to determine the eternal punishment of a soul—and she liked it. It made her feel powerful, trusted. For the briefest moment, she wondered what that made her, but she already knew. It made her his queen.

Her gaze returned to the souls in the poisonous lake.

"I wish for them to exist in a constant state of fear and panic. To experience what they inflicted upon others. They will exist, for eternity, in the Forest of Despair."

"So you shall have it," Hades said and lifted his hand for her to take. As her fingers settled into his, the souls beneath the Hydra vanished. "Let me show you something."

He took her to the library, to the basin she'd stumbled upon early in her visits to the palace. When she'd first found it, she'd assumed it was a table, but at her approach, she had discovered a partial map of the Underworld reflected in the dark surface. Then, she'd only been able to see the palace,

Asphodel, and the Rivers Styx and Lethe. When she'd asked Hades why it was not complete, he'd told her the rest would be revealed when she'd earned the right.

At that point, only Hecate and Hermes were able to view the whole of the Underworld.

Now when she looked, she saw every river and meadow and mountain. She knew the chances of the map remaining the same were small as Hades often manipulated his world—adding, moving, or erasing locations.

"Show the Forest of Despair," Hades said, and the water rippled until a harsh scene played out before her eyes. When Persephone had wandered between those trees, she'd been alone, the forest quiet around her, but now she saw it for what it was—full of thousands of souls all living some form of their personal hell. There were souls who sat at the bases of trees, knees pulled to their chest, shaking. Others hunted one another, lashing out and murdering—only to be revived and hunted again.

"Those who hunt," she said. "What is their fear?"

"Loss of control," Hades said.

"And the ones being killed?" she asked quietly.

"They were murderers in life," he responded.

There were others too—souls who drank from streams and died slow and painful deaths, souls who were caught in a part of the forest that remained perpetually on fire, souls who were tied and stretched between trees as they were poked and prodded until exposure led to their eventual death.

As each cycle ended, it began again—an endless loop of torture and death.

After a moment, Persephone turned away from the basin. "I have seen enough."

Hades joined her, taking her hand in his and kissing her knuckles.

"Are you well?"

"I am…satisfied," she answered and met his gaze. "Let's go to bed."

Hades did not argue, and as they returned to their chamber, she realized that vengeance had a taste—it was bitter and metallic with an underlying sweetness.

And she craved it.

"Persephone," Hades said her name, a tinge of concern in his voice. She knew he wondered if he'd gone too far in showing her the Forest of Despair.

She shed her robes, feeling tense. She rolled her shoulders before turning to face him.

"Hades," she replied. She needed him inside her, needed the distraction and release he would provide.

"You've been through a lot," he said, though his eyes burned with a desire so potent, her legs already shook. "Are you sure you want this tonight?"

"It's all I want," she said.

He took another step, closing the space between them, and their mouths collided, tongues sweeping together. She shivered beneath his hands, arching into him, her hips desperate to move against his. She helped him out of his robes as she kissed down his chest, making her way to his swollen sex. As her lips touched his head, he gave a sigh—it was heavy and almost raw, scraping against his throat.

She peered up at him, curious to see his expression—full of dark passion. It only encouraged the fire in the pit of her stomach. The space between her thighs dampened, her body preparing to accommodate him.

"Is this okay?" She wasn't sure why she asked. Maybe she just wanted to hear him say yes with that all-consuming fire in his eyes.

"More than," he replied, and she returned to him, tongue tasting from tip to base, teasing each ridge and lapping at velvet skin. He inhaled between his teeth when he hit the back of her throat, fingers twining into her hair. She looked up at him. His gaze was tender, loving, and yet it scorched her soul, heating every part of her until she was molten.

"You don't know the things I wish to do to you," he said.

She held his gaze, giving the crown of his cock a final hard suck, and then released him. She straightened, her head tipping toward his, their mouths level as she whispered, "Show me."

It was a dare—and Hades accepted the challenge. His hand tightening on the back of her neck, he brought her mouth to his, tongue invading and twining with her own, and then, as if she weighed nothing, he drew her to the center of the bed. Again, his mouth covered hers, sucking and caressing. She bowed against him, her fingers digging into his muscled arms until he pinned them over her head, then she felt something twinning around them—something soft but restraining. She gazed upward and found her wrists were bound with shadow magic.

A thread of unease shivered through her.

"Is this okay?" he asked, sitting back, his strong thighs straddling her, his cock heavy and erect. She swallowed, that strange thread of disquiet pulling at the back of her mind. Was it okay? She couldn't decide.

This is Hades, she reminded herself. *You are safe.*

She nodded, the unease dissipating the longer he raked her with that heated gaze.

Hades smirked, and her heart beat harder in her chest, anticipation curling tight inside her.

"I will make you writhe," he promised, crawling up her body with predatory grace. "I will make you scream. I will make you come so hard, you will feel it for days."

His mouth closed over hers, moving so that his legs were between hers, and he kissed down her body, his skin slithering deliciously against her clit as he made his way to her center—and yet her chest tightened in a way that wasn't familiar.

She tried to release the feeling that had knotted right beside her heart, but she couldn't breathe deep enough. She lifted her head, watching Hades descend, pausing to press kisses to the inside of her thighs, licking the sensitive flesh.

Safe, she thought over and over—the feeling in her chest in conflict with the fire in the bottom of her stomach. *Safe. Safe. Safe.*

Then he spread her wide, flattening her legs against the bed, and suddenly, she couldn't breathe at all. It was like she had found herself in the Styx all over again, being drawn from the surface of the black water to the dark depths in the grip of the dead who lived there. The more she struggled, the harder she was held, the darker everything became. The bindings on her wrist were rough—rope, she realized. The hands upon her thighs were clammy.

"Persephone."

The voice was muffled, but she moved toward it.

"Hades," she choked on his name.

A hand broke below the surface of the water, and she reached for it, but as she came up for air, she found herself face-to-face with Pirithous—gaunt face, pale lips, bleeding eyes—and she was suddenly returned to that wooden chair, its edges biting into her skin. Pirithous loomed on his knees before her.

"Ungrateful," his voice grated.

"No, no, *no!*"

She pressed her bare legs together, even as Pirithous's hand skimmed her from calf to thigh.

"I was protecting you," he seethed, leering over her, blood dripping from his face onto her skin. "And this is how you repay me?"

310

"Don't fucking touch me," she cried, but Pirithous's grip tightened, his fingers dug into her, and he pried her legs apart, pinning his body between them. She collapsed forward in an attempt to push away, and something sour crawled up the back of her throat.

She was going to vomit.

"No," she moaned. "Please no."

Where was Hades? Why had he allowed this to happen? He said that Pirithous could not reach her, could not hurt her anymore.

Where was her magic? She tried reaching for it, but it seemed just as paralyzed as she was.

"*Persephone*," Pirithous said, hands inching closer to her center. Her body clenched; her insides shook. "It's okay."

Then Pirithous bent to press his lips to her thigh, and she broke.

"No!"

The bindings around her wrists tore free and she swiped at Pirithous, her hand connecting with his cheek. It was then she realized there were thorns coming out of her skin—like her hands were the stem of a rose. As soon as she saw the blood, she felt as if she had surfaced from the darkness.

She was no longer in that wooden chair but at the center of a sea of black silk on her bed—and it wasn't Pirithous in front of her but Hades. His cheek bled from her strike.

The blood drained from her face as she stared at him, eyes wide, her brain scrambling to make sense of what had occurred, but it made no sense.

Safe, she thought.

She started to reach for him, wanting to wipe away the blood, to erase the evidence of her blow, but paused when she saw her hands, full of bloody thorns. Her mouth quivered, her hands shook, and then she burst into tears.

311

It took Hades a moment to move, to take her into his arms, but when he did, his body was cold and rigid.

"I did not know," Hades said, his voice low and rough. It was like he was angry but trying hard not to let it show.

I'm sorry, she wanted to say, but her mouth wouldn't work.

"I did not know," Hades repeated. "I'm sorry. I love you."

He repeated those words until his voice broke.

CHAPTER XXVI
Relics

When Persephone woke, Hades was already gone.

His absence renewed her anguish and made her chest ache. She felt horror at having Pirithous invade such a cherished space. Worse, she felt embarrassed. She'd thought she could handle anything so long as it was with Hades, and yet as soon she was restrained, she'd lost touch with reality.

How were they supposed to move on from here?

Hades always knew what to do, but last night she'd watched him freeze, and she knew him well enough to guess he would pull away.

She sighed, her whole body heavy with sadness, and rose from bed, dressing for the day in a white peplos. She checked in with Sybil, Leuce, and Zofie, who were alright but worried about her. She sent a quick text, assuring them she was fine and healed. Leuce had also sent a series of articles, and Persephone spent part of the morning reading through them and watching videos associated with the attacks at Talaria Stadium. Part of her wondered if anyone had managed to capture video of her magic, but all the footage shared was from outside the venue.

The dead were staggering—a total of one hundred and thirty people gone. Of those, three heroes had died—Damon, Aesop, and Demi. Still, there were headlines that claimed the death toll was due to the unnecessary use of magic by the gods who had attended the games.

It was a failed attempt to justify the terrorism of Triad.

Persephone set her tablet aside, needing a break from the heaviness.

She made her way outside the palace, into the gardens. Persephone had always been able to sense the aromas that belonged to varying magic, but the longer she resided in the Underworld, the more she noticed that every bloom smelled like Hades—it was an undercurrent, faint but definitely distinct. The roses, for instance, were sweet with a hint of smoke. It had been a while since she'd been able to walk these paths and visit these flowers, and as she came to the end of the trail, she halted at her plot—the one Hades had given her after she'd accepted his bargain of creating life in the Underworld.

It was barren, black sand. She imagined all the seeds she'd planted were still buried beneath, dormant, but something about bringing the garden to life at this moment did not feel right. Perhaps she would save the transformation for Hades and offer it as a wedding present, if it ever took place. Any planning had all but halted as they waited for Zeus to give his blessing, which was now deferred due to Demeter's storm—though Persephone had to admit, it did not seem so important in this environment, where gods were dying and people were being murdered.

She left the gardens, entering the Asphodel fields, where she was joined by Cerberus, Typhon, and Orthrus. They strolled through the markets of the Asphodel Valley. Some souls were going about their usual business—trading foods and textiles, watering their gardens—while others milked the cows in the meadow. The smell of baking bread and sweet cinnamon filled the air, and with it came a few faint sobs. Persephone followed the sound and found Yuri soothing a soul.

"Is everything alright?" Persephone asked. She'd never seen a soul get upset in Asphodel before, and yet even Persephone knew there was a kind of melancholy in the air she'd never felt before.

The soul immediately pulled away from Yuri and wiped her eyes, not looking at Persephone. Still, she could tell she was young—probably in her early twenties. She had black hair and blunt bangs that framed a pale face.

"Lady Persephone." Yuri curtsied, and the soul beside her mimicked her action quickly. "This is Angeliki. She just arrived in Asphodel."

Persephone didn't need any more of an explanation. The woman had been at Talaria Stadium.

"Angeliki," Persephone said. "It is nice to meet you."

"You too," the woman whispered.

"Lady Persephone is soon to be our queen," Yuri said.

Angeliki's eyes widened.

"Is there anything I can do for you, Angeliki? To help you adjust to your new home?"

That only made the woman cry harder, and Yuri embraced her once again, smoothing a hand down her arm.

"She is worried about her mother," Yuri explained. "Angeliki was her caretaker. Now that she is here, there is no one to watch over her mother."

Persephone felt a pang of sadness for this woman whose tears were not for herself but for another, and she knew she had to do something.

"What is your mother's name, Angeliki?"

"Nessa," she said. "Nessa Levidis."

"I will ensure she is looked after," Persephone said.

Angeliki's eyes widened. "You will? Truly?"

"Yes," Persephone said. "I promise."

And gods could not break promises.

The young woman threw her arms around Persephone.

"Thank you," she said, sobbing against her, body shaking. "Thank you."

"Of course," Persephone said before pulling away. "All will be well."

Angeliki took a deep breath and then offered a small laugh. "I'm going to clean up."

Persephone and Yuri watched as the soul disappeared into the house.

"That was very kind of you," Yuri said.

"It was the only thing I could think to do," Persephone said, and she wasn't sure Hades would approve, but there'd been a lot of people who'd died in the Talaria attack, and they'd left behind loved ones young and old. It wasn't like she'd offered to deliver a personal message.

She made a mental note to speak to Katerina about starting a fund to help the families of the victims—that was something Hades would approve of.

"It is good to see you," Yuri said.

"And you," Persephone said. "I am sorry I have not visited."

"It is alright," Yuri said. "We know things are not well above."

Persephone frowned. "No, they are not."

She glanced around, realizing that none of the young residents had come running to her as they usually did.

"Where are the children?"

Yuri smiled. "They are in the garden with Tyche," she said. "She has been reading to them every morning. You should visit. The children would love it."

She would like to see the children, but she'd also like to visit with Tyche. Still, Persephone worried. Was Tyche ready to answer questions about her death?

"Come. I'll walk as far as the orchard," Yuri said. "I was on my way to pick pomegranates when I stumbled upon Angeliki."

They left the main village, following a path toward a cluster of trees where Yuri stayed to harvest fruit. Beyond the orchard was the Children's Garden—which was not a garden at all but more of a park built into the surrounding forest. Since Persephone had come to the Underworld, the space had slowly transformed from a couple of swings and a seesaw to something far more magical and adventurous. It now spanned five acres, with slides and sandlots, climbing structures and suspension bridges where the children usually played, but today she found them gathered in a clearing and Tyche perched upon a large boulder. She was telling a story in the most animated way—her expressions and voices changing to match the characters as she spoke.

"Prometheus wanted the world to become a better place, and instead of spending his days on Mount Olympus, he explored and lived among men, who struggled despite all the world's beauty. One day, Prometheus realized that if only men had fire, they could warm themselves and cook food and learn to make tools. The possibilities were endless!

"But when Prometheus went to Zeus and begged him to share fire with mortals, the God of Thunder declined, fearing the strength of mortals. '*It is better,*' Zeus said, '*for mortals to rely on the gods for all they need. Let them pray for their needs and we shall grant them.*'

"But Prometheus disagreed and so he defied Zeus and gave man fire. It took many months for Zeus to look from his perch upon Mount Olympus, but when he did, he saw mortals warming themselves by fires—which were now in hearths, in the homes they had built, because Prometheus had given them fire.

"Enraged, Zeus chained Prometheus to the side of a mountain as punishment for his treason, but Prometheus was not sad about his sentence. Rather he was glad, happy, because he knew that upon the wild Earth, the mortals thrived."

Tyche's voice was even, lush, and pleasant, and Persephone found that she preferred the end to this version of Prometheus's story—the truth was far darker. After Prometheus's trickery, Zeus unleashed Pandora upon the world and gave them both fear and hope—hope, perhaps the most dangerous of weapons.

Persephone saw similarities in how Zeus viewed humanity even now. It was the god's wish to keep mortals in a position of submission. It was his reason for descending to Earth—to remind humans who was all-powerful.

It was also why Triad was retaliating.

"Tell us another story, Lady Tyche!" one child said.

"Tomorrow, young one," she said with a smile. "We have a visitor."

The Goddess of Fortune met Persephone's gaze, and the children turned to look.

"Lady Persephone!"

They raced to her, throwing their arms around her legs and pulling on her skirt.

She laughed and bent to accept their hugs.

"Have you come to play with us?" one asked.

"Please play with us!"

"I have come to speak with Lady Tyche," Persephone answered. "But we shall watch you play. You can show us all your new tricks."

That seemed to satisfy them, and they hurried away toward the playground—climbing and running, swinging and sliding.

Tyche approached. She was beautiful and tall and lithe, her body draped in black robes, her long, black hair tied into a knot at the top of her head. She curtsied.

"Lady Persephone," she said. "It is good to meet you."

"Lady Tyche," Persephone greeted. "I am so sorry."

"There is no need for sorrow," Tyche said, offering a small smile. "Come. Let us walk."

She offered her arm, and Persephone accepted. The two kept to the shade. In this part of the Underworld, the air was forever warm, and the trees had a glow to them that reminded Persephone of spring.

"I suppose you wish to know how I died," Tyche said.

The words twisted into Persephone's chest like a knife.

"I do not so much *wish* to know," Persephone said. "But…I fear it will keep happening if we do not learn from you."

"I understand," Tyche said. "I was taken down by something heavy, like a net. Then attacked by mortals—several of them. I remember feeling the first stab of pain and being shocked that they were hurting me. Then I felt another stab, then another. I was surrounded."

"Oh, Tyche," Persephone whispered.

"I could not heal myself. I think, perhaps, the Fates cut my thread."

They walked a little farther and then stopped. Tyche turned to face Persephone, her stormy eyes gentle.

"I know what you wish to ask," the goddess said.

Persephone swallowed. The words were on the tip of her tongue—*Was my mother involved? Did you sense her magic too?*

"I did sense your mother's presence," Tyche said. "I'd hoped…she was there to help me. I was not conscious enough to understand it was only her magic."

Guilt twisted through Persephone, making her stomach knot.

"I do not understand why my mother has taken this path," Persephone said, and she felt the pain of those words ricochet through her body.

There was a pause and then Tyche spoke.

"Your mother and I used to be close," she said.

Persephone's brows knitted together. She did not know that Demeter and Tyche had been friends at all. In the time she had spent in the greenhouse, she'd never once heard of or met the Goddess of Fortune.

"I...don't remember you," Persephone said.

Tyche smiled and it was sad. "We were friends long before she begged the Fates for a daughter," she said. "Long before she was so angry and hurt."

"Tell me."

Tyche took a deep breath.

"Your mother kept you secret for many reasons. You are aware of one—your eventual marriage to Hades—but Demeter was hiding long before you arrived. She was raped."

Persephone felt like her throat was raw as she swallowed this knowledge.

"What?"

"Poseidon tricked her—luring her to him in the form of a horse, then attacked her. That was the beginning of her hatred for the other Olympians. It continued after she went to Zeus, begging that he punish his brother, yet he refused. I do not tell you this to excuse her behavior toward you or toward the world. I tell you this so you will understand her why."

"I...didn't know."

"Your mother does not see strength in her survival."

Persephone had never considered what her mother had come from—the abuse she had suffered or overcome.

But this.

This was Demeter's trauma. It was the seed that had planted the roots of her fear of the world—her fear for her.

Poseidon and Zeus were both of the Three. When it came to Hades, it was likely Demeter had no room to consider him worthy.

"She was never the same," Tyche continued. "I think she buried parts of herself so she could exist, but in doing so, she lost the part of herself that also lived."

Persephone tried to inhale but failed.

"I am sorry, Persephone."

"I am glad you told me," she said, though her mind whirled with a new understanding. Despite the wrong Demeter had committed, Persephone could see the threads that led her mother down this path, and in the end, they had nothing to do with her and everything to do with trauma. Poseidon had broken her; Zeus had crushed her, and she'd had to exist in a world where they remained powerful and in control.

"Does Hades know?" Persephone asked.

"I do not know that Demeter told anyone, save me."

She wasn't sure why, but that made her breathe a little easier.

"What do I do?"

Tyche shrugged. "It is hard to know. Perhaps live with the knowledge that Demeter did her best given her circumstances and yet know that does not mean your trauma is invalid. We are all broken, Persephone. It's what we do with the pieces that matters."

Demeter was using her pieces to hurt, and Persephone knew, in the end, despite her mother's struggles, she would have to be stopped.

"Thank you, Tyche."

"It will not be easy, Persephone. The system is broken. Something new must take its place, but there are no promises in war, no guarantee that what we fight for will win."

"And yet the chance is worth it...isn't it?"

Tyche smiled, a little sad, and said, "That is hope. The greatest enemy of man."

After leaving the Children's Garden, Persephone headed for the library, wandering through the stacks, gathering material on the Titanomachy, curious about the events that had led up to the defeat of the Titans and the reign of the Olympians. Once she had a few books gathered, she sat curled up before the fire and read.

Most of the texts detailed the bitterness and strife of the battle but also Zeus's ability to charm and strategize. He had a history of manipulating and bargaining for the loyalty of both god and monster, promising power to the gods and ambrosia and nectar to the monsters. Persephone did not know this version of the God of Thunder—did he still exist? Was he so comfortable in his position and power he'd lost his edge? Or was his blissful ignorance and indulgent nature more of a ruse?

She felt Hades before she saw him. His presence crept along her neck and down her spine, as if his lips were trailing along her skin. She stiffened. Given their night together, she hadn't expected to see him today, and yet he appeared in her periphery. The God of the Dead always looked as if he'd manifested from the shadow, but something darker moved beneath his skin and behind his eyes that made her blood run cold.

Persephone lowered her book and they stared at one another for a long moment. He kept his distance, and she felt the strangeness between them, a tension that pressed against her skin and hollowed out her chest. She wanted to say something about last night—to tell him she was sorry and that she didn't understand why it had happened—but those words were too hard.

"I spoke to Tyche today," she said instead. "She thinks that the reason she could not heal herself was because the Fates cut her thread."

Hades stared for a moment, his expression blank. This was a different Hades, one that surfaced when the other couldn't be bothered to feel.

"The Fates did not cut her thread," he said.

Persephone waited for him to continue. When he didn't, she prompted, "What are you saying?"

"That Triad has managed to find a weapon that can kill the gods," Hades said matter-of-factly, no concern or anxiety present in his tone.

"You know what it is, don't you?"

"Not for certain," he replied.

"Tell me."

Hades paused a moment. It was like he didn't know where to begin—or maybe more that he did not want to tell.

"You met the Hydra," he said. "It has been in many battles in the past, lost many heads—though it just regenerates. The heads are priceless because their venom is used as a poison. I think Tyche was taken down by a new version of Hephaestus's net and stabbed with a Hydra-poisoned arrow—a relic to be specific."

"A poisoned arrow?"

"It was the biological warfare of ancient Greece," Hades said. "I have worked for years to pull relics like them out of circulation, but there are many and whole networks dedicated to the practice of sourcing and selling them. I would not be surprised if Triad has managed to get their hands on a few."

Persephone let that information sink in before she said, "I thought you said gods couldn't die unless they were thrown into Tartarus and torn apart by the Titans."

"Usually," Hades said. "But the venom of the Hydra is

potent, even to gods. It slows our healing, and likely, if a god is stabbed too many times…"

"They die."

That would make sense, why Tyche could not heal herself. After a moment, Hades spoke, and the words that came out of his mouth shocked her—not only because of what he said but because he was offering information, and he never did that.

"I believe Adonis was also killed with a relic. With my father's scythe."

"What makes you so certain?"

There was a beat of silence. "Because his soul was shattered."

Persephone understood. Adonis had gone to Elysium to rest for eternity. His soul was the magic with which poppies or pomegranates bloomed.

"Why didn't you tell me?"

Again, he was quiet, but she waited for him to speak. "I suppose I had to get to a place where I could tell you. Seeing a shattered soul is not easy. Carrying it to Elysium is even harder."

The look in his haunted eyes told her that she wouldn't understand what Hades had seen.

Persephone set her book aside and whispered his name, desperate to soothe, but as she shifted, he seemed to stiffen, eyes moving to the book.

"What were you reading?" he asked, changing the subject, and Persephone felt an echo of pain throb in her chest.

"I was looking up information on the Titanomachy," she said and watched as Hades's jaw tightened.

"Why?"

"Because…I think my mother has bigger goals than separating us."

CHAPTER XXVII
The Museum of Ancient Greece

It was late when Persephone woke and found the space beside her empty. Hades had not come to bed. She rose and went in search of him, finding him outside on the balcony, cloaked in night. She stepped behind him and slid her arms around his waist. He tensed and his hands clamped down upon hers, breaking her hold as he twisted toward her.

"Persephone."

She was a little taken aback by how quickly he'd turned.

"Will you not come to bed?" she asked, her voice a hushed whisper.

"I will be along shortly," he said, letting go. Persephone held her hand to her chest.

"I don't believe you."

He stared for a moment, his expression blank.

"I cannot sleep," he said. "I do not wish to disturb you."

"You won't disturb me," she said. "Your absence is why I cannot sleep."

She felt a little silly saying it aloud, but it was true that his presence made it easier for her to relax.

"We both know that isn't true," he said, and she flinched at his words, because she knew he was referring to Pirithous. She bit the inside of her cheek to keep her mouth from trembling. In the time since she'd met Hades, he'd never rejected her, and yet here he was, resisting. It hurt and it felt like blame.

"You're right," she said. "It isn't true."

She left him there but instead of returning to their bed, she made her way down the hallway to the queen's suite, where she crawled beneath the cold covers and wept.

Persephone sat behind her desk, a cup of coffee between her hands. She stared blankly at the steam curling into the air, unable to focus. She hadn't slept and she felt groggy. Her body wanted nothing more than to find a quiet place and nap, but her thoughts were chaotic, running on repeat through her head.

She agonized, wavering between feeling at fault or angry for Hades's distance. Perhaps she should have forced conversation around her reaction, but after he'd refused to come to bed, she'd lost her confidence and instead felt anxious about approaching the topic. She'd been triggered out of nowhere, and she'd lashed out at Hades, and while she knew that he too suffered, it was nothing compared to how embarrassed, how devastated, how violated she felt.

Another thought had occurred to her—what if he was no longer willing to explore his fantasies with her? What of her own?

A knock drew her attention, and Leuce entered carrying an armful of newspapers. She looked just as exhausted as Persephone felt.

"Are you alright?" Persephone asked.

The nymph placed the stack on her desk and shrugged. "I haven't slept well since…"

Her words drifted off, but she did not need to finish her sentence, because Persephone knew that she was struggling after the attack on Talaria Stadium.

"Some things have not changed since antiquity," Leuce said. "You still kill each other, just with different weapons."

She wasn't wrong—society was just as violent as it was peaceful.

Persephone's eyes fell to the stack of papers Leuce had brought her. The first was from *New Athens News* and the headline was about the attack on Talaria Stadium:

Death and Violence: the Consequence of Following the Gods

It was an article from Helen that claimed that the attack was designed by Triad to force change—and that without conflict, mortals would continue to live under the thumb of the gods.

The stadium was chosen because the games represented the hold the gods still had on society, and for that to change, it needed to be dismantled. The problem was, of the one hundred and thirty people who had died in that stadium, how many of them wanted to be martyrs for Triad?

Helen's response was cruel: where were your gods?

"I can't believe Demetri approved that article," Leuce said, but Persephone had a feeling Demetri hadn't had much say in this. "Helen has gone mad."

"I don't think she really believes what she's writing," Persephone said. "I don't think she thinks for herself at all."

In fact, Persephone was sure of it.

"If you ever see her again, please turn her into a tree," said Leuce.

Persephone offered a small laugh as Leuce left, closing the door behind her. For a moment, she sagged in her chair, feeling even more exhausted than before. Helen's betrayal had been shocking, but this, it was something else. Something far worse. Almost like a declaration of war.

She straightened enough and read through a few more articles, her heart feeling more and more heavy with each headline:

At Least 56 Deaths Attributed to Winter Weather—That's Just Last Week

Millions Without Power and Water Due to Dangerous Winter Weather

Many Fear Food Crisis in the Midst of Winter Storm

But it was one heading in particular that drew her attention near the bottom of the page:

Several Artifacts Stolen from Museum

Persephone thought that was strange and remembered that Hades had mentioned relics sourced from the black market, but what if they'd been taken from museums?

My mother will hide in plain sight.

Persephone dialed Ivy at the front desk.

"Yes, my lady?"

"Ivy, have Antoni bring the car around. I will be stepping out for a few minutes."

"Of course." There was a pause and then she added, "And…what should I tell Lord Hades? If he asks where you've gone?"

Persephone stiffened at the question. She was frustrated with Hades, but she also didn't want him to worry.

"You may tell him I've gone to the Museum of Ancient Greece," Persephone replied and hung up the phone.

She put on her jacket and headed downstairs, passing Ivy's desk.

"Enjoy your outing, my lady," Ivy said as she left the building.

Persephone made her way down the icy steps. Antoni waited, smiling despite the cold.

"My lady," he said, opening the door to the Lexus.

"Antoni," she said with a smile as she slid into the warm cabin.

As the cyclops entered the driver's side, he asked, "Where to, my lady?"

"The Museum of Ancient Greece."

Antoni's forehead wrinkled, a mark of his surprise.

"Research?" he asked.

"Yes," she answered. "You could call it that."

The Museum of Ancient Greece was located at the center of New Athens. Antoni let her out at the curb, and she made her way through the courtyard, toward a set of marble steps and the entrance of the building. Persephone had visited the museum many times, usually on sunny days when the square was packed with people. Today, though, the landscape was barren and slippery; the marble statues that were usually blinding beneath the light were buried under heaps of snow.

Upon entering the museum and going through security, she paused to take a breath, attempting to scent out her mother's magic, but all she could smell was coffee, cleaners, and dust. She wandered through exhibits, each one dedicated to a different era of ancient Greece. The displays were beautiful, the items arranged elegantly. Despite the intrigue, it was the people she trained her gaze upon, searching for familiarity in their expressions or their body movement. It was challenging to identify a god if they had manipulated their glamour too much.

She was not sure how long she wandered the museum, but after an hour, she'd made her rounds through every exhibit, save for the children's wing. As she stared at its entrance—brightly colored with an exaggerated font and cartoonish columns—she caught a familiar smell: a musky citrus that made her blood run cold.

Demeter.

Her heart beat harder as she stepped farther and farther into the colorful and interactive wing, passing wax statues and models of ancient buildings, following the scent of Demeter's magic until she found her at the center of a group of children. She had definitely taken steps to hide her true identity, appearing older with graying hair and a few more wrinkles, but she still maintained that haughty air that was so reminiscent of her mother.

It appeared she was giving a tour, and right now she was explaining the history of the Panhellenic Games and their importance in their culture.

This was not what Persephone had imagined, even when she'd guessed Demeter was hiding in plain sight.

Watching her with the children was like watching another god. She was no longer severe, and there was a light to her eyes Persephone had not seen since she was very young. Then Demeter looked up and met Persephone's gaze, and all that kindness melted away. The moment was brief—a flicker of disappointment and anger and disgust—before she turned her gaze back to the children, a smile dancing across her face so wide, her eyes creased.

"Why don't you spend some time exploring? I'll be here if you have any questions. Run along!"

"Thank you, Ms. Doso!" the children said in unison.

Persephone did not move once the children spirited away, but Demeter turned toward her, narrowing her eyes, lifting her chin into the air.

"Have you come to kill me?"

Persephone flinched. "No."

"Then you have come to reprimand me."

Persephone did not respond immediately.

"*Well*?" Demeter's tone was sharp.

"I know what happened to you...before I was born," Persephone said, noting the surprise in Demeter's gaze, in the way her lips parted. Still, it was only a moment of weakness, a moment where Persephone glimpsed her mother's true pain and anguish before she buried it again, scowling.

"Are you claiming to understand me now?"

"I would never pretend to know what you have gone through," Persephone said. "But I wish I had known."

"And what would that have changed?"

"Nothing, save that I might have spent less time angry with you."

Demeter offered a savage smile. "Why regret anger? It feeds so many things."

"Like your revenge?"

"Yes," she hissed.

"You know you can stop this," Persephone said. "There is no fighting Fate."

"Do you believe that?" Demeter asked. "Given the fate of Tyche?"

Persephone's lips flattened. It was Demeter's admission.

"She loved you," Persephone said.

"Perhaps, and yet she too told me I could not fight Fate, and here I am—her thread cut by my hands."

"Everyone can murder, Mother," Persephone said.

"And yet not everyone can murder a god," Demeter replied.

"So this is your path," Persephone said. "All because I fell in love with Hades?"

Demeter's lips curled. "Oh, righteous daughter, this is

beyond you. I will take down every Olympian who sided with Fate, every worshipper who holds them in high regard, and eventually, I will kill them too, and when I am finished, I will tear this world apart around you."

Persephone's anger shook her body.

"You think I will stand aside and watch?"

"Oh, flower. You will have no choice."

It was then Persephone understood there was no reclaiming the Demeter beneath the surface. That goddess was long gone, and while she appeared every so often—when she smiled at children and when she recalled her trauma—she would never be that person again. This was who she thought she had to be for survival.

Persephone had lost her mother a long time ago, and this…this was goodbye.

"The Olympians are looking for you."

Then Demeter offered a horrible smile. She looked as if she were about to speak when she was interrupted.

"Ms. Doso!" a child called, and Demeter turned. Her twisted mouth and narrowed eyes vanished, replaced by a smile and sparkling eyes.

"Yes, my darling?" Her voice was quiet and cool—a tone reserved for sweet lullabies.

"Tell us the story of Heracles!"

"Of course." She offered a laugh that sounded silvery. Her gaze shifted to Persephone, and once again her false facade melted away, and she spoke. "You should fear their search for me, Daughter."

Then the Goddess of Harvest turned, dismissing Persephone without another glance.

Demeter's words were a warning, and they cast a horrible shadow over her heart. Persephone took a deep breath, hating how her throat filled with the taste of her mother's magic, and left the museum.

CHAPTER XXVIII
A Touch of Terror

Persephone did not return to work after her visit to the museum. Instead, she teleported to the Underworld and went in search of Hecate, finding the goddess in her meadow, waiting. She was dressed in black robes today, matching Nefeli, who sat, poised behind her, like an omen. Persephone slowed upon seeing them, anxiety erupting in her chest. Hecate never waited for her. She was always doing something—gathering herbs and mushrooms, making poisons, or cursing mortals.

Persephone halted at the edge of the meadow and stared at the goddess.

"I felt your rage the moment you entered the Underworld," Hecate said.

"I am changing, Hecate," Persephone said, her voice breaking.

"You are becoming," Hecate corrected. "You feel it, don't you? The darkness rising."

"I do not wish to be like my mother."

It was her greatest fear, something she'd thought about

since the night she'd asked Hades to take her to Tartarus so she could torture Pirithous.

"I do not flinch at torture," Persephone said. "I wish for vengeance against those who have wronged me. I would kill to protect my heart. I don't know who I am anymore."

"You are Persephone," Hecate said. "The Fated Queen of Hades."

Persephone's chest rose and fell with heavy breaths.

"You should not feel ashamed of hurting people who hurt you," Hecate said. "It is the nature of battle."

They had spoken of combat and of war. They were words that had been threaded through conversations over the last few months—battle with Demeter, war with the gods.

"But does it mean I am no better than those who hurt me?"

Hecate offered a sarcastic laugh. "Whoever said so has never been hurt—not like you have and not like I have."

Persephone wanted to ask Hecate more questions—how had she been hurt? But Persephone also knew the kind of sorrow those questions unleashed, and she did not wish to bring that upon the goddess.

"Your mother wages war on the world above," Hecate said. "Do you wish to defeat her?"

"Yes," Persephone hissed.

"Then I will teach you," Hecate said, and her words were followed by a terrible surge of power as black fire gathered in her hands, casting shadows on her face. She looked terrifying, her face ashy and drained of color. "I will fight you like your mother will fight you," she said. "You will think I never loved you."

Before Persephone could think too long on those words, Hecate unleashed her shadow magic. When it hit, Persephone was thrown back, into the trunk of a tree. The pain was unbearable, a sharp ache that made her feel like her spine had broken into pieces. She couldn't move, so she immediately called up her magic, working to heal herself, but Nefeli's sudden bellow turned Persephone's blood to ice. She'd forgotten about the grim, who barreled toward her.

She wasn't completely healed as she rolled to her feet and flung out her hand, using her magic to teleport the creature to another part of the Underworld. Across the meadow, Hecate stood still, and for the first time since Persephone met the Goddess of Witchcraft, she realized she had never truly felt Hecate's magic. She'd sensed it in bursts—like ghostly lights igniting in the dark, guiding her intermittently, and smelling of sage and earth. This magic, the kind she'd summoned to fight, was different. It was ancient. It smelled bitter and acidic like wine but left a tang in the back of her throat—a metallic taste akin to blood. Sensing it left a feeling of dread embedded in her heart, and suddenly, its irregular pounding was the only thing she could focus on—that and Hecate's rapid approach.

She focused on healing and gathering her power, recounting words that Hades had used while he'd fought her in the grove.

"If you were fighting any other Olympian—any enemy—they would have never let you up."

Hecate played by this rule, sending more shadow magic barreling toward her. Persephone raised her hand, and for the slightest of seconds, everything slowed—but unlike the other times she had managed to freeze time, Hecate's magic pulsed, as if she were only using a fraction of it before, destroying her spell. The shadows crashed into her again, sending her flying backward. Persephone landed hard, the wind knocked from her lungs, the earth piling up around her as she came to a sliding stop.

As she lay there, the ground began to tremble and groan. She felt the earth yawn beneath her, and she scrambled to her hands and knees, nails digging into the dirt to keep from falling into the chasm that had opened beneath her. She looked up, finding Hecate only a few feet away. Her eyes were all black. She had broken the earth without lifting a finger. She had used powerful magic and was not lethargic. She had Persephone on her knees, and she'd only used an ounce of her abilities.

Persephone tried to pull herself up, but she only managed to fall a little farther.

"Hecate—" The goddess's name fell from her lips, but she was not moved by her plea. Instead, her answer was to hurl more flame. Persephone fell, screaming, into the chasm. It was dark for only a few seconds before she landed in the battle-worn clearing once more. She crashed several feet into the ground before coming to rest at the bottom of a crater.

She lay there for a second, blinking up at the Underworld sky. It was hazy and bright.

Again, she recalled Hades's teachings.

"How do I fight when I do not know what power you will use against me?"

"You will never know."

She teleported, appearing behind Hecate, magic stirring in her blood. As soon as she landed, the Goddess of Magic turned, and this time, instead of throwing shadow, black, thorny vines erupted from the ground. Persephone's eyes widened before she vanished once more. As she appeared a few feet away, she dug deep, calling her magic forth. A similar thorny vine burst from the ground, thicker, sharper, with red-tipped spikes. It tangled with Hecate's, a barrier between the two goddesses.

"Finally," Hecate said, and a wicked smile cut across her face.

Persephone felt Hecate's magic erupt, an energy so fierce

and deadly, it made her heart rattle in her chest. Then the tangle of thorns exploded, and Persephone hit the ground, covering her head as spikes scattered across the clearing. She felt several sharp stings as her body was lanced with thorns. She roared through the pain, her magic sweeping through her, pushing the splintered wood out of her body and sealing the wounds.

"You are the only one who can stop your mother," Hecate said. "Yet it seems to me you are waiting for the Olympians to intervene."

Persephone flinched. Hecate was not wrong, but the difference was the Olympians were far more powerful than Persephone was.

"Perhaps more powerful then, but now?" Hecate asked.

"Get out of my head," Persephone said between her teeth. The Goddess of Witchcraft ignored her.

"What if they do not side with you? What if they tear you and Hades apart?"

Persephone's hands shook, and there was a shift inside her, a change to her magic. She was drawing from a well she had only accessed once before.

It was dark.

It was a part of her where she'd stored her anger and her doubt and her fear—every negative thought and experience she'd ever had. That energy seeped from her body and into the earth. All around them, the leaves and the grass wilted and withered, and the limbs of the trees dropped as if melted.

She was draining Hades's magic from the Underworld, stealing its life to feed her own.

If Hecate noticed, she did not hesitate in her speech.

"Zeus will take the path of least resistance. You are the least resistance. You are weak."

"I am not weak."

"Prove it."

The earth at their feet was now barren. The trees that were once lush and emerald had turned to ash, the remnants carried away as a darkness gathered around Persephone, lifting her hair and tearing at her clothes.

"I am a Goddess of Life," Persephone said. "A Queen of Death."

As the shadows swirled, Persephone felt as though she herself were becoming darkness.

"I am the beginning and end of worlds."

In the next second, she charged, moving faster than she'd ever moved in her life, and as she neared Hecate, she brought her hands together. A dark energy pulsed there, shooting out and hitting the goddess in the chest. She flew back, her feet dragging along the ground, tearing up the earth. She came to land in a tangle of thorns Persephone had summoned, caging her wrists and her ankles.

As the dust settled, Persephone was left breathing hard, her body humming from the energy she'd managed to summon from the Underworld.

Hecate smiled.

"Well done, my dear," she said. "Shall we have tea?"

Persephone felt something wet beneath her nose, and as she touched her lips, they came away covered in blood.

Her brows knitted together.

"Huh," she mumbled. "Yes, tea would be lovely."

———

They retired to Hecate's cottage, leaving the meadow drained of magic.

"Should I…restore it?" Persephone asked as they walked away.

"No," Hecate said, nonchalant. "Let Hades see your handiwork."

Persephone did not argue. She was feeling tired, though not as exhausted as she had in the past when she'd used her magic. The blood was new, though, and as she sat down at Hecate's table, the goddess handed her a black cloth.

"You used a lot of power," Hecate explained. "Your body will grow used to it."

An earthy, bitter scent filled the space as Hecate prepared tea.

"Have you thought anymore on the wedding?" Hecate asked. "The souls are eager to confirm a date."

"I haven't," Persephone replied, staring down at her hands—her nails were broken, and her fingers were dirty. The wedding brought up other feelings—like blame. Suddenly, she wanted to fight again just so she didn't have to face how she was feeling.

Hecate placed a steaming mug of tea in front of her along with a jar of honey.

"You'll need to sweeten it," she said. "It's willow bark, so it will be bitter."

Persephone added the honey slowly and sipped the tea. She concentrated hard on the task, avoiding eye contact with Hecate, though she knew the goddess stared.

"Are you well, my dear?" Hecate asked, sitting across from Persephone.

She did not know how to reply, so she stayed quiet, but her eyes blurred with tears.

"My dear?" Hecate's voice was low.

"No," Persephone whispered, and her voice cracked. "I am not well."

Hecate reached across the table and covered Persephone's hand with her own.

"Do you wish to tell me?"

Persephone swallowed, tears streaming silently down her face.

"It has been a long day," she said in a hushed tone. She paused and then spoke. "I am afraid Hades will distance himself from me."

"I do not think he would be able to stay away long," Hecate replied.

"You do not know what I did."

"What did you do?"

Persephone recounted what had occurred between them the previous night. She had to pause to take deep breaths, not expecting to have such a visceral response to merely recalling the experience, but even now as she thought about how they'd begun—with healing kisses that had slowly morphed into something more passionate—and how it ended, with the horror of reliving Pirithous's abduction, she found that her heart raced, and her chest hurt.

"Dearest, you did nothing wrong."

It had not felt that way when she had woken up alone.

"It might be true that Hades is distancing himself. It is likely he is doing so because he thinks he hurt you."

She knew that was true. She would never forget how horrified he had looked after he had realized what had happened.

"I hurt him," she replied.

"You scared him," Hecate clarified. "There is a difference."

"I hate Pirithous for what he has done. First he invaded my dreams and now the most sacred part of my life with Hades."

"Hate him if it helps," Hecate said. "But Pirithous will not go away until you confront what happened to you."

Persephone swallowed thickly. "I feel…ridiculous. So many people have experienced worse—"

She thought of Lara, who had been raped by Zeus.

"Do not compare trauma, Persephone," Hecate said. "It

will do no good. You will find a way to take back your power."

"I feel powerful when I am with Hades. I feel most powerful when we have sex. I do not know why, only that I am in awe that this god worships at my feet."

"Then take that power back," Hecate said. "Sex is about pleasure as much as it is about communication. Talk to Hades. Tell him what you need."

Persephone met Hecate's gaze.

"I love him, Hecate. The world wants to take him from me, and I fear if I do not release him, there will be war."

"Oh, my dear," Hecate said, a note of melancholy in her voice. "No matter your choice, there is no avoiding war."

CHAPTER XXIX
Healing

Persephone ate dinner with the souls in Asphodel. When she returned to the palace, she bathed and changed into a white nightgown that stuck to her damp skin. Heading to her bedroom, she was not surprised to find it empty, despite feeling Hades's presence somewhere in the Underworld. She thought of her conversation with Hecate and knew she had to end this before it went any further.

Stepping out onto the balcony, she went in search of him, descending the stairs into Hades's lush garden. The stone pathway was cool against her bare feet, and the air felt damp as if it had just rained, though as far as Persephone was aware, it did not rain in the Underworld.

As she broke through the shady canopy of the garden, dusk settled in muted tones of pink and orange and blue. A skeletal moon was growing brighter, and beneath that beautiful sky was Hades. Cerberus, Typhon, and Orthrus ran in circles around him, flattening the grass as they chased after their red ball. It was Cerberus who noticed her first, then Typhon, then Orthrus, and last Hades, who turned and stared as she approached. His eyes were dark and burned every part of her exposed skin. Desire erupted in her stomach, hardening her nipples beneath the thin fabric of her nightgown.

She halted a few steps from him.

"I haven't seen you all day," she said.

"It was a busy day," he answered. "As was yours. I saw the grove."

"You do not sound impressed."

"I am, but to say I am surprised would be a lie. I know your capabilities."

Hades had always known her potential, and yet he'd been the first to teach her that her worth was not tied to her power. It was a hard lesson to learn when the value of the Divine was placed upon their abilities.

Silence stretched between them as the words Persephone wanted to say crowded her mouth. Hades looked so haunted, standing there beneath his beautiful sky. She wanted him so badly—his warmth and his scent. *Just say the words*, she thought, taking a deep breath as if to prepare, but she only managed to let it out in a slow stream of air.

"Did you come to say good night?" Hades asked.

Persephone looked at him, surprised. She never sought him out to say good night because she did not have to—he always went to bed with her, even if he did not stay.

"Will you not come to bed with me?" she asked, watching as Hades's throat bobbed.

"I will join you shortly," he replied, but he did not look at her. Instead, he stared off at the fading horizon. It was the second night he'd lied.

Her throat tightened.

She considered leaving—fleeing, really. In the face of the wall Hades was building, it seemed easier to run away than attempt to tear it down. Except she knew that wasn't true.

"I want to talk about the other night," she said, imbuing her voice with as much confidence as she could.

Her request drew Hades's attention—his fierce gaze, his clenched jaw, his tense body. He opened his mouth and then closed it before looking away.

"I did not mean to hurt you," he said, and those words opened a raw wound in her chest.

"I know," Persephone said, tears burning her eyes. In turn, Hades's own breath came fast, as if he were holding back a dam of emotion.

"I was so lost in my desire, in what I wished to do with you, I didn't see what was happening. I pushed you too far. It will never happen again."

No, she wanted to scream. It was what she feared—that Hades would halt exploring with her out of fear.

"What if that's what I want?" she asked.

Hades stared at her, searching her gaze, and she continued.

"I want to try so many things with you, but I am afraid you will not want me."

"Persephone—" Hades took a tentative step forward, then another.

"I know it isn't true, but I cannot help how I think, and I thought it was better to say what was on my mind than keep it to myself. I don't want to stop learning with you."

His hands came to rest upon her face, a gentle touch, as if she were porcelain. He tilted her head so that her gaze would meet his and spoke.

"I will always want you."

He pressed a kiss to her forehead, and as he pulled away, Persephone latched on to his forearms.

"I know you hurt for me, but I need you."

"I am here."

She held his gaze and guided his hands from her face to her breasts.

"Touch me," she whispered. "We can go slow."

She did not release his hands as he gently squeezed her breasts or when his thumb and forefinger brushed her nipples.

"What else?" he asked, voice low and husky.

"Kiss me," she said, and he did. His lips pressed gently to hers, and his tongue slid over the seam of her mouth. She opened for him, tasting him, their rhythm a slow, intoxicating exchange. Hades's hands remained on her breasts, kneading and caressing.

Then he shifted closer, one hand moving into her hair, and froze suddenly, pulling away.

"I'm sorry. I did not ask if that was okay."

"It's okay," she whispered. "I'm okay."

She reached for him and brought their lips together. This time, she led, driving her tongue into his mouth. Her fingers thrust through his silken hair, releasing it from its tight binding. She used it to pull him closer and kiss him harder, and then her hands shifted—skimming down his chest to his cock, which strained, desperate for release.

This time, his hand came to rest over hers, grinding against her palm.

"Touch me," he said.

And she did, first through the fabric, but when that wasn't enough, she unbuttoned his pants and freed his sex. He was warm and soft and hard, and as her hand moved, working from root to tip, they continued to kiss until Hades pulled away, his face glistening with sweat.

"Kneel," she whispered, and they both hit their knees, kissing desperately until Persephone eased Hades onto his back. She lifted her gown and straddled him, sliding over his sex with her own. The friction was delicious, and without delay, she guided him inside her. She let out a breath so deep, it felt like her soul had left her body. Hades groaned, his fingers digging into her thighs.

"Yes," he hissed as she moved, rolling her hips to feel him deeper. Their eyes held and their breath quickened. Persephone took his hands, guiding them over her body—to her breasts, down her sides, over her ass.

"*Fuck.*" Hades's curse was low and breathless.

She leaned forward and kissed him, devoured him, drowned in him. There was nothing but him beneath the skeletal moon and starry sky, and when she grew too weak to move, Hades sat up, gripped her neck and her back, and helped her slide along his cock until he came.

They sat in the middle of the field, joined, until their breathing eased. After, Persephone stood on wobbly legs. Hades held her hands from the ground.

"Are you well?"

She smiled down at him.

"Yes. Very."

Hades followed her to her feet and restored his appearance. After a moment, he held out his hand.

"Are you ready for bed, my darling?"

"As long as you are coming too."

"Of course," he replied.

As they made their way back through the garden, Hades's pace slowed to a stop. Persephone looked at him, wary.

"What is it?"

"When you said you wanted to…*try*…things with me. What *things*, exactly?"

Persephone's face flushed—it was ironic, given that they'd just had sex in the field outside the palace.

"What are you willing to teach?" she asked.

"Anything," he said. "Everything."

"Perhaps we should begin where we failed," she answered. "With…bondage."

Hades stared at her for a long moment before brushing a piece of her hair from her face.

"Are you sure?"

She nodded. "I will tell you when I feel afraid."

Hades rested his forehead against hers, and as he spoke, his breath warmed her lips.

"You hold my heart in your hands, Persephone."

"And your cock too, apparently," Hermes said.

They turned to find the God of Mischief standing a few steps away, looking thoroughly amused. He was dressed as if he'd stepped out of antiquity, in gold robes that shimmered in the night and sandals that squeezed his calves.

"Hermes," Hades growled.

"I thought interrupting now was probably better than a few minutes ago," he said.

"You were *watching*?" Persephone asked, torn between feeling angry and embarrassed.

"To be fair...you were having sex *in the middle of the Underworld*," Hermes pointed out.

"And I have thrown you just as far," Hades said. "Need a reminder?"

"Ah, no. If you are going to be angry at anyone, be angry at Zeus. He sent me."

Persephone's stomach dropped.

"Why?" she asked.

"He's called for a feast," he said.

"A feast? *Tonight*?"

"Yes." Hermes looked at his wrist, which Persephone noted had no watch. "In exactly an hour."

"And we must be in attendance?" she asked.

"Well, I didn't just watch you have sex for nothing," Hermes said mildly.

Persephone rolled her eyes. "Why must we attend? And why at such short notice?"

"He did not say, but perhaps he has finally decided to

bless your union." Hermes paused to chuckle. "I mean, why would he call for a banquet if he was going to say no?"

"Have you met my brother?" Hades asked, clearly not amused.

"Unfortunately, yes. He's my father," Hermes responded, then he clapped his hands together. "Well, I'll see you two soon."

Hermes vanished.

Persephone turned fully to Hades.

"Do you think it is true? That he is summoning us to bless our marriage?"

Hades's jaw visibly relaxed before he answered, "I will not venture to guess."

To Persephone, that translated to *I will not hope*, and she would have been lying if she didn't admit that it only made her feel more uneasy.

"What do I wear?" Persephone asked.

Hades looked down at her. "Let me dress you."

She smirked. "Do you really think that is wise?"

"Yes," he said, drawing her close with an arm around her waist. "For one, it will not take long, which means we have approximately fifty-nine minutes for anything you may desire."

"Anything?" she asked, leaning close.

"Yes," Hades breathed.

"Then I desire…a bath."

While she'd just left them, she had spent the last few minutes rolling around in the grass with Hades. Needless to say, she felt a little dirty.

Hades chuckled. "Coming up, my queen."

CHAPTER XXX
A Feast upon Olympus

Hades walked a circle around Persephone.

She stood still, the center of his world, wearing a gown he had manifested with his magic. It was soft and black, accentuating the curve of her body. An elegant sweetheart neckline and long, capped sleeves created a regal silhouette. A shiver vibrated down her spine, causing her shoulders to straighten and her back to arch slightly. She thought that Hades might have noticed when he spoke, because his words came out in a low, sensual growl.

"Drop your glamour," he said.

She obeyed without hesitation, letting her glamour slip away to reveal her Divine form. Like Hades, she didn't use this form often, save for events in the Underworld. It felt most natural here, among the people who recognized and worshipped her as a goddess.

As Hades came to a stop before her, the force of his presence stole her breath. He was stunning, robed in black and crowned with iron. His bright blue gaze trailed from her horns to her feet, snagging on her breasts and the curve of her hips.

"Just one more thing," he said, lifting his hands, and as he did, a crown appeared. It matched his—all jagged black edges.

Her lips curled as he placed it upon her head. She was surprised by how light it felt.

"Are you making a statement, my lord?" she asked as his hands fell to his sides.

"I thought that was obvious."

"That I belong to you?"

Hades placed a finger beneath her chin as he spoke.

"No, that we belong to each other." He kissed her, and as he pulled away, his gentle gaze connected with hers. "You are beautiful, my darling."

She traced the shape of his face, the curve of his nose, the bow of his lips. She was certain she had memorized every dip and hollow and curve, but suddenly, she felt the need to be sure she had internalized all parts of him for fear of never seeing him again.

Hades's brows drew together, and his fingers brushed down the side of her face.

"Are you well?"

"Yes. Perfect," she replied, though they both knew she wasn't being completely honest. She was afraid. "Are you ready?"

"I am never ready for Olympus," Hades said. "Do not leave my side."

She would have no problem with that—unless, of course, Hermes pulled her away.

Her grip tightened on his arm as he teleported, her heart stuttering in her chest, anxious at returning to the home of the gods, even though a few of them were friends.

They arrived in the marble courtyard on Mount Olympus, where an arc of twelve statues rose before them, each carved to resemble the Olympians. Persephone recognized it as the space where Tyche's body had been burned. It was the lowest part of Olympus—the rest of the city was built into the mountainside and accessed by a number of steep passages. Stories above them, there was a loud clamor of voices and music. At the very top of the mountain was a temple where warm light streamed from the arched columns of an open porch.

"I am assuming that is our destination?" Persephone asked.

"Unfortunately," Hades replied.

The walk was pleasant—a winding stair that took them past pretty doors and exceptional views. Up this high, the clouds were close, the stars brilliant, the sky inky blue. She found herself wondering what the sunrise and sunset looked like from here. She could just imagine—the burning bronze of the sun probably bathed the marble in gold, and all around would be clouds of the same color. It would be a gilded palace in the sky, beautiful and unworthy of those who ruled it.

The final ascension to the temple was a wide set of stairs flanked with two large basins of fire that led to an open porch. At the top, Persephone found a room crowded with gods, demigods, immortal creatures, and favored mortals. She recognized all the gods and a few of the favored—Ajax and Hector in particular, who wore short white chitons and gold circlets in their hair. Other guests were dressed more extravagantly and more modern—in gowns that glittered with sequins and beads, suits with velvet or a sleek sheen.

There was laughter, excitement, and an electricity charged the air that had nothing to do with magic—until they appeared.

Then, one by one, heads turned to stare, and silence swept through the crowd. There were a number of expressions—intrigue, fear, and disapproving frowns. Though her heart hammered in her chest and she squeezed Hades's hand tight, she kept her head held high and looked at him, smiling.

"It seems I am not the only one who can't help staring at you, my love," she said. "I think the whole room is enthralled."

Hades chuckled. "Oh, my darling. They are staring at you."

Their exchange encouraged a wave of whispers as they made their way onto the floor. The crowd parted for them, as if they feared the brush of either god would turn them to ash. It reminded Persephone of a time when she'd been frustrated with Hades for letting the world think he was cruel. Now she considered that it was probably his greatest weapon—the power of fear.

"Sephy!"

She turned in time, releasing Hades's hand as she did, to find Hermes zipping through the crowd. He was wearing the brightest suit she'd ever seen—in a shade of yellow that resembled the skin of a lemon. It had black lapels and flowers embroidered on the jacket in colors of teal, red, and green.

"You look stunning!" he said, taking her hands into his and lifting them as if to inspect her gown.

She grinned. "Thank you, Hermes, but I should warn you—you are complimenting Hades's handiwork. He made the dress."

There were a few gasps—the crowd, still quiet since their arrival, was listening.

"Of course he did, and in his favorite color," Hermes observed, a brow raised.

"Actually, Hermes, black is not my favorite color," Hades said, his voice quiet but somehow resonant, and Persephone felt as if the room was collectively holding their breath.

"Then what is it?" The question came from a nymph Persephone did not recognize, but judging by her ashy hair, she'd guess she was a melia, an ash tree nymph.

The corner of Hades's lips lifted as he answered. "Red."

"Red?" another demanded. "Why red?"

Hades's smile grew, and he looked down at Persephone, his hand settled on her waist. She imagined he did not like this attention, but he was doing well under the scrutiny.

"I think I began to favor the color when Persephone wore it at the Olympian Gala."

She blushed—she couldn't help it. That night had been the night she'd given in to her desire for him, and in the aftermath, she'd felt life for the first time—a faint heartbeat in the world around her.

A few people sighed longingly while some scoffed.

"Who would have thought my brother to be so senti-mental?" The question came from Poseidon, who stood nearly halfway across the room. He wore an aqua-blue suit, his hair was thrust back into a wave of blond, and corkscrew-like horns jutted from his head. On his arm was a woman Persephone knew to be Amphitrite. She was beautiful, regal, with bright red hair and a delicate face. She clung to Poseidon, and Persephone could not tell if it was from devotion or fear of his wandering eye.

Once Poseidon spoke, he offered a laugh, devoid of any humor, and drank from his glass.

"Ignore him," Hermes said. "He's had too much ambrosia."

"Do not make excuses for him," Hades said. "Poseidon is always an ass."

"Brother!" boomed another voice, and Persephone cringed as Zeus's large frame barreled through the crowd. He was dressed in a light blue chiton that clasped over one shoulder, leaving part of his chest exposed. His shoulder-length hair and full beard were dark in color but threaded through with silver. Persephone could not help thinking that his boisterous manner was all an act of deception. Beneath the surface of this god was something dark. "And gorgeous Persephone. So glad you could make it."

"I was under the impression we did not have a choice," Persephone said.

"You're rubbing off on her, Brother," Zeus laughed, jabbing Hades in the side. His eyes ignited, angry by the touch. "Why wouldn't you come? This is your engagement feast after all!"

Persephone thought that was ironic, given their quiet welcome.

"Then that must mean we have your blessing," Persephone said. "To marry."

Again, Zeus laughed. "That is not for me to decide, dear. It is my oracle who will decide."

"Don't call me dear," Persephone said.

"It is only a word. I mean no offense."

"I don't care what you intended," Persephone countered. "The word offends me."

Stark silence stretched between all the gods, and then Zeus laughed. "Hades, your plaything is far too sensitive."

There was a blur as Hades's hand moved to grip Zeus by the neck. The whole room went silent. Hermes grasped Persephone's arm, ready to pull her away the second these two went to battle.

"What did you call my fiancée?" Hades asked.

Then Persephone saw it—the look she'd been waiting to see. The truth of Zeus's nature beneath the facade. His eyes darkened, burning with a light so fierce and ancient, she felt fear in the very depths of her soul. The jovial expression he usually maintained melted into something evil, darkening the hollows of his cheeks and the space beneath his eyes.

"Careful, Hades. I still rule your fate."

"Wrong, Brother. Apologize."

A few more seconds ticked by, and Persephone did

not think Zeus would cave. He seemed more like the kind of god who would go to war over a few words than what really mattered—the death and destruction her mother was wreaking on the world below.

But after a few moments, the God of Thunder cleared his throat.

"Persephone," he said. "Forgive me."

She did not, but Hades released his throat.

Zeus regained his composure easily, his rage melting away into his usually jovial expression. He even laughed, energetic and full. "Let us feast!"

———

Dinner was held in a banquet hall adjacent to the porch. A large, horizontal table rose above the rest on the far side of the room at which most of the Olympians were already seated.

Persephone looked at Hades.

"It appears we will not be sitting together," she said.

"How so?"

She nodded toward the front of the room.

"I am not an Olympian."

"Being one is overrated," he said. "I shall sit with you. Wherever you'd like."

"Won't that make Zeus angry?"

"Yes."

"Do you want to marry me?" Persephone asked. Making Zeus mad didn't seem like the best way to gain his blessing.

"Darling, I will marry you despite what Zeus says."

Persephone did not doubt that, but she did have a question.

"What does he do when he does not bless a marriage?"

"He arranges a marriage for the woman," Hades said.

Persephone ground her teeth, and Hades placed his hand

on the small of her back, directing her to a chair at one of the round tables on the floor. He helped her sit and then took his place beside her. There were two others at the table Hades had chosen—a man and woman. They were young and looked similar, like siblings—their hair curled in the same pattern, golden in color, and their green eyes were wide. Both appeared to be petrified and awed by their presence.

Persephone smiled at them. "Hi," she greeted. "I'm—"

"Persephone," the man said. "We know who you are."

"Yes," she said, her voice a little high, unsure of what to make of the man's words or his tone. "What are your names?"

They hesitated.

"That is Thales, and that is Callista," Hades said. "They are children of Apeliotes."

"Apeliotes?" Persephone did not recognize the name.

"The God of the Southeast Wind," Hades replied mildly.

Again, their eyes widened.

"Y-you know us?" Callista asked.

Hades looked annoyed. "Of course."

The two exchanged a look, but before they could say anything else, they were interrupted.

"Hades, what are you doing?"

The question came from Aphrodite, who had paused at their table. She was dressed in a beautifully pleated gown with an empire, belted waist. The fabric was gold and glistened beneath the light as she moved. Beside her was Hephaestus, who stood stoic and quiet, dressed in a simple gray tunic and black trousers.

"Sitting," Hades replied.

"But you are at the wrong table."

"As long as I am with Persephone, I am right," he replied.

Aphrodite frowned.

"How is Harmonia, Aphrodite?" Persephone asked.

The goddess's sea-green eyes shifted to meet her gaze. "Fine, I suppose. She has been spending much of her time with your friend Sybil."

Persephone hesitated. "I think they have become very good friends."

Aphrodite offered a small smile. "Friends," she repeated. "Have you forgotten I am the Goddess of Love?"

With that, the two departed. Persephone watched as Hephaestus walked Aphrodite to the Olympians' table, helped her sit, and then left to find a table for himself.

She turned to Hades. "Do you think Aphrodite is... opposed to Harmonia's choice of partner?"

"Do you mean is she opposed because Sybil is a woman? No. Aphrodite believes love is love. If Aphrodite is upset, it is because Harmonia's relationship means she has less time for her."

Persephone frowned, and for a moment, she thought she could understand how Aphrodite felt. Harmonia's attack had brought the goddess back into her life, and that had meant companionship, and as much as Aphrodite liked to pretend she did not mind her independence, Persephone— *everyone*—knew she craved attention, specifically the attention of Hephaestus.

"Do you think Aphrodite and Hephaestus will ever reconcile?"

"We can all only hope. They are both completely unbearable."

Persephone rolled her eyes and nudged him with her elbow, but the God of the Dead only chuckled.

Dinner appeared before them—lamb, lemon potatoes, roasted carrots, and *eliopsomo*, a bread baked with black olives. The smells were savory and made Persephone realize just how hungry she was.

Hades reached for a silver pitcher on the table.

"Ambrosia?" he asked.

She raised a brow. "Straight?"

Ambrosia was not like wine. It was stronger than mortal alcohol. Persephone had only had a small amount in the past—and that had been due to Lexa, who had bought a bottle of Dionysus's famous wine, which had been mixed with a drop of the divine liquid.

"Just a little," he said and poured a small amount in her goblet.

Hades filled his own to the brim.

"What?" he asked when he noticed Persephone staring.

"You are an alcoholic," she said.

"Functioning."

Persephone shook her head and sipped the ambrosia. The taste filled her mouth with a cool, honeyed sensation.

"Do you like it?" Hades asked. His voice was low, almost sensual, and drew her attention.

"Yes," she breathed.

Callista cleared her throat, and Persephone turned to look at her.

"So how did you two meet?" Callista asked.

Hermes snorted, appearing beside Persephone holding his plate and silverware. "You sit before gods and that is the question you choose to ask?"

"Hermes, what are you doing?" Persephone asked.

"I missed you," he said and shrugged.

As soon as the God of Mischief sat beside her, Apollo left the Olympian table to sit beside Ajax.

"I think you started a movement, Hades," Persephone said. One Zeus did not seem happy about, as his lips twisted into a scowl.

Hades looked at her and smiled.

"I have a question," Thales said, grinning, his eyes glinting as he looked at Hades. "How will I die?"

"Horribly," Hades replied.

The young man's face fell.

"Hades!" Persephone elbowed him.

"Is–is that true?" the man asked.

"He is just kidding," Persephone said. "Aren't you, Hades?"

"No," he replied, his tone far too serious.

They ate in silence for a few awkward minutes until Zeus stood, clanking a gold spoon against a goblet of ambrosia so loud, Persephone thought the glass would shatter.

"Oh no," Hermes muttered.

"What?" Persephone asked.

"Zeus is going to give a speech. They're always horrible."

The room went quiet, and all eyes turned to the God of Thunder.

"We are gathered to celebrate my brother Hades," he said. "Who has found a beautiful maiden he wishes to marry, Persephone—Goddess of Spring, daughter of dread Demeter."

Dread Demeter was right. Just the sound of her name made Persephone's stomach twist.

Hermes leaned over. "Did he just say maiden? As in a virgin? He has to know that isn't true, right?"

"Hermes!" Persephone seethed.

Zeus continued.

"Tonight, we celebrate love and those who have found it. May we all be so lucky, and, Hades—"

Zeus lifted his glass and stared directly at them.

"May the oracle bless your union."

After dinner, they returned to the open porch. Music began again, a sweet sound that swept through the air. As she searched for the source, she found Apollo played upon his lyre. His eyes were closed, his face relaxed, and she realized she had never seen him without tension in his face.

She watched him for a long moment, until he opened his violet eyes and saw that they darkened with jealousy. Her gaze shifted to where Ajax stood across the room, signing animatedly with a man she did not recognize. Persephone was sure Ajax was just happy to communicate with someone without having to read their lips, but she was also not aware of how Apollo's conversation with him—or Hector—had gone, or rather if he'd had it at all.

"Shall we dance?" Hades asked, offering his hand to Persephone.

"I would like nothing more," she said as the God of the Dead led her into the crowd. He drew her close, and she felt his need press into her stomach. She met his gaze, heavy with desire, and raised a brow.

"Aroused, my love?"

Hades smirked—and she did not know if he smiled because of her candid question or her term of endearment.

"Always, my darling," he replied.

Persephone reached between them, grasping his cock, her hand hidden in his robes.

"What are you doing?" he asked, a sultry edge to his voice.

"I don't think I need to explain myself," she said.

"Are you trying to provoke me in front of these Olympians?"

"Provoke you?" Persephone's voice was breathy as she stroked him. She hated the fabric between them and wanted to feel his warmth in her palm. "I would never."

Hades's jaw ticked and he gritted his teeth. His arms tightened around her; the closeness made it hard for her to move. She stared into his eyes as she spoke.

"I am just trying to please you."

"You please me," he said.

Their faces were inches apart, and as Persephone's eyes dipped to Hades's lips, he closed his mouth over hers. The kiss was savage and demanding and not appropriate, and when he tore away, he spoke.

"Enough!"

The whole room grew silent, and Persephone's eyes widened.

But then he was kissing her again, his hands grasping low beneath her ass as he drew her legs around his waist, grinding into her so hard, she gasped.

"Hades! Everyone can see!"

"Smoke and mirrors," he mumbled as he left her mouth, trailing kisses down her neck and shoulder. In the next second, they had teleported to a dark room, and Hades had her pinned against a wall.

"Not so interested in exhibitionism?" she asked.

"I cannot focus on you the way I wish and maintain the illusion," he said as his fingers parted her hot flesh. Persephone moaned.

"So wet." He hissed. "I could drink from you, but for now, I'll settle with tasting."

He pulled his fingers free and placed them into his mouth before planting that hand against the wall and kissing her.

"Hades, I want you inside me," she said, reaching between them. His robes seemed endless and were far more frustrating to part. "You once told me to dress for sex. Why can't you?"

Hades chuckled. "Perhaps if you were not so eager, darling, finding my flesh would be much easier," he said as he easily unclasped his robes, revealing his muscled chest and engorged flesh.

Her fingers closed around him greedily, and then he was inside her. They both groaned, and for a moment, neither moved.

"I love you," Hades said.

She smiled, brushing pieces of his hair from his face. "I love you too."

Then he thrust, his fingers digging deep into her skin.

"You feel so good," he said.

She could only manage one word as she focused on the feel of him pushing inside her.

"More."

Hades groaned. "Come for me," he said. "So that I may bathe in your warmth."

His command was reinforced with the movement of his thumb against her clit. A few teasing pulses and she was undone, her legs shakily hanging on, her body so heavy, she would have fallen had Hades not been holding her.

"Yes, my darling," Hades said, his fingers biting into her ass as he pumped into her harder, faster, coming inside her so hard, she felt the warmth of it, thick and heavy inside her. After, Hades let her legs go, keeping her upright with an arm around his waist. He brushed her hair away from her face, smoothing it into something that did not look so mussed.

"Are you well?" he asked, still breathless.

"Yes, of course," she said and giggled. "And you?"

"I am well," he said and kissed her forehead before releasing her.

Hades clasped his robes and helped Persephone clean up. Then her eyes shifted to the room where he had brought them. Though it was dark, the moonlight streamed in through windows all around, illuminating the entryway of a house. It was unlike anything she'd ever seen—partially open to the sky, with a floor of black-and-white marble that led to a staircase and other interior rooms.

"Where are we?" she asked.

"These are my accommodations," he said.

She stared at him. "You have a house on Olympus?"

"Yes," he said. "Though I rarely come here."

"How many houses do you have?"

She could tell he was counting, which meant he had more than the three she was aware of—his palace in the Underworld, the home on the island of Lampri, and this one here on Olympus.

"Six," he said. "I think."

"You...*think*?"

He shrugged. "I don't use them all."

She folded her arms over her chest. "Anything else you want to tell me?"

"At this very moment?" he asked. "No."

"Who manages your estate?" she asked.

"Ilias," Hades replied.

"Perhaps I should ask him about your empire."

"You could, but he would tell you nothing."

"I am certain I could persuade him," she said.

Hades frowned. "Careful, darling. I'm not opposed to castrating anyone you decide to tease."

"Jealous?"

"Yes. Very."

She shook her head, and then there was a knock on the door behind them. Hades groaned and opened the door. The God of Trickery stood opposite them, grinning.

"Dinner wasn't satisfying enough?"

"Shut up, Hermes," Hades snapped.

"I was sent to retrieve you," he said.

"We were just on our way."

"Sure," he said. "And I am a law-abiding citizen."

The three left Hades's residence. Outside the home, they found themselves in a narrow alleyway. The stone walls on either side were covered in flowering ivy. She could hear the music of the celebration, the laughter and murmur of the crowd. They were not far from the temple.

"Why do I get the feeling Zeus does not want Hades and I to wed?"

"Probably because he's a creep," Hermes replied. "And would rather have you himself."

"I am not opposed to murdering a god," Hades said. "Fuck the Fates."

"Calm down, Hades," Hermes said. "I'm just pointing out the obvious."

Persephone frowned even deeper.

"Don't worry, Sephy. Let's just see what the oracle says."

Once they had returned, Zeus's response was immediate.

"Now that you have decided to rejoin us," he said, "perhaps you are ready to hear what the oracle will say about your marriage."

"I am *very* eager," Persephone said, glaring at him.

The god's eyes glinted.

"Then follow me, Lady Persephone."

They exited the temple, making their way across a courtyard full of beautiful flowers, lemon trees, and statues of cherub-faced children surrounding deities of fertility—Aphrodite, Aphaea, Artemis, Demeter, and Dionysus.

Once they exited, they came to a narrow passage that let out into a barren marble courtyard. At its center was a round temple. Twenty columns surrounded the structure, and it was set high upon a platform. Wide steps led straight to oak doors—the left engraved with the image of an eagle, the right with the image of a bull. Inside the temple, a basin of oil sat at the center, and a set of ten lit torches hung in holders around the room. Overhead, there was an opening in the ceiling where the dark sky peeked through.

Persephone was surprised to find that Hera and Poseidon joined them. Neither of them looked particularly pleased—not Hera with her head tilted stoically or Poseidon with his thick arms crossed over his chest.

"My council," Zeus said, when he saw Persephone hesitate.

"I thought the oracle was your council," she said.

"The oracle speaks of the future, yes," Zeus said. "But I have lived a long life, and I am aware that the threads of that future are ever-changing. My wife and brother know that too."

That was far wiser than Persephone expected—which, she reminded herself, was the danger of Zeus.

She watched as the God of Thunder retrieved a torch from the wall.

"A drop of your blood, if you will," Zeus said, standing beside the basin. Persephone looked to Hades, who reached for her hand. They approached the basin, and as she did, she noticed a sharp needle-like object protruding from the edge. Hades placed his finger upon it and pressed until his blood slid down the gleaming metal. Holding his hand over the basin, he let a drop of blood fall into the oil. She followed his example, wincing as the needle pierced her skin. Once the blood was in the basin, Hades took her hand into his, drawing her finger into his mouth.

"Hades!" She whispered his name, but when he released her hand, the cut was healed.

"I do not wish to see you bleed."

"It was only a drop," she whispered.

The god did not reply, but she knew there was no way she could understand how he truly felt, seeing her injured, even so small.

They stepped away from the basin, and Zeus lit the oil. It blazed quickly and burned in an unearthly shade of green. The smoke was thick and billowed. Slowly, the flames began to resemble a person—a woman cloaked in flames.

"Pyrrha," Zeus said. "Give us the prophecy of Hades and Persephone."

"Hades and Persephone," the oracle repeated. Their voice was clear, cold, and ancient. "A powerful union—a marriage that will produce a god more powerful than Zeus himself."

And that was it. With the prophecy given, the fire vanished.

There was a long silence where Persephone could stare at nothing but the basin.

A marriage that will produce a power greater than Zeus himself.

They were doomed. She knew the moment the words were spoken. Even Hades had stiffened.

"Zeus." Hades's voice was dark, a frightening tone she had never heard before in her life.

"Hades." Zeus's tone matched.

"You will not take her from me," Hades said.

"I am king, Hades. Perhaps you need reminding."

"If that is your wish. I am more than happy to be the end of your reign."

A tense silence followed.

"Are you pregnant?" Hera asked.

Persephone's eyes widened. "Excuse me?"

"Need I repeat myself?" Hera asked, annoyed.

"That question is not appropriate," Persephone said.

"And yet it is important when considering the prophecy," Hera replied.

Persephone glared at the goddess.

"Why is that?"

"The prophecy states that your marriage will produce a god more powerful than Zeus. A child born of this union would be a very powerful god—a giver of life and death."

Persephone looked at Hades.

"There is no child," Hades said. "There will be no children."

Poseidon chuckled. "Even the most careful of men have children, Hades. How can you possibly ensure that when you cannot even get through a dance without leaving to fuck?"

"I do not have to be careful," Hades said. "It is the Fates

who have taken my ability to have children. It is the Fates who wove Persephone into my world."

"Do you wish to remain childless?" The question came from Hera. Persephone could tell she was curious.

"I want to marry Hades," she said. "If I must remain childless, then I will."

But as she spoke the words, her chest ached—not for herself but for Hades. When he'd told her of the bargain he'd made, he had agonized, and she had quickly recognized that it was Hades who had wanted children.

"You are certain you cannot have children, Brother?" Zeus asked.

"Very," Hades gritted out.

"Let them marry, Zeus," Poseidon said. "Obviously they wish to fuck as husband and wife."

Persephone really hated Poseidon.

"And if the marriage produces a child?" Zeus asked. "I do not trust the Fates. Their threads are ever-moving, ever-changing."

"Then we take the child," Hera said.

Persephone held on to Hades's hand so tight, she thought his fingers might break. All she could think was *do not speak—do not protest.*

"There will be no child," Hades repeated, adamant.

There was a long moment where Hades and Zeus stood opposite one another, glaring. It was so hot in this room, and each breath Persephone took felt like it was clawing its way out of her throat. She needed to get out of here.

"I will bless this union," Zeus said at last. "But if the goddess ever becomes pregnant, the infant must be terminated."

At Zeus's words, Hades wasted no time leaving. One second, they stood in the temple on Olympus, and the next, they were in the Underworld.

Dizzy, Persephone hit the ground and vomited.

CHAPTER XXXI
A Touch of Forever

"It's okay," Hades said. He knelt beside her, gathering her to him, brushing her hair out of her sweaty face as she sobbed.

"It's not," she said. "It isn't."

They had demanded her child. She did not even know if it was possible for her to ever conceive, but the idea that Zeus would take her child devastated her.

"I will destroy him," she said. "I will end him."

"My darling, I have no doubt," Hades said. "Come, on your feet."

She rose with him, and Hades took her face between his hands. "Persephone, I would never—*will never*—let them have any part of you. Do you understand?"

She nodded, despite wondering how he could stop them. Zeus was determined to eliminate any and all threats—except the ones that mattered. There was a part of her that did not even trust his blessing.

Hades took her to the baths, to a smaller pool than the one they usually used. This one was round and raised.

"Let me," Hades said, helping her out of her gown and

into the pool. The water was warm and came to her breasts. Hades knelt, lathering a bar of soap between the folds of a cloth. She shivered as he began washing her—starting with her back, her shoulders, her arms. When he reached her breasts, his movements slowed, and he ran the cloth over her in soft passes until her nipples beaded beneath his touch. When she could take no more, she reached for his wrists.

"Hades," she breathed.

His eyes burned into hers, and he leaned forward and kissed her. Persephone's arms wound around his neck, and she drew him closer, covering him in soap.

"I want you," she breathed as his lips left hers.

"Marry me," he said.

She laughed. "I already said yes."

"You have, so marry me. Tonight."

Her brows knitted together as she studied him, gauging his seriousness.

"I do not trust Zeus or Poseidon or Hera, but I trust us," he said. "Marry me tonight, and they cannot take it away."

There was something else at work inside her—an excitement that rose at the thought of finally being Hades's wife. At not having to plan anymore, to worry about flowers or venues or *approval*.

"Yes," she said, and as Hades's smile broke across his face, she felt like she was falling in love with him all over again. He kissed her, and for a long moment, she wondered if they would leave the baths, but Hades eventually pulled away.

"I will have you tonight as my wife," he said. "Come. I will summon Hecate."

She rinsed off and changed into a robe Hades held for her. The Goddess of Witchcraft was already waiting as they left the baths.

"Oh, my dear!" Hecate said, wrapping her arms around Persephone. "Can you believe it? You will be married tonight! Let's get you ready," she said, looping Persephone's arm through her own. She glared at Hades. "And if I see—or sense—you anywhere near the queen's suite, I will banish you to Arachne's Pit."

"I will not peek," Hades said, grinning at Persephone, his eyes alight, and then his voice dipped. "I'll see you soon."

They parted then, and Persephone found herself in the familiar space of the queen's suite—the space Hades had made before he knew he would ever have a lover, before he knew of her existence. This room was his hope.

Hope, she thought. *The most dangerous weapon.*

She wasn't sure what brought on that thought, but it sent a tremor up her spine that even Hecate noticed.

"Nervous, dear?"

"No," Persephone said. "I'm more ready than ever."

Hecate grinned. "Sit. The lampades are ready."

She gestured to the white vanity where the fairylike creatures hovered. They were tiny silver-skinned nymphs with almost invisible wings. White flowers burst against their dark hair. As Persephone sat, they went to work; their magic tingled against her skin and molded her hair. They were quick and efficient, and when they fluttered to hover behind her head, she admired their work—simple makeup that accentuated the curve of her eyes, the bow of her lips, the height of her cheekbones, and the soft, pale waves of her hair. Upon her head, at the base of her horns, was a crown of baby's breath.

"Beautiful," she said, and then her eyes shifted to Hecate, who hovered in the reflection of the mirror. She held a white gown draped over her arms.

Persephone turned fully.

"Hecate, when did you—"

"Alma and I worked on it together," she said. "Let's see how it fits."

Hecate helped Persephone into the gown, guiding it over

370

her head. The material was silk and felt cool and soft against her skin. As she turned to face the mirror, she gasped quietly. The dress was beautiful and simple, having a pretty silhouette that seemed to be made specifically for the curve of her breasts and the flair of her hips. The neckline was an elegantly cut V the straps thin, and a short train trailed behind her.

"A final touch," Hecate said as she brought forth a shimmering veil embroidered with green vines and flowers in colors of red, pink, and white.

The final look was dreamy—it was everything and more than Persephone had ever imagined. She was a goddess, a queen, but most importantly, she was Persephone.

"Oh, Hecate, it is beautiful," she said, and as she stared in the mirror, she found it hard to completely grasp that this was her wedding day.

She faced the goddess, who was holding a bouquet of white narcissus, roses, and leafy greenery.

"Yuri had the children pick the narcissus," Hecate said.

Persephone smiled and felt tears prick her eyes as she took the flowers.

"No tears, my love," Hecate said. "These are happy times."

"But I am happy."

Hecate smiled and took her face between her hands. "I knew the moment Hades spoke of you that I would love you. I never doubted for a moment that this day would come."

Persephone's lips quivered but she did her best not to cry. Instead, she took a breath.

"Thank you, Hecate. For everything."

"It's time," Hecate said. "Come."

"Hecate," Persephone said, hesitating. There was something she wanted—needed—but she was afraid to say it.

"Yes, dear?"

"I'd...*like* to have Lexa present. Do you think Thanatos would let her leave Elysium?"

"Dear, you are Queen of the Underworld. You decide."

"Then we have a stop to make."

Persephone waited behind a line of trees with Lexa, who wore a dress that looked like a version of her veil, only the fabric was black. She had yet to peek around the branches to see the grove in which she would actually wed Hades, but Lexa did.

She inhaled and whipped around to face her.

"Oh my gods, Persephone," she exclaimed. "It's gorgeous and there are so many...people."

Persephone guessed Lexa was torn between calling them people and souls.

She peeked again.

"I cannot believe I'm actually getting married," Persephone said, holding her flowers so tight, her palms had started to sweat. When she thought of what she'd come from, it was even more surreal. She had never considered marriage, never dreamed of this day, but meeting Hades had changed all that.

"Are you nervous?" Lexa asked, looking at her over her shoulder.

"Yes."

"Don't be," she said and came to Persephone's side. "When you step beyond those trees, just look for Hades. You'll think of nothing else, want no one else, but him."

It was something the old Lexa would say, and it gave Persephone comfort. Still, she glanced at her friend curiously.

"What?" Lexa asked when she noticed.

"Nothing," Persephone said. "It just sounds like you are speaking from experience."

A strange, thick silence followed.

"I think I know what it is like to want no one else," Lexa said quietly.

"Thanatos?" Persephone asked, still watching Lexa closely.

Lexa nodded. It wasn't that hard to guess, given how they'd talked about one another over the last month. Persephone wanted to say something—to ask more questions. Had she talked to Thanatos about her feelings? Had they kissed? But a sweet, beautiful sound filled the air, sending chills rippling through her body.

"That's our cue," Lexa said, tugging on Persephone's arm.

Persephone held her flowers and her breath tighter, and as she rounded the corner, it was knocked out of her. They were in a huge grove surrounded by tall trees, each decorated with garlands of blooming lavender and pink flowers, and overhead, the lampades glowed like lantern lights. Then there was Hades—dreadfully handsome—wreathed by an arch of greenery and flora, Cerberus, Typhon, and Orthrus sitting stoically at his feet.

As soon as her gaze collided with his, he was all she wanted.

His smile—wide and gleaming—lit up his entire face. Even his eyes seemed brighter and tracked her as she approached him. He'd chosen a suit for the occasion, black with a single red polyanthus flower in the pocket of his suit jacket. His hair was slick and tied at the back. His horns were on display—beautiful, lethal things that loomed over his head.

The whole procession felt frantic and wild and perfect.

She paused to hug those she could reach—Yuri and Alma, Isaac and Lily and the other children of the Underworld, Charon and Tyche. Then she faced Apollo, who smiled, his violet eyes warm and sincere.

"Congratulations, Seph."

"Thank you, Apollo."

When she came to Hermes, she hugged him longest.

"You look beautiful, Sephy," he said and pulled away. He was still wearing his yellow suit.

"You're the best, Hermes. Truly."

He smiled and brushed his knuckle over the curve of her cheek. "I know."

They laughed, and when she turned, she realized she was now face-to-face with Hades. She started toward him when Lexa tugged her back, taking her bouquet.

"Eager, darling?" Hades asked and the crowd laughed.

"Always," she said.

He took her hands, and her gaze did not waver from his face. His smile—*oh*, his smile was brilliant and something she rarely saw, and as he looked at her from head to toe, sapphire eyes as deep as the coldest parts of the ocean, she knew he was hers forever.

"Hi," she said quietly, almost shyly.

"Hi," he replied, raising a brow. "You are beautiful."

"So are you."

Hades looked thoroughly amused.

They found themselves interrupted by Hecate, who had stepped into the space before them, clearing her throat, and when they turned to look at her, she smiled, warm and happy.

"I knew this moment would come," Hecate said. "Eventually."

The Goddess of Witchcraft looked to Hades.

"I have seen love—all forms and degrees—but there is something dear about this love—the kind you two share. It is desperate and fierce and passionate." She paused to laugh— and so did everyone behind them. Persephone blushed, but Hades remained passive. "And perhaps it is because I know you, but it is my favorite kind of love to watch. It blossoms and blazes, challenges and teases, hurts and heals. There are no two souls better matched. Apart, you are light and dark, life and death, a beginning and an end. Together, you are a foundation that will weave an empire, unite a people, and weld worlds together. You are a cycle that never ends— eternal and infinite. Hades."

Hecate held out her hand, and at the center of her palm was the ring Hades had made for her. He took it and held it between his thumb and forefinger.

Persephone's gaze collided with his—*a ring!* She did not have a ring, and yet the tilt to the corner of his lips told her everything would be okay.

"Do you take Persephone to be your wife?" Hecate asked.

"I do," he said. His deep voice slid against her skin, making her shiver as he slipped the ring upon her finger.

"Persephone," Hecate said and held out her other hand. A black ring rested at the center of her palm. It was heavy, and as Persephone held it, her hand shook.

"Do you take Hades to be your husband?"

"I do," she said and slid the ring upon his finger. She stared at it for a long moment, feeling a deep sense of pride at seeing it there—it meant he belonged to her.

"You may kiss the bride, Hades."

Persephone's eyes were fastened to Hades as his expression turned thoughtful, almost grim, but Persephone knew it wasn't because he was upset; it was a mark of how serious he took this moment. A weight settled upon her chest as she realized how long he had waited. While their courtship was a second in his vast life, he had spent most of that alone, yearning for companionship, for love reciprocated, and when their lips met, it would be an end to that vast void.

He cupped her face, and she latched on to his wrists, smiling up at him.

"I love you," he said and sealed his mouth to hers.

At first, she thought he would end the kiss there—something simple and sweet before the entire Underworld—but then his hand moved from her face to the back of her head, while the other wrapped around her waist. His tongue slid against her mouth, and she opened for him, smiling for a moment before he deepened the kiss.

Around them, the souls applauded.

"Get a room!" Hermes yelled.

When Hades pulled away, there was a smirk on his face, and he bent forward to press a kiss to her forehead before taking her hand. They turned to face the massive crowd.

"May I present Hades and Persephone, King and Queen of the Underworld."

The cheers were deafening. Hades guided Persephone down the aisle, which felt so much shorter than when she'd first walked it. Once they were behind the line of trees, he pulled her against him and kissed her again.

"I have never seen anything more beautiful than you," he said.

Her smile widened. "I love you. So much."

"Come," Hecate said as she rounded the corner.

She used her magic to teleport them and ushered them into the library.

"You have a few minutes to yourselves until I return to collect you for the festivities," Hecate said at the doors. "If I were you, I'd keep your clothes on." She paused for a moment and added, "And your feet on the ground."

As the door shut, Hades looked at Persephone.

"That," he said, "sounded like a challenge."

Persephone arched a brow. "Are you up for it, husband?"

But at the word, he closed his eyes and exhaled.

"Are you okay?"

His eyes were still closed as he spoke. "Say it again. Call me your husband."

She smiled.

"I said, are you up for the challenge, husband?"

Hades opened his eyes. They had darkened from blue to black, burning with desire. He reached for her hips, bunching the silk of her dress into his hands.

"As much as I want you now," he said, "I have something else planned for us tonight."

Persephone swept her hands over his chest and behind his neck.

"Does it involve…something new?" she asked.

Hades raised a brow. "Are you asking…for something new?"

"Yes," she whispered.

Hades reached for her hand and kissed the inside of her wrist. "And what is it you wish to try?"

She swallowed. "Restraints."

CHAPTER XXXII
In a Sea of Stars

Hecate retrieved them from the library and led them to the first-floor entrance of the ballroom. On the other side of the doors, she heard Hermes's voice.

"Introducing your Lord and Lady of the Underworld, King Hades and Queen Persephone."

Persephone was certain she would never tire of hearing her name spoken in tandem with Hades's, and as the doors swung open, she was faced with her people—every soul in the Underworld she had grown to love. They clapped and cheered again as they entered the throng, spilling out into the courtyard, where they came to a stop, and there beneath the Underworld sky and before all the souls—new and old—Hades drew Persephone close.

The music was soft—a beautiful melody that seemed to twine them together.

"What are you thinking?" Persephone asked.

"I am thinking of many things, wife," he said.

"Like?"

The corners of his lips curled.

"I am thinking of how happy I am," he answered, the words warming her chest. Still, she arched a brow.

"Is that all?"

"I wasn't finished," he said, tightening his hold and bending so that his cheek pressed against hers, his breath brushing her ear. "I am wondering if you are wet for me. If your stomach is wound tight with desire. If you're fantasizing about tonight as much as I am—and are your thoughts just as vulgar?"

When he pulled away, she was flushed, the heat pooling in the core of her body. Still, she held his stare, and as the music came to an end, they halted at the center of the courtyard. Persephone craned her neck, her lips close to his as she answered his questions.

"Yes."

His eyes darkened, and Persephone grinned just as her attention was taken by a group of children begging for a dance. She broke away from Hades and held hands with the children as they moved around the courtyard, oblivious to rhythm or footwork. Still, Persephone did not care—she laughed and smiled and felt more joy than she had in months.

When the song ended, another began, and the children broke away to play on their own.

"May I have this dance, Queen Persephone?"

She turned to find Hermes, who bowed low in her presence.

"Of course, Lord Hermes," she countered, taking his outstretched hand.

"I am proud of you, Sephy," he said.

"Proud? Whatever for?"

"You did well in front of the Olympians tonight," he said.

"I think I made enemies."

He shrugged and guided her into a spin. "Having

enemies is a universal truth," he said. "It means you have something worth fighting for."

"You know," Persephone said, "for all your humor, Hermes, you have a lot of wisdom."

The god grinned. "Another universal truth."

After dancing with Hermes, Persephone was passed to Charon, and when she found herself standing face-to-face with Thanatos, her smile faded.

He was pale and handsome and looked a little sad.

The god bowed his head. "Lady Persephone, will you dance with me?"

Thanatos had not approached her since the day he'd told her she could not see Lexa. Facing him now felt awkward.

She hesitated and Thanatos noticed, adding, "I understand if you wish to decline."

"I do not expect you to be kind because I am your queen," she said.

"I did not ask you to dance because you are my queen," he said. "I asked you to dance so I could apologize."

"Apologize then, and we shall dance."

He frowned, his blue eyes sincere as he spoke. "I am sorry for my actions and my words. I took protecting Lexa to an extreme, and I regret how I hurt you."

"Apology accepted," she said, and Thanatos offered a sad smile.

"It does not appear my apology has made you feel better," Persephone said as they danced.

"I think I am appalled by my behavior," said the god.

"Love does that to the best of us," she said. Thanatos's eyes widened, and Persephone offered a small laugh. "I know you care for her."

The God of Death did not speak, so Persephone added something she knew all too well. "Sometimes, it is hard to explain our actions when they are guided by our hearts."

"She will reincarnate one day," Thanatos said.

"And?"

"She will not remember me."

"I do not understand what you are trying to say."

"I am saying that she and I—we cannot be."

Persephone's brows knitted together. "You would deprive yourself of a moment of happiness?"

"To escape a lifetime of pain? Yes."

Persephone did not say anything for a long moment.

"Does she know of the decision you have made?"

Thanatos did not seem to like that question, because he pressed his lips into a hard line.

"You should at least tell her," Persephone said. "Because while you are choosing to escape pain, she is living in it."

Once her dance with Thanatos ended, she wandered beyond the courtyard, needing rest and distance from the crowd, into the garden where large roses bloomed, emitting a sweet scent. Ahead of her, Cerberus, Typhon, and Orthrus wandered, noses to the ground. She was surprised when she noted the familiar silhouette of her husband ahead of her. He stood with his hands in his pockets, staring up at the sky.

After a moment, he turned, his eyes glittering.

"Are you well?" he asked.

"I am," she replied.

"Are you ready?"

"I am."

He held out his hand, and as she pressed her fingers into his palm, they vanished.

Persephone wasn't sure what to expect when they teleported—a room warmly lit by firelight, perhaps a return to the island of Lampri. Instead, she found herself standing upon a platform with a large bed that was open to the sky. Overhead were clouds of clustered stars in colors of orange and blue and white. They were also reflected in the pool of dark water that surrounded them. It was as if they were floating in the sky itself.

"Are we…in the middle of a lake?" Persephone asked.

"Yes," Hades answered.

Persephone stared. "Is this your magic?"

"It is," he said. "Do you like it?"

"It is beautiful," she said. "But where are we, really?"

"We are in the Underworld," he said. "In a space I made."

"How long have you planned this?"

"I have thought about it for a while," he replied.

Persephone approached the bed and smoothed her hand over the soft silk sheets before looking at Hades over her shoulder.

"Help me out of my dress," she said.

Hades approached and drew the zipper of her gown down until it hit her lower back. His hands skimmed along her spine and across her shoulders, dipping beneath the thin straps. The fabric whispered over her skin as it puddled to the floor.

Beneath her dress she wore nothing, and Hades's hands went to her breasts, his mouth to hers. He kissed her with a slow hunger that curled into the bottom of her stomach.

When he pulled away, he drew something from his pocket—a small, black box.

"These are Chains of Truth," Hades said. "They are a powerful weapon against any god unless they have the password. I am telling you that password now so that if you begin to feel afraid, you can release yourself from their grasp. Eleftherose ton—say it."

"Eleftherose ton," she repeated.

"Perfect."

"Why are they called Chains of Truth?" she asked because she thought she could guess, and Hades's smile confirmed her suspicions.

"The only truth they shall draw from your lips is your pleasure. Lie down."

Persephone did as he instructed. Hades followed, straddling her body, his clothes scraping against her skin, sensitive with need.

"Spread your arms," he said.

He placed the box above her head, and in the next second, her wrists were restrained with heavy chains.

"Forgive me, my darling," Hades said as he touched each cuff, turning them into soft bindings.

"Are you ready?" he asked.

"For you?" she asked. "Always."

"Always," Hades repeated.

He sat back on his heels, still straddling her, and loosened his tie, then his cuff links before making his way to the buttons of his shirt.

"What are you thinking?" he asked.

"I want you to move faster." The words were out of Persephone's mouth before she even had time to think. Her eyes widened, and then she remembered that the restraints around her wrists would pull the truth from her mouth. She narrowed her eyes. "Is there any chance you get to wear these?"

Hades chuckled. "If that is what you want," he said as he pulled off his shirt and cast it aside. "But you do not need chains to draw the truth from me, especially when it comes to what I plan to do to you."

"I'd rather not hear your plans," Persephone said, her eyes roving hungrily over his muscled chest.

"What do you want, wife?"

"Action," she said, wiggling beneath him. If she could, she would reach for him, but her wrists strained against the bindings.

Hades chuckled and then pressed a kiss between her

breasts. She rose against his touch, her legs twined around his; she wanted the friction of his body against hers. But Hades continued, trailing his lips down her stomach as he untangled himself from her grasp. She let him go and allowed her legs to fall open, shameless, ready, desperate. Hades stared at her hungrily before hooking his arms beneath her hips, lifting her ass, and licking her slick folds.

A low growl came from somewhere deep in his chest.

"This. I love this."

He descended, tongue parting her and teasing her clit. He spread her wider so he could go deeper, and soon his fingers were inside her, curling. Persephone's heels dug into the bed, her fingers twined around the chains, and her head pressed hard into the pillow beneath her. She felt so wound up, so tight, so flushed, then Hades's warm mouth closed over her clit, and he sucked—it was gentle and followed by slow circling. Her breath caught on a loud moan, and Hades pulled away, his fingers still working inside her.

"That's it, darling. Tell me how it feels."

"It's good. So good."

She managed to look at him, perspiration building across his forehead, eyes lustful and gleaming. Then his mouth closed over her clit again, tongue vibrating against it. Her head fell back as she moaned. His pace was consistent, and the pressure built and twisted until her limbs shook with release.

Hades pressed kisses to the inside of her thighs, back up her stomach, her breasts, her neck before finding his way to her lips. He kissed her before standing.

"Where are you going?"

"Not far, wife," Hades promised as he stepped out of his slacks. Her eyes scanned every part of his body. He was huge and imposing, the muscles of his arms, abs, and legs cut and conditioned—his body a tool and weapon. Her gaze caught on his swollen cock and heavy balls.

"Tell me your thoughts," he said.

Persephone shuddered as the words came from her mouth. "It doesn't matter how often you are inside me. I can't...it's not enough."

Hades chuckled and climbed on top of her again, settling between her legs. He pressed his body flush against hers.

"I love you," he said.

"I love you."

She'd said the words so often and meant them deeply, but this time, they brought tears to her eyes. Tonight, they hit differently. Tonight, she felt as though she understood love in a way she never had before—it was wild and free, passionate and desperate. It encompassed every emotion in its attempt to make sense of a world that challenged it.

"Are you well?" Hades asked, his voice a rough whisper.

Persephone nodded. "Yes. I am just thinking of how much I truly love you."

Hades's expression intensified, his gaze stripping away every layer of her soul, and then he kissed her before lifting himself and guiding his head against her opening. She pressed her heels into his ass in an attempt to push him inside, but he resisted, chuckling, only to lift her legs so that they were propped against his shoulders, sliding inside her as his eyes held hers, hungry and carnal.

Persephone gasped—a guttural sound that scraped against her throat. Her fingers curled into fists, the bindings cutting into her wrists. The pleasure of his thrusts was deep and lush, each stroke unearthing a moan, a sigh, a wave of pleasure.

"You feel so good," Hades said through his teeth, his face glistening, his long hair coming loose from its binds as he moved. "So tight, so wet. Eleftherose ton!" he commanded, and her restraints were suddenly gone. He released her legs and let them fall around him. Their mouths collided in a hot kiss, and Persephone's hands combed through his hair until it fell down around his shoulders.

"Fuck!"

His curse shivered through her, and then he left her body completely, and she made an animalistic sound. She reached for him as he sat back and pulled her into his lap, wrapping her legs around his waist. Then he was inside her again and she moved against him. Every sensation was delicious—the way her muscles gripped him, the way her nipples grazed his chest, the light scrape of his hair on her clit. Their lips collided awkwardly as Hades began to help her along his length, moving faster the closer he came to release until he emptied himself inside her.

After, their breaths were heavy, their bodies slick. Hades fell back against the bed with Persephone in his arms. She felt dazed and boneless and so happy, she began to laugh.

"I will refrain from thinking you are laughing at my performance, wife," Hades said.

That made her laugh harder.

"No," she said, lifting herself so she could look at him.

His face was free of tension, and his smile seemed so easy, a lazy curve of his lips that was only for her. She reached to brush her fingers along his brow and cheek. Then she rested her head against his chest and said, "You were everything."

Hades rolled so that they were on their sides, facing each other, their legs tangled.

"You are my everything," he said. "My first love, my wife, the first and last Queen of the Underworld."

The words struck her, each one a part of her identity—an identity she had created from the ashes of her past. It was beautiful and breathtaking.

Her heavy eyes closed with those words on repeat: Goddess. Wife. Queen.

CHAPTER XXXIII
Abducted and Unmasked

When Persephone woke, Hades's body was pressed tight against hers.

She smiled, blissful, and stretched, her ass pressing into Hades's cock. The god's arm tightened around her waist.

"Are you asking?" he murmured, his voice sleepy.

She twisted in his arms and threw her leg over his hip, hand going to his cock. She didn't wait for foreplay—she dove in, feeling reckless, warm, ready. Hades groaned; the position kept him from thrusting. Instead, they ground into one another, kissing languidly and breathing heavily. The longer they were joined, the more desperate their movements became, and Persephone's eyes fluttered closed.

"I want to watch you come," Hades said, and she opened her eyes. Their gazes held until she found release and he followed.

After, they rose and went about getting ready for their day as if nothing had changed, as if she weren't Hades's wife, the Queen of the Underworld. It was strange to feel much the same and yet different.

"You're quiet," Hades said. He stood, fully dressed, near the fireplace, a glass of whiskey in his hand, watching her roll her thick stockings up her thigh. She lifted her gaze to his.

"I am just thinking of how surreal this is," she said. "I am your wife."

Hades took a sip from his drink and then set it aside, approaching her to cup her face.

"It is surreal," he said.

"What are you thinking?" she countered.

For a beat, Hades was quiet, and then he spoke.

"That I will do anything to keep you," he answered.

With his words, a cold reality settled on her.

"You are thinking Zeus will try to separate us?"

"Yes," he said without hesitation, and then he tipped her head back so she would look into his eyes. "But you are mine and I intend to keep you forever."

She had no doubt that was what Hades intended, but his words left something dark upon her heart. She thought of the oracle's words—short, simple—*a powerful union—a marriage that will produce a god more powerful than Zeus himself.* Persephone knew how Zeus handled prophecies that predicted his downfall—he eliminated the threat.

"Why do you think he let us leave?" Persephone asked.

"Because of who I am," Hades said. "Challenging me is not like challenging another god. I am one of the Three—our power is equal. He will have to take time deciding how to punish me."

Again, Persephone felt dread.

Hades pressed a kiss to her forehead. "Do not worry, my darling. All will be well."

"Eventually," she said, smiling wryly.

Her mother's storm still raged, and now she wondered how much worse it would get once word got out that she and Hades had wed.

"Shall I take you to work?" Hades asked.

"No," she said. "I am going to breakfast with Sybil."

Hades raised his brows. "Will you tell her that we are married?"

"Can I?"

Persephone wasn't sure how or if they would tell anyone outside of those who had been in attendance. Still, it seemed wrong not to tell Sybil who had known of their connection from the beginning.

"Sybil is trustworthy," Hades said. "It is her greatest attribute."

"She will be ecstatic," Persephone said, grinning.

They teleported outside Nevernight, where Antoni was already waiting, the car warm, the heat from the exhaust turning to thick smoke as it met the icy morning. Antoni stood outside the back passenger door, hands crossed in front of him.

"Good morning, my lord, my lady," Antoni said, smiling, his kind eyes crinkling.

"Good morning!" Persephone said, smiling wide.

"I shall see you tonight, my wife," Hades said and drew her in for a kiss. Then he reached for the door and helped her into the cabin.

"I love you," she whispered.

"I love you," he said and shut the door.

Antoni squeezed into the driver's seat.

"Where to, my lady?" he asked, looking into the rearview mirror.

"Ambrosia & Nectar."

"Of course. One of my favorites," he said as he put the car into drive and started down the street. "I believe congratulations are in order. The wedding was beautiful."

She couldn't help blushing. "Thank you, Antoni. I am still floating."

"We are very pleased," he said. "We have waited a long while for this day."

From the beginning, those who admired Hades had been deeply invested in his happiness—and the fact that she was part of that happiness made her chest blossom with pride.

He'd chosen her, and he would continue to choose her.

Even if the Fates unraveled our destiny, I would find a way back to you.

Those words filled her heart, made it beat—a truth no one could deny.

It did not take long to arrive at Ambrosia & Nectar. It was a small modern restaurant, built with salvaged blocks of marble. Antoni helped her out of the car and walked the few steps to hold the door open for her.

"Thank you, Antoni."

"Of course...my queen."

They grinned at one another before she entered the café.

Inside, the space was cozy with warm lighting, wood tones, and soft seating. When she was settled, she ordered a coffee and pulled out her phone to text Sybil that she had arrived.

While she waited, she took out her tablet and began to read through the morning news, starting with *New Athens News*. She was already anxious at the thought of what might feature on the front page, given the last two articles Helen had written, but she did not expect what she saw today.

GODDESS PLAYING MORTAL: THE TRUTH OF PERSEPHONE ROSI

Persephone drew in a shaky breath, and her heart hammered painfully as she read.

For four years, Persephone Rosi posed as a college student, journalist, and entrepreneur. She claimed to be dedicated to the truth, outing the Divine for their injustices, a mortal suffering just as the rest of us, but the reality is, she is none of these things—not even mortal.

Persephone is a goddess, born of Demeter, the Goddess of Harvest.

The article continued, claiming to have begun the investigation by asking the question, would Hades really marry a mortal? Beyond that, they attacked her work.

She accused Hades of deception, but over the course of her articles, she fell in love with the God of the Dead. She wrote of Apollo's harassment of women, but when public outrage became too much, she fell silent. Now she is often seen out and about with the God of Music. Persephone's attempts at outing the gods seem to have been nothing more than a way for a minor god to reach the rank of an Olympian.

The last line ignited a fine rage inside her, mostly because she knew this was Helen's truth—she was the one searching for a way to rise, and she'd chosen the wrong side.

Persephone looked up and noticed people staring. She started to feel uncomfortable and checked the time. Sybil was almost fifteen minutes late, and she hadn't responded to Persephone's text. Both were unlike her.

She texted again: *You okay?*

Then she called, and her phone went straight to voicemail.

Strange.

Persephone hung up and dialed Ivy at Alexandria Tower.

"Good morning, Lady Persephone," she chimed.

"Ivy, has Sybil arrived?"

"Not yet," she said. "But I will double-check."

The nymph placed her on hold, and as Persephone waited, her stomach roiled with dread. She already knew Sybil hadn't arrived at work. No one got past Ivy, a truth that was confirmed when she returned to the phone.

"She has not arrived yet, my lady. Would you like me to call when she does?"

"No, that's okay. I'll be there soon."

Persephone hung up the phone and frowned. She did not like the feeling curling in the bottom of her stomach. It took hold of her lungs, making it hard to breathe and swallow.

Perhaps she stayed the night with Harmonia. Maybe they lost track of time.

"Zofie." Persephone called the Amazon's name, and she appeared instantly. Onlookers gasped in surprise, but Persephone ignored them.

"Yes, my lady?"

"Can you locate Harmonia?"

"I will do my best," Zofie said. "Shall I escort you to the tower?"

"No, I'd rather you find Harmonia as quickly as possible."

"As you wish," she said and vanished.

Zofie will find them, Persephone thought.

She attempted to comfort herself with those thoughts as she paid for her coffee and made the short walk to Alexandria Tower in the bitter cold. As soon as she arrived, she welcomed the heat tingling across her face, melting her frozen skin.

"Lady Persephone," Ivy said. "I have put in a call to Miss Kyros but her phone seems to be off."

It was the one fact that kept her from completely believing she was with Harmonia. Sybil's phone was never off.

Maybe she forgot her charger, she reasoned. Still, her fear grew.

"I'll try again in a few minutes," Ivy said. "I left coffee on your desk."

"Thank you, Ivy."

Persephone headed upstairs and entered her office. She started to take off her jacket but paused as she came around her desk, noticing a small black box. It was tied with a red ribbon and sat beside her coffee. Had Ivy left a gift and said nothing of it? She picked it up and was even more confused when she found a sticky substance on the bottom—then horrified, as she realized what it was.

Blood.

"Good morning—" Leuce's voice halted abruptly as she entered Persephone's office and saw the crimson stain on her desk. "Is that…*blood?*"

It was suddenly very hard for Persephone to breathe, and there was a ringing in her ears that hurt.

"Leuce. Get Ivy."

"Of course."

Persephone held the box gingerly, her hands already shaking. She pulled the ribbon free and removed the lid. Inside was white, bloodstained paper. She parted the leaves and found a severed finger. An ache started in the back of her throat, and she dropped the box, stepping away from her desk.

Just then, Ivy and Leuce returned.

"What is it, my lady?"

Persephone could feel thick tears gathering.

"Was this box here when you brought my coffee this morning?"

"Well…yes," Ivy said. "I assumed it was from Hades."

"Has anyone else been in my office?" Persephone looked from one nymph to the other as they answered in unison.

"No," they said.

"Your door was closed when I got here," said Leuce.

Persephone felt dizzy and her mind raced. Her gaze fell again to the box and the ashy limb peeking through the paper.

"I have to check on Sybil."

"Persephone, wait—"

She didn't.

She teleported to Sybil's apartment and found herself in the middle of the oracle's living room. It was completely destroyed—the coffee table was in pieces, the television shattered. The doors of the console table upon which it had rested appeared to have been ripped from their hinges. The curtains had been torn from their rods. Shattered glass littered the floor. It was in this chaos she noticed something shivering, curled up on the couch—Opal, Harmonia's dog. Persephone gathered her into her arms. "It's okay," she soothed, but even she did not believe the words. She started to explore the rest of the apartment.

"Sybil!" Persephone called, her shoes crunching on the debris as she moved down the hallway, gathering her magic into her palms, a hectic energy that matched how she felt. She checked the bathroom and found the mirror shattered, the vanity spattered with blood. Her eyes shifted to the bathtub, concealed behind a shower curtain. Time seemed to slow as she approached, her magic hot in her hand.

She jerked the curtain back but found the tub empty—spotless.

Still, she felt on edge as she moved out of the bathroom further down the hallway to where Sybil's bedroom was. The door was ajar, and as she kicked it open a little more, she found it demolished, but there was no Sybil.

No Sybil.

Then she recalled the words of the false oracle.

The loss of one friend will lead you to lose many—and you, you will cease to shine, an ember taken by the night.

Ben.

Persephone summoned Zofie, handing off Opal before teleporting to Four Olives, the restaurant where Ben worked and where he'd met Sybil. There were gasps as she manifested and scanned the crowd. Mortals withdrew their phones to snap pictures or film her.

"No," she commanded and sent a rush of power throughout the entire room. Suddenly, tiny saplings grew from inside their devices. Some mortals dropped their phones in shock, while others called out.

"She's a goddess!"

"The stories are true!"

She ignored them, searching for Ben, who had just exited the kitchen, carrying a serving platter full of food. When he saw her, he halted, and his blue eyes widened. He dropped the tray and swiveled on his feet in an attempt to reenter the kitchen, but instead he collapsed to the ground, his ankles held in place by thin roots that had grown from the floor beneath him.

Persephone stalked toward him. With each step, she felt her anger—and her power—growing.

"Where is she?" Persephone asked as she approached. By the time she was in front of him, he was struggling to free himself, his fingers bleeding from the splintered wood. "Where is Sybil?"

"I-I don't know!"

"She is missing. Her house is in disarray, and you might as well have been stalking her. What did you do?"

"Nothing, I swear!"

Her magic swelled, and the vines that trapped his ankles now trapped his wrists, growing rapidly until they circled his neck.

"Tell me the truth! Did you capture her to prove your prophecy?"

"Never! I gave you the words I heard. I swear it upon my life."

"Then it is good I hold it in my hands," she said, and the vines squeezed his neck harder. Ben's eyes grew wide and bulging, and the veins in his forehead popped.

"Who gave you the words? Who is your god?"

"D-Demeter," he rasped, barely able to utter words as he turned purple in front of her.

"Demeter?" Persephone repeated, and she released the mortal's throat.

Ben gasped and fell to his side. Tears streamed down his face as he groveled, hands and feet still bound.

"You knew who I was," Persephone said.

Ben had a reason to attach himself to Sybil. It was because Sybil was close to *her*.

It is only a matter of time before someone with a vendetta against me tries to harm you.

They were words Hades had spoken—a fear he'd had as their relationship became more public. Persephone had never considered that those words would ring true for her.

"Tell me everything!" Persephone demanded.

Ben attempted to scurry away, but he was held in place by her vines.

"There is nothing to tell! I gave you the prophecy!"

"You did not *give* me a prophecy. You gave me a threat from my mother," she raged.

"I was only given words to speak," he cried. "Your mother threatened Sybil, not me!"

As she stared down at the man, she noted a wetness pooling beneath him. The mortal had pissed himself, but it wasn't his fear that convinced her he was telling the truth. It was that she knew he believed he was a true oracle—he did not recognize that he, himself, was a tool of her mother.

"Trust, mortal, if anything happens to Sybil, I will

personally greet you at the gates of the Underworld and escort you to Tartarus."

His punishment would be brutal, and it would involve severed limbs.

She rose then, her anger subsiding into something that felt a lot like grief—what if she couldn't find Sybil? Ben had been her only lead. Then her gaze shifted to the other mortals in the café, and she found that while some glared at her, others were riveted to the television, where breaking news streamed.

Deadly Avalanche Strikes, Thousands Presumed Dead

No.

No, no, no.

"Heavy snowfall is believed to be the cause of the deadly avalanche, which has buried the cities of Sparta and Thebes under several hundred feet of snow. Rescue workers have been dispatched."

Persephone's whole body felt warm, primed with anger and magic.

And then something struck her in the head. She looked in time to see an orange hit the ground and roll away.

Her head snapped in the direction it had come, and a man yelled, "God fucker!"

"This is your fault!" a woman yelled, picking up her plate and throwing it at Persephone. It hit her arm and fell to the floor, shattering.

More food, objects, and words followed.

"Lemming!" another yelled, throwing their coffee at her.

The ground began to shake, and Persephone knew if she didn't leave, she would bring the whole building down, and despite their assault, they did not deserve death. With a final look at the television, she teleported.

CHAPTER XXXIV
A Battle Between Gods

She arrived at the site of the avalanche, which stretched for miles—every direction was a blanket of bright white. There were signs of a city; toppled buildings, broken trees, wood and twisted metal jutted out from the snow, but the worst part of it all was the silence. It was the sound of death—of an end.

As she stood there amid the devastation, pieces of food that had stuck to her hair and clothing fell to the ground, and it spurred something inside her—a desire to end her mother's reign once and for all. She reached for her magic, for what life remained around her, drawing upon its energy, upon her anger, upon the darkness inside her that wished for revenge, and as she released it, she thought of every beautiful thing she had ever wanted to create—the nymphs she had wanted to protect from her mother, the flowers she had wanted to grow, the lives she had wanted to save.

The magic built behind a dam of emotion, and when it burst, it streamed from her in a wave of bright light that made her eyes water and her skin hot. The snow began to melt beneath her feet, and in the gruesome aftermath of the avalanche, amid the rubble and debris, grass grew, flowers sprouted, and trees straightened and bloomed. Even the sky above split at her command, the clouds parting to show blue skies.

Then vines rose from the ground, lifting and righting whole buildings and houses, repairing the structures until they were covered in greenery and flowering blooms. The landscape no longer resembled a white desert or a metal city but a forest of colorful and fragrant flowers, emerald vegetation, and pure, bright sunlight.

Still, the silence reigned, and there was a new sensation that played upon the edges of her mind, much like the life that fluttered there—but this one was dark, a curl of smoke, teasing and mocking.

It was death.

She might be able to bring life to part of this world but not all of it.

She was distracted from her sorrow when she felt a terrible power coming from the sky. It was both wicked and pure, and it crowded into her soul, raising the hair on her arms and the back of her neck. Then Olympians fell from the sky, landing in a circle around her—except for Hermes and Apollo, who landed on either side of her, slightly in front, as if to defend.

Hermes was dressed in gold armor and a leather linothorax. His helm boasted a set of wings that matched the ones sprouting from his back. Beside him, Apollo wore a similar outfit, only a halo of spikes protruded along the top like a sunburst.

Hermes looked over his shoulder and grinned.

"Hey, Sephy," he said.

"Hey, Hermes," she replied quietly, unsure of what to make of the presence of the gods and yet knowing this was not good.

Directly across from her was Zeus, who was bare-chested,

saving for a fur pelt he wore as a cape and a skirt made of leather strips called pteruges around his waist. Beside him was Hera, who wore a complicated mix of silver, gold, and leather armor. Despite Persephone's fear of Zeus, she felt as though the Goddess of Marriage looked the most battle hungry. Then there was Poseidon with his predatory gaze. He too was bare-chested and wore a white tunic, secured in place by a belt of gold and teal. In his hand, he gripped his trident, a weapon that gleamed with malice. Ares was here too, his bright red cape and feathered helm fluttering in the wind. Then there was Aphrodite, draped in gold and blush, and Artemis, whose bow was slung on her back. Persephone could tell she was tense, ready to reach for the weapon if given the signal. Athena looked regal if not completely passive as she stood with Hestia, who was the only goddess not dressed for battle.

Her mother was the only Olympian missing—and Hades.

Then she felt his unmistakable presence—a darkness so delicious, it felt like home as it curled around her waist, and suddenly, she was pulled back against his solid chest. Persephone tilted her head back and felt Hades's jaw scrape her cheek as his lips settled near her ear.

"Angry, darling?"

"A little," she replied breathlessly.

Despite his teasing comment, she felt the tension in his body.

"That was quite a display of power, little goddess," Zeus said.

"Call me little one more time." Persephone glared at the God of Thunder, who chuckled at her anger. "I am not sure why you are laughing," she continued. "I have asked for your respect before. I will not ask again."

"Are you threatening your king?" Hera asked.

"He is not *my* king," Persephone said.

Zeus's eyes darkened. "I should have never allowed you

to leave that temple. That prophecy was not about your children. It was about you."

"Leave it, Zeus," Hades said. "This will not end well for you."

"Your goddess is a threat to all Olympians," Zeus responded.

"She is a threat to *you*," Hades said.

"Step away, Hades," Zeus said. "I will not hesitate to end you too."

"If you make war against them, you make war against me." The words came from Apollo, whose golden bow materialized within his hands.

"And me," Hermes said, drawing his blade.

There was a stark silence.

Then Zeus spoke, "You would commit treason?"

"It wouldn't be the first time," Apollo mused.

"You would protect a goddess whose power might destroy you?" Hera asked.

"With my life," Hermes said. "Sephy is my friend."

"And mine," said Apollo.

"And mine," said Aphrodite, who broke from the line and crossed to Persephone's side. As she came to stand beside Apollo, she called Hephaestus's name, and the God of Fire also appeared, filling the space beside her.

"I will not battle," Hestia said.

"Nor I," Athena said.

"Cowards," Ares shot back.

"Battle should serve a purpose beyond bloodshed," said Athena.

"The oracle has spoken and pinned this goddess as a threat. War eliminates threats."

"So does peace," said Hestia.

The two goddesses vanished, and then it was Zeus, Hera, Poseidon, Artemis, and Ares who faced them.

"You are sure this is what you want, Apollo?" Artemis asked.

"Seph gave me a chance when she shouldn't have. I owe her."

"Is her chance worth your life?"

"In my case?" he asked. "Yes."

"You will regret this, little goddess," Zeus promised.

Persephone's eyes narrowed.

"I *said* don't call me little."

Her power moved and broke the earth beneath Zeus and the other Olympians' feet. They jumped to avoid falling into an open abyss, rose into the air with ease, and attacked. Zeus seemed intent upon striking Persephone, and his first attack came in the form of a powerful bolt of violet lightning that struck the ground near her feet, causing the earth to shake.

"You are as dogged as your mother," Zeus snarled.

"I believe the word you are looking for is strong willed," Persephone said.

Zeus reared back, but instead of striking her, his arm met a wall of sharp thorns—and they shattered, but it was enough of a barrier for Persephone to avoid the god's blow. As she did, Hades stepped between them, his glamour fading into black armor, but the shadows that fell away from him barreled toward Zeus. One managed to pass through his body, causing him to stumble back, but he recovered in time to deflect the other two with the cuffs that braced his arms.

"The rule of women, Hades, is you never give them your heart."

Persephone didn't have time to wonder how Hades responded, because as she stumbled back from the two, she came face-to-face with Poseidon, who swung his trident at her. The edges cut into her upper arm as she tried to move, and she gasped in pain, but she used that sting to begin to heal and summoned vines from the ground that tangled around the trident, pulling it from Poseidon's grasp. The god was quick to anger and punched his hand into the vines, ripping his weapon from their hold and slamming it into the ground. The earth began to shake and crack open, and the land that Persephone had healed was now broken. A giant fissure appeared between her and the God of the Sea, and as he took a step closer to her, fire sprang from its depths, and a flaming whip cut through the air, wrapping around Poseidon's neck, sending him flying backward. He crashed into one of the vine-covered buildings Persephone had resurrected.

At first she did not know who had come to her rescue, but then her eyes fell upon Hephaestus, whose eyes glowed with raw power and flame. He turned his back to her and faced Poseidon, who rose from the rubble, his trident gleaming.

Suddenly, her head was yanked back, and she stared into Hera's cruel eyes as she lifted a blade and brought it down upon Persephone's neck. She reached for Hera's hand and summoned spires from her fingertips. They sank deep into the goddess's flesh and she screamed, wrenching away, her sword going flying. Rage flashed in Hera's eyes, and she picked Persephone up by the arm and threw her. She flew through the air, the wind sharp against her skin. She landed on her feet but in a crater, and as she jumped from it, Hera continued toward her. Persephone gathered her magic, and blackened limbs burst from the earth, tangling around Hera's arms and ankles, holding her aloft in the sky. The goddess struggled, and her scream sounded animalistic, until the vines closed over her mouth, silencing her.

There was a moment when Persephone stood at the edge of the abyss her body had created, staring out at the destruction brought about by the gods. The earth was barren and cracked, and fires raged, cutting across the land like rivers of flame, the sky heavy with smoke. The magic of the gods was heavy in the air, an energy that felt like doom and sounded like thunder.

Across the field, the Olympians were locked in battle with one another—blades and spears clanked and clashed, while bursts of powerful magic countered attacks. Apollo released arrows upon Ares, who blocked them with his spear. Hephaestus used his fire-like whip to block blow after blow of Poseidon's trident, while Artemis and Aphrodite crossed blades. Then there was Hades, who was still locked in a fierce battle with Zeus. The two struck at each other with their weapons—Hades's bident and Zeus's lightning bolt. Each time they clashed, there was an explosion of power, and it seemed to feed their anger.

Persephone focused on the two, her magic rising to grip Zeus's ankles and arms. The god broke her hold easily, but she persisted, and Zeus roared with anger. Hades used the opportunity to send shadows shuddering through him until he stumbled backward. As he fell, the ground yawned open, urged by Persephone's magic, and the god fell into the abyss, dirt and rubble filling the hole, burying him alive.

Hades turned to Persephone just as the ground began to shake, and Zeus tore free from the ground in an explosion of earth, showering the gods with dirt and rock. Lightning crackled around the King of the Gods, and his eyes glowed. A terrible fear shivered through Persephone when she saw him and felt his power. It was like a poison, making her stomach sour.

"Persephone!" Hades roared.

The lightning hit fast. Her body shook uncontrollably, and her limbs froze in place, eyes wide, mouth open. She could only see the flash of violet light, smell burning hair and flesh. She did not know how long she suffered beneath the shock, but something happened, a shift in her body as it adjusted to the feel of the magic that had initially accosted her body, and suddenly, she could harness it. As Zeus's attack ended, Persephone felt aglow, her body zinging with electricity. Her eyes narrowed upon Zeus in the sky, and she gathered his magic as if it were her own, sending it striking toward him.

His eyes widened just as he was hit, and his body convulsed in the sky.

When the assault ended, Zeus fell, his landing shaking the Earth. Persephone's vision swam and her lungs rattled. She turned, searching for Hades, only to find Ares releasing his golden spear. It cut through the air at an inhuman speed—too fast for Persephone to move.

In the next second, she was pushed to the ground, and she twisted to see Aphrodite's body arch as she was pierced by the spear. It lodged in the ground behind her, and she was pinned at its center, her arms hanging limp beside her, blood dripping from her mouth.

"No!" Hephaestus's roar was so loud and so deafening, it halted the battle. Everyone watched as he tore his way toward her, wreathed in flame. Reaching for the spear, he pulled it free from her body. One arm was wrapped around her shoulders, the other pressed on her stomach.

"Aphrodite—" Ares spoke her name as his feet touched the ground. "I didn't mean—"

"If you take another step, I will slit your throat," Hephaestus threatened.

"Aphrodite," Persephone whispered, her throat thick with tears. "No."

"Persephone," Hades said, suddenly beside her, urging her to her feet. "Come."

"Aphrodite!" she screamed.

"We must go," Hades said.

"Apollo! Heal her!" Persephone cried.

Hades gathered her into his arms.

"No!" she roared even as they vanished.

CHAPTER XXXV
A Favor

She was still screaming when they appeared in their bedchamber.

"It's going to be okay," Hades said, his arms tight around her, holding her up.

"She took that spear for me," Persephone cried, burying her face in his chest.

"Aphrodite will be well," Hades said. "It is not yet her time to die."

Even hearing those words, it took a while for Persephone to calm down. The day had begun on such a beautiful note—a euphoria she'd never felt before—and it had quickly spiraled. Sybil was still missing, there were thousands of dead buried beneath that avalanche, and the Olympians were now divided.

"Sit," Hades said, guiding her to the edge of the bed.

"Hades, we cannot stay here," Persephone said. "We have to find Sybil."

"I know, I know. Just let me make sure you are well," he said.

Persephone's brows knitted together. She felt fine, then

her eyes lowered to her shirt, and she realized it was covered in blood.

"I'm fine. I healed myself."

"Please."

The word was quiet, breathless, and so she nodded and let him unbutton her shirt. He seemed to relax when he found unmarred skin.

"Hades." She started to reach for his face, but he stood.

"Fuck!" he yelled.

She flinched.

"I never fucking wanted this for you," he said, raking his fingers through his unbound hair.

"Hades, this is not your fault."

"I wanted to protect you from this."

"You had no control over how the gods would act today, Hades." He kept his eyes averted, glaring, jaw ticking. "I made a choice to use my power. Zeus made a choice to end me."

"I will destroy him."

"I have no doubt," she said and rose to her feet. "And I will be beside you when you do."

She expected Hades to say no, but instead he reached to stroke her cheek.

"Beside me," he repeated and let his hand fall. "Tell me about Sybil."

Persephone explained what she'd found on the desk this morning—the black box, tied neatly with a red ribbon, containing Sybil's finger.

"You are certain it was Sybil's?"

"Yes." Persephone knew Sybil's energy for one, but she also recognized the polish on the bloodied nail.

"Where is it now?"

"It's still in my office." She'd been too frantic to think to bring it with her when she left to check Sybil's apartment.

"We'll have to retrieve it," Hades said. "Hecate can cast

a tracing spell that will at least tell us where her finger was removed."

It was hard to believe they were speaking so casually about Sybil's abduction and what, essentially, was torture. The reality sent a shiver of rage through Persephone.

"What do we do if she isn't there?" Persephone asked.

"I cannot say," Hades replied. "It depends on what we find when we trace her."

Persephone knew why Sybil had been taken—it was a way to lure her, but where? Persephone suspected the kidnapping was Demeter's idea based on the prophecy she'd given to Ben, but who had taken her? The same people who had mercilessly attacked Adonis and Harmonia and Tyche?

"Come. We must hurry. We cannot spend much time outside the Underworld given how we left the Olympians," Hades said.

As soon as they appeared in her office, Persephone knew something was wrong. Hades stiffened beside her, and his grasp tightened around her waist. There was a dried, bloody rectangle on her desk where Sybil's finger had rested in the box too long, and it was gone. Her eyes shifted to the couch, where Theseus sat. He looked much the same as when she'd met him, if not more relaxed, one leg crossed over the other, arms stretching out on the back of the seat.

Persephone scowled. "You."

The demigod looked amused, his dark brows rising over aquamarine eyes.

"Me," Theseus said, mouth tilting into a smirk.

"Where is Sybil?" Persephone demanded.

"She's right here," he said and held up the finger.

Persephone's eyes darkened.

"What do you want with her?"

"Your cooperation," Theseus said. "I will need it after I collect my favor."

Favor?

That word made Persephone's blood run cold.

The demigod's eyes shifted to Hades, and there was a horrible silence. Whatever Theseus was here to collect caused Hades's grip to tighten on her, his fingers digging into her side painfully. Persephone looked at the god, but all she could see was the bottom of his jaw as he glared at the demigod.

"What favor?" she asked.

"The favor Hades owes me," Theseus explained, his voice still so casual. "For my aid in saving your relationship."

"What is he talking about?" Persephone looked at Hades again. When he didn't respond, she whispered his name. "Hades?"

"He returned a relic that fell into the wrong hands to me," Hades gritted out, then he added, as if to explain why he'd felt obligated to grant such a monumental gift, "You have learned the devastation such a piece can cause."

She had. The relics had resulted in Harmonia's injuries and Tyche's death.

Persephone's eyes returned to Theseus, whose smile was wicked. He took pleasure from this, she realized with disgust.

"What is it you want from him?"

"You," the demigod replied, as if it were obvious.

"Me?" Persephone repeated.

"No," Hades said, and Persephone felt his magic rise.

"Favors are binding, Hades," Theseus said. "You are obligated to fulfill my request."

"I know the nature of favors, Theseus," Hades hissed.

"You would face Divine death?" Theseus asked, rising from his spot on the couch.

"Hades, no!" Persephone said. She clutched his robes, but he would not look at her, his gaze trained upon Theseus, his body tense and ready for battle. Horrible memories ravished her mind. They were false memories, drawn from her greatest fears when she'd battled Hades in her grove, but they'd felt real. She still remembered the weight of his head in her lap and the way his blood darkened as it dried.

"For Persephone?" Hades asked. "Yes."

"I'm only asking to borrow her. You can have her back when I'm through."

Disgust made Persephone's stomach roil.

"Why me?" she asked.

"That is a conversation for another time. For now, you must leave here with me, and Hades cannot follow. If you do not do as I say, I will murder your friend in front of you."

Persephone's eyes burned, and she turned to Hades, gripping his arm until he stared down at her.

"Persephone." He said her name, desperate and pained.

"It's going to be okay."

"No, Persephone."

"I have lost too many people. This way...I can keep you all."

He held her, his fingers digging into her arms. She knew what he was thinking—this was the last time he would see her. She pressed her lips to his and they kissed softly. As she pulled away, she whispered.

"Trust me."

"I trust you," he said.

"Then let me go."

And to her surprise, he did.

Behind them, Theseus chuckled and opened the door, waiting for her to pass through.

"You have made the right decision."

She brushed past Hades, and as much as she'd encouraged

him to let her go, she felt the weight of his absence immediately. All she wanted was to return to him. She paused when she came to stand beside Theseus, which only seemed to make Hades grow more tense.

"Persephone," Hades said her name again, and her heart ached in a way it never had before, like it was wrapped in thread pulled so tight, it could barely beat.

"I love you," she said. "And I know you."

The second this door was closed, he would come after her, and she could not risk it. Sybil would die, and Hades would face an eternity of being hunted by Nemesis.

She couldn't let that happen.

His eyes widened at her words, and then great black vines sprouted from the ground, wrapping around his feet and wrists. Their weight anchored him to the ground, causing it to buckle beneath his feet. He struggled against the bindings, his muscles rippling, veins popping, but he could not break free of them.

"Persephone!" Hades bellowed as the door slammed closed, blocking him from her view. Guilt slammed into her, and tears welled in her eyes. She was left facing Theseus, whose lips were curled, eyes alight with amusement.

"Well done. He will never forgive you for that."

PART III

"Men are so quick to blame the gods: they say
that we devise their misery. But they
themselves—in their depravity—design
grief greater than the griefs that fate assigns."

—HOMER, *THE ODYSSEY*

CHAPTER XXXVI
Persephone

Theseus ushered Persephone out of Alexandria Tower and into a waiting SUV. Inside, the windows were so dark, she couldn't see out. Theseus climbed into the vehicle behind her and held out his hand.

"Your ring," he demanded.

"My—why?"

"Your ring or I will cut your finger off too."

Persephone glared at him. She wanted so badly to use her magic against this demigod, but she couldn't bring herself to do it, not without knowing if Sybil was okay.

She twisted her ring from her finger and handed it over, feeling as if she were giving away a piece of her heart. She watched as Theseus placed it in the inside pocket of his jacket.

"Where are you taking me?" she demanded.

"We will be going to the Diadem Hotel," he said. "Until I am ready to execute my plans with you."

"And what are those?" She couldn't keep her voice from shaking.

He chuckled. "I am not one to show my hand before I am ready, Queen Persephone."

She ignored his use of her title; it was likely not serious—just a way to get under her skin.

"Is Sybil there? At the hotel?"

"Yes," he said. "You will get to see her. You will need to see her so you can remember why you must follow through on your mission."

Persephone let the silence stretch for a moment before speaking again.

"You are working with my mother?"

"We have common goals," he said.

"You both want to overthrow the gods," she said.

"Not overthrow," he said. "Destroy."

"Why? What do you have against the gods? You were born from one."

Even if Theseus had wanted to, he could not deny his parentage.

"I do not hate all gods, just the inflexible ones," he said.

"You mean the ones who will not let you have your way?"

"You make me sound selfish. Have I not always spoken of helping the greater good?"

"We both know you want power, Theseus. You are only playing at offering mortals what other gods will not grant."

Theseus grinned. "Ever the skeptic, Lady Persephone."

She was not sure how long they drove, but at some point, the car came to a stop. Theseus leaned toward her and captured her chin between his fingers, squeezing hard and forcing her to meet his gaze.

"We have a bit of a stroll to make," he said. "Just know I will be counting the number of times you misbehave, and for each offense, I will cut another finger from your friend. If I run out of fingers, I will move on to toes."

He released her and she glared, breathing hard.

"I trust you will obey."

Just as he spoke, someone opened her door, and she almost fell from the vehicle, but she caught herself and shifted, stepping from the cabin gracefully, the threat from Theseus still in her mind.

The Diadem Hotel was grand, a palace-like structure that spanned miles. Persephone had never been inside before, but she knew that the place boasted several upscale restaurants and was an escape for both local residents and vacationers.

Theseus came around the SUV and looped his arm with hers.

"Does Hera know you are using her facility for treasonous activities?"

Theseus laughed—a deep belly laugh that Persephone found appalling despite its warmth. Then he said, "Of all the gods, Hera has been on our side the longest."

They entered the extravagant lobby of the hotel. Large crystal chandeliers hung midway from a seven-story ceiling that was crowned with stained glass. There were several sitting areas, and many of them were full, crowded with people, chatting and drinking.

It was a magnificent place.

And somewhere inside was Sybil, bleeding.

As Persephone's eyes wandered, she noticed people noticing her. She wouldn't be surprised if someone had already snapped pictures of her arriving here with Theseus sans ring and on the demigod's arm. Paparazzi looked for that sort of thing. She turned her head toward Theseus.

"I assumed you would be more discreet," she said between her teeth. "Since you *are* breaking the law."

He smiled and leaned close, his hot breath on her ear. Onlookers would think he was whispering sweet nothings, but his words enraged her.

"You broke the law. You engaged in battle with the gods."

"You kidnapped my friend."

"Is it a crime if no one knows?" he asked.

She hated him.

"Do not waste your thoughts on how you will torture me when I die. Hades has already claimed that honor."

Finally, Persephone found something to laugh about. "Oh, I will not torture you when you die. I will torture you while you live."

Theseus did not respond, not that her words seemed to affect him. He was unafraid—and why should he fear? Right now, he was winning.

They continued along the lobby's edge toward a grand staircase that branched off in opposite directions. They took the one on the right. The climb was four stories, and Persephone's legs burned, but nothing could overpower the deep sense of dread that was stirring in her stomach. They topped the staircase, and Theseus led her down a hallway of doors, stopping at one on the left—number 505. He entered the room and held the door open for her.

Persephone kept her eyes trained on Theseus until she was past the threshold. There was a small entryway that spilled into a larger room, where a man stood against a wall. He was unfamiliar, large, but he stood as still as a soldier on guard. As she came into the room, her eyes connected with Sybil, whose name exploded from her mouth in a broken wail. She ran to her and dropped to her knees.

The oracle sat with her legs and arms restrained. Her head was bent to the side, resting against her shoulder. Her blond hair was matted with dried blood and covered part of her face. Persephone brushed the locks away, revealing bruised eyes, a busted lip, and a bloodied nose. Tears built and burned in the back of her throat.

"Sybil," Persephone's voice was more of a whine, but the oracle's eyes opened into slits, and she tried to smile but winced and then moaned.

Persephone rose and whirled to face Theseus, her anger acute, but found another person in the room with them.

"Harmonia!"

The Goddess of Harmony was in the opposite corner, also restrained. She was bruised and beaten, far worse than she had been the night Persephone had met her in Aphrodite's home. She bled from a wound in her side.

"Oh yes," Theseus sneered. "That one was with her when we showed up. Made a mess of things, so I was forced to make a mess of her."

Persephone ground her teeth, her fingers curling into her palm.

"You didn't have to hurt them," she said, her voice quaking.

"But I did. You will understand what it takes one day to win a war," he said and then indicated to the large, silent man who stood against the wall. "Tannis here is your bodyguard. Tannis."

Theseus said his name as a command, and he brandished a knife, approached Sybil, and held her wrist. She whimpered as he placed his blade against her ring finger—her middle finger was already missing.

"No!" Persephone started to move toward them, but Theseus's voice stopped her.

"Ah-ah-ah," he chided. "Tannis is a butcher's son. He is an expert carver. He has been ordered to dismember your friend *if* you misbehave. Of course, not all at once. I will return shortly," the demigod promised and left.

In the silence that followed, Persephone kept her back to the wall, facing the man whose hands were still upon Sybil. She wondered if he intended to remain like that while Theseus was gone.

"You should be ashamed," she spat. "If it is the gods you hate, their actions you despise, you have placed yourself on their level."

Tannis did not speak.

"Don't try to reason, Seph," Sybil managed, her voice haggard. "They have been brainwashed."

At her comment, Theo squeezed Sybil's hand.

"Stop!" Persephone begged. Sybil's screams clawed at her heart. "Stop, please! *Please!*"

When he let it go, Sybil sobbed.

After that, none of them spoke.

Persephone sat on the edge of the hotel bed. She stared down at her naked finger, missing the comfort of the weight of her ring and fearful for Hades. She wondered if he had escaped her bindings. She closed her eyes against the memory of his expression—the shock, the desperation. He had not wanted her to walk away, and yet she'd continued, taking step after step until the door was closed. She'd told herself it wouldn't be long—*we won't be parted for long.* He would free himself from the bindings and he would come.

But the minutes turned into hours, and still they sat with no sign of Hades. Persephone fought sleep, unwilling to rest while her friends suffered beneath the gaze of her enemies. Each time she nodded off, she felt like she was falling and woke with a start. When she couldn't stand sitting anymore, she stood. When she couldn't stand anymore, she paced.

She wasn't sure how many times she crossed the floor or how many hours they'd been locked in this hotel room, but the door finally opened, revealing Theseus and another large man who could have been Tannis's twin. He passed Persephone and went straight for Sybil.

"What are you doing?"

"You are about to find out why I needed you," Theseus said.

Persephone grit her teeth, glaring at the demigod. She hated him so much.

Then something shifted in the air, a change she couldn't quite place, but she knew it came from Theseus, who stiffened suddenly and then twisted as the door burst open. Everything happened so fast, all Persephone could do was stare in horror as the demigod threw out his hand. His magic crackled through the air, a current like lightning meeting water, and froze Zofie, who had kicked in the door with her feet, brandishing her blade.

Persephone could tell by the expression on her face—eyes wide, mouth open—that she had not expected to face such power when she'd come to her rescue. Then Theseus manifested a blade, held it like a spear, and threw it at Zofie, striking her in the chest.

She fell to the ground in the doorway of the hotel room.

Persephone's screams were cut off by a hand that went around her mouth. She fought against Tannis, tears streaming down her face.

"Shut up!" Theseus seethed, reaching for her arm. "If you don't want your other friends to join her, you'll shut up!"

Persephone shook.

"Clean this up," Theseus ordered, staring down at Zofie with disgust.

Persephone wanted to hold her, to brush her hair from her face, tell her what an accomplished warrior she was—but Theseus kept his grip on her arm.

"Let's go."

He pulled her along and they filed out of the room, past Zofie, down the stairwell, into a parking garage where a limo waited. Theseus shoved Persephone inside where she came face-to-face with her mother. Seeing her was like a blast of cold air, and she recoiled.

She knew her mother would think it a weakness, that

she drew back out of fear, but it wasn't that—it was disgust. This goddess, the harvester, the nurturer, had the blood of thousands on her hands.

"Sit," Theseus commanded, pushing her into the space opposite her mother.

The demigod took a seat beside Demeter while Sybil and Harmonia were dragged into the limo and practically tossed into the cab opposite one another. Persephone knew why they kept them apart—they were afraid Harmonia would teleport with Sybil. Though she didn't think the Goddess of Harmony had enough energy to use her magic.

When the doors were shut, they sped off, and Theseus spoke.

"I am taking you to Lerna Lake," he said.

"That is an entrance to the Underworld," Persephone said. She had never seen it in person but knew it was an ancient way into Hades's realm. Knowing the god as she did, she could not imagine what kind of traps he'd set to prevent entry, but she could imagine they were deadly.

"Yes," he said.

"Why not go through Nevernight?" she asked.

"Because there are too many people there who will try to protect you," he said. "After all, you are their queen."

Demeter scowled. "Do not speak such things. It makes me sick."

Persephone glared. "Why do you wish to enter the Underworld? Are you hoping to retrieve a soul?"

"I am not so predictable," he said. "You will lead me to Hades's arsenal, and you will ensure my safe passage."

"You want weapons?"

"I want a weapon," Theseus said. "The Helm of Darkness."

She swallowed thickly.

"You wish to wear Hades's helm," she said. "And what? Steal the other weapons?"

"I will not have to steal them. They will be given to me," he said.

She should have guessed. Poseidon was his father, keeper of the trident, and Hera would ensure he had Zeus's lightning bolt. They were weapons of war that aided the Olympians in defeating the Titans—it made sense that Theseus would think he could use them to overthrow the Olympians.

"Those weapons will not help you win a war against the Olympians. The gods are far stronger now."

"I never rely on one method to defeat my enemy," Theseus said.

She was not surprised that he did not elaborate. Theseus was not one to wax poetic about his plans.

Once he'd given her the mission, no one spoke again. Persephone feared saying something that might cause Theseus to pull over and cut up Sybil or Harmonia.

She looked at them, staring hard to make sure they were both breathing. Harmonia rested her head against the window while Sybil sagged against the leather.

The car came to a stop, and the doors on both sides of the vehicle opened. Persephone was dragged out of the car by Tannis. They'd stopped close to the shore of Lerna Lake, and she was guided with a heavy hand on her shoulder, down a rickety pier where a rowboat waited. A lantern hung at its prow and illuminated a small part of the black lake.

"In," Tannis commanded, again giving Persephone a little push.

She glared at the man but stepped into the boat. She was followed by Theseus, who helped Demeter. Then came Sybil and Harmonia. Sybil shook as she stepped down, but she managed to do so without trouble. Then she turned to reach for Harmonia, who was pale and still bleeding from whatever wound had been inflicted at her side.

"Do not touch her," Theseus commanded. "Demeter."

The Goddess of Harvest reached for Harmonia's arm and yanked her down into the boat. Persephone leaned forward and managed to catch the goddess before she smacked the side of the boat.

"I said don't touch her," Theseus said and swung. Persephone ducked as the oar flew over her head. When he tried to hit her again, she reached out and grabbed it, stopping his attack, her eyes gleaming.

"If you want that helm, I suggest you start rowing," she said. "You don't have long before Hades breaks my binds."

At her words, Theseus seemed to become amused and jerked the oar from her grasp.

"As you wish, Queen of the Underworld."

Theseus pushed off the pier. The water was dark and thick, as if it weren't water at all but oil. Persephone watched the surface, feeling a presence below; something monstrous lived within its depths. It wasn't until they were almost across the lake—the cave entrance looming—that whatever lived in the water made itself known by rocking the boat hard, causing water to splash them.

Theseus's eyes found Persephone.

"What did I say?"

Before she had a chance to react, a horrible cry came from the darkness around them, and the boat was flipped.

Persephone hit the water hard but broke the surface quickly, in time to see Sybil struggling to hold Harmonia up.

"Sybil!" Persephone called, but just as she started to swim toward the two, a shock of power sent them flying back. Persephone fought the waves as a creature roared, exploding from the water—followed by Demeter, who stood atop a plume of water. The creature was something Persephone didn't recognize. She was a goddess with large, downturned horns that stuck out on either side of her head. Her hair was long and fell over her shoulders, down her naked breasts, falling to the edge of her scaly tentacles—which she'd used to hold Theseus prisoner.

"Ceto," Demeter said. "I will not hesitate to sever your tentacles from your body."

"You can try, dread Demeter," she said. "But you are not welcome here."

Her mother summoned a blade and jumped, moving in a blur. In the next second, the tentacle that held Theseus was severed, falling into the black lake below. Ceto roared and lashed out at Demeter, sending the goddess flying. In her rage, the waves rose, high and fast, burying Persephone, Sybil, and Harmonia beneath the surface once more.

"Stop!" Persephone cried, water rushing into her mouth, but the two goddesses continued to engage, creating chaos in the lake around them. Ceto's tentacles swept out, catching Persephone around her waist and lifting her from the lake.

"Ceto!" she cried, her lungs burning as she coughed, spitting up water. "I command you to stop!"

The goddess froze and turned toward Persephone; her eyes widened.

"My lady," Ceto said, placing her hand to her chest and bowing her head. "Forgive me. I did not sense you."

Persephone started to speak when she felt a rush of Demeter's power. Her head snapped in her mother's direction in time to see the goddess wielding her sword in midair.

"*No*," she snapped, and her mother froze, eyes wide and wild, face contorted in an angry scowl. Persephone turned back to Ceto. "My friends are in this lake," Persephone said. "Will you find them for me?"

"Of course, my queen," Ceto said, but her eyes shifted to Demeter, who was still suspended in the air.

"She will not bother you again," Persephone promised.

Ceto moved Persephone to the shore, before the cave-like entrance to the Underworld, and disappeared below the water. It wasn't long before the monster returned with Sybil and Harmonia. As she set them on the sandy beach, they both collapsed, exhausted from fighting the water's unnatural current. Sybil rolled onto her hands and knees and crawled to Harmonia, who looked pale, almost blue. Persephone ran, falling to her knees beside them.

"Harmonia! Open your eyes!" she begged. "Harmonia!"

But the goddess would not respond. Persephone looked frantically from her face to her chest, sensing the faint pulse of life—but it was quickly fading.

"Sybil, move!" Persephone commanded, pushing the oracle out of the way. She placed her hands upon the goddess's chest and closed her eyes, seeking the life that remained inside her, and when she pinned it down, her body began to feel warm—the same way it felt when she healed. She pushed that heat into Harmonia, and after a moment, her stomach turned, and she was forced to pull away and vomit into the sand. It was nothing but water, but it burned the back of her throat and dripped from her nose. As she did, Harmonia took a deep breath.

They barely had time to recover before Theseus appeared, dragging Sybil up by her hair, drawing a knife against her throat.

"No, please! Please!" Persephone begged. She was on her hands and knees before the demigod, frantic.

"I told you safe passage," Theseus said through gritted teeth.

"I did not know!" she screamed, her voice breaking.

"It doesn't matter what you know," he snapped. "She will suffer for your ignorance!"

He released Sybil's hair and grabbed her hand, cutting off a second finger and throwing it at Persephone's feet.

Sybil screamed, Harmonia sobbed, and Persephone raged, her eyes burning with tears.

Once it was done, Theseus seemed to calm.

"Get up," he commanded. Then he turned to where Demeter still hung, suspended in the air. "Release her."

Persephone did as he asked, and the goddess plummeted into the lake. It took a few minutes for her to join them onshore, her eyes bright and gleaming with just as much anger as Persephone felt.

"Lead us into the Underworld," Theseus commanded.

CHAPTER XXXVII
Hades

Motherfucking Theseus.

Forget an eternity of misery in Tartarus, Hades would not rest until his nephew ceased to exist. He would shatter his soul, cut his thread into a million pieces, and consume them. It would be the most savory meal he'd ever eaten.

Fucking favor.

Fucking Fates.

He strained against Persephone's bindings, his limbs shook, and his muscles tightened, but they would not give.

Fuck. Fuck. Fuck.

She was powerful, and he would have felt more pride if she hadn't left with that bastard demigod. He knew why she'd done it. She'd wanted to protect him, and the thought filled him with a conflict that made his chest ache. He loved her so much, and he raged that she would put herself in danger, even if he understood it.

What would Theseus do to her?

The thought sent another wave of fury through him, and he fought against her bindings once more. This time, he heard the distinct snap of one, and his foot was free. He wrenched his arm, veins rising to the surface of his skin, and the vine cut into his wrist until it finally broke. He tore at the remaining bindings after that, and once he was free, he teleported.

Persephone had a knack for hiding her own personal energy signature. He had not yet discovered if it was merely one of her powers or a result of having her powers dormant for so long. Either way, it made it impossible to find her—except when she wore her ring. He focused on the unique energy of the stones—the pureness of the tourmaline and the sweet caress of the dioptase. He had not set out to track her when he'd given it to her. He would have been able to trace any precious metal or gem so long as he became familiar with it.

He manifested among ruins.

It did not take him long to recognize where he'd arrived: the crumbling Palace of Knossos. In the night, it was impossible to make out the detailed and colorful paintings that covered what was left of the ancient walls or exactly how many miles the grounds stretched, but Hades knew because he'd known this place in its prime and throughout its inevitable destruction.

It was here he sensed Persephone's ring, but faintly. He knew these ruins went deep into the belly of the earth, a twisted maze meant to confuse. He imagined Persephone somewhere within, and his anger drew him into the shell of the palace.

Though it was dark, his eyes adjusted, and as he crossed a broken, blue mosaic floor, he came to a dark pit. It seemed to be a part of the floor that had given away. He spoke to the shadows, commanding them to descend. He watched through them as the chasm turned into another level of the palace, then dipped farther into an even deeper level.

Hades jumped, landing quietly upon another mosaic

floor. Here, the palace was more intact—its columned walls and rooms were more pronounced. As Hades crept through each, following the energies from Persephone's ring, unease crept through him. He sensed life here—ancient life—and profound death. That was not unusual, given this site dated back to antiquity. Hundreds had died here, but this death, some of it was fresh—harsh, acute, acidic.

Hades continued to descend until he came to the edge of another dark pit. The smell of death was stronger here, but so was Persephone's ring. Hades's rage and fear twined through his body, and a dread thick and foul gathered in the back of his throat. Memories from the night he'd found her in the basement of Club Aphrodisia accosted him, and for a moment, it was like he was there again, Persephone on her knees before him, broken. He could smell her blood, and his mind spiraled into a dark and violent place. It was the kind of anger he needed, the rush he would use to tear the world to pieces if he found her harmed.

He stepped into the darkness; this time when he landed, it shook the earth. As he straightened, he found several narrow hallways.

A labyrinth.

He was familiar with this craftsmanship too, recognizing Daedalus's work, an ancient inventor and architect known for his innovation—innovation that eventually led to the death of his son.

Fuck, Hades thought, turning in a circle, studying each path. It was colder here, and the air was full of dust. It felt unclean and a little suffocating. Still, he could sense Persephone's ring, and the energy was strongest down the path that stretched out to his right. As he stepped into the deeper dark, he noted that parts of the tunnel were broken—as if they had been hit by a large object.

Something monstrous had lived here.

Perhaps it still did.

Hades gathered his shadows to him and sent them down the corridor, but they seemed to become disoriented and faded into the darkness. Their behavior raised the hair on the back of Hades's neck. There was a wrongness here, and he didn't like it.

Suddenly, the wall to his left exploded, sending him flying through the opposite barrier, and as he landed, he came face-to-face with a bull—or at least the head of one. The rest of its body was human.

It was a Minotaur, a monster.

It bellowed and clawed the ground with one of its hoofed feet, wielding a double ax that was chipped and caked with blood. Hades imagined the creature had been using it to kill since his imprisonment here, which, if he had to guess by the state of the creature—matted hair, filthy skin, and crazed eyes—was a very long time.

The creature roared and swung his ax. Hades pushed off the wall and ducked, sending his shadow-wraiths barreling toward him. If it had been any other creature, his magic would have jarred it to the soul. The usual reaction was a complete loss of the senses, but as they passed through this monster, he only seemed to grow angrier, losing his balance momentarily.

Hades charged, slamming into the Minotaur. They flew backward, hitting wall after wall after wall. When they finally landed, it was in a pile of rubble, and Hades rolled away, creating as much distance between them as possible.

The Minotaur was also quick and rose to its hoofed feet. He might not have magic, but he was fast and seemed to draw from a never-ending well of strength. He roared, snorted, and charged again, this time, keeping his head down, his horns on display. Hades crossed his arms over his chest, creating a field of energy that sent the creature soaring once more.

As quick as he crashed, he was on his feet, and this time the snarl that came from the Minotaur was deafening and full of fury. He tossed his ax, the weapon cutting through the air audibly. At the same time, he charged at Hades, who braced himself for impact. As the creature barreled into him, Hades called forth his magic, digging the sharp ends of his fingers into the Minotaur's neck. As he pulled free, blood spattered his face. The creature roared but continued to run at full speed into each labyrinth wall. The impact against Hades's back began to send a sharp pain down his spine. He gritted his teeth against it and continued to shove the spikes into the Minotaur's neck over and over again.

Hades could tell when the creature began to lose his energy. He slowed; his breath came roughly, snorting exhales through his nose and mouth where blood also dripped. Just as Hades was about to let go, the Minotaur stumbled, and he found himself falling with the monster into another pit. This one narrowed quickly, causing Hades to hit the sides like a pinball, knocking the air from his lungs. They twisted and turned sharply, until they were both thrown from the tunnel into a larger room. The Minotaur landed first and Hades after, hitting a wall that did not give, which told him whatever they'd landed in wasn't concrete or stone.

Adamant, Hades realized.

Adamant was a material used to create many ancient weapons. It was also the only metal that could bind gods.

Hades rose to his feet quickly, ready to continue the fight with the Minotaur, but the creature did not rise.

He was dead.

His eyes adjusted to this new darkness. It was somehow thicker. Perhaps that had something to do with how far below the earth they were located, or maybe it was the adamant. Either way, the cell was simple—a small square with a sandy floor. At first glance, as far as Hades could tell, there was no way out—but he'd have to look longer. For the moment, his attention was drawn to Persephone's presence. It was strong here, as if her heart beat within the walls of this cell. Then he saw it—a gleam from one of the jewels in her ring.

If her ring was here, where was she? What had Theseus done?

As he started toward it, there was a faint mechanical sound, and a net fell from the ceiling above, sending him to the ground. He landed with a harsh crack against the floor. As he tried to call upon his magic, his body convulsed—the net paralyzed him.

He had never felt so helpless, and that made him angry.

He thrashed and cursed but to no avail. Finally, he lay still, not because he did not wish to fight but because he was too exhausted to move. He closed his eyes for a moment. When he opened them again, he had the sense that he'd fallen asleep. It took him a moment to adjust, his vision swimming even in the darkness. As he lay there, breathing shallow, he noticed a faint flicker of light a short distance from him.

Persephone's ring.

He started to reach for it, but the net kept his arm locked in place. Sweat broke out across his forehead, his body losing strength. Once again, he closed his eyes, the sand from the floor coating his lips and tongue as he worked to catch his breath.

"Persephone," he whispered her name.

His wife, his queen.

He thought of how stunning she'd looked in her white gown as she had walked to him down the aisle, flanked by souls and gods who'd come to love her. He remembered how her smile had made his heart race, how her bottle-green eyes, aglow and so happy, had made his chest swell with pride. He thought of everything they'd been through and fought for—the promises they'd made to burn worlds and love forever—and here he was, parted from her, not knowing if she was safe.

He gritted his teeth, a fresh wave of anger coursing through his veins. He ripped open his eyes and reached for the ring again. This time, though his hand shook, he managed to strain and grasp a handful of sand, and as he let it sift through his fingers, he found the gem-encrusted ring.

Breathing hard and shaking, he brought the ring to his lips, curled it safely into his palm, and held it to his heart before he fell into darkness once more.

CHAPTER XXXVIII
Persephone

Persephone entered the dark mouth of the cave and the others followed. Theseus kept Sybil nearby, a hand constantly on her forearm, a reminder that if Persephone messed up, her friend would bear the consequences.

The cave was large, and each sniffle, whimper, and sob echoed in Persephone's ears, feeding her fury. She had to think up a plan and began to wonder if this entrance to the Underworld was like the one in Nevernight. Was it a portal that would take her anywhere she envisioned?

They walked until they came face-to-face with a rock wall that appeared to block their entry.

"What is this?" Theseus demanded.

"This is the entrance to the Underworld," Persephone explained quickly. She reached forward, hands sinking into the wall. The portal was cold, and the magic swirling around her skin was like the flutter of wings. It was comforting because it was Hades's magic, and it made her chest ache.

Where was Hades? She'd bound him in the Upperworld only to ensure he granted Theseus's favor, which had been fulfilled the moment she'd left Alexandria Tower.

Perhaps he is waiting for us in the Underworld, she told herself.

"I will step through first," she said.

"No," Theseus commanded. "Demeter will go."

"That is not wise," Persephone argued. "Monsters guard these gates."

"Worried for me, my flower?" Demeter asked, her voice thick with sarcasm.

"No," Persephone said. "I worry for my monsters."

For Cerberus, Typhon, and Orthrus specifically.

"I will not risk Sybil's pain," Persephone said. "You have nothing to worry about from me."

"Fine," he said, the word slipping between his teeth like a curse. "Just remember, I'm a little bored cutting fingers."

With that, Persephone entered the portal. It was like wading through water, and she moved slow, basking in the feel of Hades magic, before coming out on the other side in Hecate's meadow. It seemed so bright after experiencing the night in the Upperworld and the dark of the cave.

"Persephone," Hecate said. "What's wrong?"

She blinked, turning toward the Goddess of Witchcraft, who stood dressed in dark robes with Nefeli at her side.

"Hecate," Persephone began but quickly slammed her mouth shut as Theseus, Sybil, Demeter, and Harmonia entered behind her. As they appeared, a deadly growl erupted from around them. It came from Nefeli and from Cerberus, Typhon, and Orthrus, who crept out from between the trees.

"No, Cerberus!" Persephone commanded.

The dogs halted, still tense, still poised for attack, but did not growl.

"What is this?" Theseus asked. "A trap?"

"No!" Persephone said. "No. It is not a trap!"

She stared at Hecate, her eyes wide and desperate,

communicating what she could, knowing the goddess could read her mind. She showed her what had happened in the last several hours—from the time Sybil had gone missing, to finding her severed finger at work, the avalanche and battle between the Olympians, to Theseus's favor.

Persephone turned to face the demigod.

"Hecate is my companion. She only came to ensure I was well."

"Yes, of course." Hecate managed a tight smile, then her eyes shifted to Demeter. "What a treat. The Goddess of Harvest in the Realm of the Dead. Come to pay your respects to the hundreds you've murdered in the last month?"

Demeter offered a cold smile. "I have no desire to dwell upon the past."

"If only that were true," Hecate replied. "Are you not here because of the past?"

Demeter scowled and spoke to Theseus. "She is a powerful goddess. Perhaps you should choose a limb from the mortal so Persephone behaves."

"No," Persephone said, her voice dark. "Hecate will not bother us, will you? She will remain in her meadow while we travel to the palace."

"Of course, I will do as my queen commands," Hecate replied. "However, it would be quicker for you to teleport."

"No teleporting," Theseus said. "I cannot trust that we will end up where we should."

"If my lady commands it, you can trust I will take you exactly where you want to go," Hecate said, her voice pleasant, but Persephone sensed the undercurrent of darkness within.

Persephone looked to Theseus. He hesitated, uncertain.

"Do not trust this goddess's magic. She is evil," Demeter said.

"Shut up!" Theseus commanded.

Demeter's eyes narrowed.

"Command her," he said. "But remember, I hold your friend's life within my hands."

"Hecate, takes us to Hades's arsenal."

As Hecate's magic surrounded them, Persephone shivered. She remembered fighting the goddess in this very meadow, feeling the strength and age of her power. It left a darkness upon the heart that was hard to shake, but right now, it was comforting—comforting because she knew Hecate would fight, and the results would be deadly.

They appeared outside the arsenal. The door to the vault was round and gold, inlaid with thick, clear glass that showed all the locks and gears.

Theseus whirled upon Persephone and Hecate, his fingers biting into Sybil's arm.

"I thought you said you would take us to the arsenal."

"I have," Hecate said calmly. "But even I am prevented from teleporting inside. The queen or king himself are the only two who can open the vault."

Persephone started to protest, but Theseus once again threatened Sybil.

"Open it!" he screamed, his madness returning. He was so close to what he wanted, he could barely contain himself.

Persephone looked at Hecate, desperate.

I don't know how.

You don't have to know, Hecate said.

Persephone stepped forward and placed her hand upon a pad beside the door. Once it had scanned her handprint, the door began to grind, winding open like a wheel to reveal Hades's arsenal. Persephone stepped into the familiar round room with its black marble floor and walls covered in weapons, but her eyes—like Theseus's—went to the center, where Hades's armor loomed and the Helm of Darkness rested at its feet.

Theseus pushed Sybil toward Demeter as he entered.

"Hold her!" he barked.

Hecate hovered near Harmonia.

"It is more magnificent than I could have imagined," Theseus said as he stepped toward the display. Persephone's gaze held Hecate's, unwavering.

Get them out of here, she begged.

Of course, the goddess said.

When Theseus touched Hades's helm, Hecate's magic was like a thrust, sweeping Harmonia and Sybil out of the arsenal to safety. Theseus's hands slipped, and Hades's helm fell from its place upon the pedestal, rolling onto the ground with a loud crack.

"No!" Theseus growled.

Persephone's magic erupted, and thorns rose from gashes in the marble, sealing the exits. Demeter's lips peeled away from her gleaming teeth as she smiled wickedly.

"I will teach you a final lesson, Daughter. Perhaps it will keep you complacent."

If magic was a language, then Demeter's confessed hatred. Immediately her power gushed in a wave of fierce energy, knocking Persephone back into a wall, which crumbled beneath her weight. She landed upon her feet, only to find Theseus armed with a blade from Hades's collection.

"God-fucking bitch!" he growled as he swung.

Persephone lashed out; the tips of her fingers spiked with black tips that released like bullets into the demigod's chest. He stumbled back, his shirt darkening with blood, and his eyes flashed, glowing unnaturally bright. Then he struck the ground with his fist, and the earth began to tremble, jarring the weapons on the wall and causing Persephone to lose her footing.

At the same time, Demeter called forth another blast of energy. It struck her hard, sending her flying once again. As she landed, Theseus lifted his weapon over his head to strike. Persephone held up her hands, and as his blade met the energy she had gathered there, he crashed into Hades's armor. Persephone called forth vines that restrained him where he landed.

Then Persephone turned her full attention to Demeter. Their magic clashed—each burst of energy met and exploded, each vine and thorn tangled and crumbled. The Goddess of Harvest threw out another blast; this one stirred the air, causing it to gust, tangling Persephone's hair and clothing. Demeter reached for the blade Theseus had used during his attack, swinging it at Persephone. She countered with her magic—with whatever she could summon fast.

"The gods will destroy you," Demeter said. "I would have kept you safe!"

"What good is safe when the rest of the world is under threat?"

"The rest of the world doesn't matter!" Demeter seethed.

It was the first time Persephone saw Demeter's true fear for her, and for a brief second, they both ceased to fight. They stared at one another, both on edge, but the words that came out of Demeter's mouth were broken, and they broke Persephone.

"You matter. You are my daughter. I *begged* for you."

There was a raw truth to those words, and while Persephone could understand her mother's action to a point, there were some things she would never agree with. Hades too had begged for her. Hades too wanted to protect her—but he was willing to let her fight, to watch her suffer, if it meant seeing her rise.

"Mom," she said, shaking her head.

"Leave with me," Demeter said, desperate. "Leave with me now, and we can forget this ever happened."

Persephone was already shaking her head. "I *can't*."

For her mother to suggest this was actually insane, but Persephone had grown to understand something about the goddess. Despite how long she'd lived, she was no longer well. She was broken, and she never would be whole again.

Demeter's features hardened, and she threw out her hand, sending a bolt of magic toward Persephone while lifting her blade. Persephone blocked the magic and summoned her own, calling to the darkness, which manifested in shadow. The wraiths charged Demeter, and as they shuddered through her, she stumbled, falling to her knees.

When Demeter met Persephone's gaze again, her eyes glowed. She rose, screaming her anger, her magic gathered fast like a screaming wind.

"You were right about one thing, Mother," Persephone said.

"And what is that?"

"Revenge is sweet."

In the next second, the sharpest weapons rose to Persephone's call—spears and knives and swords—and descended, striking Demeter, pinning her to the ground.

A horrible silence followed as the wind died suddenly. Persephone dropped to her knees, breathing hard.

"Mom," she rasped, crawling toward her.

Demeter did not move and did not speak. She lay with her arms spread wide, her fingers still clasping her blade. Her eyes were wide, as if she were in shock, and blood dripped from her mouth.

"Mom," Persephone breathed.

She managed to stand and start to pull the weapons free. When she was finished, the goddess lay on the cold, marble ground, and Persephone sat with her, waiting for her to heal.

But she never moved.

"Mom!" Persephone grew frantic, rising onto her knees, shaking the goddess. She had wanted a lot of things from Demeter—for her to change, to be a mother, to let her live her life, but never death. Never this.

Then she remembered something that Hades had said about the weapons here—that some were relics and could prevent a god from healing.

"Mom, wake up!"

"Come, Persephone," Hecate said, appearing behind her. She hadn't even felt the goddess approach.

"Wake her up!" Persephone demanded. She placed her hands upon Demeter's body, which was now growing cold, attempting to use her own magic, willing her mother to breathe again, but nothing worked.

"Her thread is cut, Persephone. There is no bringing Demeter back."

"This isn't what I wanted!" Persephone cried.

Then Hecate placed her hands upon Persephone's face, forcing her gaze to hers.

"You will see Demeter again. All dead come to the Underworld, Persephone, but right now, Sybil and Harmonia need you."

Persephone took a few deep breaths, her eyes stinging. Finally, she nodded and let the goddess help her to her feet, but as they started toward the door, she halted.

"Theseus!"

She whirled to where she'd restrained him earlier and found that he was gone.

"The helm!"

The two goddesses started to search the arsenal when the Underworld shook violently, and there was a horrible cracking sound.

Persephone's heart pounded in her chest, and when her gaze connected with Hecate's, the goddess was pale.

"What was that?" Persephone whispered.

"That," Hecate said, "is the sound of Theseus releasing the Titans."

BONUS CONTENT

The following are scenes that either did not make it into the book or had to be reworked into the book.

Housewarming

"What is this called again?" Hades asked as they waited.

"It's called a housewarming party," she said.

He eyed the box in her hands.

"You brought cupcakes and not wood?"

Persephone tried not to laugh, especially since this was the second time she'd been asked this question.

"Why would I bring wood, Hades?"

"To warm the house."

She couldn't help giggling now. "You're so old!"

Hades raised a brow, and she knew she would pay for that comment later.

"People don't bring wood to housewarming parties anymore, Hades. They bring gifts and alcohol. They get drunk and play games."

"And us? Will we get drunk and play games?"

She had been watching Hades drink since sunup, and he was perfectly sober. She was certain he couldn't get drunk anymore—and that he was possibly an alcoholic.

She eyed him. "You aren't going to trick anyone into a bargain, are you?"

He narrowed his eyes, a playful smirk on his face. "I promise nothing."

"Hades." Persephone spoke his name like a warning, and turned toward him. He surprised her by clasping her face between his fingers and kissing her.

When he pulled away, he said, "I will be on my best behavior."

She snorted. "Well, that's reassuring."

A Shower Scene

When the spray hit her, she groaned at its heat, and Hades took the chance to deepen their kiss, hands gripping her breasts, fingers teasing her hardened nipples. She reached between them, stroking his thick sex as it beaded with moisture. She wanted to take him into her mouth, but Hades's hand moved to her throat, fingers splayed across her jaw as he plied her mouth with this tongue.

Then he pulled away suddenly, and Persephone growled, reaching for his cock.

He chuckled, hand covering hers. "A moment, darling. You are covered in blood."

"You didn't seem to mind," she pointed out.

"I don't mind, but I'll take any opportunity to touch you everywhere while I wash you."

They stood outside the spray as he reached for the soap and wet a cloth. He started with her shoulder, gently washing the blood away. He moved to her breasts, groping and squeezing, his slick hands teasing each one before moving on to her stomach and sides, her thighs and her calves. On his knees before her, he gave an order.

"Turn." She obeyed the command, placing her hands flat on the wall as he made his way back up her body. He spent time washing between her thighs, fingers parting her flesh to circle her clit and slide into her slickness before pressing his hard cock against the curve of her ass, hands returning to her breasts.

"How bad do you want me?" he asked, his lips close to her ear. She turned her head toward him, feeling the scrape of his beard against her cheek, and arched her back against him, pressing harder into his cock.

"More than anything," she said.

Hades twisted her head toward him and captured her mouth, kissing her hard before he released her, only to kick her legs apart to guide himself inside her. Persephone rested her head against her hands, which were pressed firmly against the tile wall as he slid into place, filling and stretching with the sweetest burn.

"I would keep my cock buried inside your sweetness for eternity if I could," he said, gripping her hips, thrusting into her so hard, she felt his balls slap against her ass. "Tell me how I feel inside you."

There were so many words for it, so many pleasurable things, but the only thing she could manage to say was "Good."

Hades's fingers tightened in her hair.

"I want to feel you come on my cock," he said against her ear. "Can you do that? Can you come for me?"

These were words he'd never spoken before. Hades had always been a very sexual person, but these words—they were raw and primal and dark, and she wanted more of them.

She wanted his darkness.

"I'll come for you," she said and moaned.

This time, he groaned—a guttural sound that she felt in the bottom of her stomach. His hand drifted down to her clit, and as his thumb brushed over the sensitive nerves, she bent back harder, feeling Hades's thrusts deeper. His mouth was everywhere, sucking her ear, her neck, her shoulder.

"You are fucking glorious," he said. "You are mine."

Persephone's orgasm came hard, and her legs shook so hard, she almost fell, but Hades held her up, one of his hands pressed to the tile for support.

"Come inside me," Persephone ordered. "If I am yours. Come."

Hades managed a strangled laugh. "Anything, my queen."

The last few thrusts were hard and deep and fast, but she felt him pulse inside her, and his body relaxed against hers, his release finally realized.

For a moment, they stayed like that, bodies pressed together, leaning against the tile wall while the spray from the shower grew cold. When Hades pulled out, Persephone turned and slid to the tile floor, too drained to remain standing.

Hades knelt before her.

"Are you well?"

"Yes," she said, smiling sleepily. "I just need a moment."

A Lyre

"That sounds horrible," Apollo said.

Persephone stopped plucking at the lyre the God of Music had given her and glared. "I'm doing exactly as you instruct. It must be the teacher."

"If you were doing exactly as I instructed, your song would sound like this," he countered and strummed a few pretty and clean notes.

"We're not all gods of music, Apollo."

"Clearly," he spouted, dark brows rising.

"Someone's moody today—more than usual," Persephone countered.

It was Apollo's turn to glare.

Persephone set the lyre aside. "What's wrong? This isn't about Ajax, is it?"

Apollo's lips tightened. "Why would I be upset about a mortal?"

"You seemed pretty upset when Hector attacked him."

"I was worried for my hero," Apollo snapped.

"So you don't think Hector has a chance against Ajax in the games?"

Apollo opened his mouth and then slammed it shut.

"You watch him," Persephone said. "You smelled like him that day you brought me to the palaestra."

Apollo's jaw clenched, and he did not speak.

"I guess if you don't want to talk," she said and picked up the lyre again and started to play it—horribly.

"Stop! Is this your idea of torturing answers from me?" he demanded.

"Is it working?"

He glared and then sighed, suddenly looking very tired.

"The last time I fell in love, it ended in bloodshed. It always ends that way."

"Hyacinth's death wasn't your fault, Apollo."

"Yes, it was. I was not the only god who loved Hyacinth, and when he chose me, Zephyrus, the God of the West Wind, grew jealous. It was his wind that changed the trajectory of my throw, his wind that resulted in the death of Hyacinth."

"Then his death is Zephyrus's fault," Persephone said.

Apollo shook his head. "You do not understand. Even now I see it happening with Ajax. Hector grows jealous everyday. The fight he picked with him at the palaestra was not the first."

"What if Ajax likes you?" Persephone asked. "Will you decide not to pursue him out of fear."

"It is not fear—" Apollo started and then looked away angrily.

"Then what is it?"

"I don't want to fuck this up. I'm not…a good person now. What happens when I lose again? Do I become…evil then?"

"Apollo," Persephone said as gently as she could. "If you are worried that you will become evil, then you have more humanity than you think."

Apollo gave her a look that begged to differ.

"You should talk to Ajax."

"About what? We're not in a relationship."

"You smelled like him," Persephone pointed out.

"And?"

"Well, that suggests you've at least had…physical contact."

Apollo rolled his eyes. "I haven't slept with him, if that's what you're asking."

"It wasn't a question."

"It was implied," he shot back. "But…we did kiss."

"And? How did you feel while he kissed you?"

Apollo sighed and scrubbed his face. "Like…breathing and drowning all at the same time." He paused. "That sounds so…silly, doesn't it?"

"No," Persephone said quietly. "Not at all. It sounds to me like there's something between you two worth exploring."

"Even if it ends in disaster?"

"Even so," she said. "Look at what my mother is doing to the Upperworld as a result of my choice to marry Hades."

"You must have regrets," he said. "I know how you mourn humanity."

"I regret that she chose this path," Persephone said. "Because it means I must tear her apart."

Author's Note

Gods. Where do I begin with this one?

First, let me just say thank you to my readers. There are so many of you and I appreciate all of you—the reviews, the posts, the messages—all of it keeps me writing. It's because of you that I was able to become a full-time author, and it's because of you that I can continue doing what I love.

Also, a huge thank you to my Street Team. You all are the best hype team I could have ever asked for. I appreciate all the time you spend investing in me and my books. Y'all are the best.

About the Book

Writing this book was a blur—it was a messy mix of exhaustion and agony and grief and some hope it would all get better. Reflecting on the process, I cannot say how I got here, but I'm really glad I did. I'm *very* proud of this book—beyond proud. I know we all have our opinions about Ruin, but I hope you can tell *why* we suffered, why that journey was so important—it was to get to this. To the power of

Malice. Looking back on who Persephone was in Darkness, her struggles in Ruin, and who she is at the end of this book, it makes me proud. Her journey gives me hope—that the hardship and the trauma and the grief just makes us powerful.

The Rest

As you all know, I play upon several myths, and I like to go over those myths and how I adapted or changed them in my books. I'll start with the Titanomachy.

The Titanomachy: The Ten-Year War

The main question I asked myself as I prepared for Malice was—what would lead to another Titanomachy? We all know that the gods go through this cycle—the primordials were overthrown by the Titans, the Titans overthrown by the Olympians.

If you read about the Titanomachy, especially Zeus's role, you see how charismatic he is, which is very off-putting, because you don't really want him to be so charming, but he understood what it would take to overpower the Titans, and he promised those who would support him and the Olympians that they would be rewarded by being able to keep their status and power—Hecate and Helios were two Titans who joined him. It is said, specifically too, that Zeus held Hecate in high regard—which is why she is the only person who can really put him in his place. This is why I decided she would be able to castrate him. I chose castration for Zeus's punishment from Hecate because Cronus also castrated his father, Uranus (with the scythe that is used to kill Adonis).

I also felt that Demeter's snowstorm would create an environment of unrest that would contribute to another Titanomachy. In myth, when Persephone is taken by Hades to the Underworld, the Goddess of Harvest actually just neglects the world, and it is plunged into a drought. I felt like while a drought would be bad, technology could combat that easier than it could combat a snowstorm. I think I felt this way because I live in Oklahoma, and we suffer during snowstorms because we don't have the infrastructure to handle them. I felt that Demeter, as the Goddess of Harvest, obviously has control over weather, so why not have her bring a raging winter storm upon New Athens? It would then set the stage for unrest among the mortals, who were already encouraged by Triad.

Speaking of Demeter. When Persephone goes missing in myth, she actually wanders the world aimlessly in a bit of a depression. She goes to Celeus disguised as an old woman called Doso (hence her name choice in Malice). While there, she begins to take care of the king's two children, although she is caught trying to make one of the children immortal by placing him in the fire and outs herself as a goddess. She gets really mad about this and forces the king and his people to build a temple in her honor.

I struggled with how the gods were going to react to Demeter's rampage, but I tried to stay close to how I felt the myth unfolded—which was that the gods let this go for a long time, until they were faced with the extinction of the human race, and as a result, no worshippers. At first, Zeus tried to use words to calm the goddess. He also sent other gods to attempt to convince her to come back to Olympus, but she refused. As a last resort, Zeus then sent Hermes to retrieve Persephone from the Underworld. I played upon Zeus's same lazy decision making within my book. Zeus might need worshippers, but he's not afraid of losing his power, so he does not act fast.

More on Demeter

The rape of Demeter is something I touched upon in this book. Poseidon actually rapes Demeter while she is searching for Persephone, but I felt that if this had happened before Persephone were born, it would give Demeter a reason to retract from the world and want to protect her daughter from the three.

Hermes and Pan

I just wanted to make a quick note that I did reference Pan, the God of the Wild, as Hermes's son, which, as parentage goes in all mythology, may or may not have been his actual father. Still, I'd like to take a moment to say that of the Greek gods, Pan is the only one known to die. His death is not detailed—in fact, no one knows how he died. It was basically just a game of telephone that eventually reached the masses. The idea is, however, that with the birth of Christ, Pan had to die.

Don't ask me. I just read the myths.

Apollo and Ajax and Hector

I do not know what made me ship Apollo with Ajax, but I did know that Ajax and Hector duel in mythology during the Trojan War, so I thought that would be an interesting dynamic. In myth, Hector is also favored by Apollo because Apollo is in support of the Trojans, while Ajax fights for the Greeks.

I also decided that Ajax, described as colossal and strong, should be deaf because I wanted to show that deafness does not mean incapable. That being said, I didn't want Ajax to have any kind of superhero-like powers other than what he was given in myth—his strength, his size, and his reflexes. I didn't think his deafness should change that he had trained like the hearing warriors around him.

Aphrodite and Harmonia

In myth, Harmonia is said to be the daughter of Ares and Aphrodite—OR Zeus and Electra. Since I don't ship Ares and Aphrodite, I went with the second option and made her Aphrodite's sister. Harmonia was also married off to Cadmus, who I believe she really loved, because when he was turned into a serpent, she kind of went insane and was also turned into a serpent. I don't know that I will touch on this particular myth in any of my books, but I thought it important to mention here.

In my retelling, I really felt like Harmonia was pansexual. I also felt like while Sybil had never considered falling in love with a woman before, when she met Harmonia, she just couldn't help herself, and it's really, really cute.

The Palace of Knossos and the Minotaur

First, here is a great article about the history of the Palace of Knossos and why it was originally through to be the "labyrinth": livescience.com/27955-knossos-palace-of-the-minoans.html. I'm adding this here because it was originally thought that the labyrinth was just a maze-like palace built by Daedalus. I brought in the story of the Minotaur because we also have Theseus, who, as we know, was sent to kill the Minotaur. He succeeded with the help of Ariadne, who gave him a reel of string to help him escape the labyrinth once he defeated the monster.

Theseus and Helen

Maybe some of you are surprised by Helen's trajectory, so I'll explain here. There is a myth where Theseus and Pirithous abduct daughters of Zeus. Theseus chooses Helen of Troy, while, as we know, Pirithous chooses Persephone. The other famous myth is the one where Paris falls in love with Helen and he takes her from Sparta to Troy, beginning a war.

Depending on readings and interpretations of the myth, I just felt like Helen might be someone who looks for the best way to the top. After all, she is a Spartan woman. She is strong and capable and intelligent. She knows how to use her beauty as a tool and her mind as a weapon. Given my impression of her, you can understand her trajectory in Malice.

The Monsters

There are a lot of monsters mentioned in this book aside from the Minotaur: the Hydra, Lamia, Ceto, and Arachne. I just wanted to take a moment to give a short overview of each.

The Hydra resided in Lerna Lake, which you will recognize as one of the entrances to the Underworld. I chose to have this monster in the Underworld because it's very venomous. Additionally, the monster was eventually killed by Heracles as part of his labors.

Lamia was the queen of Libya. As I stated in the book, she had an affair with Zeus that resulted in her being cursed by Hera to lose all her children. The myths vary on if they were killed or if they were kidnapped as well as how she eventually came to begin to devour children. Whatever the case, she did go insane and began to kidnap and eat children. Zeus gave her the power to remove her eyes—apparently to help alleviate her sleeplessness (Hera also cursed her with insomnia). He also gifted her with prophecy, which, I suppose is a gift all child-eating monsters deserve?

Ceto is a primordial goddess and is Queen of Sea Monsters. She also gave birth to a lot of monsters including the Gorgons and the Graeae who you might recall are the three sisters who share an eye and a tooth between them.

Last, I mention Arachne. She features in Ovid's *Metamorphoses* which I quote at the beginning of this book. She was a woman who challenged Athena to a weaving contest. The reason I wanted to mention her is that Arachne chose to weave scenes that illustrated the misdeeds of the gods, much as I choose to do in these books. Anyway, the rest of the story goes that Arachne's weaving was flawless, and this enraged Athena. The versions of how Arachne became a spider vary, but she is transformed nonetheless. In the book, I mention Arachne's Pit, which I like to think of as a punishment in Tartarus.

Miscellaneous

Okeanos and his twin Sandros are made up modern demigods, but they were based off another set of twin sons of Zeus, Amphion and Zethus. I did not use Amphion and Zethus as modern demigods because I already reference a myth that is sort of connected to them that happened in antiquity and that is the death of Amphion and Niobe's children by the hands of Apollo and Artemis.

Apeliotes is an actual god—the God of the Southeast Wind. It's kind of hilarious because he was thought to bring refreshing rain. I made up the two children, Thales and Callista, in the book, though.

I briefly mention Hecuba, who was the wife of King Priam. There are a couple of myths about her that all end with her becoming a dog, which is one of Hecate's symbols. At the point of this book, Hecuba is ready to rest as a soul in the Underworld, and so Hecate finds Nefeli, who she describes as a woman who begged for the goddess to take her pain away after she lost a loved one. This is a direct reference to one of the Hecuba myths in which she watches her son die and goes mad, after which she was transformed into a dog.

About the Author

Scarlett St. Clair lives in Oklahoma with her husband. She has a master's degree in library science and information studies. She is obsessed with Greek mythology, murder mysteries, love, and the afterlife. For information on books, tour dates, and content, please visit scarlettstclair.com.